The Stars of My Heart

To the ones who are brave enough
to love like fire.

Chapter one

The stars are always there. Something to wish on.
A beautiful sight to look at. They are something I
admire, but tonight they are different. Instead of
twinkling lights, I see burning balls of destruction.
They send fear, confusion—

"What are you looking at?"

And apparently a thorn in my side. I breathe in
the cool air composing myself for my next job.

"I'm assessing the plan one more time. Are you
sure you know what your job is?"

He glares at me. An expression of *are you really
asking me that question.* "Of course I know what my
job is," he starts. "Stay by the door. Send the signal
if something is wrong. Don't get caught." He points
to each of his fingers, counting off each job.

"Make sure you focus on that last one." I have
been stuck with my partner John for two years now.
I have faith in him, but *trust* on the other hand
doesn't come easily in our house. I can only trust
myself. I am the only one I can count on, so leaving
John with the job of lookout makes me want to rip
my skin off at the nervousness of his "expert
watching abilities." I guess I also wouldn't like it if
he were the one to steal the four million dollar
diamond from the Exploratory Museum, so I'll take
what I can get."

The wind shifts, blowing a crisp bite at our faces. Squinting my eyes, I hover my hand over my forehead. There, I see it. The grand stone entrance sign of the Exploratory Museum. An attraction it is, and one I am glad for. At least this location was easy to find.

"We're almost there," I whisper. Pointing ahead of us, I start assessing the plan with John. "Go that way one more block and meet me at the back door. I'll let you know when I get inside. Two knocks."

We nod our heads in agreement. *Set a diversion. Draw attention away from yourself.*

That is what my father, Damian, always taught me, but it's been a long time since he's taught me anything useful. I passed every test whether physical or mental whether I was sick or well. After that, nothing. I was then sent out to be the ruthless spy and thief I am today, or the spy and thief he made me. But tonight is about agility. Tonight is about being invisible. A shadow in the night, and if there is anything I can do, I can disappear.

I match my breathing and steps making myself as silent as a spider as I round the corner. I slowly draw the pin from my pocket hidden in the sleeve of my jacket. I fluff the heavy leather around me to seem as big as possible before I reach the pin to the lock.

Conceal yourself. Don't let anyone know or even guess at your identity. At the thought, my hair pulls at my scalp. It had been braided so tightly to my head and wrapped around to make me appear as if I were a boy.

With steady hands I reach out and soundlessly pick the lock, all silent, but that satisfying click. The click of approval. I open the door slowly to check if there is any creaking. I hold my breath and pull. To my surprise it is as smooth as butter. I knock on the outside of the door twice with the delicacy of a feather before slipping in.

The museum reminds me of a school. The white walls that soak up any kind of joy, the whole room looking bland and heartless. The smell of bleach fills the air stinging my eyes as I peer through the open room. Posters line the walls filled with portraits and articles that no one in their right mind would stop and read. This is just a grown-up version of school where rich people like to act like they are entertained by the information and education when they really aren't, just like school. I only went through elementary school. After that it was vigorous training. Wake up at six, practice physical combat with the gang, practice sneaking methods and sleight of hand. And for what? This?

I mean, I guess it's better than being in school. What 17-year-old wouldn't want to go out in the night knowing there is a possibility they wouldn't be coming home? What 17-year-old wouldn't want to have to know how to break the law every day and get away with it? What 17-year-old wouldn't want to be a criminal?

I don't want to be a criminal, but I also don't want to be dead, and if I don't get this diamond, I may as well be.

Examine the security system.

I scrunch myself up against the wall sucking in my breath until my chest burns. Sidestepping across the floor, I soon reach the back room. This is exactly where I need to be. The big "employees only" sign confirms it. The lock is easy to crack. Nothing fancy even for a place like this. Drawing the pin out of my pocket, I again wait for that satisfactory click. Pushing the door open I give myself a pat on the back. There must be twenty computer screens that all secure the museum, yet none of them detected me once. I'll have to remember to brag to John about that when we get out of here. I sit down in the big office chair, the leather lining squeaking against my own leather pants. My fingers glide across the keyboard, moving like they were destined to hack into security. Every programming task, and memorization skill has led up to moments like these, and I have never been one to disappoint.

Hack into the security system, turn off the cameras, and then turn off the alarm system. I know I've accomplished just that when the computers go black, my own blurry reflection staring back at me. "Bingo," I say under my breath. Before I get up I lean back in the chair sighing, sinking into the cushions. I try to silence the voice in my head.

The voice that screams at me. The voice that tells me that I shouldn't be doing this. I've had it for years, and every time it has said the same thing. *"Do what's right, even if it hurts."*

It hurts. It hurts too much. This is the only way, and it's gotten me to where I am now, and I've learned to manage the hurt.

Stomping my boots back onto the floor, I leave the security room shaking my head. I wish on every star for the voice to go away, to just leave me alone.

"Hello." But it seems the stars have a different plan.

Gasping, I cover my mouth jumping back. I look at who greets me only to see John's stupid face staring back at me. I take in a slow breath and shoot a glare. He sends back an awkward smile, the left side of his face curling up more than the right.

"Aren't you supposed to be outside?" I ask through gritted teeth, my hands balling into fists.

"It's cold out there," he says in a whiney voice. Why did Damian ever pair us together? I love him, but stars, I hate him. He's like the brother I never had.

Suppressing my frustration, I take a deep breath. "Just help me, then we'll leave," I say in a dramatic sigh.

"What exhibit are we looking for?" he asks.

"Fossils and Minerals. Right down that hall."

I set my pace, my limbs stretched tall. Powerwalking over there, I just wish to be done, to go back to the mansion tonight, and fall into a deep sleep, or as deep as I can.

"There." John points to where the diamond is. Front and center for everyone to see. It's their loss really. They should be smarter with their displays, especially with how many gangs are known to be in the city, but I guess that just makes our job easier.

We approach the beauty both gasping, holding back tiny laughs of accomplishments. I slip my leather gloves onto my hands. The fresh smell of them reminds me of falling asleep in my mother's arms as a child. Her chest would rise and fall as I breathed in the luxurious smell of her leather jacket. Always soft. Always warm.

The memory weighs my heart down. I carry these gloves not just to hide my fingerprints, but to have a piece of her with me. Maybe if I was returning the diamond back to her, things would be different. She would make this stolen gem into something beautiful. I bet she would beg my dad to make a ring for some homeless guy on the street to either profess his undying love for the lady at the bakery, or to just get him some cash… but not Damian.

I know exactly what Damian is going to do. He probably has a buyer secured to meet him tonight. He's going to get paid thousands of dollars, and then use that money to drink and gamble at the casino. I take the spotless display glass covering the diamond off and set it on the ground, being gentle as to not make any scratches and just as I touch it, the voice comes back. It screams, yet it is gentle.

Toying with my mind, the voice makes me hesitate, because the voice is not just some shadow, or some note of a stranger, or even my own voice. The screams and pleads are from the person I loved most in this world, but she is gone. Just like the smell of her jacket and the rise and fall of her chest, it's all gone. The only thing remaining are her pleads and prayers for me to stop, for me to put the gem down, and never return back to the mansion. But if I don't... if I don't come back with this gem, have another successful break in, and keep Damian's name as Alpha of all Mafia bosses... I will be by myself. No family, no house, no money, nothing.
I have to.

I am Zaria Farewell, daughter of the most feared Mafia boss, and I can do any crime.

I reach my arm forward slowly, inching my hand closer to caressing the giant jewel. I look at it serenely and watch red and blue light sparkle into the surroundings.

The colors dance like fireworks on the Fourth of July. Every moonlit beam, reflecting off the lustrous jewel. I get caught in the amazement, my mind feeling hypnotized until it hits me.

Wait a minute, red and blue lights?

Chapter two

Sirens. The scream of sirens fills every alleyway of Flesherg. I honestly don't know whether the sirens or the beat of my racing heart was louder. My steps are fast and frantic as I run down the streets. We've never been caught before. Damian was always there, but now I'm doing jobs on my own…well not entirely on my own.

"Keep up you fool or we'll be spending the night in sinner's paradise."

"The bar?"

His sarcasm is beyond me. My steps get faster, and I hear the car shriek. That can only mean they're going by foot.

"I thought you took care of the security!" He screams at me.

"I did!"

I frantically look around. The only thing visible are the tall buildings of Flesherg. A tiny streetway the only escape.

"Go down that alley. Run and don't look back. I'll see you back at the house." I order at John. He gives a slight nod and quickens his pace. I, on the other hand, take to the wall. I climb, my limbs shaking. I focus to make sure I'm moving faster than the police steps behind me. They are progressively getting quieter which gives me a bit of relief.

I take hold of any crack or spur in the wall to grab on to. Risking a glance down, I see how high I've climbed wishing I hadn't looked down at all. I turn my head back up, but as I do I see movement. I lose my grip but quickly find it again with a burning sweat surging through me. I quicken my pace to get to the top of the building. When I do, two figures running on the roofs of the opposite street buildings. They can't be the police. They wear all black and move too catlike to be police officers with heavy equipment.

I watch them swiftly run, hopping gracefully from roof to roof. Then I see it. A small bun bobs up and down as they run away. Burney. Top spy of the Huva gang. Top gang on our backs. Those little rats sold us out.

I jump from rooftop to rooftop with relative ease. I have always had long legs, the one thing I can appreciate from my father. Building after building, I eventually see John from up above. His running is consistent, like he does this every day, and that's the truth. We *do* this every day.

I whistle. Loud enough for him to hear me, quiet enough to sound like a bird.

He looks up, meeting my eyes. Stopping, he waits for me to climb down. Shame in our hearts, we walk back to Damian's mansion, the police no longer on our tail.

Breaking the silence John whispers, "What do you think he will do?" He slouches his arms at his side, his head hanging down.

"I don't know…." I say it again, this time sounding like a prayer. "I don't know."

***

"You're getting really bad at this."

Damian looks down at me with disgust in his eyes. He holds his arms crossed over his chest like he always did when I disappointed him as a little girl. I sit in a chair across from him slouched, trying to show the part of me that is unfazed. The table is ridiculously long. Something Damian had wanted to make himself seem like he was in charge. The room painted a dark burgundy color, the candlelight making it seem more brown than red.

Wine bottles line the room. Damian's collection. The thing he will show off first to any guests that have the nerve to enter. My heart still beating faster than it should be, I cross my right leg over my left, glaring at him directly just like he taught me to do with city rats.

"Don't give me that look. You put yourself in this situation," he says, his voice gruff and stern. I leave my glance on him for another second then turn to look away. I have nothing to say to him. It's not my fault that the Huva gang sent one of their spies out to catch us. It's not my fault they called the cops on us. It's not my fault that he has made us the most powerful gang in Flesherg with everyone on our tail. If anything, this whole ordeal is his fault.

His doing. His problem.

I stare at the wall, taking in the ornate brass swirls that boarder the top. It's just a show. All the beauty, all the flash, just to make us look like we have a damn good reputation. But what good is our reputation if he has nothing good to offer in return. Not riches and niceties, but a break. A caring hand. Someone to talk to. I scoff at the idea. Not anymore. That dream has been well squelched.

"I have a job for you." His eyes stare daggers into mine. "Depending on your actions, this might be the last job you have."

"What?" I didn't have time to think about whether it was a better idea to stay silent or not. "Papa, I'm your daughter!"

"I am well aware of that, which is why you shouldn't be this reckless. You have one more chance. Got it?"

He looks away from me, swirling his glass of wine. With the adrenaline wearing off I can feel the pins in my head throbbing. I look down at my hands, cut and bruised from the escape tonight. I don't meet his eyes with mine. I can't. His jet black hair is slicked back with the gel he has been obsessed over since the beginning of time, and his perfect tailored suit. His closet is full of them all thanks to John and I. Not a scratch remains on his body. All tells of his accident gone.

He had never even told us what the accident was. It was shortly after my mother's death. He came home beat up and about ready to pass out. One of the other members of the gang took him to the emergency room, and the story of what happened always remained a mystery.

There is no doubt in my mind that Damian was the one to get himself into trouble. We all had our suspicions. Alcohol, drugs, some members of the gang even thought that he didn't need to be under any influence for his temper to get out of control, and though the bruising and scars might have gone away, his temper never did, and it has just become our reality.

This is absolutely foolish. I scoff at thinking what he would do without me. I do his dirty work, and I do it well. I can't be perfect all the time, but to him, making a mistake was a matter of life or death. I can feel my cheeks heat as I struggle to contain my anger.

The hard metal of my gun presses against my hip I decipher whether I should pull it out and fire. The singing of a bullet through the roof is sure to get my message across. He sees me go to reach and raises his eyebrows. I know that look all too well. The "think about what you're going to do before you do it" look. I let my hand graze the gun and eventually drop it to my crossed leg.

"What?" I grumble. "What do you want me to do?" I ask, still glaring at the wall.

"You're agreeing?" He places his hand around the half-filled wine glass, circling the top of it with his finger. I know this trick. The subtle way to tell the other party that you are in charge. Two can play at that game. I put my hand over my gun again. His eyes twitch with a sly grin, and we stay like this for a second that feels like eternity. I decide to break the silence first.

"I would like to know what you're having me do before I agree to one of *your* jobs," I bite. Grinning, he responds, "At least you haven't lost all of your brain. This is a very important job that could get us everything we ever wanted."

I listen to him and roll my eyes. Everything he does is always for the benefit of himself. The exact reason why, when I became old enough, he sent me to do the hard jobs for him. Ever since his accident he decided that it wasn't safe for him to go on the streets. When has it ever been safe for him to go on the streets? And better yet, he sends John and I out with all his enemies lurking at every corner, but he doesn't know that. He will never know that.

"What's in it for you?" I direct my eyes past him, but I can still see the smirk that arrives on his face.

He chuckles. "Always knowing my next move?"

"You could say I've grown up having to know that there are always strings attached."

He chuckles again, this time I don't know if it's because he finds what I said funny or because he's about to expose every part of my weaknesses.

Luckily by the drumming of his fingers on the table, I can tell he wants to hurry this conversation up, because if we sat and talked about everything I've done wrong we might as well move to the dining room table and gather the whole gang to watch me crumble in embarrassment.

"If you pull this off, it will give you the most power you've ever seen. You will take over this gang and be the leader, following in my legacy." He lifts his arms, gesturing to all he has created this mansion to be.

"And if I refuse?" I ask. He thinks anyone will fall at his feet for anything that comes spewing out of his mouth. Just because he's the most feared in all of Flesherg doesn't mean I'm scared of him.

"You don't want to take over the gang?" he asks me this with an inquisitive look on his face. Leaning forward he awaits my answer ready to be bowed down to.

"I don't want to be played," I remark, mirroring his body language. "So, what's in it for you?"

"The riches."

Of course. He runs to money like a child in a candy store.

I start to pick at my nails. "What is this… *job* you want me to do?"

"I'm glad you're interested." He leans back in his chair. "This can get you far. Farther than me. Do you know of the Prince of Lumbridge?"

"Can't say I do." All this cryptic talk boils my bones till they are just a jumbled mess; however, this is how he is. A trickster. Even as my own father.

"I'll get to the point. I can tell you're getting antsy."

I roll my eyes.

He slides a manila folder in my direction. "Get the prince to fall in love with you. Learn his routine, his habits, and his darkest secrets that would make the royal guard slice a sword through his heart. Steal the riches of the kingdom wherever they may be. Stage your death. Come back, and Flesherg is yours."

His explanation was long. Easy to follow, but confusing as hell. For a moment I stare at him, wondering what he is thinking. I almost let out a chuckle.

"Great, great story. Just how am I going to get into the castle, much less close to the prince?"

He tilts his head back. "Ah, I was hoping you would ask. The Prince of Lumbridge is looking for a new advisor. Someone to follow him around. Write down his meetings, royal events he has to attend, making note of his favorite breakfast strudel." He sends a devilish smirk my way.

"Do you want me to fail?" I stammer, slamming my fist onto the table. "I am a thief. A gang master. How do you expect—

"And a gang master you shall be. I have taught you well daughter." He spits at the title. "Steal the money. Make this gang dine in riches, and the key to Flesherg is yours."

It should be simple. A yes or no question. Not even a yes or no, but listening to what I'm told, but that has stopped a long time ago. My father has made me into himself. A monstrous thief. No heart. Just brains and muscle.

"Do I have a choice?"

"Actually you do. You can take on this job, succeed and be wealthy, or, you could walk away. Live on the streets, find a place of your own and never step foot in here again."

A scoff escapes my nose. Smirking, I shake my head in a serpentine rhythm. Slow, but enticing.

"You know that's hardly an option."

"Then I guess you know what to do. Pack your bags. You leave in the morning."

Chapter three

A bone-shattering slam follows after my conversation with my father. If it was even a conversation at all. The sound would have startled me, but this time it was from me. Maybe slamming the door to my bedroom was a little childish, but it was the only thing I could think of to get the "last word" in. Every one of my movements finishes with the finesse of attitude.

Throwing my suitcase on the bed, I make sure I do it as loudly as possible. I toss what little clothes I have into the air, watching them come down like little parachutes. I go to my bookshelf. Each book I throw like a heavy frisbee. They hit the wall, each making a statement, before they slide down. Even through my fit, I stop to make sure the pages are intact. Holding them in my hands I frill through the pages, some of the corners and edges folded and smooshed. I run my hands over them hoping smoothing out the rough edges but thy still crease. My mother gave me these books. I can almost hear her voice;

One should always have a world to escape to. One where you can be whoever you want.

I often think about that. I would be better off, prison-wise, if I dumped this whole gang and moved out. I would start again. A clean record, but then I would have nothing. There is always a bit of regret whenever I steal something, a bit of my mother still in me.

When I was younger, still in training, my contact with my mother was diminished. Damian had said that I could not feel any remorse, and that spending time with her would soften my heart. I started getting stronger. Not just physically, but mentally as well. There would be days where Damian would have his gang members scream at me all day for anything that wasn't just so. One of those days I had made it through training, but I had retired early to my bedroom. I'd like to think that I kept my tears to myself, but I think everyone knew what was happening when I closed my door. I laid in my bed, my pillows a soggy mess when the soft footsteps of my mother sounded from the hall.

She came into my room and sat next to me. Her frail hands wiped my tears and held me close until my sobs dwindled to a soft murmur. She then gave me a book. A leather bound with the most intricate details on it. The letters of the title swirled together like a whip of magic. She said it was her favorite book when she was a child. She thought I might like to read it. A way for me to calm down after a hard day. And so I did.

When I had finished it, I came racing to her lap. I told her all about it. My favorite parts, the funny parts, anything that I could remember. After that, anytime I had a truly rough day, she would sneak in and give me a new book.

I know Damian found out at some point. He never said anything, but anytime he comes into my room he always peeks at the shelf. Sometimes I wonder if he misses her. How does he cope? How does he go on with a sharp mind and stone heart when his wife is dead? In a way, I wish to be him. He's powerful, respected, something I can only hope I will be one day.

A knock comes at my door interrupting me from my thoughts.

"Come in," I say. I already know it's John. I could tell by the loopy swing of his steps. Always sounding like he's dancing to jazz music playing in his head.

He turns the knob slowly. His eyes peek around the room, gawking at the mess I had made. Swiftly, he comes in and closes the door to my room. He drops his voice to a low whisper that I can barely even hear.

"You know you don't have to do this."

"Really?" I retort, not being as quiet as him. "Do I have a choice? Damian made it pretty clear on that matter."

"You know what I mean. I could…" He searches for words. "I could help you. We could find a place together —

"I'm going to stop you there." I reach my arm between us, keeping the space. "John, even if we leave, we would still have to steal. It's not like anyone is going to want members of the Flesherg gang serving up people's morning coffee. They'll probably think we would poison their customers. This is how we grew up. At least here we are safe."

"Are you?" he takes a pause. "Are you safe here?"

His eyes glazed with tears, he stands right in front of me. Grabbing my arm with his calloused hands, he tries again.

"Is this really what you want?"

His voice is shaky. Sure I've thought about this question. Every day since the day I started training with father, I had asked myself the same thing. But Damian is right. I have no choice. I make my voice as even as possible. Commanding and deliberate.

"Yes. This is what I want."

He looks in my eyes a bit longer, hoping he can find some sort of lie in them, but I do not falter. Letting go of my arm as if saying goodbye, he walks backwards not breaking eye contact until he exits my room. Only then do the tears come. Not in a sob, but slow growing pools that collect in my eyes. The ones that make my eyes sting, before they let go, making trails of sorrow down my cheeks.

I take the time to imagine what it would be like if I just ran away. Leaving the city never turning back. What would life be like? What would it be like with John? I've known him since we were little. Living with him would be like living with family.

I can imagine us finding a worn down place, trying to make it as cozy as possible. We would steal ice cream, getting brain freezes every night. We would sing as loud as we wanted to, just to get yelled at by passersby. That life sounds so much simpler. The thought makes me want to dash into John's room telling him I have changed my mind. The voice in my head tells me to take up his offer. Take my bags to somewhere safe, somewhere I can make a home, instead of going on a suicide mission to the Kingdom of Lumbridge. It's my mother's voice. I would drop and do anything for my mother.

But if I were to run away, what if something happens? What happens if John gets shot for stealing one too many plums at the market? I've seen him get shot for more foolish things. I don't have the support to take care of both of us and I can't put him in danger at my expense.

I curl up on my bed like I used to when I slept with my mom years ago. Damian scheduled hand to hand combat trials in the morning all throughout training. The night before, my mom would come in and lay with me. She would stroke my hair singing soft lullabies. I long for that. I miss being hugged. I miss being told everything is going to be alright.

Every day for us is a challenge. You win if you get to lie on your own bed at the end of the day. Even still, when you are on your own bed you're never truly safe... like mother. I try to convince myself that I am safe. Safer here than out there.

It is a cruel world out there, and I'm used to the cruelty here. Sometimes I really just wish my mother was back in the mansion. To make warm food. To tell evening stories. To have a shoulder to cry on, but she's not. Not anymore, and I have a feeling I will never receive that kindness again.

***

There are times in life where I question what I'm doing. Why am I putting myself through this? I've decided that after this mission I will take my share of money. I will leave. John's offer sits heavy on my heart.

Are you safe here?

It's something I had always questioned, but I knew Damian would protect me. That's what I had always thought until last night.

Damian comes up from behind me, while I wait outside the plane runway. "I applaud you for agreeing to this mission, but I must warn you. If you fail, if you get caught, you won't be coming back."

"You won't let me back into Flesherg because I failed an impossible mission?" I say, the sarcasm in my voice dry.

He cocks his head. "Not just Flesherg. You won't make it out of the castle... if you know what I mean."

I look up at him pouting my lips, mocking. "You wouldn't want your reputation to be stained."

"Let's just say I'm sending someone to make sure, if you don't get the job done, you will not keep getting in my way."

My lips curve up into a sly smirk.

"I mean it this time. I have had enough of you failing missions. If you are no help, there is no need for you to take up space here."

I stare at him. Really stare at him, wondering if this is what the death of my mother did to him. Instead of loving even more, he would rather have nobody. Faintly, I hear the loopy tap of footsteps. They are not springy today. Like his jazz music has turned into some funeral procession tune.

"Ah, here he is." My father looks down at me.

"John is the one who will be watching you."

***

I board the private jet, baffled. Of course Damian would do this. He knows this job not only haunts John's dreams, but that it will be the perfect way to hurt me as well. I buckle my seatbelt, looking out the window. He doesn't speak, or even look in my direction. That, I am glad for. We both half listen to the bland voice listing out the instructions for safety if something goes wrong with the flight.

Our take off is rocky. I try not to take it as a warning sign of this mission. A red flag saying "Abort. Change directions. Go to the desert for all I care, just not Lumbridge." But of course I can't say that.

The whole point doing this mission is to keep John safe, and now he sits next to me, accompanying me on my mission. Also in charge of offing me, if I do not succeed.

"I'm sorry," I voice in barely a whisper.

"What?" He turns his head finally looking at me.

"I'm sorry." I say again. "I'm sorry I drug you down with me. I didn't know you were coming until before we boarded." I heave a sigh, folding my fingers together. "Is that why? Is that why you tried to convince me to leave?"

He looks down, and back out the window. "Yes."

It's his only response. For a while I think it's all I am going to get until he speaks again.

"It's not your fault. I just want you to be safe. That's all I ask. And, that you get the mission done because… if you don't."

"Don't worry… I have a plan."

"You're not going to get yourself killed are you?"

"Not intentionally. No."

I try a smile but it fails me, John seeing right through my charade. I can tell he doesn't have much faith in me. He is contemplating what he will do when the time comes. And not if it comes, but just *when* I am going to mess up. Loyalty is big in our gang, but to whom is he loyal? I guess I will find out.

***

I crash on the jet. I don't know how long I have been out, but a sheet of darkness greets me out the window.

"You're up." John says, exhaustion written on his face.

"I am." I suppress a yawn that tries to fill my lungs.

He turns his body to face me, leaning in close. He lowers his voice, but I really don't see why. Damian has hired the same pilot every time we need to travel. He has seen the clothes we wear, the guns we carry, I don't think he's blind to what is going on. He gets paid stacks though, so it doesn't surprise me that he stays quiet.

"Damian asked me to give you this information before we land."

"Could he not have done it himself?"
The attitude in my voice shows. The second I say it, I wish I could bring it back. John just rolls his eyes. I'm not sure if that is directed at me or Damian, but he's used to both of our mood swings.

"Continue," I say.

"As you know, the prince is looking for a new advisor."

"What happened to the old one?" I ask.

He looks down to avoid eye contact.

"You know that trip Damian went on two weeks ago…"

"Don't tell me," I start.

"Yeah… um anyway. You're going to have to make a good impression on the King. It's always a possibility that if you don't play your cards right, this mission could be over sooner than it started."

I hadn't thought about that. I had been so angry at Damian, I hadn't stopped to realize I'm going to be with the royal family all day. I'm going to have to sit with the prince every day. Talk to him. Talk to the King. How am I, a thief, a street rat, a nobody, supposed to pretend to be proper? The worry shows on my face. John is as lost as I am, maybe even more. I always have expectations. The life of the daughter of a gang master isn't elegant. There would be times that I would be so bruised from combat, picking up my fork for dinner would send tears to my eyes. John didn't have it any easier, but he didn't have the name attached to him. If we got in trouble together, I was to blame, to be punished, to be beaten.

"What do I have to say?"

"The King likes people who follow directions. If his power is ever questioned, he will no doubt send you away."

"Makes sense." I nod to myself. "What else?"

"I will be on guard at the dining hall. It shouldn't be too busy in there, so I'm sure we will get breaks."

"Lucky you," I shoot back, my voice sarcastic.

"I think you mean lucky you. You're going to have to rant about rearranging the prince's socks by color to someone."

We share a sly look. Our look. In that moment I can tell we are on the same page. We're both two rascal kids who are going on a mission against all odds. I can't wait to see Damian's face when I succeed because I will succeed. I have to.

***

The pilot voices over the loudspeaker. "One hour until landing." I take a deep breath.
"You might want to change into something more suitable."
"And what might you suggest?"
John pulls out his suitcase. Inside is a satin black suit, tailored to the sharpest look. Next to it is a baby blue colored dress, looking like a jumble of fabric. He picks it up and hands it to me.
"John?"
"Yes?" he asks, not sure how to respond.
"Did you steal these?"
"I borrowed them."
"You stole them."
"That's not the point. The point is, you need to look your best to get this job. Go change."
I turn around, the beautiful dress in my hand. Stopping in my tracks, I pivot.
"If this is about my success, why did you get yourself a suit?"
"They weren't sold separately," a grin appearing on his face.
"Funny."

I slip the dress on. It's the softest thing I've ever worn, the silk hanging loosely at my less than curvy sides. The heels are what get me, my toes screeching in pain already. There is no mirror, but I know the dress can't fix anything about my bruised arms or scarred face. As for John, he can pull anything off.

It's a little strange to see him in evening attire; however, he looks fantastic. The edges of the suit bring out the sharpness in his jaw, and unlike me, the scar on his cheek actually looks quite charming. He looks as though he could be related to royalty with his head held high and his dark brown hair perfectly framing his face. Sure to get the job. I just wonder what he'll do if he gets hired and I don't. Will he drop out and go back to Damian, killing me in the process? If he is smart, he will stay right where he is. At least there, he will be provided for, putting his skills to great use. As long as he can keep his Flesherg identity on the low, he will be perfectly fine. I, on the other hand, am a wreck. One mistake from me, and I can kiss this world goodbye.

"You look rather gorgeous." John interrupts me mid-thought.

A blush goes to my cheeks. "Yeah I think the battle scars really complete the ensemble."

"I'm being for real. That color looks nice on you. You look… sweet."

I look down, examining the dress again, my hair falling over my shoulders.

"All passengers, we are coming in for a landing. Buckle your seatbelt, and move your seats to the correct position."

This is it. Fate awaits.

***

John and I take landing. My heart thumps in my chest, butterflies stuck in my stomach. I am going to have to play a part for how long? Weeks? Months? I look over to my left. John's piercing eyes say the same. They show the terror, and also the mask that shadows the terror. The one that shows no fear.

Stepping off of the plane, the warm air hits me. The sun shines on my face warming my cheeks from the cool air conditioner that was blowing on the plane. We must have traveled quite far for it to be so warm. I take a glance at John following close behind. His hand rests on my back guiding me to where a black limousine waits. There is a slight relief in my stomach. It must be Charlie. He is always the one that drives us places for our top secret missions.

He steps out of the limo, closing the door behind him. "If it isn't Zaria and John. How are you guys doing?" His smile is so bright along with the neon collared shirt from his trip to Mt. Espren.

He embraces us in a group hug. Unlike the pilot, Charlie is very friendly.

I don't even know the pilot's name, but when I met Charlie, it was the first thing he said, along with his favorite food, and how cool it is to drive a limo.

"We're great, thank you Charlie," I heave, the breath squeezing out of my chest.

"I hear you're heading to Lumbridge. Big mission?"

John speaks up this time. "Extremely. Can we get going now?"

Charlie opens the door with exquisite finesse.

"Your adventure awaits."

The limo ride is short. Either we weren't far away, or Charlie was speeding. The windows are all black, even on the inside, and I wouldn't put it past him to speed like a maniac. Lumbridge? I've never heard of it, and I don't even know where we are or where we're going.

John sits next to me. We don't say anything, but we both rest against each other worrying about what lies ahead of us. We keep the silence until we feels the limo slow and the engine cut off.

"Alright you two," Charlie turns around looking back at John and I, his hands still on the newly detailed wheel. He had it specially painted an obnoxious bright blue just like his collared shirt. Mt. Espren really changed him. He came back... different.

"Hey, you know if there is anything you guys need help with, you can always call me up."

Charlie has been trying to get into *the know* of the gang for years now. He awkwardly smiles at us.

I catch a glance at John who sits next to me, his arms crossed. He looks down at me, his eyebrows turned up as if saying, *you deal with him.*

I clear my throat. "It's not that we wouldn't want you pulling up making a grand entrance in style with your limo, but we are going to need a ride back home and we can't do that with you splat on the concrete."

"Oh well that's insulting that you think I wouldn't make it." Turning back around he slowly rolls up the tiny window that separates the driver's seat from the rest. We sit in silence listening to the tiny "*rrrrrrrr,*" sound of the motor. Before it gets all the way up he presses his face against the glass. "It's you loss," he whispers dramatically before finally closing the window.

John looks down at me. Rolling his eyes, he shakes his head and smirks before he unbuckles his seatbelt.

When I step out, he is right by my side. I am grateful for his presence. A rock to hold onto when I'm stuck in a riptide. We stare at the castle in front of us. I have never seen such elegant architecture.

It is a square building made of ancient stones. Each carefully placed like the hardest puzzle on earth. Towers are posted on each corner of the castle. Flags dancing in the air at the top of the peaks. The lightest blue imaginable with a golden bridge as their crest.

The windows reflect the beams of the sun, the doors a solid portal into our lives for the next couple of weeks. Everything about this place seems perfect.

A wonder and awe enters my heart. The architecture is absolutely unbelievable, but there is also a bit of a sting. A feeling deep down that I can't quite place. Frustration? Jealousy?

I see people on the street of Flesherg holding up signs to anybody that might have a kind soul, searching for help. The people in this castle have probably never known what it is like to go hungry, to be cold. Everything is done for them.

We walk towards the front entrance. The gate is as elaborate as the rest of the castle. The feeling of entering a new and different world, the second we cross through. Happy sunflowers stand in the front garden. White, wispy flowers filling in the gaps.

Guards line the perimeter. I feel their eyes are on us as we approach. Hiding behind the cover of night as a regular makes being seen by hundreds of eyes terrifying. My breath hitches. John squeezes my hand for a split second before letting go. How can he act so confidently? He has built his mask so much stronger than I have, his eyes the only tell to his tale. They remind me of a breezy day. When he gets flustered, the wind picks up. His eyes are stormy. Dark and focused. He is playing his part. It is time I play mine.

"Hello," I say, sounding as polite as possible as we make it to the front gate "My friend and I have an appointment with the King for new jobs."

The guard stares us down. Only then do I remember I have my dress on. His eyes linger on me a second too long for John's liking. Grabbing my hand, his own feel clammy.

"Whenever possible, are we allowed access to meet with the King today?" John asks, his voice steady

"Are your names John and Zaria?" His voice sends a shrill down my spine. The very reason why he is posted by the front gate. The sternness in his voice. One that would shake anyone's nerves.

"Yes sir."

"ID?"

Both John and I retrieve our phony IDs, both of us being underage, and not to mention, part of a mafia gang. Handing them over to be examined, the guard takes a look, pondering at each of our papers like he's searching for something out of place. Anything that would end up getting him fired if he didn't catch it. By the time we are done, the likelihood of him being fired is 80%.

"Come with me." He waits for us to walk in front of him so we are not behind. Smart move. *Never let your enemies behind you.*

Climbing the stairs, another set of guards open the front door. All in uniform, it is hard to tell any of them apart. Only a few features define them. One has a bigger nose. The other, having bushier eyebrows.

Other than that, they all look like clones. All decked in black suits, golden armor lying on top. Their swords are hilted next to them. A line of enemies ready to attack.

We enter into a room with the highest ceilings I have ever seen. Even higher than the Exploratory Museum. Baby angels are painted, circling above us. The like of which I have only read in books. My heart can't help but melt at the fairytale that comes to life.

Gold chandeliers hang, bringing the whole art piece together. I walk with my head held up, not able to take my eyes off the roof that contains us.

"This is the common area, wait here. A servant will come and get you when it is time."

He walks away, his movements stiff and robotic. We wait for his steps to fade in the echo before we decide to let out our breath.

Finally taking in the rest of the room, I gawk at the velvet seats and couches that are placed along the perimeter. John and I sit down on one of the sofas, melting in the cushion it brings. Both of us release a sigh. A sigh of relief, and also of pain.

***

The second my name is called, my heart leaps into my throat. Standing up from the chair I am aware of every movement I make.

The way my arms fall stiffly at my side. The clunky and unbalanced steps I have in my heels as they echo through the high ceilings. My dress swishes with every step I take, making me feel lost in a swirling sea. The fabric brushes against my leg making me long for my comfortable pants again. I am brought into a room. It has no windows, only a long table that resembles Damian's. I guess it really is a power move. Rows of chairs line down the table. I see the King meet my eyes at the other end of the table. I keep my mask on. The mask of a polite woman who needs a job and will do anything to get it. The servant who escorted me pulls out a chair opposite from the King. I smile the warmest I can towards her.

"Thank you," I insist as I sit down, aligning my skirt. A habit I'm not used to.

The servant waits at the edge of the room with her head down, long blonde curls falling like spirals down her front. The King clears his throat turning my attention back over to my main mission. I am surprised by his warm smile, the flash of his white teeth being almost as perfect as the walls surrounding us. He wears a blue tuxedo, a white cape flowing over his shoulders. Looking down at my own lap I take note that I wear the same color. Smart move John.

"You are, Miss Zaria?" he starts, his voice as pleasant as early birds chirping.

"Yes, Your Highness." I almost stutter.

"Let me start by giving you a warm welcome to
my kingdom. How was your trip?"
I struggle to keep my voice high. Sweet and airy,
like a butterfly.

"It was quite well," I begin. "I've never seen a
kingdom as beautiful as yours." Or any for that
matter.

"Why, thank you," his eyes gleam in my direction
before tidying the stack of papers that lay before
him. The questions of what are on those papers
flood my mind. They can't be anything but lies. He
smiles as he reads whatever is written before him,
nodding to himself. Definitely lies.

"Let's get down to business." Folding his hands in
front of him, he straightens his back. "You came
here to fill in the role of my son's new advisor. Is
that correct?"

"That is correct, sir."

"And what kind of experience do you have?
You'll be with the prince. The future King of
Lumbridge. What makes you special?" Looking me
up and down his words are said with delightful
interest, yet I can sense the speculation under his
eyes. The protectiveness of his son.

This is the question I was preparing for. Of course
I can't tell him I have no experience as an advisor. I
can't tell the King that I run around the street with a
target on my back every waking moment, so
instead —

"I was previously stationed at a prison where I am from. My friend John and I both worked there together dealing with the enemies of our nation."

A half-truth, if dealing with the enemies of our nation was dealing and stealing from people all over the city.

"It seems as though you would be a better fit for a soldier than an advisor."

I quickly hide my surprise with an unfazed glance. A smile at best, referring back to what my father told me under pressure. *Turn the tables away from you, then ask a question.*

"I can see how you would think that sir," I smile trying to be convincing. "I am looking for something a little bit more laid back." I reveal my bruises and scars. "As advisor, would I be fighting much?"

The King's face widens, his eyes in shock. He looks almost sorry. Like he has felt the pain that is now part of me. He takes a deep breath and continues.

"No, you wouldn't. Not unless needed."
I speak fast, hoping not to interject whatever follows.

"I will protect the prince at any cost, my own life included. I just need some time to heal. I am good at taking notes, and making suggestions. I work well with a tight schedule. I can handle being under pressure."

The whole time I speak, the King just looks. His eyes are pure. It's weird to look across a table and not see condescending eyes staring back at me, playing games.

"Your friend is also here for an interview, yes?"

"Correct, Your Highness. We protected each other the same as we will protect this kingdom. I could always count on him to have my back… more than you know." The image of him standing in my room last night, begging me to run away, to abandon all of this mess and start new, weighs heavy on my mind.

He looks again at my scars. It's like he can see right through me. The one in particular he is looking at, is the one I got after losing every practice combat battle. The slash proudly sits upon my right shoulder. That night, my dad had slashed me with his pocket knife. He told me if I lost every battle out on a job, worse would happen. It was to teach me a lesson. To scare me.

John had heard my cries and came into the room to comfort me. I tried to warn him as much as I could. To turn around and lock himself in his room, but before I could, Damian slashed him as well telling him that is what happens when you are caught eavesdropping. When Damian left, we stayed lying on the floor calming each other. He wrapped me up and read one of the stories my mother had given me. That day I knew that I had someone. Someone in this crazy world that would be right beside me.

"I think you will make an excellent advisor for my son."

The King's voice startled me back into reality.

"What?"

"Lucy, could you get one of the rooms ready on the top floor?"

"Yes, Your Highness." She bows before stepping out of the room

I match the name to the face. I look at the King wondering if I should follow her, or stay, or —

"Before you go, Zaria," My eyes peer back at him.

"I would like to admire your bravery, and I trust that you will be just fine as my son's advisor."
For once in my life I am left speechless. He stands, starting to walk over to me. Holding out his hand, he smiles. I take his hand in mine, my grip a little tighter than it should be.

"Thank you," I say, a stupid smile plastered on my face.

He gently blinks at me. "Follow Lucy. She will show you to your room."

***

I walk down the halls, turn after turn, up a huge flight of stairs, another turn. The rest of the palace looks as magnificent as the common room. Stunningly beautiful flowers fill every vase stationed through the halls. Everything feels like a dream, but despite the romantic feeling of the palace, I find myself itchy and restless.

Without Lucy I would be lost in this never ending maze. She is very quiet. Her head still down, she navigates through the castle. Hopefully, in a few days I will be able to have the navigation skills she has acquired.

I try to break the silence.

"I'm Zaria, by the way," I start, my voice sounding awkward in the echoing halls. "I hear your name is Lucy. That's a lovely name."
She finally looks up, her eyes glazed. "Is it really?" she asks, her voice nothing above a whisper.

"Of course."

I wince at her response. The mellow tone that comes out of her, like it has been weeks since she has seen the light of day. My stomach tosses at the question of how badly she must be treated.

"Here is your room, Miss Zaria."

She opens a door that lies on the left hand side of the long hallway. There is no creak, unlike my bedroom back in Flesherg. Instead, it is perfect, just like everything else. The handle is coated in gold, the light bending and bouncing off of it. Trying not to roll my eyes, I instead force a gasp out of my mouth.

"Woah..."

"It truly is something," she comments, lifting her head ever so slightly. Just the tiniest bit, that I catch her indigo eyes.

A true complement to her blonde curled hair. Her cheeks blush a bright pink when she catches me looking. "If you wish to do an activity while your room is being prepared, I can show you where to go."

Quickly correcting her posture back to her slumped shoulders, she adverts her face to the ground again.

"Um actually… I can unpack my things myself." I catch myself, "That is, if it doesn't cause any trouble."

I don't need eyes on me. Not here, and definitely not now.

"Really?"

"Yeah. You've been such a help already."

She still just stands there. For a moment I think she won't move. She fidgets, running her fingers up and down, alongside her arm.

"Oh… okay."

She walks away, eyeing the floor as she had done our whole introduction. Her steps are small and dainty, barely leaving a sound on the marble tile. Did I really just upset her? A wave of frustration boils through me. Everything. Every little thing I do, is somehow wrong. To someone, in some way, it is always not quite right.

Once the door is closed behind me, I collapse face first onto the bed. I go to cry, but the bed is so soft it interrupts my tears. Only for a second do I relish in the fluffy cloud, then the tears come out in sobs.

I fight to not make any noise.It feels as though any and every thought and emotion I have ever felt is all coming out, and I have only just begun.

I wipe my tears, sliding my fingers across my now soaking cheeks. I need to make quick work. I go to unpack my things, mindful of the fact that I may be being watched. I'll have to look for any cameras or recorders later. The few clothes that I did bring jumbled inside my suitcase. Then it dawns on me, I can't wear my clothes.

"Ahhhhhh." I groan from deep in my throat. My back starts to itch, my shoulders sore from the straps. Looking at the clock that hangs on the wall, it has only been three hours. Holding my leather pants, I almost go into another fit of anger. I can't even wear my combat boots. Walking up the stairs had been such a struggle, regardless of all the physical training I do on the regular.

The only reason I even remotely know how to walk in heels is because John and I were sent on a job to steal Mr. Rodmen's watch. He is a man of wealth, which of course made him a target to Damian. We staged as guests at a multimillion dollar party. In the end we got the watch, but my feet payed the price. I always thought John had it so easy. A suit and dress shoes isn't that much different from his regular street wear. He can still run a mile in dress clothes, where as I put on heels and have to rebalance every step.

In the pile of my ratty clothes, I see it. The one thing that truly matters. My mother's necklace. Damian had given it to her as a mother's day gift. It had been the only thing that truly reminded me of her, besides the gloves. A ruby embedded in gold plating and chain. The only worldly possession that could shine a fraction as bright as she could.

Some nights she would sing to me in the dead of night. There was no candlelight, no moonlight, but I swear it sparkled. That's just what my mother did. She could make anything sparkle. My sparkle died the day I found her body in the living room, lifeless and bloody. I had never seen such horror before.

I wait in my room. Waiting for someone to come in and tell me my assignment, but the hours pass and no one comes. The beating of the sun in the window turned to a soft glow shadowing my room. I hadn't had dinner, but I don't have the nerve to descend those stairs and find it.

I wonder if I will start tomorrow. Am I going to need training? Damian didn't give me a time limit. As long as I complete the mission, I can keep my head.

Maybe it's better if I make him wait. I would love to see him squirm, watching, waiting to see if I will slip up. But if I do wait, I'm stuck in this castle. Stuck knowing the job I need to complete, because I know the consequences all too well if I don't. As I draw a bath, I wonder which option is worse. Any option at getting back at Damian is better, so I sink into the bubbles letting out a sigh.

I let them stick to my skin, the sweet smell filling my nose. Honey and jasmine? It definitely has a flowery scent. For the first time in a while the tension in my muscles eases. I close my eyes to the outside world I have called home. A shameful home, but a home none the less. A tune comes to my head. I've never been really good at singing, but this castle is big enough that no one will hear me. I try to remember the lullaby I would drift off to. It reminded me of Celtic mermaids, somewhere under the sea where it is calm, quiet. The bliss of the memory blocks out all my senses making me paralyzed all except this overwhelming hum. All that remains is the melody in my ears and the mystery scent lingering in my nose.

"Hello?"

I snap out of the dream I was in. Confused at first, I answer, "Hello?"

"Are you in the bath?"

The voice sure isn't from Lucy. It's instead low and confident. It could be another servant. Delivering clothes maybe?

"Um… yes."

"I will wait out here until you are finished."

I quick get out of the tub, slipping and sliding on my blistered feet. Fresh towels are stacked neatly next to the sink. I make a watery trail across the floor, the cold air shocking me. Wrapping myself with the towels they are surprisingly very warm.

I am grateful I left my dress in here instead of out on my bed, like I would normally do at home. The last thing I want is for someone to steal my dress, and then I would have nothing. I'd have to bow down to the King in my leather pants and jacket. That wouldn't get a great response. I brush tiny tangles out of my hair. For once I let in fall loose down my back, instead of in a tight braid. Coming out, I wish I never did.

In front of me stands my mission. The Prince of Lumbridge. Heir to the throne and my next victim. I stand in the doorway, his eyes meeting mine. His hair is as golden as sun-kissed meadows, a gentle wave over his forehead. His dress is a mirror of his fathers. The only difference being his cape cut half the length of the king's, and draped on one shoulder instead of both. He has to tilt his head downward even from far away to meet my eyes.

He clears his throat. "From my understanding, you will be my new advisor."

I almost forget to respond, his voice a secret melody. I stutter as I start.

"Yes….yes Your Highness." I bow, trying to make up for our unfortunate meeting. As I rise, I almost see a wince on his face. I wait for him to continue, but he doesn't. Our eyes both wander, the silence almost suffocating.

"I didn't expect for you to be so young." He says.

"Why aren't you in school?"

I hadn't had anyone ask me that before, the question taking me by surprise. I have never once had to come up with a cover as to why I was not in school. I could say I was an early gradate, but I could be doing a lot more with that kind of resume than an advisor. The only response I can come up with is—

"Unfortunately, where I grew up, school only ran until high school. After that you get a low paying job and make the best of it."

A thin line appears on his face. Of course it would be hard for him to try to imagine any struggle. The thought almost makes me scoff.

"Well I'm glad you are here. You will get well taken care of in this palace. My father will make sure of it."

I gesture a polite nod, unsure what else to say. An awkward silence fills the room. Picking at my nails, I face slightly away from him, not knowing where to look.

"I brought up dinner for you," he speaks up. Lowering his head down at me, he looks me up and down. "I saw that you did not arrive for your welcome banquet."

"I didn't know I was invited." The sentence comes out a little harsher than I expected. The corners of his mouth lower. Now I know I didn't make a good first impression. "I didn't know where dinner was served," I try again in a more polite voice.

"I can take you for a tour tomorrow, if you want."

"That would be great. What time should I meet you?"

His arms cross behind his back, making his form seem broader than before.

"Don't worry, I will get you. Be ready by seven."
I internally groan. What a great mission this is.

He looks back at the steamed bathroom before looking back at me. "Just out of curiosity, what song were you humming before?"

I feel my cheeks heat, my thoughts scattered all over the place. "I… I don't know?"

He nods slowly, glancing away again he says, "Well I won't disturb you anymore."

"Thank you for the dinner. I wish you a restful sleep." I tell him, hoping it ushers him out quicker.

"Thank you." He replies. "Goodnight Zaria."

He turns around, walking swiftly back to the door. "Wait—

He turns looking back at me, his fingers still resting on the door handle.

I almost choke at the stupidity of the question I am about to ask. "Pardon me, but I didn't get your name."

He laughs, his head angled up towards the ceiling. Opening the door, he slips out.

"I guess you will find out tomorrow."

With that, he closes my door.

That has got to be the most disrespectful thing I could have said. I hide under my sheets agonizing about tomorrow. The lullaby faint in my mind. I lay still in my evening dress, but unless I want to look like a hobo, it's my only option. I shut my eyes cursing myself.

At some point I must have fallen asleep. I awake to a creak. This place is so quiet it's hard to fall asleep. Any noise made, sounds like a storm compared to the calm sea of the night. I had become used to falling asleep to sirens outside my window. Shouts for someone's dear life echoing in my dreams. All part of living in Flesherg. More, all part of living with Damian. A hand grasps over my mouth.

I only look over, my eyes glaring at John.

"You should be glad I knew it was you," I whisper after his hand comes off.

"Yeah, yeah, big tough guy." He smirks. "How are you making out so far? Want to quit?"

I stand from the bed, rocking back and forth on my feet. Deep sleep had taken me so far, my feet forgot how to work. Stepping on the fresh blisters wakes me up real fast.

"John, don't tease me like that. I don't want to be here anymore than you do." I pause for a second.

"How did your interview go? I'm guessing you got the job."

"I didn't have an interview," he says flopping his hand.

"What?"

He leans back against the pillows, stretching his arms, his face smug.

"The King came out and said I was hired. Must have been my huge muscles he couldn't resist."

"Mmmhh, was there anything else he said? Anything that would have helped you get hired?"

He clicks his tongue against the roof of his mouth, acting like he's trying to think. Typical John. Always making a big production out of everything.

"I don't recall. No." His eyes wander to the plate of food that was left uneaten.

"That's a shame."

"I want to hate this place, but it's hard to when the bed is so comfy," he says sleepily. "And the food so good," he continues picking up pieces of meat and eating it.

I plop back on the cozy mattress in agreeance. "This is the best sleep I had in years, ever since my…" I choke on my words not able to get them out.

"Your mother," he finishes for me.

"Yeah."

A long silence fills the air. I listen to the smooth breathing of John beside me. Relaxed and content. Even if I don't want to stay here long, it could possibly be the best for him. He's like my family. I need to protect him. If he is happy here, I will drag this on for as long as I can. For him. For him I would do anything.

"When do you think you will start?" John whispers.

"The mission?"

Nodding, he looks back up to the ceiling. I do the same. The roof looking so pristine. No sign of gunfire, or holes from objects being thrown.

"I don't know," I answer, a yawn escaping my throat. "Give me some time. I'll go from there."
Next to me, he grunts in pain. His eyes sealed shut, his forehead creasing.

"What's wrong?" I roll over trying to get a better look.

He struggles at first for words until it seems like he snaps out of whatever had just consumed him.

"I've had this crazy headache. It keeps coming in and out."

"Are you sure you're okay?" the worry in my voice sounding, a bit more than I would like.

"I should get back to my room." He says, his face squeezing again.

"Okay." I hesitate, watching him slowly lift himself off the bed. "I'll see you tomorrow."

He smiles, some of the pain from before leaving his face. "Tomorrow I get my uniform."

The happiness on his face, in his eyes is contagious. I smile with him.

"I'm glad you're happy."

"I'm glad you aren't mad at me." His smile fades into a shameful frown.

"Why would I be mad at you?"

He looks around perplexed that I didn't put the pieces together. I sit in silence waiting for a response.

"Is it Damian?" I ask, already knowing the answer. A nod of his head confirms it.

"John, what my father does has nothing to do with you. I would never blame you for something that was his fault, so you can stop worrying."

His smile reappears. Forceful at first, then a slight chuckle follows.

"Goodnight Zaria."

For the second time today someone has said goodnight to me. That is twice more than I had in five years. Before I can say it back, John has successfully snuck out of my room. I hope he doesn't do anything stupid in the castle. We made a pact on the jet. No stealing, except for what's inside their safe, of course. If he's lucky, he might actually start to like it here. There are a million possibilities of what I could do, but also a quick way of ending it all. The thing is, I know John would never kill me even if Damian had a gun to his head. That's who he is. The one part I didn't have to think to lie about, is how reliable John is. He can be stupid and drive me insane, but his heart is gold.

I roll over on the bed, snuggling into the blankets. The spot where John laid still warm. I relax all my muscles, breathing in his scent.

Never in a million years did I think I would sleep in the presence of royalty, let alone in a castle. I wonder if Damian feels any jealousy. I would if I were him. Tomorrow I will find out his name. Step one, in this monstrous plan. For now I sleep in comfort, knowing that Damian is far, far away, probably drunk out of his mind.

Chapter four

Lucy arrives in the morning with a fresh new dress and a clipboard. I blink the sleep from my eyes, preparing to have to wear my mask of smiles and laughter.

"Good morning Lucy."

She stands in the corner, eyes down. I guess I'm going to have to get used to that. Without raising her voice much, she speaks. "Good morning, Miss Zaria. Would you like any assistance getting ready?"

I think of her walking away last time I told her I was okay on my own. She could always be an ally to me, another path for information. The whole, making the prince fall in love with me, and then faking my death is just the icing on the cake to make the kingdom fall.

"I would be delighted," I tell her, satisfied.

With that, her head rises ever so slightly. All I can see is the crease on her forehead. Her eyebrows raised in surprise.

"I will go in the tub and then get dressed. After that, would you mind doing my hair?"

"Certainly."

I gather the new dress she has laid out for me, glad that they provide dresses to me. I would be out of luck if they didn't. Drawing the bath, I catch the smell of that sweet fragrance again. It's the most calming thing on earth. Each breath, I feel like I am drifting into a dream. I try not to get lost in a trance, so I bathe as fast as possible. If I could, I would stay in this bath forever. No Damian, no prince, just this beautiful dream. But it's been a while since any dream of mine has come true.

I throw the new dress over my head. This one a blush pink that goes down to my knees. Chiffon fabric, draped from my waist, moving harmonically with every step. I have to admit the dresses are very lovely, but if I can't wear pants soon, I might just decide to ask John to do the deed. I spin to set the dress in place. Bracing myself to talk to Lucy, I step out.

I walk over to what I think is a vanity. I have lived in a mansion all my life, but have never once requested a vanity. It always seemed too girlish to me. I didn't wear makeup, and all my clothes looked the same, so there was really no point. I sit down on the cushion, forced to look at myself in the mirror. The feeling is foreign, one I am not used to. It is only now that I notice the little details about myself reflecting back in the spotless glass. The little bit of redness under my cheek, from crying every night. The way my jaw is higher on the one side compared to the other from constant tension.

I don't look how I imagined I once did. I had once thought that I would be poised, maybe even beautiful. That was when I was little, dreaming of being a princess. Now, I am literally in a castle, living my six-year-old dream, but I don't fit. I have gone too far on the other side. A side that I think has no return.

Once I get situated, Lucy pulls my hair back into a ponytail. Opening a pot of paints, she reaches for a brush.

"No!" I stammer, before I can even think what I said through.

"Is something wrong Miss Zaria?" Looking up, I am met with her whole face. For a split second, I see it. The pain, the brokenness. The misery that has been hidden. But just like last night, it only lasts for a second.

Frantically I start thinking. I get up looking for my shoes to stall more time. I find them easily, cursing under my breath. Slowly I slide my feet into the death trap to get yet another set of blisters.

"I... um... have an allergy." I fluster my voice to make the whole lie seem more realistic. "I have tried makeup once. Face blew up like a balloon at the fair."

"I am... so sorry Miss." She starts jumbling the pots and brush back together in a tizzy.

The truth is I have no ill will towards make up. Most of the women in the gang wore it, and my mother always looked stunningly beautiful with a fresh layer of paint on. I just can't bring myself to do it. To cover my scars would be to cover who I am. It's the only thing left to remind me of the pain every day. To remind me of the *"why." Why* I keep doing this. *Why* I have no other choice. And if I don't have the marks, I have nothing left.

"I would still love if you could do my hair." I try to reassure her, stepping back over to where she stands.

"Yes, Miss." And with that she closes her mouth, the corners of her eyes drooping.

She slides my hair out of the pony tail she had done before. The brush in her hand ever so slightly grazes my head. I try to catch her gaze in the mirror, but it is no use. I don't even know if I try to talk to her, if she will feel like she is noticed, or just get even more flustered. I throw in all my cards and decide to try.

"What's your favorite part of working in the castle?"

An easy question. One I should be asking anyway. Our jobs aren't that different.

She's slow at first, but eventually she answers, "I would have to say the best part is keeping track of the garden."

"Ooh, what do you do?"

Perfect. *Get your opponent to talk about what they like.*

"I decide what flowers will be in each section of the castle. Everyone's preferences, and the meaning behind them"

"That sounds like a lot of fun," I proclaim, sounding as enthusiastic as possible.

"It is," she says, her fingers running through the length of my hair. "Sunflowers have always been my favorite. The happy nature we receive from them. It's warm and delightful."

I think on her words. "I have never thought of flowers as such before."

"Your hair is ready Miss."

I look in the mirror at what she had done. My hair remains down, but she has pulled two strands of hair into the back, pinning it with tiny crystals.

"This is absolutely stunning." I say, not even lifting a finger to lie.

"Thank you, Miss."

"Please," I look at her through the mirror catching another small glimpse of those sparkling blue eyes.

"Call me Zaria."

She halts for a minute, her hands on the clipboard she had brought in.

"Here is the prince's schedule. For the first couple of days he will help walk you through what he expects of you, so you can relax while you settle in."

Lucy hands me the board. A stack of papers lays on top of it, almost too big for the clip to hold them all.

The first page is filled with script. Line after line, the scribbles so tiny, I have to squint to read it. I frill through the pages to see if there is any break in the pattern, but the long list continues. How am I supposed to be able to connect with the prince, when there are so many tasks to be done? I guess I am now the one with a distressed face because Lucy puts her hand on my shoulder.

"It seems like a lot, but if you ever need help, you can always ask me."

I hesitate, my hands grasping the clipboard. I hear Damian's voice in my head. To stay on guard, and not accept help from anyone, bedsides John. But despite the aching feeling in my chest, my heart still warms at her offer.

"Thank you, Lucy."

I then hear a knock at the door. I stand from the vanity, Lucy walking to the wall, her head down again. The door opens, and just like last night, there is the prince.

"Your tour awaits."

***

Walking behind the prince, my heart starts to beat. His cologne wafts back behind him as he walks, the aroma hitching in my throat. Those blonde waves that lay perfectly on top of his head are freshly styled, looking wet in the early morning.

His legs are long, I have to skip to keep up. Making it to the stairs, I wish I could cancel this whole day, and crawl back into my warm blanketed bed. The dreaded fifty steps I counted on the way up when I first arrived. He stops at the top of them, waiting for me to catch up. The embarrassment of the wobble in my steps makes me clutch my board tighter, taking all my frustration out on the tiny slab of wood. He waits until I stand next to him before offering his elbow to my side.

I pause for a second, looking at his hands. His skin looks so soft and smooth, like it has seen no torment. His veins stick out, two golden rings wrapped around his fingers. It would be rude if I did not accept and the anxiety of the heels make me grudgingly accept his arm. I move my clipboard to the other side, holding stiff my other arm around the prince. Unlike me, he stays firm, a calm cool expression on his face. Not one ounce of worry.

I try to think of something to say. Something to break the awkwardness of my shaky hands.

"You haven't walked in heels before, have you?"

My mouth forms into a thin line, my lips pressed tightly together. I never expected to have the prince of Lumbridge speak in such a manner, or lack thereof. He looks down at me, obviously awaiting me to prove him right. A pest from the start.

"No. I don't walk in heels often."

We make it to the final step. A sigh of relief escapes my lungs. Still looking at me he chuckles.

"Don't worry. You now have your own personal railing," he says, bowing at me, mockingly.

This little—

"Shall we start the tour?"

I gather all my loose threads, weaving my kind, and elegant mask back on. "Yes, Your Highness."

He leads me down another grand hall. This one has a golden chandelier hanging from the roof. Little candle sticks nestle into the nooks and crannies, their flames licking the air. I wonder who lights those candles. The twinge of smoke fills the air confiming it is indeed real. As we round the corner the bite of smoke exits my throat finally allowing me to breathe just as Axil starts the tour.

"This is the royal kitchen. Mostly only chefs are allowed in here." He leans down putting his lips next to my ear. "But I won't tell my father if I happen to hear unsteady footsteps coming from inside."

I can't help but glare at him. His perfect blue eyes avoiding my rudeness. A shame really. I recall my glare to be quite menacing according to John.

He leads me into another room, then another, then another, explaining all of the rooms to me. The council room, where the royal court will have weekly meetings. The day room, a room that is made of mostly windows. It is filled with loads of frilly ladies sipping their tea and gossiping about the latest news.

The women stop their banter, admiring the prince, then sending dirty looks in my direction.

"How are we today, ladies?" he asks, a gentle smile forming on his lips.

Squeals ring out. Bunches of tulle and lace frolicking about as they usher themselves to him. Stepping aside, I give them plenty of room.

"We were just having some morning tea and cakes. You are welcome to join us if you like."
If it was just the statement being said, I would think these girls have a kind heart. But judging by the slight panic that bubbles in the prince's eyes as they wrap their arms around his, I decide to step in.

"I'm Zaria," I say, holding out my hand, interrupting their pounce. "I don't think we have been introduced."

One of the ladies looks me up and down, her smile falling. Makeup cakes her cheeks, her chestnut ringlets falling around her face.

"No, I don't think we have." Scoffing, she refuses to shake my hand.

"Who are you?" I ask, genuinely curious, and a little just to tick her off.

Raising her eyebrows, she purses her lips. "*I* am the Princess of Hemway. And if I am correct, you should be bowing to me."

Gritting my teeth, I curse her with my eyes. Slightly lowering my head, I see her raise her own.

"Well Brielle, it was a pleasure seeing you, but we must be going," the prince insists.

Her two friends look me up and down, as Brielle once did. I try not to fidget at their stare, but they catch it anyway.

"I'm guessing you are the new advisor," She spits out the last part.

The prince scoops his arm around mine again, ushering me out. "And I'm guessing you are not only a princess, but also a pain in the ass."

A tiny laugh escapes the prince, recovered by a convenient cough.

Stomping her foot, she yells before we are out of the room, "Good luck being an advisor. I wouldn't be surprised if they put you as a slave with that dirty mouth of yours."

Shutting the door, the prince walks out, dragging me along with him. Letting out a breath, he finally lets himself chuckle, his face scarlet.

"I have never heard anyone ever talk to Brielle like that," he gets out between gasps of breath.

"Well now you have." I smile at my own accomplishment. "Who is she anyway?" I ask, pulling myself back together.

"She's from a neighboring kingdom. Her parents sent her away while they rebuild their own grounds. Every day she has tried to make some type of move on any of the men here. I should have run while I had the chance."

"Who knows, maybe one day you will receive an invitation to one of her tea parties, signed *yours truly*."

"Maybe one day," he remarks. "Shall we continue the tour?"

I was right when I first arrived, I could really get lost in here for days. Luckily, between each room, I have had time to sketch out a map. The lines look all scraggily along with my handwriting, looking like chicken scratches, but it's clear enough to get the picture.

Placing his hands on a set of double doors, he throws them open. "And here we have the sparring room."

I stumble back amazed at what stands in front of me. We enter a massive room. Swords of all shapes and sizes hang upon the walls. No space left for any fancy writing or painting that was on all the other walls of the palace. I grip the clipboard to make sure I don't drop it. For once I stepped in front of him. Not caring if I was being disrespectful.

Crash mats line the floors. Makes sense, but also another reminder of the luxury this prince has over everyone else. Most of my scars are from sliding or falling on the concrete. That was the only way I learned to stay on my feet, unless I wanted another gash from the swamp of alligator teeth, I call the pavement.

"Have you ever sparred?"

An exasperated laugh comes out of my lungs. I try my best to hold my tongue.

"Once or twice before." I shrug, a smug face forming on my lips.

"Want to try?"

I look at him shocked. "Is that allowed?"

"As long as you don't cut my arm off, I think we're okay."

He tosses me a sword that was lying on one of the mats. I catch it with ease, even with the clipboard in my other hand. I set it down against the nearest wall, taking my shoes off as well. There is no way I could win this with those death traps. He takes his time retrieving a sword for himself.

He wraps his hands around a shiny gold handle. One of the strongest swords I have ever seen. Holding it firm, he sends a glance towards me.

We end up in the middle of the room circling each other. Both of us waiting for the first move. Lucky for me, he takes pity on me, and swings first. Using his swing as an opening, I go for his side. He clashes his sword up against mine. My heart starts to speed. Not from fear, but from excitement. The feeling of the attack, making my nerves fire, my body coming to life. Serve after serve, our swords screeching against our lashes. I backed him to the wall. He has underestimated me, and he was aware of it now. I cross my sword over his body, immobilizing his arm. With my free hand I secure the sword on the other side, kicking the handle of the sword that he grasps. He lets go, his sword making one finale clang. Picking it up, my eyes still fix on his movements.

"Wow. My father had said something about you fighting before. You're better than I thought you would be."

Breathless, I respond, "Thank you."

"We better get going. It's almost lunch time. I will tell you all that's on that clipboard while we eat."

I hand him the swords, going back to the clipboard that I tossed to the side. I put my shoes back on, dreading standing back up. Sliding my feet back in, one thing is for sure. I had showed the Prince of Lumbridge just how powerful I can be.

***

We make our way back to the dining hall for lunch. When we arrive, I look around frantically trying to spot John. And just like I had confirmed when we first got here, everyone looks the same in uniform, and now John is lost in the lineup of guards. I am surprised when the prince starts speaking.

"You are the new soldier. Am I correct?"

He stands in front of a man that looks exactly like the rest. Only then do I see his dark brown eyes. The eyes that almost appear black. The boy I had always seen John to be, now looking like a man amongst the rest. I see him glance at me, the look of pain from last night surging through him again for a second. I reach out for him but the moment I do, his eyes open and he responds, "Yes, Your Highness," his voice revealing nothing of what had just washed over him.

"You came in with Zaria. You were her partner at your old job." The prince looks back at me before retuning his attention to John.

John shoots me a worried glance. "Yes."

He chuckles to himself. "I guess that explains why she is so good at wielding a sword."

This time John's eyes are not just worried, but petrified. Petrified for me. Petrified for himself.

"Yes, well..." He struggles for words, trying to keep his head held high. Only then do I notice tiny flinches from the other guards listening in, ready to memorize whatever information is told. "We had to do a lot of training together. Every day was an uphill battle."

"I'm sorry to hear that." Looking back at me, his expression has changed to a sorrow which I can only guess is for show. Clearing his throat, he continues, "Zaria and I are going to have lunch together for her to learn the schedule."

"I will be out here on guard." He looks at the prince, shadows loom back over his eyes as he lowers his head squinting again.

"That's the spirit," the prince says, patting him on the shoulder.

I try to advert my eyes from his gaze. Like my glare, his eyes can tell a thousand stories as well. This one being a not so happy one. The prince steps into the dining hall. I follow, trying to tell John that I'm sorry, but he refuses to look at me. His eyes have focused back to staring right ahead. I linger by the threshold for any sign from him, but none comes. I lower my eyes towards the floor, stepping in the prince's footsteps.

I follow him to the end of the table. He pulls out a chair for me, cushioned with a velvet covering. It reminds me of the beautiful common room. Just like my heels, adjusting to the frilly skirts of the dresses seem to yield a problem. I shift on the chair, readjusting the skirt, but nothing feels right. Striding gracefully to his own chair, he sits at the head of the table to my immediate right.

"Hey… what *is* your name? You said you would tell me today."

He sets his goblet back onto the table, his eyes searching the room.

"How about this. You tell me why you don't like the dress that our staff has picked for you, and I'll tell you my name."

Heat rushes to my cheeks. The sheer embarrassment showing plainly on my face. "I don't know what you are talking about."

He takes a sip from his goblet, I watch waiting to see how I have revealed myself.

"You shift, you fidget, and you have a permanent frown on your face, like a fly buzzing at your ear. You obviously aren't comfortable, so I ask. Why don't you like the niceties the palace provides for you?"

"Oh no, but I do," I retort, trying my best to gain back control. "Didn't you just hear that I fought alongside John?"

"Yes, indeed, but that can't be the only reason. Every girl likes to dress up on occasion, and this palace is the perfect excuse for it." Lifting his goblet in the air, he scans his hand across the dining hall. My thoughts don't catch up until the words leave my mouth, spewing far more than I should have.

"They don't make me feel safe. I don't have the agility I do in a dress, as I have in pants. It's how I grew up. How do I know if I am safe, if I am not in any position to defend myself?"

He watches me as I talk, like he's listening. He doesn't answer as he looks at the tablecloth that lay before us. Nodding his head, he takes another sip. Just as he does, our food arrives. A beautiful spread is placed in front of me. The aroma so much more defined than the smells coming from the kitchen.

Glasses of wine are placed off to the side of our plates. Technically I am not old enough to drink in Flesherg, but that never stopped me, and judging by the look of the prince, he shouldn't be allowed to either.

"I'm not old enough to drink," I blurt out. The sentence sounding childish, my pride flushed down the toilet.

A soft smile appears on his face. "Palace rules are different. No one inside the palace is leaving unless invited outside of the premises. As long as you don't have too much... or do anything reckless, drinking is totally fine."

He raises his glass to make a cheers. "To Zaria. Prince Axil's new advisor."

I retire to my bedroom after a long day of reviewing the schedule. Axil and I spent all day talking about his daily routine and what will be my job as his advisor. Turns out I'm just going to be running after him making sure that everything gets done.

I place my clipboard on the side table. The bookshelf in this bedroom puts mine to shame. I had packed some of the books my mother had given me. They sit on the shelf proudly. The only stable thing in this big mess.

My fingers run over the spines on all the books stopping on one in particular. I pull it out feeling the weight of it in my hands. My fingertips frill through the pages until the instinctually stop on one of the pages. Though I had folded the page to bookmark it, it never mattered. I always landed on this page. The page my mom had quoted since day one. "Do what is right, even if it hurts."

I look at the text. The words, the phrase. It's just ink on a page I tell myself before her voice comes flooding back into my mind. I brace myself. Eyes squinting, knuckles clenched around cover, but the pain never comes. Instead of the plea, there is instead a whisper. Light as a feather it sends chills up my spine. Instead of her voice pleading the same phrase, it continues on in a soft voice, calm and soothing.

I sit upon my bed, my eyes following the voice down the page. Never in years had I dared read anything else in the book besides that one phrase, torturing myself with it until I would eventually pass out on my bed.

My mind starts to drift. Back into the world that I had only allowed myself to visit once. Into the pouring of heart into the text and the flow of the love this book wrapped up in the tiny pages. She tells the story in my mind as if she has memorized every line, and I almost fall asleep before a knock comes at the door.

"Oh." Axil walks in, quickly stopping in his tracks. "I didn't mean to wake you."

Blinking myself out of a daze I answer, "I wasn't sleeping."

Taking that as an invitation he strides in towards the middle of my room. "I was just... reading." Reading. I actually did it. I had made it past the line. The line that has haunted me for years.

"Ah, what a lovely way to pass the time," he says standing in place. He looks around observing the room. "It has been quite some time since I have stepped foot into one of the guest bedrooms."

"I see." Looking down at the book that still lies in my hand I notice the page. Once folded, it now splays open perfectly. I blink, flipping the page over and over try to figure out what had just happened.

"Are you alright?"

"Oh… yes," I say. Slamming the book shut and tossing it further on the bed. I look back at him. "Is there a reason you came in here?"

"I just came to check if there is anything you might need."

I scan my room like I can find some answer hidden in the walls. "Umm. No, I think I'm good."

"Okay," he says before walking his way back out. "I will make sure to meet you up here before dinner. My mother and I had planned a postponed welcome dinner, and I would want to make sure you could find your way. "

"The Queen will be there?" I ask. A small layer of sweat building on my forehead.

"Of course. She'll see you down there."
After that, he walks away. I wait for the door to be closed before shaking my head and lying back down. I don't touch the book. Can't bring myself to even think about it. I shut my eyes laying my head back and sleep.

***

I only have a few minutes before dinner is served and I will meet the Queen. Axil had wanted to plan a welcome meal for me and John to make up for the other one that I didn't attend. The royal family will be accompanying us.

Checking the clock, the minutes tick by faster than I had thought. I hurry to my wardrobe, throwing open the doors. I need to find something a little more *evening wear*. Inside I find a fancy dress. The color of rubies, and bedazzled from top to bottom. This has to be some mistake. I shift the hanger from side to side, trying to catch the light on all angles. On the front of the dress there is a note secured with a shiny safety pin. I pluck it off.

Dear Zaria,

I am so sorry for what I did this morning. I did not mean to endanger you in any way. If you would like a new servant, I understand, but I pray that you give me a second chance. I found this in the design room. I thought you would look lovely in it if you wore it tonight.

From, Lucy

I didn't know this morning upset her so much. I am going to have to get used to the soft-hearted nature of people here. How I spoke to her this morning is no different than I speak to John, and he's my best friend. That's always the dynamic between us. Always has been, probably always will be. I write a note back.

Dear Lucy,

Please don't be sorry. I apologize that I upset you. You are a wonderful person, and a lovely servant to me. Hopefully in my time here we can become friends. Thank you for the gown. The thought is beautiful.

From, Zaria

I will stick it on her door this evening. Time is ticking faster than ever now. The letter took twice as long to write than normal, but I don't think Lucy would understand my chicken scratch of a writing.

My hand already cramped from taking notes at lunch with Axil.

I slide into the evening gown. It's the most gorgeous thing I've ever seen aside from the sparring room. I honestly don't think Damian would be mad if I just came home with this smuggled into my bag. It's got to be worth one thousand… maybe even two?

Standing in front of the mirror I don't recognize myself. I look like a princess. Someone like me should not be dripped in jewels, or expensive fabric. I pick at my hair, brushing it with my fingers. My arms look too boxy to be feminine, my scars too ugly. Nothing can cover up who I am. Damian's voice rings in my head. *You are a thief. You will never be anything else.* I had always hated him for it. For choosing the path in which my life goes, but now I see the truth. I am not built for anything other than what he has made me to be.

I step out of the room, my note to Lucy gripped tightly in my fingers. I stride away from my room, taking deep breaths. I have to just suck it up. Walking in heels will get easier, right?

At the top of the stairs Axil waits for me. The same blue suit as he always wears, this time just a few minor details differing from his other suits. The shoulder seams come out a bit more, making his shoulders appear broader. His cape is now lined with gold trim, instead of the one that just hangs solidly on his back. The sparkle of his crown catches my eye. Never seeing him in it before, it sends a wave of nerves. Like the crown snapped me back into who I was dealing with. Just a singular object differentiating a person in a suit, from the Prince of Lumbridge.

"I have to deliver this to Lucy before dinner starts," I voice, my breath still catching up.

He looks at me worried, the corners of his eyes creasing. "Dinner has already started."
My eyes fly open, and I take off down the flight of stairs without Axil. I know I look like a dinosaur wrecking everything in its path. I sure feel like it. I hear his delicate footsteps behind me, not missing a beat. They get closer and closer, until he grabs my hand, steadying me going down the last few stairs. I have got to start getting better at walking in these. Not letting go, he leads me in a brisk pace to the dining hall.

We walk in together, only then does he let go of my hand. I take my seat, ashamed.
"I'm so sorry I'm late," I exclaim breathless.

I peer at all the eyes on me, John's sticking out the most. Shaking his head, he looks at me the same as he did this afternoon. The shadows still loom in his eyes but the pain is gone. His glare is exactly like Damian's. Hard and disappointed. Silent curses in every blink.

The Queen's eyes look over me. Not speaking, but giving the same feeling as John. Judgmental eyes that make me question every little thing about myself. It is the King who speaks first.

"We understand. You can sure get lost easily in here."

I nod, trying to move onto another subject.

"Where did you used to work?"

It was the Queen asking. It is only now I really see her. The exact definition of power. Her posture straight, a similar crown placed atop her head. The only difference being the triangular shape of hers, and the millions of tiny jewels that cling to it like gnats on a light pole. Her golden hair pinned perfectly to her scalp. She is not only power, but beauty. Her face is as delicate as a rose, but her stare is as sharp as the thorns.

John breaks the silence, "Zaria and I worked—

The Queen cut him off with a flick of her finger.

"Her." The Queen's eyes target to me. "I want to hear it from her."

A lump forms in my throat. My hands ball into fists as I try to come up with a lie. A lie that I can continue. Something strong enough to last my stay.

"We worked at the local imprisonment. We were security guards there. A fight broke out every two or three days. John and I were always called in." I see her gaze drop to my arms and the part of my leg exposed from the slit that runs down the dress. The insecurity comes boiling back. The knowledge of how stupid and out of place I look.

It still surprises me how easily I can come up with a lie. John's face for once today looks slightly satisfied. I guess Damian is right. I am a mirror of him. He would be proud if he heard what I came up with. The Queen nods her head, slowly examining every word as I speak, then examining every scar that is visible on my person. We stare at each other a bit longer. Her icy eyes pierce into my soul. The King clears his throat, interrupting our little banter.

"How would you say your stay is so far? Are you liking the kingdom?"

I glance over at John. It's his turn to answer a question. The whole day, he just has to stand and be still. I would like to see him contribute and help this mission along, like he is supposed to be doing.

"Your kingdom is very strong, Sire. As for my stay, I feel very welcome and comfortable."

He winks at me, knowing what I was thinking. One of the things that had always annoyed me about John is his confidence. Confidence I never had. Confidence that Damian has tried to drill in me. I never got it back.

John has no family. As a child he was abandoned, never knowing his parents. He struggles knowing that he was never wanted. That part of his past haunts him every now and then, but he wasn't ripped from his family. He was offered a clean slate. A new beginning. I, on the other hand, had to adapt to a way of life that shouldn't have to be lived.

They say every girl needs a mother, and when I needed her most, she was gone. Not even the women in the gang comforted me, or tried to fill in for her. I was lost. Damian tried to help me find my way back, how to look forward, have a stone mind. My wall has been crumbling lately, and he's taken note on that. That's why he sent me here. To get my head straight. To not ponder on the past. He thinks, if I can make myself a fortune and start my own life, I will move on. Wash away the tears and never cry again. If only it was that easy.

The King looks at me. Looks as if he's waiting, has been waiting. Snapping out of it, I question, "What?"

"Do you need a rest?" the King asks, his eyes earnest and gentle. "Your mind seems elsewhere."

He sends a sharp glare directed at his wife.

I look down at my plate. I hadn't eaten anything, just moved bits of food around on my plate, shoving my fork back and forth.

Axil leans down to whisper in my ear. "Why don't you go lie down? I'll deliver the note on my way back."

I look up at him, holding back the tears that the memory has brought up. Looking back at me, he does a quick nod. A suggestion, or an order, I can't tell. But despite it all, I nod back. Leaving the note under my plate, I get up trying to turn invisible, but the gift of invisibility is only given to good thieves.

Chapter five

Burning tears roll down my face. I rip off the dress, slipping into one of my old tee shirts and gym shorts. Sneaking out of my room, I make my steps as quiet as possible, my sniffles itching to get out. I climb down the stairs with ease this time, my bare feet leaving barely a sound on them. I run into the garden. I long for the smell of flowers, and to see all that Lucy has done. The cool air greets me as I exit, sending calm through my veins. The air has always reminded me of freedom.

Oftentimes when John had a tough day of training, he would sit outside. I remember he told me that he would sit and breathe until all the air that was in his lungs, all the air that had been beaten, all the air that had been starved, was gone. Blown away into the world, to be lost and never found. Ever since he told me that, I had done the same thing. Each breath, I would attach a wish. I wish I could be better. I wish I will make my father proud. I wish… my mother was here. Standing with me. I feel her presence almost too real to be true because when I turn around, it is not her. The Queen stands upon the front entrance. I blink the tears from my eyes to see her face soften. The hardness in her scowl has now vanished and instead resembles the King's worried expression.

"I'm sorry." In a sweet voice like no other, she speaks. "You remind me of my daughter. You know… the marks." She waves her palm over my arms.

"I didn't know you had a daughter." A long pause fills the air between us. Gears shift in her mind deciding what to tell me.

"Not so many years ago, she still stood before her throne. That is, until a threat came. She was always one to stand up for what she believed in, very determined, very strong. One day, she was kidnapped. Taken out of the kingdom and beaten to death." Her eyes wallow, her voice getting softer and softer. "When they found her body, she was a broken mess. I just wondered, perhaps hoped, that whoever you had worked with might have been the culprit." She frowns at her own words. The taste of poison in her mouth. "A sick and twisted thought, but the resemblance burned in my memory. I hope you can forgive me."

For a while, I just stare in shock. I never thought the Queen of Lumbridge would ever apologize to me. Especially if she knew what I was planning.

"I'm so sorry, my Queen. I too, know what the loss of a family member feels like. Not in a natural death, but one from hate and spite. I understand your pain."

She does the unthinkable. Stepping forward, she hugs me. Embracing me in her arms. The feeling is warm, the comfort comes rolling back in.

It almost feels wrong to feel the way I did with my own mother. This feeling is special to *her*. Maybe it's because I'm so deprived of affection that I can't hold in my emotions. She slowly pulls away, her hands still resting upon my shoulders. Tears well in my eyes. My lip quivers as I try to contain myself.

"Go rest, child."

She pats me before letting me go. Here I stand in front of the Queen in my street clothes, messy hair, and no shoes, and yet feeling, just for a second, like I'm twelve again. My mother alive, arms wide open. The shattered wall feels more hollow than ever, but a bit of it not so broken. I wipe my tears and bow before heading off to bed. There is one more person I need to talk to.

***

I barge into John's room. I had found out his room number from the guard at the front entrance. He apparently knows the ins and outs of the whole castle. I might need to remember that for future reference. John sits in a recliner at the corner of his room.

"I knew you would come."

"*I knew you would come.* Shut up," I stammer mockingly. "Go ahead. Go ahead. Yell at me. Tell me I need to do better. Tell me you will kill me if I don't. Whatever you need to say, just say it."

His face goes very angry, his lips pressed in a tight line. "You revealed too much today. How do I know you won't only get yourself killed, but that you will drag me down with you?"

The air in my lungs sinks like a rock. "You think I would go and get you killed?" My empty stomach roils with rage, a sick smile forming on my lips.

"The whole point I'm here is because of you. I was thinking of accepting your offer, but I can't provide for you. I can't make sure you are safe on our own. At least here I know you are being taken care of."

His eyes burned harder than I have ever seen them. "You don't need to treat me like a child who needs coddled!" he stammers with gritted teeth.

"Then stop treating *me* like it." I grit back at him. My hands ball into fists, my limbs starting to shake with bottled up anger.

"Zaria—

"No! Do you think I wanted to do this? Do you think I want to be in Damian's control, being his puppet at any given moment? No! What I *want* is freedom. What I *want* is to be my own person, with my own name. So I'm sorry if you think I'm sabotaging *your* chance in this mission, but leave me the hell out of your childish games."

I turn around, slamming the door in his face. I'm tired. So tired, but at the same time, I could run. Run and never stop, so that's what I do. I run through the halls to the only place that will allow release. The sparring room.

Chapter six

I swing my sword over and over in the air, never quite satisfied. Hearing the whooshes in the air gives me encouragement, making the next one even louder. Never giving up.

During one of my training sessions I was given a machete. For as many perfect hits I got, was how many bites I got to eat at dinner. He gave me all day. Every one of my swings was critiqued. Not one of them being perfect. When the sun went down, my arms hung beside me like heavy weights. Damian had come to assess my work.

Not once did I accomplish a perfect swing, but I had fought all day, never giving up. Sweat was dripping down my face, my lungs heaving, dry from lack of water. I had done it though. And the feeling of making Damian the slightest bit impressed, made me continue to never give up.
It was hard when I was growing up. Finding my purpose to fight, but now it was easy.

In my head I was fighting whoever murdered my mother. It pains me to not know who it was, but I would also be a murderer right now if I had. That was how I fought. Any task, any job. I fought for her, for when she couldn't fight.

"Nice moves."

I turn, baffled. I hadn't heard anyone come in, but now the quiet little mouse stands before me with her head raised fully, for once.

"Thank you," I say, taking in all of Lucy's features. Her high cheekbones and sharp jawline. The subtle curve of her nose, and the almond shape of her eyes.

"I got your note. Thank you for not hating me."

"Sure," I say, still a bit irritated. She looks down, her eyes wandering all around the floor. Cupping her hands together, her thumb runs over the side of her fingers. Reassuring her, I fill the silence. "It's been a long day."

"I'm sure." Nodding her head she changes the subject. "Would you like me to prepare your bed for you?"

I put the sword down where I found it. The exact same sword I had been admiring in Axil's hands earlier this morning. "It's fine. I've got it."
She goes to walk out. Before she reaches the door, I stop her.

"What time does the prince wake up?"
Her face looks puzzled, like my question took her by surprise.

"I'm not exactly sure. I would guess sometime before seven. That's when his breakfast is served."

Catching my breath, I respond, "Thank you. Goodnight Lucy."

"Goodnight Zaria."

I tidy myself up to go back to my room. I close the door as quietly as possible. All the lights are now off in the palace, the darkness making me more comfortable to go back into my room. Slipping in the doorway, I pull out a pen and paper. I write myself a reminder to get up at six a.m. I also make a mental note. One that only my thoughts can contain.

Why was Lucy going into the sparring room when the palace lights turned off?

***

I don't sleep much. I'm going over my plan. I will succeed, but it won't be for Damian. It will be for myself. Whenever the sun comes up, I am out of bed and ready. Another day of uncomfortable clothes, and fake smiles. Exiting my room, I stand as tall as possible. I have started this mission, and it's time to play.

My clipboard rests in my left arm, a new pen clipped onto the paper. I wait outside Axil's room. It wasn't hard to find it. Double doors, gold plated, a giant cursive "A" written on the door. Holding back the roll of my eyes, I perch myself by the door. The royal family gave me a week to settle in, but I will show them I don't need it. Show them how dedicated I can be. A young, poised girl, who would never do any harm. The perfect thing I need before I strike.

I wait, twiddling my pen back and forth until I hear the door open. Axil stands in front of me brushing off his new pressed suit. His hair freshly styled, and his cologne a strong aroma.

"Zaria." Knowing he has company, he makes a quick effort to straighten his suit, and run his fingers through his hair. "I wasn't expecting you this early."

"It is an advisor's job to wake early, and accompany the prince wherever he may go, unless given the permission to leave." I recite the passage from one of the papers. "Page sixty-one."

I tap the clipboard, finding right where it says it.

Looking back at me, he smiles. "I can see you are dressed. I guess the surprise is going to have to wait."

I flip the papers back in order, my thumb stopping in between them, as he speaks. "What surprise?"

"You'll find out at the end of the day."

He walks away, leaving me standing still at his doorway. I jog, trying to catch up. "What surprise?" I ask again. He only chuckles.

I arrive at the dining hall. Checking to see if John is here yet, I catch his gaze.

"Good morning, John." He can tell by my voice, I am still peeved about what he said.

"Good morning Zaria, Your Highness."

"Thank you, John," Axil says cheerfully. The spring in his voice is beyond me at this hour.

I sit down with Axil, getting out my pen to start planning the day.

"Your important events for today are a council meeting at nine and a horse lesson at two."
He ponders over his glass, swirling whatever liquid is inside.

"What happened last night?" he inquires.
Right at that moment, my ink pen bursts. My hands turning black and stained. I try to save the paper, but couldn't help the few splatters that ran through the pages.

"Oh my." He assists me at my side, a cloth in his hands. "Let me get that for you."
His hands wrap around mine, the feeling making me want to squirm. The damp cloth wiping away the ink leaving a smeary mess. He must have doused whatever was in his glass on the napkin. He gently tries to clean my hands, but it's no use.

"I'll go wash up in my room. I'll meet you at the council meeting."

Before he can respond, I whiz out the door. I had left my stuff sitting at the table. Letting out a breath, I make note to return to the dining hall before the council meeting.

Running past the guards, I know John must have seen me. He's probably shaking his head in disappointment. I don't care. As long as I get this mission done, he can stuff it.

Inside my room, I scrub for what seems to be hours. My hands feel raw from the friction, the ink still refusing to fade.

I frustratingly shut off the water. Grabbing one of the fluffy white towels, it becomes... not so white. The towel now looks like a cow had been printed on it. Black splotches smearing onto the cotton. The ink looks a little faded being exposed to the air, but it has seeped deep into my scars. The skin, being fresh, had taken a liking to the darkness.

I fix my hair before I head back down to retrieve my clipboard. Never had I looked at myself so many times. I realize how little fat is on me. I look like a toothpick on steroids. My eyes are sunken in, my cheekbones very prominent. I don't look right.

My door closes harder than expected. I walk down the staircase with a little more grace than normal. On my trip to retrieve my belongings, I hear what seems to be a wail.

Stopping in my tracks, I then hear the scream get closer and closer to me. A girl about my age runs out of one of the halls. Not having time to brace herself, she crashes into me. Both of us end up on the floor. I get up first, offering my hand to her. Something I wish was done for me more often.

"Thank you," her voice sounding in pain.

Grabbing my hand, her billions of bangle bracelets clang up against each other. The gold, a complement of her hazelnut skin. "Are you okay?" I ask.

"Oh yeah," she giggles. "Just a failed spell. *Whoo!* I could set fire to this palace if I'm not careful."

I look her up and down. She wears a black dress with a purple overskirt. A tiny witch hat floats above her tousled curly hair. Bobbing up and down, it follows her as she bends down to wipe the dust off of her dress.

"You're a sorcerer."

Her eyes light up, a smile filling up half her face. She has got to be the brightest person I have ever met besides Charlie.

"You guessed it! Normally, people don't know the exact term. I get called a witch. Don't get me wrong, I love that as well, but there is something about the word *sorcerer* that brings a whole new magic to what I do."

Of course I knew what a sorcerer was. My favorite book from my mother. A story of a sorcerer who had cast a spell to turn back time. Each time she turned back, she took the role as a new person. It was really gruesome and horrid actually, but strangely one of my favorites.

"If you can stop by today, I can show you where I work. I've always wanted a friend to show it to for so long."

She grabs my hand, quickly pulling away. My hands aren't the only ones who now have an inky mess on them.

"Oh goodness." Looking down at my hands she asks, "What happened?"

"My pen exploded," I explain, embarrassed.

"Let me fix that up for you."

She holds out her now ink stained hands, hovering above my own. Closing her eyes, concentration squeezes her face. A whoosh of magic swirls around my hands, at least that's what I think it is. Like a shooting star of sparkles it wraps around me, each pass revealing my own skin. Energy shoots through my arm connecting deep into my chest. Only a couple of seconds later does her face relax. I look down examining my now clean hands. Back and forth I turn them in awe.

"I didn't know magic was real," I blurt out, still awestruck.

"But you knew I was a sorcerer," she says, giggling to herself. "You are so funny." Patting my back, she flounces around. "Can you come by later today?"

I draw my eyes away from my hands, only able to nod.

"Great, see you then."

She skips down the hall. I watch to see where she goes as she disappears into thin air. My eyes widen, and in that moment, I swear I can hear her giggle. Shaking my head, I jump back into reality. I check my watch. 8:30 on the dot. Rushing into the dining hall, I race to retrieve my clipboard, but it's gone.

"I'm guessing you were looking for this."

Hearing his voice sends annoyance down my spine. I turn around back into the hallway. Snatching my board out of John's hands, I curse under my breath. Rolling his eyes, his grip loosens.

"Shut up, and let me pass."

He stares at me a long time, his eyes looking more and more like Damian's every day. That is one thing I'm glad that I did not inherit. Damian's eyes were a dark brown that felt like black holes when he was upset. I remember once when they were not. When his eyes were as soften as melted chocolate. That was when mother was still around. Her emerald eyes sparkled in any room she stepped in. They shined until one day they couldn't. After that, my eyes did the same. They have been a dull green ever since.

John's eyes have always been a dark brown, but his eyes paired with the stern look he adopted makes him intimidating, making me feel like some stupid child. Whenever he gives up our staring contest, he lets out a huge sigh.

"Zaria, please —

"I said let me through."

His face squints for a second. He inhales sharply but before I can ask if he is okay, he steps aside without saying a word. Hitting his forearm against my own, I stagger down the empty halls. I will wait at the council room until nine. It's strange that only a couple of days ago, I thought John was on my side. He had told me he believed in me. Not two days before, did he ask me to run away with him. I need to talk to him, but not here, and definitely not now.

***

I lean against the wall outside of the council room. It makes my heart beat a little to imagine sitting in front of all the rule makers. The exact people that can imprison me if they find out what I am doing. I had led countless meetings before. Talking out plans, jobs, times, and weapons. I was the lead. Now standing here, I know that I am nobody to them. My job will be to stand on alert behind Axil, taking notes on whatever is said, and agreed upon. I look down to see a blue pen attached to the board. At least John was kind enough to get me a new pen. I guess he has a heart, although sometimes it's hard to tell how big.

"Good morning, Miss Zaria."

"Good morning, Your Highness," I bow to the King. "Is there anything I can get for you?"

He folds his hands together, "You are too kind. I am quite well at the moment. Thank you."

He opens the door, holding it open for me, "Would you like to come in?"

I look down both ways of the hall clutching the board to my chest. "I think I will wait until the prince arrives."

"Yes, my dear, good idea." He turns entering the room, doors shutting behind him. But through a tiny window, I can still see him. He stands in front of a desk. Picking up papers, he frills through, skimming each page he reads. Instead of placing them back down, he opens a drawer and sticks them in.

"You're here." Axil stands next to me, again seeming to come out of nowhere. "I've been looking all over for you."

"Oh… Are you ready to enter?"

He pauses for a moment, looking down at the floor, then back up. "…Yeah."

I step in front of him, opening the door. He walks through, his head held high.

"Father." He tips his head in acknowledgment.

"How are you, my son?"

"Great." It was his only response, one I can tell is a lie.

I file in after him, hearing people behind me. I hold the door open from the inside. Three more people come in. They all sit, settling in at the table. Their hushed voices make white noise as I peer out the window. Looking out, I imagine, seriously imagine, what I can turn my life into after all of this. Somewhere out there, in the open trees, with the wind in my hair. Maybe then… possibly…

The King's voice snaps me out of my daydream, my posture standing back at attention. "It looks like everyone is here. Let the meeting commence."

***

I stand behind Axil, my pen in hand. A lot of what they talk about is additional security, alliances with other kingdoms, threats to the kingdom.

"As you all know, Malaka is still trying to make an attack against us. We will need to find extra forces to guard this kingdom for the next couple of years." I take notes, my pen moving fast. I scribble down "more guards," and "Malaka." I wonder if that was the threat on his daughter. Axil's sister. I know too well what it is like to have a target on your family's back. I have fought every day to make sure Flesherg stayed safe. I wonder now if everyone is okay. I didn't really have positive relationships with anyone beside John, a relationship which is questionable at the moment.

I was in charge. My father was, of course, the Alpha. The Alpha that didn't do anything. I took the lead. It's what I do. I can't stop myself.

"Might I suggest," all eyes look back. Some glaring, some surprised I even raised my voice, myself included. "I agree with the idea that you get more guards; however, if you post a thousand new guards along the perimeter of the castle, word will spread fast to Malaka. It will make them want to attack even sooner. If you train new soldiers, keep them on the inside of the castle, honing their skill every day in secret. The time when Malaka does attack, the extra soldiers will be a surprise to their troops, and we will have had more time to collect extra resources."

The room goes quiet. Questioning eyes still look at me. Heads start nodding either in spite or consideration of my idea. I cross my fingers for the second option. The only person I can't seem to look away from is Axil. He sits in front of me, turned around in his chair. A quick grin appears on his face.

Not wavering his gaze from mine, he addresses his father. "Zaria is right. The more advantages we have on Malaka, the better. It's best to keep it hidden, using it as an element of surprise."

The King looks me straight in the eye. "Happy to have you on our team, Zaria."

I look down, a tiny smile forming on my mouth. It felt good to be in control. To be heard. Gaining their trust, is step one.

After the meeting, the King dismisses everyone. Axil and I walk out of the door last.

"What are you doing now?" He leans down closer to my ear so he doesn't have to talk so loud.

"I'm supposed to be meeting a friend, actually."

His face falls in slight disappointment, his eyebrows drooping. "But, I can meet you at the stables at two. Don't forget about your riding lessons."

"Yeah, yeah. See you then."

He starts off, his steps still in composure. His grace will always be a mystery to me.

I navigate the long maze of the palace back up to my room, avoiding walking past the dining hall. I only had to whip out my map twice, so I guess that's progress. I sigh in relief as I close my door, a tiny break from the mask I have to wear. I set my board down on the table right next to the entrance, making it easy to pick up before I leave. On my bed lies a huge box. There is a note on it, in a clean script.

Dear Zaria,

It has come to my attention that you are not the most comfortable in fancy clothing. Comfort is one of the most important things we want you to feel during your stay. You are welcome to any of these clothes inside. I did my best to make the outfits match, but please do not judge. I hope you like them.

Axil

I hold onto the letter just a bit longer, admiring his thought. The thought that I had planted in his mind. He is falling right into my hands. Opening the flaps of the box, a baby blue chiffon blouse is folded neatly. The color is mesmerizing, almost the same as the color Axil wears himself. I slip out of my dress as fast as I can. I button up the blouse, my finger remembering happily what buttons feel like. I dig in the box some more. I complete the ensemble with a pair of white slacks, and a gold belt.

Turning around in the mirror, I feel back to myself. Most of my scars are hidden, so I guess I look more "normal." I secure my hair in a loose braid, having it fall over my shoulder. I turn around back to my bed, a sight stopping me in my tracks.

There is a trail of leaves from my feet to the door. Yellow and orange in color, but illuminated as if the sun itself were lighting up the leaves. I step to pick it up, wondering what exactly it is. As I step, it disappears. I gasp staggering back with my hand held over my mouth. A crumb trail. Someone else here knows how to play games, and I know exactly the person.

***

Following the trail of leaves, I keep my eyes on my back making sure no one else sees what I'm seeing. I would be told I was crazy, and… I might just be.
The trail leads to a part of the palace that I had not seen before. I trek down the hall, pondering why Axil didn't take me this way. All the more reason to investigate.

I come across a wooden door, unlike all the pristine white ones. This one is a natural wood color with rusty black hinges on the side. On the door hangs a circular door knocker. I reach up to grab the handle when the door suddenly swings open.

"You made it." The same bright smile welcoming me in.

"It was kind of hard not to with your leaf trail." A giggle follows. "How did you do it? I mean, was it a spell… or a mind trick?"

She walks me inside her chamber. Amazement washes over my face. Shelves line the walls, each filled with tiny glass bottles with corks. Red liquids, blue, green, some sparkly, some—

"Why do you have a giant bottle of spiders?"

"Oh… the key ingredient of many spells. The legs bubble an extract that binds the ingredients together."

I nod my head tightly, my gaze still taking in the room. A purple bed sits in the corner, curtains hanging over it like a canopy. In the center of the room sits a giant caldron. It is so large, I could curl up in a ball and fit inside. I hope nothing like that has ever happened, the last thing I need is to be an ingredient along with those spindly spiders.

"I must say, this is quite the room you have here."

"Thank you. Most of it has been passed down for generations. The older the ingredients, the better the magic."

"I hope you don't use any cheese."

Her eyes dart to one of the shelves. Looking back at me, she cracks a smirk. Both of us end up laughing.

"Would you like a taste?" Still cackling to herself, she reaches for her jars.

"No!" I respond, trying to hold back my laughter. Catching my breath, I try to keep the conversation flowing. "What is your job anyway?"

She looks over at me, puzzled. "What do you mean?"

"Doesn't the King give you special orders?"

She laughs again. I don't understand what is so funny, or how someone can laugh so much. She holds her stomach, catching her breath.

"I am under orders of Axil." I still eye her, looking for some sort of answer to my question. "He's my cousin."

"Oh…" Embarrassed, I bow before her.

"Please don't do that. Like I said, I am a sorcerer. I may be a royal sorcerer, but I am also a witch. More witch than crown. My job is simple. Practice my magic until I am needed."

"Do you like practicing?"

She strides over to her bed, sitting down. I follow her, sitting on the opposite side. Her bed sinks in as I sit down. The comfort of the mattress still surprising me.

Her head lowers, the floating hat following her drooped head. She picks up a nearby wand, what looks to be just a finely crafted stick. She waves her wand, closing her eyes. A strip of purple magic shoots out like a comet, twinkling lights flying across the room. It hits a lone brown vase. For a split second, a plant appears inside the pot green as ever, then as quickly as it appeared, a whirlwind starts. A tiny tornado twirls in her room. Papers fly in every direction, the bottles chattering against their shelf.

I spring from the mattress, catching any fallen objects. Meanwhile, she still stays on her bed, just watching. After a minute of chaos goes by, the wind gives up. The magic disappearing as quickly as it started.

"I am not that steady with my magic. If I can't perfect it, and we lose against Malaka, I could never forgive myself. I have the gift to save people's lives, turn back time, transform objects, teleport... but I can't control it."

I look at her. She sits hugging her knees to her chest, defeated, looking at the newly made mess.

"What about the ink this morning, or the leaves? I literally saw you disappear into thin air. That seemed to be good, really good."

She takes a deep breath, "It's better when there is a constant. If I can make one leaf, all I have to do is multiply it. Same with the ink. If I can concentrate on one molecule of ink and make it disappear, all I have to do is multiply its effects." Pausing, she lowers her voice, sounding a bit ashamed. "Making something out of nothing is where it gets hard."

I try to find my words. I know how hard it is to focus, to concentrate, to not let anything around you distract. The feeling of failure biting at your mind, feeding you lies. I had not come here to make new friends or loathe in another person's wallow, but I can't shake the feeling that I am looking in the mirror.

I open my mouth knowing I am going to regret what comes next. "How about I help. I can show you the techniques I used for fighting. It took me years before I mastered my skill. You, on the other hand, have the talent already, it's just your mindset. If you will let me, I can help."

She ponders for a moment. In the silence, I can practically hear John saying it's a bad idea. I know I will get another lecture about this, and I don't care. Just like this mission, I just have to not get caught. He doesn't have to know, and since when was he the boss of me?

"Would you really?" Her eyes have teared up, her cheeks becoming a dark shade of rose.

"Of course. That is, if you want me to?"

"Yes, yes, of course! Thank you."

She slides over, wrapping her arms around me. Though she squeezes me tightly, I can feel her body relax. We spend the rest of the time talking on her bed. She talks about ancient stories of her ancestors, and her life in the castle. I listen as best I can, egging her to keep talking so she doesn't ask me about myself.

"Wait, wait, wait... so you're telling me that sorcerer's are more common than anyone thinks. Just how many of them are there?"

She giggles. "Well it's all genetics, but when the gates to our world were open, someone decided that we might need a little extra help. A little extra guidance."

"Are there any others in the palace?" I ask wondering if I had been misled once again.

"There used to be." She says a frown forming on her face. Taking a deep breath she continues. "When I was little my mother used to live here. She taught me all I know along with her friend. My dad is human. Well... I guess we're all human but he was... normal. He lives on the outskirts of Lumbridge. He loved living simply. The whole palace thing was more my mother's scene."

"Do you visit him? Your father, I mean."
The brightness comes back into her face. "Oh yes. He is a grand old fellow. I could take you to meet him sometime. Oh he would love to know that there is another girl my age at the palace!"

She squeezes my arm. Great. Another way in.

"That sounds great but I've got to get going. I have to meet Axil at the stables in half an hour."
Heading for the door, I hear her start to talk again.

"How is it? Being his advisor, I mean?"

I pick at my nails as I collect my thoughts. "It's good, very complex but... good."

"I thank you again for deciding to help me. Maybe now I have a shot." She looks off for a second. I glance at what has caught her eye. An old photograph sits upon her nightstand. I can only catch a glimpse before she looks back at me.

"I didn't ask. What is your name?"

"Zaria."

"I'm Crista."

We share a moment smiling back and forth. A moment that makes me question, just for a second, if I am actually feeling something instead of...

"I'll meet you tomorrow," I say, opening the door. It creaks as I push it. Shutting the door behind me, feels like I left some type of world. A whisper sounds deep inside of me to turn around and go back in. For a moment I consider, until I once again remember the time.

I walk down the hallway feeling as if I am floating. Because of the flat shoes Axil has gifted me, my feet sigh in relief with each step.

I shake my head trying to snap back into a reality that I never left. That was all real. It's hard to imagine, but it was all real. Maybe once John isn't in such a mood I can tell him about her.

I make it to the stable. When I arrive, I see Axil riding on a white horse, the caretaker on a brown one. He sits tall on the horse, his blazer a vivid blue against the white. He sees me. Catching my eye, he nods his head, going back to listening what he is being told. I see his sword in his other hand. I can only imagine fighting on horseback. The thought of not being able to feel my feet on the ground sends dread to my stomach.

I lean up against the fence, resting my forearms on the wooden gate. For a while, I breathe in the fresh air. My feet squish into the soft earth beneath me.

It sounds silly, but the smell of grass calms me down. A life filled with city air, chemicals being pushed out of every vent, the smell of the earth is like a dream.

My eyes close as I rest my head on my folded arms, soaking in the sun. I feel as though I could fall asleep. For a moment, I imagine growing up like this, knowing no pain, no crime, just serenity with nature. Would I still have my perfect family? Would my best friend not hate me right now? It's hard to imagine a world in which I didn't grow up, but for some reason, it has always consumed my thoughts.

A tap on my shoulder startles me. My body tenses again but slowly relaxes. Axil stands to my left, copying my stance on the fence.

His face glows in the mid-day sun, the light cascading off of his pure skin like he is one with the universe. Perfect. He is perfect, and though that should be something that makes me feel joy, I can't help but have a smidge of hate towards him. My stomach turning every time I am in his presence.

"Would you like to go for a ride?" his voice soft as the birds chirping. "I know a trail that loops around the palace walls. We can go together."

"Sure, should I get an extra sword?"

"Please don't. As we know, you might beat me to a pulp with your swordplay."

I roll my eyes.

He leads me to the stalls. Stopping in front of a black horse, he waits and smiles.

"Go ahead, pet him."

The midnight stallion looks at me. Out of nowhere, my fingertips start to tingle, my nerves firing in every direction. The size of the animal makes me feel tiny, out of control. We never saw horses in Flesherg. Involuntarily, I step back, keeping eye contact with the horse.

"Are you scared?"

"No, I'm not scared," I retort, the fluster showing in my voice.

"Here." He grabs my hand, leading me back over to the horse. He places my palm on the center of its face. I pet it's nose, making all of my movements slow and over-exaggerated.

I have never liked the feeling. The fear of being small, insignificant. It is everything Damian has taught me not to be. He taught me to be in control. To send fear into people the second I walk in a room. It has been a while since the tables have been turned. I could always muster up my courage, and get on the horse, but I would look just like when I was a frightened little girl, and that's not the role I'm here to play.

"Maybe when you feel more comfortable, we will go for a ride." I listen to his voice still in a daze. The giant horse stands. Passively, he leans his head into my hand, longing for more pets. "I think he likes you." Axil says smiling.

For a while I just look at the horse. He doesn't seem as scary as before, just big. All I remember about horses is this old western movie Damian had made me watch, especially the part where the rider gets thrown off, hitting the ground and crouching in pain. I don't remember if it was supposed to be a lesson, but it was probably just to scare me.

"How about a walk instead?" He offers his hand again. I take it, his grip firm but loose. Nothing like the members of Damian's gang when they would hold me down mocking me to get back up, never making it easy. The feeling is much better. An offer, rather than an order.

We walk down the trail that we would have taken with the horses. The trees overhead conjoin to the other side, making a canopy over the path. He lets go of my hand, the warmth still fresh, compared to the autumn chill.

"How was your visit with John?"

"What?" I ask, unsure of what he means.

"This morning you said you were meeting a friend. I'm assuming it was John?"

His tone is tight, like he knows the answer before he has heard it.

"Yes, but I actually met Crista. You didn't tell me you had a magical cousin."

"You never asked. Did she… show you her special gift?"

"You mean the fact that she can make things appear out of nowhere, or make something disappear, or literally do anything?" I take a moment to catch my breath. Calming down I add, "She seems like a nice girl."

His face softens, a breath escaping his lips. He nods his head before asking, "Was she a bit... extra?"

A giggle bubbles its way out. "I guess you could say that; however, I don't see it as a bad thing."

"She can be a bit much sometimes. That's why I didn't have you meet her when you first arrived. I didn't want you to feel overwhelmed by her."

"So that's why," I say, "Well thank you for your consideration."

We walk side by side, listening to the birds chirping. Everything is alive, the forest seeming to have a spirit of its own, not able to hide. It's refreshing.

"You never answered my question this morning."

"Which question?"

He tenses for a moment, "What happened last night?"

I am quiet for a bit. I can't say that during dinner John was judging every word I said, or that I felt self-conscious in front of his mother. Both of those answers would send him into a frenzy.

"I had a tiny bug all night. I stayed in the bathroom most of the evening. I feel fine today, though."

"I'm glad." Kicking an acorn, he lowers his head to the thick leafy trail. "You know… if you ever feel sick again, you can always ask the chefs to make you some soup."

"I'll keep that in mind."

We walk the loop back to the palace just in time for dinner.

"I wanted to thank you."

He stops, his blue eyes focusing on mine. "For what?"

"Well if it weren't for you, I wouldn't have been able to take a walk." I point down to my new shoes. The shoes he gifted me.

He smiles, his teeth as white as snow. "No problem. I'm glad you like them."

The guards open the door for us. Entering into the common room, my limbs welcome the heat back into my body.

"I'll meet you at dinner," he says before walking off.

"See you."

***

I walk into my room, a small smile still on my lips.

"How's the mission going?"

"Nice to see you too." I reply.

John glares at me, his eyes looking like they are on fire. "What have you found?"

"How about if you're so much better at jobs than I am, you figure it out."

He hits the bed, standing up abruptly. "What is wrong with you? Why are you so mad at me?"

"Because you're treating me like you're Damian." I throw my arms up. Like hell he didn't know what he did. "You are constantly judging my every move. What happened to 'together'?" After you were sent to keep watch on me, you suddenly think you have authority over me. What happened? Did you put on some silly costume, and now you think you know everything?"

"Do *you*?" He stands right in front of me, eyes blazing. His head is tilted down, making me feel even more belittled.

"Do you even know what *you* are doing?" A pause falls over us. I have never seen this side of John. The side that punches where it hurts, the side that makes me feel like I'm some kind of prey.

"You should at least have something. Any information to pass on. A guess at a combination, or where they might keep the money. You have to have something."

His words bite with every letter. Just a few days ago we laid on this bed laughing and chatting the night away. He was my rock, my equal.

I debate telling him about the papers I saw at the council meeting, but what good would that do? For all I know, they could just be documents of hierarchies, or the King's schedule, or the council topics. It could be nothing. I hang my head, refusing to meet his eyes anymore.

He lets out a scoff. Turning around, he shakes his head rubbing at his temples. "Damian was right." Raising my head, I wait for him to continue. He turns around, his gaze piercing into the depths of my soul. "He was right from the very beginning. You are not fit to be a leader. You are just like your mother." He pauses for a moment. "Soft and worthless."

Tears well in my eyes, my hands balling into fists. I wish to scream, to argue, to punch and fight him but it wouldn't do anything. The second I retract the claws that dig in my brain his words sound again. *Soft and worthless. You are nothing but soft and worthless.*

"If in a week's time you do not have any information, I am taking over." My heart stops, a cold sweat dripping down my face. Turning back to meet my gaze, he sneers. Standing tall, he looks down at me. Belittling me. "I suggest you get started. Instead of gaggling with the prince, or hanging out with other girls in the palace. It would do you best to get some work done."

"Wasn't that the plan? To earn their trust and make the prince fall in love with me? I need time for that to happen first."

"You earned enough trust from them when you became the prince's advisor. You do not need him for this mission."

His stance is tense, unbreakable. Walking to the door, he pushes past me like he had done this morning. Stopping before he exists, he turns back around. "You either finish this mission or I will." The door is shut behind him softly, opposing to the hurricane that just ripped through.

How could he talk about my mother like that? She was a mother to him when he had no one. She was the only person to be his saving grace when he was abandoned. It wasn't Damian that fought for John it was mother. I thought he was always there for me. We were always there for each other, and I thought he would have a bit more respect for the decisions that I choose.

It is apparent that the plan has been changed. Why my father didn't tell me is quite obvious. He wants me to fail, and I guess, so does John.

Tonight I requested dinner be brought to my room. I need to think about what has to be done. My original plan was to take the money for me and John, but now it seems that is not happening. Now the question remains, do *I* steal the money, or do I have John do it? I could run away on my own. John was all I had at Flesherg. If he is going to stay like this, there is no reason for me to stay at Flesherg anymore. He would most likely become the new leader, and the gang would protect him but it wouldn't be the life he would want. His life would get worse and he would never find anything to satisfy him… but he would be safe. It's not enough. It is never enough.

My mother's faint whispers speak to me. Her words only a blur. Her last words. *Do what is right, even if it hurts.* She had kissed my forehead before tucking me in to sleep. I never wanted this, it was my only choice. I got used to not having to make decisions, the path already chosen for me. Now I am left with a huge choice. The decision of *my* future.

I reopen the book reading past the page that I never could. I read over it. Over and over for so many years, but now I look past. At some point I welcome the peace of sleep, unaware of when my eyes had shut. A knock comes at the door, quiet and steady. I try to wake up, but my eyes won't open. At this point I don't care, my mind still numb from this evening. The footsteps get louder as I hear them approach.

Warm arms wrap around me, and suddenly I am lifted into the air like I am floating. I am set down on my bed, hands lingering on my arm. They exit the room, and I fall into a deep sleep.

I dream of tall grass fields. I run through feeling free, the wind in my face. Peace washes over me, my heart in one piece. The joy that I had longed for years finally racing back into my memory, but the second it's there, I feel it being torn away. Before I know it, the meadow goes quiet, not a soul moving. Dark clouds canopy over the dazzling blue sky, swallowing all the happiness that was once in the air. I don't have time to react.

I freeze looking up to see the teeth of a lion chomping down on me, because at the end of the day, I will always be the mouse in a lions' den.

Chapter seven

"Zaria?"

A hand shaking me awake, almost makes me fall out of bed. Lucy stands at my bedside.

"It is nine o' clock."

"Oh shit!"

I race to my wardrobe picking up anything I can. As I button up my new shirt, Lucy pulls at my hair, securing it in a braid. I am out the door faster than I startled awake. Lucy runs to catch up with me, handing me my board.

"Thank you!" I quickly check the time. 9:05. Looking down at the schedule placed before me, I skim the 9:00 column. He is in the sparring room for training. I run down the vast hallways, seemingly longer today than any other day, the twinge of smoke still making my lungs contract for a brief moment until I finally round the corner and make it to the correct hallway. Breathlessly, I walk down until I make it to the grand double doors. I take a moment to take a deep breath and prepare myself to go in. Slowly, I ease open the door wondering what I would be walking in on.

The sparring room is darkly lit. One beam of light illuminates the mat that Axil and his opponent spar on.

Axil stands ready at one side of the square. Unlike his usual blue, he instead wears a light white button up closed halfway up his chest. His slacks remarkably move with every movement, not restricting his lunges at all. His sword glistens in his hand, strong and sturdy. The look of strength etched on his face. I watch as he and his opponent spar. They show each other no mercy. This is a true fight. No holding back, or fake swords, but ruthless battling. That's what happens when you have to train for the approach of evil.

After some direct hits towards Axil, I see the struggle start to show on his face. Sweat beads on his forehead, his lip starting to quiver. His opponent takes advantage of his tiredness, knocking his sword out of his hand, as I once had. He falls to his knees, huddling into a ball.

I walk from the sidelines over to him, crouching beside his weakened body, resting my hand upon his back.

His chest heaves up and down, gasping for air. The supply never being enough. Struggling with his breath he still manages to get out, "I try… and try… I never get better. Never." Walking to get some water, the trainer gives us some space.
His cry rings in my head, the moment bringing back a memory.

One day during my training I learned how to fire a gun. I was only thirteen.

Damian had talked me through how to shoot someone effectively. He even showed me what it looked like when someone got shot. That whole week I was given a target to shoot at, and every day when I raised the gun, I could never get myself to pull the trigger.

Taking somebody's life felt wrong. Not only did it feel wrong, but I knew it was wrong. That was when her voice started, when I finally decided to pull the trigger. Since then, it has never stopped. It was another one of those nights that John and I spent holding each other half crying at life, and half trying to get the other person to laugh so that we could move on. I wish we could just have another moment like that but with all the crossings of John's arms, I don't think he will be in the mood for any hugs whatsoever.

"I think it best for the prince to have a rest," I say, nodding in the trainer's direction.

The trainer nods his head, leaving the two of us in the room. Axil leans over to where I crouch, and instead of John lying in my lap like I had remembered, it's Axil. My body goes stiff, my breath held and shocked. All is quiet as he lay tense over me. I have never been one to know how to comfort, but it's almost like the voice of my mother is back. Not to beg me not to do something, but encourage me. Without thinking, I place my hand on top of his head slowly moving my fingers through his soft golden hair.

He doesn't say anything, he doesn't pull away, but in the silence I hear that plea again.

It takes me a moment to notice that it is not the voice in my head from my mother, but the own silent cries of Axil. His back trembles as he tries to stifle his cries. Damian always had discipline for tears, but Damian is not here, and he is not in control. I let him cry. Moving one of my hands to rub his back I breath out loud coaxing him to follow my breath. I wait until the rise and fall of his back slows staring off into space. It is only his shaky voice that draws me back into reality.

"I don't know how to get better. You've seen me fight…" His speech falters, not able to finish what he had been saying before.

I had thought he was going easy on me. I thought he was simply defending my attacks as to not attack me. I didn't even think that he struggled with fighting.

"Please… please help me learn." His face still covered, he begs. Just like Crista, the resemblance is like looking in a mirror. He is broken just like me. Someone I thought was perfect is really just another human being as well. Someone going through training, and stumbling along the way.

"Come on." I drag him up with me, pulling him to his feet. I retrieve his sword that had been left behind. Feeling its weight, I am reminded of my own sword. The one that's teetering on my mind.

I can feel it sinking into my back, slowly ripping at everything left in me. I came here to rob them. To take all they have and not look back.

Now my best friend is threatening to take over the mission, and I'm helping the royal sorcerer and crown prince with their acquired skills.

I hand him his sword. Wiping his tears, he meets my eyes. That blue ocean, a restless sea.

"Now…" I clear my throat steading my voice, the picture of him lying on my lap flashing before me.

"Your stance is a little off. You need to bear most of your weight on your back foot until you attack. You then will take a step, shifting your weight to your front leg, quickly recovering on your back again."

He listens to my instructions. He follows through each of my commands. Attacking and retreating. Defending and advancing. One after the other he follows. All of these skills I recite like a bedtime story. Swords weren't a popular choice back in Flesherg. Way too old fashioned and slow compared to a hand gun, but it has always been my favorite. I watch his feet, using his steps as a way to clear Damian from my mind. He has always found a way to sink his claws in no matter how tightly I build my walls, and even being thousands of miles away I can still feel the prowl of his anger. Slowly but surely, his feet find a rhythm, and I force myself to block him out.

I stop the drills, walking over to get a plastic sword.

"Oh, don't destroy my ego like that," he stammers, pointing his sword at me.

"It's nice to know you still have a sense of humor. Come on. Spar one."

I do the honors of attacking first. He successfully defends the blow, taking a step forward, making me step backward, leaving space between us. He goes to attack, clashing his sword with mine, the ring echoing in the room. I take two steps forward, but he attacks again. It seems as though I'm not the only one with inner demons. I can see his eyes darken. Focused and ready to fight. Good.

I hit his sword more forcefully, sharing my anger. Everything that John has said, has done. Each strike has a meaning, a purpose. Once again I fight for my mother. John had opened a fresh wound with his words last night. Words that won't be so easily forgiven. We both fight until he is out of breath.

"That was a lot better," I say.

"... Thank you..."

We sit at the edge of one of the crash mats. I run over to the fountain to get us some water. Axil speaks.

"I'm sorry you didn't feel well last night. John said you came back to your room and got a nasty headache."

Did he now? Two can play this game.

"Yeah, I promise I'll be at dinner tonight, though."

Sitting on the mat, I stretch my legs. Long jobs like this have me miss training.

It is impressive how just a few days of rest can change my performance. Although, if I help him out, if I teach him how to fight, it will help me stay in shape while I am here. An aid to complete whatever task I decide to do.

"Can you help me train from now on? Your teaching is a lot better than Michael's."

"Throwing staff under the bus now, are we?"

Giving me a playful shove he starts to laugh. The smile back on his face eases my heart. The corners of his eyes crinkle, his bright white teeth flashing in the overhead light.

"Sure." I take a sip of water, offering a cup to him as well. A silent cheer ringing in my ears.

"Where did you learn? I mean, you mentioned that you worked at the prison. Was this part of your training?"

I take a long sip, the cold water rushing down, making me calm a bit. "I guess you could say that. I learned how to fight at a very young age. I could skip past most of the training for my job. That's also how I was able to work so young."

He nods, himself now taking a gulp of water.

"I say, we work on stamina together. Start with running. How about tomorrow morning after breakfast?"

I pick up my clipboard to make sure nothing is taking up that time. Everything looks free, so I wait for his nod of approval.

"That sounds great."

I walk through the halls with my head down, my choice heavy on my mind. Either way, I would be doing something wrong. Silence fills my thoughts, forcing me to stop thinking.

"I will have to see what Zaria says."

The voice comes from the room I pass. The door is cracked open. I peek my eye inside. The room is filled with papers, top to bottom. Inside stands the Queen and her advisor. I haven't met the latter before, but she shares the same clipboard as me. They stand facing away from the door. My throat closes, thinking up all the different things they could be talking about.

"All we can do is ask her. Hopefully she will tell the truth."

Oh no. I take quick steps away from the door. Pack your stuff and leave. No one has to find you. Keep going, don't look back.

"Miss Zaria."

My mind tells me to take off running, but I know that voice, and if I run away from the Queen, I will be in more trouble than I am already. Slowly I turn around, bracing for whatever comes out of her mouth. When I face her, she stands tall, her gown encasing her like a sea of waves. Her hands are crossed, interlocking her fingers.

"Yes, Your Highness?" I bow my head, still planning to run if I have to.

Her smile is there, but how many times have I seen Damian smile before he ended someone's life? Way too many to count. Her golden hair flows down her back, tamed and smooth. I curse myself at my own tangled hair.

"It has come to my attention that you seem to have extra time on your hands."
What am I getting myself into?

"I'm sorry my Queen. If you need me to work more, I will."

"That is not the problem, my dear."

She opens her arms now, gesturing to her own advisor. She comes out the door, waving her hand at me. Her blonde hair is tied in a low ponytail. She wears a suit like me, instead of a dress.

"Rosalyn and I are in need of some assistance planning our upcoming ball. We were wondering if you would spare us your time and opinion, helping us with planning."

It takes my brain a while to catch up to what she is saying, still shocked she is not coming for my head. I look at the Queen, then at Rosalyn. They both look back, hopeful eyes watching my every move.
I stutter on my answer. "If — if that is your wish, I'm sure I can help."

"Marvelous," the Queen says, clapping her hands together. "Come in. Come in."

She grabs my arm, guiding me into the chaotic room. Dim lighting shadows overhead, making the ambiance very relaxing yet suspicious. I still keep an eye on everyone.

Just in case, I check for an escape. There is one window, but we are on the third floor. That jump would probably be the last thing I do. I scan more of the room filled with furniture and tables, like some strange royal office. My muscles ease at the fact that this would be probably the worst room to end me, but the perfect spot to interrogate.

"As you can see, the room is not quite as organized as I would like it to be. There is just so much planning."

Rosalyn raises her voice, "We have sorted everything into piles. Different ideas for each theme we have come up with."

Papers stack a mile high on top of the two desks that occupy the room.

"That is a lot of ideas." My eyes wander around the room, looking up and down. Almost every shelf or counter is filled with inked paper and pens. Yeah, something tells me that I am still safe.

The Queen sits down in one of the cushioned chairs, "I do wish I didn't have to rip you away from your free time, but if you help, I can assure you a tip in your payment."

I try to smile, my insides unsettled. I always have to consider the bad before I can even allow the good to come to mind. Always feeling like I have a target on my back, I have always needed to find the loophole in every situation.

But, something deep inside me whispers that it is real. That there are no tricks here, just a community of people who are in need of some help, and I don't know how to feel about it.

The feeling looms in my stomach for the rest of the afternoon. I help sort through all of their ideas. In two weeks' time the air will become chilly, and snow will be on the ground. We decide to go with a snowy theme. Silver, gold, blue, and white will fill the ballroom. Rosalyn has assigned me the job of invitations. The thought already making me wish I didn't pass by this room in the first place. She wants all of them handwritten, in script. I start by collecting paper from the archive room. Just like the study room, it is filled with shelved paper, ceiling to floor. Some rose pink, others literal gold sheets.

I examine them, top to bottom, stalling as much as possible. In the corner of the room, I spot the blues and silvers and decide to pick one of those styles. In the end, I am left with an icy blue sheet of paper. It was the only style that had enough for everyone to have the same invitation. The Queen had compiled a list of two thousand guests, so the stack I have to carry back is very heavy. Training, this is part of training.

I must be in luck. When I return, the Queen decides for a break.

"Thank you for chipping in on such short notice, Zaria."

I frill through the papers in my hand, guessing at how many I was able to get in one trip.

"Oh, it's no problem. Thank you for trusting me to help."

"Get some rest, my dear. I want to be able to see you at dinner this evening."

I look back before leaving the room. "I will."

If only I could be telling the truth. I fake my way through the halls, acting as if I'm going to my room. I change course halfway. I have to meet Crista. I have a favor to ask.

I arrive at her door, the sight awing me again. It mirrors much of her personality. Unique and different, yet in unison with everyone. I knock on her door, wishing she will be inside.

"You're here." She pulls me into a surprise hug, her squeeze a little desperate. "I was starting to think you wouldn't make it."

Welcoming me in, she quickly closes the door. "I got stopped by the Queen on the way. I am on royal ball duty as of now."

"Ah." She walks over to where I sit. "We have a ball every year. It's supposed to signify our growth as a kingdom. A night of peace and unity."

Nodding my head, I try to slowly transition into my question. "Listen, I kind of have a favor to ask. Also, it can be our first lesson."

"Hit me."

I pick at the side of my nail. "Well… I was assigned to make all the invitations, and my handwriting really sucks. I was wondering if you could enchant a pen for me to use, that will write in perfect script every time."

She listens, her eyes looking blank. "I can try, but I can't promise anything."

"All I ask is a try," I say, plead in my voice.
She inhales a deep breath, reaching for a pen on her side table. Picking it up, she places it on the bed in-between us. For a while, all I hear is the clock ticking, she sits staring at the pen leaving me to wonder what is really happening inside her head.

"Any advice?" She finally looks up.

"What do you struggle with? I don't know if I can really help you with magic, but I can be your cheerleader." Waving my arms in the air, I act as if I have pom-poms in my hands.

A small smile appears on her face. "Mostly it's my concentration. When I try to focus, it's like everything around me is amplified, pulling my attention away from my task."

I remember learning to focus. The time I learned to pick locks, Damian had played sirens in my ear while I tried to break in. The whole point of a siren is to scare you. To get your heartrate up, letting you know something is wrong. The pick required 100% of my concentration. The moment I would get flustered, he would turn up the volume. We sat there all evening until the sun went down. I only broke it open once. John had got it three times. For that, I got a smaller plate of food. In Flesherg, we were fed according to our performance. The better you were at being a criminal, the better you ate.

"Try to listen to the pen. Of all the sounds around you, try to hear its whisper, its call. Feel the weight of it. The smooth point as it glides across the paper." I almost cringe at my own words, but nothing else comes to mind. Again, it's just that weird feeling of acting before thinking. As if my own mind had been shut off and controlled by something else. Something foreign yet familiar.

She closes her eyes again. This time, there is a much greater silence, one that swells in my core. Out of nowhere, a burst of purple sparkles hits the pen. It swirls around the cylindrical shape. After it gets to the edge, it takes off to her glass jars. I sit up, rushing over to her shelves. I catch as many jars as I can, the magic still bouncing off of anything it can. Crista grabs her trashcan, dumping out all that's in it. The magic bounces to the floor, Crista pouncing on it, trapping it inside the can. The room goes quiet. Putting her jars back on the shelves, I see her slowly lift up the can. Inside, there is nothing.

"*Whoo!* What a chase."

"You caught it pretty well," I say, still lining up her collection.

Smirking, she stands from the floor. "I've gotten in the habit of chasing down runaway magic."

She walks back over to the bed, picking up the pen.

"For you." She shoves it in my direction. I clear my hands, taking it from her.

"How do you know if it worked?" I ask, trying not to sound rude.

"I just… know," she says, cautious delight on her face.

"Are you sure?" I sweep my hands around her room.

"Hey!" She jokingly punches my arm.

"Thank you. You don't know how much of a lifesaver you are."

She takes a deep breath, joking aside. "I'm glad I can save at least one life."

***

I dress for dinner. No matter what, I am going tonight. I stride into the dining hall, it looking as magnificent as it did the last time I was here. Soft lights fill the room, vases of flowers and napkins sit delicately on each round table made for conversation. Surprisingly, John hasn't arrived when I enter. I scan the room until I see Crista waving me over with frantic arms. Sitting down next to her, we start chatting away.

"Good evening ladies."

Axil approaches from behind us. He sits down to my right.

"I see you have found a friend, cousin."

"Remember, she is my friend, not yours," Crista retorts.

I laugh at their tiny argument. It reminds me of John and me. If only we could be like that now. I wish I knew what got into him. I really hope to talk to him, but I also feel like being miles away.

Speak of the devil. John walks in by himself, sitting at the opposite end of the table. I feel his heated glare on me, his anger still fresh and looming.

Catching my glance at John, Axil whisper in my ear, "You can sit by John if you want. You don't have to sit with us."

"I am perfectly fine here." Finally taking my eyes away from John's I look over to Crista. "Hey, catch."

I throw a chunk of cheese that sits upon the platter. Apparently, I startle Crista. Her purple magic wraps around the chuck of cheese, levitating it in the air. She shoots a glare. I stick my tongue out in response. "Better."

Her eyes go from annoyance to gratitude. I don't think it registered with her that she even used her magic. I wonder if it is like a reflex. I'll have to ask her sometime.

I turn to Axil. He sits tall, scanning all of his future subjects. Looking at him, I catch a glimpse of John's tight face. He really is like a lion, stalking his prey. I tap Axil's shoulder.

"I want to go riding tomorrow."

A smile appears on his face, showing his bright teeth.

"Of course, after our run I'll plan a trail."

I nod, fixing my gaze on anything else but John and Axil.

"Hey." Lowering his head back down to me, he quiets his voice.

Turning back, I curse myself.

"I just want to thank you for this morning. Your teaching is quite magnificent. I enjoyed it."

I can feel my cheeks flush. "I'll teach you all I know."

We smile at each other. I never noticed the tiny freckles across his nose. The imperfections on his face make him look even more perfect.

The doors open, chefs filing in with carts. The King stands up at the front of the table.

"Dinner is served."

Chapter eight

I awake the next morning feeling fully rested. The moon peeks though my window, a hint of light in the darkness. I put on a soft shirt and stretchy pants for my run with Axil this morning.

The routine reminds me of Flesherg. I tie my shoes tight. For once, not to sneak around alleyways or lurk in the shadows of the night, but instead, do something on my own without Damian breathing down my neck.

I am still undecided. I don't have many days left. For some reason I can't shake a guilt feeling from me. I should be able to decide what to do, yet the feeling of being stuck clouds my vision. A glint of hope shines though. A stupid hope that one day I will wake up, and this will be my real job. That I am actually *someone*, not just a targeted shadow. Hope that one day I can live like anyone else, and I will finally not just be free but feel free.

I tie my hair in a braid, feeling the weight of it on my back. I feel so heavy. Yes or no. Steal or flee. Succeed… or die.

I slide on a jacket, the crisp air seeping through my window. The cool air excites me, filling my lungs with a fresh breeze.

I tiptoe down the stairs in my sneakers, careful not to wake anyone up. The halls are still dark, only the faint glow of the moon illuminating my path. At that moment, something shakes my judgment. A bright light peers into the hall, from what was a closed door. Now open, I see a shadow of a silhouette. The light turns off, only the sound of the door closing ever so slightly.

I hold my breath, peering at whom it may be. It is hard to make out, the suspect not even making a sound on the tile. The shadow starts to take off into a hurried skip, long curled hair swishing with the movements. Lucy.

This hall is not filled with bedrooms. I remember Axil walking me through this hall, explaining all the rooms filled with different activities such as the sparring room connected to the archery room filled with different targets, the study room, and finally the dining room. But there seems to be one more. Another room that Axil had kept from me. Curious, I step into the room she left. Turning the knob, a sliver of light comes out into the hallway. I slip in, so no one sees me. The sight almost takes my breath away.

Hanging on the wall is a giant tapestry. Small stitches weave in and out of the fabric, colors I've never seen before making an incredible scene. I stare at it a little longer, my mouth hanging open.

The tapestry is of a dragon flying overhead the kingdom, a night sky in the background with stars sparkling like tiny crystals. But what catches my gaze and makes me stop is not the colors or shimmer of tinsel, it's those green reptilian eyes. They seem so lifelike, telling an entire story without speaking one word.

Did she work on this all night? It's gorgeous. I wish not to but I back my way out of the room, eyes still glued to the dragon. Dazed, I make my way to the common area. I had told Axil I would meet him here whenever he was ready. I close my eyes for a brief moment on those soft velvet sofa. Those same eyes from the tapestry stare at me, they look at me in a way that makes me feel translucent. Unable to hide, like it can sense my beating heart that is slowly getting faster or the sweat accumulation on my forehead. Goosebumps run up and down my arms and legs.

"Zaria?"

I startle awake, at first confused where I am, and how I am back to reality from a dream that was not quite fake.

"Oh, it's you," I sigh, relaxing my shoulders.

"Are you ready?" Looking down at my clothing, the memories of early this morning play in my mind. The routine I had awoken for, to make sure I was down here early enough. Crossing his arms over his chest, he continues, "If you're too tired, we can do this another time."

Standing from the sofa I had snoozed on, I look him in the eye. "I'll beat you to the gate."

With that, I take off running like I used to from the police. Even with his royal training, I know he can't keep up with me. I burst open the door, welcoming the rush of cold air. Filling my lungs, I run past the guards, giggling and screaming. Looking behind my shoulder, I see him close on my tracks, arms stretched out ready to tag me. I turn my focus to the gates. A few more strides, and I've got him beat.

Just as I feel the adrenaline of victory, a tug comes at my sleeve. Axil digs his heels into the ground, his grip tight on the fabric. Pulling me back, he runs like the wind, tapping the gate.

"I won." Waving his hands in the air, he points his fingers up to sign number one.

"You cheated."

"Says who?" he taps my nose, reaching in his pocket for his keys. Aggravated, I take a pin out of my hair holding my long bangs in place.

"Allow me." I shove him out of the way, inserting my hair pin into the lock. I jiggle it around waiting for the click. When I hear it, I quickly turn my hand. Pushing at the door, I pull my pin out. Axil stands, a sly smirk on his face.

"You're lucky I know you worked at a prison."
I nervously giggle trying to hide my panic.
Putting his hand on my shoulder, he stops me.

"Hey… thank you."

"For what?" I ask, trying to ignore the butterflies that entangle in my stomach. The panic from earlier subsiding.

"For fun. For making my life fun."

And with that, he walks through the gateway leaving my heart fluttering the same as it did yesterday with him. Shaking my head I catch up, brushing his arm as I do and we start on our jog.

Leaving the palace walls, we take off at a steady pace. I listen to the whistle of the wind, and the sound of our steps. I focus on my breathing, reverting back to my training. I can tell Axil tries to do the same, but his breath is still all over the place.

"Try to match your breath with your step. Every two steps, an inhale, the next two, exhale."

For a while we run in silence, listening to each other's breathing.

"How hard was your training? You seem like the kind of person that has seen and done a lot," he asks out of breath.

For a moment I don't answer. No one has really asked this question. At Flesherg, you don't talk about your pain. That is why Damian had such a hard time with my tears to my mother. He didn't want his gang to see his daughter, their next leader, as weak.

"There were a lot of things at the prison I wish I didn't have to do." Looking off into the distance, I try to hide the escaping tears that slip out of my eyes. I sniff the cool air begging it to wash through me. "But hey, now I can teach you." Lightly tapping his shoulder I try to smile.

"Nothing too extreme, please." He pouts his lips, making puppy dog eyes.

"Of course not."

Another silence fills the air, memories of Flesherg coming back. The horrible training days and the life threatening nights. The times I would go to sleep with a knife as if it was a teddy bear praying I would know how to wield it if I must.

"My father taught me to fight." I came out of nowhere. When the words leave my mouth I wish I could eat them right back up.

He shifts his head to look at me, his eyes landing on my face, trying to read my features. Taking a leap of faith, I continue.

"He wasn't the best man. He would push me until I couldn't be pushed anymore. Day in and day out, fighting until the sun set."

His eyes soften. The last thing I want is pity.

"Why?"

Tears well in my eyes. I have known it since it happened. It took a while to accept. Weeks of crying myself to sleep. I had always carried the burden by myself. John would slip into my room and talk to me, joke with me, but we never talked about it. Never about her.

"My mother was murdered."

Saying it out loud made the tears come in fast. My pace slows, my cheeks freezing as the wind bites at my tears. Axil steps in front of me, blocking my path. He takes my arms, pulling me into him. Wrapping his arms around me, he rests his chin on my head. I fall apart.

I had never said out loud that my mother was dead. The weight feels lifted, but it's suffocating me. I could drown in my tears, and I couldn't care less. It means I would be with her. Away from this world. This world of chaotic disaster.

I lean into his hold. My head buried in his chest. I hear his heartbeat quicken, the jog finally catching up to him. He rubs slow circles on my back. We stand there in the middle of the trees, hidden from everyone else.

"I'm sorry for your loss, truly. I can't imagine not having my mother growing up."

I wish to reciprocate his words. Tell him I'm sorry for the loss of his sister, but my throat tightens. No words come out. Maybe I *am* suffocating. What would John do if he found me dead? What would Damian do? Would they even care? I know the answer, but I still hope I would mean something to them. It hits me now that I have no one. No one cares about me. Dead or alive, I would mean nothing to them. I sink deeper into his arms, wrapping mine around him as well.

"I'm sorry your childhood was such a nightmare, but believe me when I say, I'm glad you're here with me now."

We stand like that for a little longer, holding each other. Relieving each other's pain. I step back, wiping away my tears, my cheeks burning yet cold to the touch.

"Why don't we head back to the castle? I can make us some hot cocoa," he says, trying to coax a smile out of me.

It does. For the first time in a while, a weight has been lifted off my chest. I nod my head, stepping back where I was on the trail. We walk back slowly. I look over to Axil, his eyes burning with rage. Did I upset him? I can't be a burden to anyone else.

"I'm sorry," I say quietly, my voice failing me. "I'm sorry for dumping all of this on you. I am supposed to be your advisor, not the other way around."

He grabs my arm, stopping me again. "Listen to me. If you ever need to talk to me, you can. Don't think for a moment you are ever unsafe here." He takes a moment looking off into the distance. "I may totally suck at fighting, but I will protect you as long as you live under the palace roof. Do you understand?"

His words send a shock to my heart, one that I do not know how to handle. One I have never felt before. All I can do is nod my head.

We make it back to the palace. Inside I watch as Axil stirs hot chocolate in two cozy mugs. He hands one to me. I greedily take a sip, welcoming the warmth of the beverage into my freezing body.

"I can relate to you." Breaking the silence, his eyes refuse to meet mine. "Not exactly, of course, but I can relate."

Finally looking at me, he leans against the counter.

"Ever since I was young, my father has been training me to become King one day. Our monarchy isn't like most. My father will not die for me to become King, rather when I come of age."

"How old?" I ask, holding the mug, warming my hands.

"Twenty," he responds. "Ever since I was four, it has been sparring, language, manners. Not just the basics, but how to go above and beyond. Use those simple skills to become a great leader people can only imagine having."

His eyes get lost in his mug, swirling it around, watching the bubbles spin in the cup. "I never had a childhood. Not one that was carefree. Sure, I had my free time. Time to grow up with Crista, or attend tea parties with my mother, but it was never easy. The responsibility at such a young age was quite overwhelming."

"I got used to it, of course, I guess that's just part of the reason I am so thankful to you. Nothing in my schedule has changed, but instead of my duties seeming like a chore, they now seem… fun."

There is a silence, yet the room is not empty. It feels as though we are still talking, just not with our words, but with our thoughts. Just in case he didn't get my message, I say it out loud.

"You are doing a great job. You will be a wonderful King, and I promise you, to make your title, a life worth living." Smiling at me, he dips his face back into his mug, a flush of warmth coming to my cheeks. Sitting atop the counter with hot cocoa, in the same room as the Prince of Lumbridge, I allow myself to hope that both of our promises can be real.

***

After our hot cocoa we head back outside. I need to get on that horse. All this hot cocoa talk is making me forget the danger of being here. If I ever do need to escape, by horse is best. I can't be scared.
Entering the stable, my hands start to shake. I take a deep breath. Noticing my worry, Axil takes my hand. I reach out my other hand, stroking the soft fur of the horse. A small chuff comes out of his mouth.

"Aww, I told you he really likes you."

He watches as I slowly stroke the horse, giving me time for my breathing to slow and my muscles to get less tense.

"Are you sure you are ready?"

Axil had put all the equipment on the horse. I stood watching in awe at the gentle nature of the stallion, even while getting piled on with a whole bunch of equipment. Just thinking about the word stallion, makes me shudder. A word meaning strength. Meaning power. Everything I pretend to be but am not.

In a slow steady voice I reply, "I am ready."

I hook my foot into the stirrup, checking to make sure it is secured. I grab onto the saddle, Axil's strength assisting me up onto it. When I sit atop the horse, a thrill runs through my veins just like the times that I would impress Damian. I try to forget the times. The years that I spent on a power kick. A puppet for Damian. I would do it willingly. In fact, I asked to do more. Anything to get my mind off the grief. Anything to try to stop hearing her voice in my head and feeling her warm hand on my back. I had to stop. For the better sake of myself it had to be done, but there's a little part that wants it back. The thrill, the adrenaline, the rush.

While I settle on my horse, Axil hops onto his. The same pure white horse from before, its long lashes embarking every inch of beauty.

"Now you want to keep hold of the reins. Light movements."

He demonstrates how to communicate with the horses, going over the basics. Walk, run, canter, and stop. He taught me how to turn. He lets me practice inside of the fenced meadow, but I long to run free. Feel the wind in my hair, the exhilaration pumping my heart.

"Can we go onto the trail?" I ask. That electric thrill running through me again.

His forehead creases, his face scrunching up. "The boats are coming in at the dock today for winter trade. It can really spook the horses. I don't think it's the best idea."

"Oh come on, I will be super careful."

Gears turn in his mind, his eyes gazing at the path we took this morning.

"One quick lap."

We slowly ride our way down to the trail. I listen to the leaves crunch with every step of the horses. I know I could be putting myself in danger, but it all goes out the window when we enter the trail. I ignore Axil's instruction about staying close to the inside edge. I recall back to what he taught me about how to canter.

I squeeze my legs down, the speed surprising me. My grip tightens around the reins so much, my knuckles turn white, and that's when I feel it, the freedom.

Fresh air fills my lungs, my blood boiling hot. My eyes widen as I take in the quick pictures that blur past my vision, a soft painting of auburn and gold. I hear yells coming from behind me, but I don't care. The only thing that matters is the freedom.

I close my eyes for a brief second, taking in the sweet smell of maple that fills the forest air, until I get the feeling of falling.

I open my eyes, seeing everything backwards. I feel weightless. That's when I know it isn't euphoria, but I am actually slipping through the air. A squeal comes out of the horse I am riding. Sharp pains pierce my skin, as I hit the ground, all the autumn air escaping my lungs. My eyes shut to the outside world, an overwhelming nightmare of pain welcoming me in my dreams.

***

My throat feels dry, every limb from my body aching. I try to open my eyes, but I can't find the strength. A panic surges through me. The last I remember was hitting the ground.

Why? Why did I do that? I take a deep breath, my lungs tightening as I try. I have to know. I have to know what happened.

With all my strength, I open my eyes. My vision blurs, slowly trying to knit the pieces back together. I see a young woman standing at the opposite side of my bed.

"Lucy?"

Gasping, she starts to move to the side of my bed. "You are awake!"

The voice doesn't come from Lucy, but from right next to me. All of a sudden, I come to my senses. An arm rests around my shoulders, warmth heating my left side. I turn my eyes to look. Axil stares back at me, eyes wide.

"Thank the sky, you are okay."

He pulls me into him, hugging me. His big hands gripping my shoulders.

"Is there anything I can get you?"

This time it is Lucy. Axil still holds me close, my own voice coming out hoarse.

"What happened?"

He pushes me away. "Exactly what I said would happen. You took off riding really fast. A boat came into the harbor, and the horse threw you off." I try to listen to his explanation, but the only thing I can focus on is his anger. His brows form tight lines as he rushes his story out. The longer he talks, the stronger his grip becomes on me. I try not to wince in pain. "What were you thinking?"

My eyes falter, not able to look at his eyes anymore.

"I'm... I'm sorry."

Lucy comes to sit down on the opposite side of me.

Out of the corner of my eye, I catch her shoot Axil a sideways glare, something I have never seen anyone do. "Are you okay?" She places her hand on my forearm.

Am I okay? Not at all. No. None of this was worth it. Nothing I did proved anything. All I proved was that I am a wreck.

"Everything hurts."

Patting my arm she gets up. "I'll get you some medicine."

She closes my door softly, but to me it sounds like a hurricane raging in my ears.

"Don't do that ever again."

Mustering up my courage, I look him in the eye. When I do, it makes me want to look down again, two pools of tears settling in his eyes. "When I saw you fall, I didn't know what to do. I didn't know if you were hurt, or if you were breathing!" A sniffle comes from his nose. "When I got to you, pieces of bark were embedded in your skin, blood ran down your nose. I ca—

He chokes off. Holding a fist to his forehead, he tries to calm himself. His breathing is ragged, an uneven mess.

"Zaria?"

My door opens. Thinking it is Lucy, I sit up in my bed, but Crista comes in tiptoeing on the floor. She looks at me, then at Axil. "I need you to leave."

"Excuse me," Axil scoffs in remark, quickly pulling himself together in front of his cousin.

"Get out." She grabs him by the sleeve, pulling him up from my bed. She pushes him out, closing the door aggressively this time.

"Where does it hurt?"

"What?" I look up at her, wondering how she had heard of what happened.

"Where does it hurt? I will heal you."

I stop to think. I have seen her do magic. Times where it rips apart her room, other times where she leaves a trail of leaves across the castle floor. I think back to when I was put under pressure.

There was a time on one of my jobs where John got stuck behind a door. I wasn't just going to leave him there. I burst into the control room. I had never learned how to hack into a security system before. I kept pressing buttons. One after the other, until I heard the door slide open. John and I booked it out of there. All I can do is trust her. I really have no other option. If I wait to take Lucy's medication, I will have no more time to convince John to stay a little longer.

Axil looks me over one more time before mouthing the word *I'll be back*, and closing the door.

One she hears the click of the door she raises her eyebrows at me, waiting for some kind of answer to her question.

"Everywhere. Everything hurts, my back mostly."

She helps me roll over, my limbs refusing any movement. I hear her open a bottle. I keep my eyes fixed on the pillow, hoping it's not filled with those dreaded spiders. A cool liquid rolls across my back. Relishing in the cold, I turn my head back to where she works.

Her hands hover over me, radiating a soft glow of lilac. Not as prominent as her other magic, which resembles a deep purple. This seems soft and light. Her eyes are closed, focused on her task. There is no strain nor any fumbles. She just *is*. That eases my mind a bit. What feels to be knots untying in my back makes me wince. My body feels in more pain than before.

"Are you okay?" she asks as calmly as possible, the giggling Crista I knew hiding somewhere beneath. A tight squeezing pressure gripping onto my insides. A tear runs down my cheek.

"I'm fine," I mutter. Gripping onto my pillow, I bury my head. In that moment, everything relaxes. A cold rush rolls through my veins. Tingling, my body feels electrified. I release my breath that I was holding so tightly. This time, allowing a gasp of air into my lungs, without pain.

"How do you feel?"

Finding my words, I take a moment to sink into the mattress that lies underneath me. "You did it." I sit up, opening my arms as if to hug her. She stagger back looking at me. Looking away, I put my arms down, but she steps towards me embracing me.

In that moment, I wish. I don't know what for, but I wish.

That night I fall into a deep sleep. I don't dream. I don't turn. I lie still. Relaxed and wishing.

***

I flurry my eyelids awake. There is no pain, just a longing for sleep to take me again. I thank the sky Crista could heal me. I was very stupid yesterday. I knew the consequences and decided to still do it. Axil must think of me as a toddler, a little kid who threw a temper tantrum, having to drag me out of trouble all day. I decide to get ready early. I have no events to attend to with Axil today.

I get dressed and head to the study room. Turning on a singular lamp, I hold the pen Crista had enchanted in my hands. I lay a crisp paper in front of me, the blank page taunting with evil remarks. I don't know what to do, but as I hover over the page it just… happens. I start to write, the pen gracefully dancing across the page. It looks that of a poet. Synchronized in a melody, each loop of letters bringing in another section of music. At the end of the page, I have a full orchestra. The script is beautiful, one hundred times better than what I could ever do, and I had gotten it done so fast.

"Good morning Zaria. I didn't expect you this early."

I bow as the Queen enters the study.

"Would you like to read over the invitation?"

I hand her the paper filled with magic. I watch her eyes read over the scripted letters, picking at my nails as I wait. Her face is relaxed, so I take that as a clue that she likes it.

"Marvelous. Finish writing down everyone's invitation. Then, we can address and deliver them. This ball is coming up in only a few days' time."

It will be at the end of the week, the week John will push me for information I don't have. I don't even know if I want to search for information. Stealing from such a nice family makes my stomach turn. Not just a family, but the kingdom. I ponder on how the King feared war. If I were to steal all the kingdom's money, there is no way they will be able to recover.

My mind wanders as I write out the rest of the two thousand invitations. What to do. What not to do. I can hear him. *You're being played. You're feeling all of this for nothing. Remember how we were? You were happy and an excellent worker just like me.* And then it's her. *This is not for nothing. This feeling in your heart is not a joke. I saw you suffer. That wasn't happiness. Please... Do what is right, even if it hurts.* It's always like this. Damian gambling his luck on me, and my mother pleading me with all she has left of her soul. And then I'm left in the middle wondering where I went so wrong.

***

The rest of the week passes by quickly. I walk around the village in the kingdom two days prior to hand out the invitations. Apparently, the Queen wanted it to be a surprise as to when the ball would be. I sure did surprise them with such a short notice.

When Axil had heard about my trip to the village, he had decided to tag along, saying he wanted to watch his future subjects. So, we now walk the dirt path around all the little cottages that dwell just outside the palace walls.

"How often do you leave the palace?" I ask, a huge basket of invitations in my hand, with more in Axil's basket as well.

He holds his other hand in his pocket, lifting his face up to the warm sun. "Not much," he replies. "I'm lucky if I get out twice a year."

"Why can't you just go? These people are your future subjects. Why would you not want to observe and interact with them? Start your relationship strong before you even take the throne."

"I told you. Training has taken up most of my time, and… there have been some restrictions over the past couple of years regarding me being by myself. Higher security, safer premises… that kind of thing."

His sister. That is why. I find myself in the same situation, not of myself, but my own mother. It must have been hard for her to see me go off with Damian doing God knows what.

She was forced to sit at home knowing her little girl would one day be breaking the law for her job. I wonder, if it was up to her, would she have let me go with him, or would she have fought to keep me by her side, safe and protected.

Nudging his arm, I try to brighten the mood. "What's so special about this occasion?"

"You." He looks down at me, a smug smirk on his face.

"Me?"

"Your background, specifically. And the chance of anything happening today is pretty slim. The ships are still coming into our harbor, so most of the occupants will be down there receiving goods, or already at the marketplace."

"Well, I'm glad you could come out. Being cooped up all the time can't be any good for you."

We pass a stand filled with baked goods. Cakes, bread, and candies galore. An old lady sits by her table. Humbly she rests her arms on her lap, a wilting daisy in her hand.

"Maybe not, but you know what is good?" Picking up a cookie from the nearby stand, he offers the sweet to me.

I look at the lady. Smiling, she nods her head. "What's the price?" I ask.

In a slow sweet voice she waves her hand. "I do not work for a price. I do this just to see smiles form on the people's faces."

My heart drops, accepting Axil's offer. I step over to her, outstretching an invitation. Taking the envelope, she carefully peels open the wax seal I had worked so hard at perfecting.

"The annual ball. I've seen many of these. Who knows, maybe this one will be my last." Looking up at me she smiles, her wrinkled lips as warm and inviting as a spring day. "I'll be there."

"Bring some of the sweets. They are delicious." I look over my shoulder to see Axil shoving his face full of half her stand.

"Axil!"

"You bet ya," she giggles at Axil.

Pulling him away, we walk through the rest of the town, giving as many invitations as I can to the people, then circling back to post the extra invitations at any available doorsteps.

Stopping at the park, which lies in the middle of the whole village, we sit on the ledge of a water fountain. A sculpture of what looks to be the Queen sits above us. Axil leans back, his body looking more relaxed than I have ever seen it.

"I've missed this," he says after a breeze blows through our hair. "The open air, the smell of the village, the little children that run around the park."

"It's the reason you keep your head straight," I say, eyeing the way the leaves blow in the gentle breeze.

"How do you mean?" Curiosity outlines his features. Sitting up, he points his body towards me.

"All the training and lessons. You do it without complaint to ensure the happiness of your people. *These* people."

"Yes." A short pause fills the air. "What about you? Why did you decide to come here? I think I would have remembered a face like yours in the village."

Glancing at him, I roll my eyes. It takes me a moment to collect my answer, but surprisingly I didn't have to lie, not anymore. "The kindness. I came here for the kindness that your kingdom offers."

He puts his hand over mine, resting on the fountain brim, and for a minute, I think we both remember the promises we had made to each other.

***

Every day I helped Axil with his sparing, and Crista with her magic. I never thought I would be that much help, but the time spent together always lifted my spirits. I never noticed how rough the people in the palace have it. On the streets, it's easy to think that they live a life of luxury. On some accounts, the fact is still true, but the more I talk to Axil, the more I see a broken teenager, just like myself. Crista had opened up about her mother, who had passed as well. I now had someone who knows what it's like to grieve a mother.

Shockingly, we had lost our mothers at about the same age. I have never felt so listened to before. Heard and accepted for my emotions and opinions.

Today is the day of the ball. I had kept myself awake most of the night, helping prepare for the formal. Stringing lights, taste testing different fruit punch, listening to previews the musicians had to offer. I had drifted off to sleep for a few hours before I was awakened. I expected to turn around and see Lucy. My heart stops when I see the Queen herself in my bedroom.

"Good morning, Your Highness." I bow, shaking the sleep from my mind. "Was there something I forgot to do last night?"

"Oh not at all." Her voice as gentle as the morning sunrise, she folds her hands in front of her. "I just wanted to give you this."

She picks up from the table a large box. Setting it down on my messy bed, her graceful hands open the box.

"Take a look what's inside."

I step, hunching over so I can see. A beautiful dark blue dress is folded neatly inside. I pull it out. Sparkles hit the morning sun, dazzling across my room. Shiny silver crystals sewn on from the waist to the middle of the skirt, imitating snow. A matching silver sash runs across the waist, a deep blue rose attached to it.

"I had this specially made for you. You have helped Rosalyn and me so much these past few days. I might have also heard from my son, you have been coaching him with his sword, and Crista with her magic. Your stay here has been remarkably brilliant. I want to welcome you as part of this kingdom. A member of this palace."

I am left speechless. Her kind words engulfing me in a sea of emotion. I hold the dress in my hands trying not to cry.

"It's stunning. Thank you so much."

She smiles at me, running her hand across my cheek. "I look forward to seeing you at the ball." With a wink she turns around, leaving me an emotional wreck.

Once the sun had risen over the mountain, I take a walk in the garden. It amazes me that the flowers are still in bloom in late autumn. I wonder if Crista has anything to do with it. It seems like something she would do, bring life to something that should be dead. I stroll, weighing my options, knowing that I have already made a decision.

A rustle from a nearby bush catches my attention. I quickly turn to see Axil plucking one of the nearby roses.

"Zaria."

"Why are you destroying Lucy's flowers?" I ask, examining him hunched awkwardly over the rose bush.

His cheeks redden. "I was um... I just wanted to..."

"Come on, spit it out."

He takes a deep breath, closing his eyes. "Zaria, will you be my plus one to the ball tonight?"

My heart stops for a beat, uneven breaths coming out of my mouth.

"Is that allowed? Shouldn't you be taking a princess?"

"My mother said I shall pick anyone I so wish, and you, Zaria, are that wish."

He takes hold of my hand, offering me the rose. I can't help but smile. I look up at him to see his smile, too. His aqua eyes shining right back at me.

In another world, I would be ecstatic. I am ecstatic, but my guilt comes bubbling into my stomach. In another world, I would allow myself to be happy, happy about tonight, but I can't. I go to deny, but I can't stop myself because there is no other world. I only have this one, and I can change it right now. Change it into a world that I am just a normal girl with a normal job. No gangs, no crime, no record, just a life.

"I accept your offer." Taking the rose into my hands, the weight of my decision doesn't feel so heavy anymore. "Next time, don't go digging in Lucy's garden. She works really hard on it."

"Noted." A huge smile splays on his face. He squeezes my hand a bit tighter before letting go. "I'll meet you at your room to escort you down the stairway. We all know how hard it is for you."

"Shut up." We smile at each other before I watch him walk away. I raise the rose to my nose, smelling its sweet perfume. I know in my heart what to do.

***

I walk back inside, the bustle of preparation filling the halls. A smile is on everyone's face. I can't help but feel their joy. They all seem like one big family. I guess that's part of the reason for this ball anyway.

In Flesherg, we never had any celebrations. I grew up knowing only the sad tunes of funeral processions. The morbidly dark colors shaking me to my bones. Not even on holidays do we celebrate. In fact, the holidays are a perfect time to do many burglaries. Food stores, the mall, jewelers. It never stopped. It was never enough for Damian. I would see tired faces pass me through the mansion. We turned into robots for him. Our blank expressionless eyes that tell no story.

It's nice to know the whole world isn't like that. Nice to know that there are people out there that are happy, warm, and safe.

"Zaria!"

Running footsteps sound from behind me. I zip around seeing Crista running right at me.

"Zaria!"

She slams into me like the first time we met. Her run so momentous, she knocks me over.

"What is it?" I ask, a bit worried.

"Come with me."

She takes off running again, holding my hand. She drags me through the halls. Many times I have to correct my footing, to not stumble over. She pushes me into her room, slamming the door behind her. I am about to ask if everything is okay, but when she turns around, her face is scrunched up looking like a little kid with candy.

"Axil asked you to be his plus one!"

"Uh, yeah."

"EEEEEEEHHH!"

She takes my arms, jumping up and down. Her eyes squinted, a soft squeal coming from her mouth.

"Axil has never had a plus one before. He must *like* you."

She taps my nose on that last part. I roll my eyes.

"I don't think so," I tell her, grabbing her finger and pulling it away from my face. "He probably asked me to go because I am his advisor. He was just being polite."

I wish the words I say are false, but I can't shake the feeling that I'm being set up.

She flattens her face, calling out my bullshit. "He never invited his last advisor."

Remembering what John had said on the airplane, I ask, "What ever happened to her? Was she nice?"

"I don't know," she says. I never really ran into her, so when she went missing I didn't even notice." She laughs to herself for a moment. "Axil never really liked her. He would hide out in my room any time he could to get away from her."

"That bad huh?"

She shrugs her shoulder, flouncing about as she usually does.

"Let me make you look perfect." Her eyes widen. I can tell it's been a while since she has had girl time. Especially with the loss of her mother, I can relate that you fend for yourself. No one to talk to, no one to gossip with. I am not fond of girlish parties, but I can tell she is dying to have some fun.

"Okay," I say. A bit of hesitation in my voice.

She starts frolicking around the room. When I turn to observe, I see her on her tiptoes reaching for the jar of spiders.

"No way!" My stomach turns seeing them crawl around in the jar. Imaging them crawling on my face makes me want to hurl.

"Oh relax. They're not going on your face. Remember I said they were the main ingredient in a potion."

She's making a potion. I thought she was just going to sit down and do my makeup, like regular girls. Then again, there is nothing regular about Crista. I see her reach at the top of her head. She grabs her floating top hat, pulling out a little bottle of what looks to be sparkles.

"What is that?"

She holds up the elixir she just pulled out, "This? It's stardust. Everyone needs a little sparkle. Especially when the prince invites you to a ball."

"OKAY!" I stammer annoyingly, interrupting her. All she does is giggle to herself, still taking a tour of her room.

Once she gathers everything, she sets them down on a table next to her cauldron.

"Does the cauldron have magic, or is it just you?" I ask, curious.

"Mostly me, although it is rumored that the spirits of past sorcerers live inside, giving your spell that extra flavor."

The flavor of dead sorcerers. My stomach doesn't know how to settle with that.

I see her open up her book, presumably filled with different spells. Some of her pages look a little charred. I wonder what spell went awry, that ended up burning part of her book.

I stand back, giving her room to concentrate, one of the things I have learned with her over the past week. Her magic has gotten substantially better. I don't think the problem was even her magic. I think she was just... I don't know, lonely. I'm glad I could make her feel like she's got someone, and I think that's what I needed as well.

I hadn't seen John all this week. I had only passed him in the halls a few times, and at dinner all of which he looked to be so annoyed that the creases on his forehead made a permanent dent.

"Hey, have you talked to any of the guards at the dining hall recently?" I ask, trying to be a subtle as possible.

She side-eyes me, squinting. "If you're thinking of asking John to go with you and Axil, I am afraid that I will have to step in and object."

"No, no, no." I shake my head. "I mean… Is it just me or… does he look, not himself."

She stops stirring. "I don't really know his appearance that well, although I did pick up on some negative energy on him. Remind me to gift him some sage."

I let out a short breathy laugh. Something tells me that he's going to need more than sage and meditation to relax whatever is looming inside of him.

Focusing back on Crista I watch as petals fall into the cauldron, each carefully placed in a specific way, then the dreaded spiders are released. They crawl around the inside, trying to escape. Crista every once in a while has to flick one back in. I try not to gag. Finally the stardust is added, the sparkles making a hazy fog that billows over the cauldron. It looks like it has come to life. She raises one of her fingers, dipping it into what looks to be plain water. One drop falls from her finger. She then starts to swirl her finger in a circular motion. Seconds later, I hear the contents inside start to follow her lead. A small hum fills the air. It makes my bones rumble, a vibration deep in my core. The liquid starts bubbling. A quick motion of her arms sweeping across settles the boil.

A few seconds pass. I watch her peer inside.

"I think it's all done."

She picks up a ladle, and an empty bottle. Carefully dipping into the potion, she funnels some inside the jar. Putting a cork on top, she hands it to me.

"What does it do?"

"I guess you will have to find out. Before you leave, apply three drops. One in the center of your forehead and one on each palm."

I pause, speechless. *This feeling in your heart is not a joke.*

"Now go, go. You must get ready."

She pushes at my back, opening the door, and shoving me out. I close my hand around the bottle. It is only as big as my thumb. A tiny little thing, that knowing Crista, will do wonders.

***

I fall asleep before the hours of the ball. I want to be able to enjoy myself tonight. To be able to relax with friends. Friends? I never thought I would use that word to describe the people here. It's kind of hard to have friends when you are a thief. I want to be able to laugh, to dance, to be filled with joy. Even if it is only one night.

I am shaken awake by Lucy, her warm fingers wrapped around my arm.

"How are you feeling, Miss Zaria?"

"I thought I told you, you don't need to use 'Miss.'"

Blushing, she holds up her arms. "Sorry, sorry. Habit."

I didn't think I would, but I had grown a liking to Lucy. She doesn't hide her face anymore, so I guess her shyness had nothing to do with the kingdom itself, just that her shyness is who she is, and as I think about that, I'm actually glad. Glad to have someone who is so laid back and quiet. For tiny moments of everyday I can relax and not have to worry about keeping my energy up, she just allows me to relax.

"It is time to get ready. I would ask if you would like my assistance, but there is no way you are getting into that dress by yourself."

Lucy ties up the back of my dress. I have never once worn a corseted dress. It feels weird, restricting a bit, but I feel like a lady. I have never felt like that before. I have prided myself in being a female thief. A young woman who can get stuff done. That was who I was… but not anymore.

I have never allowed myself to want to be feminine. The concept doesn't work well, while trying to hide my identity. Every night I would dress up like a guy. The best way to get people off my back, is for them to think I am someone else. I have hidden behind a mask for a long time, shadowed by the darkness of the night. Tonight, I want to shine. To be myself. Not who Damian has shaped me to be, but truly me. The girl who lost her mother. The girl who fought for her life, and the girl who has now found a home.

Lucy fixes my hair, her cool fingers combing through my strands. I ask for my hair down, and she obliges. She makes a cluster of tiny diamond around the crown of my head. Once she leaves, I take a second to look in the mirror. My face looks a lot fuller, my eyes less sunken in. I knew I wasn't being treated well at Flesherg, but I never thought to consider that life was that bad.

I don't look like myself, but I don't look like somebody else, either. Is this what I actually look like? I reach for the little potion Crista had made me. I pop it open, wondering what it will do. I tip the bottle, my finger blocking the top. I follow her instruction as to where to place the potion, letting the liquid drip down my face.

At first nothing happens. I wait in silence, looking at myself in the mirror. I almost give up hope. Maybe the potion can't doll up beat-up girls like me? Mid-thought, three lights shoot into the air. A line of sparkles connects from my head, to my arms. The same hum from before, rings in my ears. The magic swirls around me in a spiral. I feel electrified, on fire, but not burning. I open my eyes when it is over.

I look back into the mirror. I look the same, with a sharpened flare. My skin has been blurred of all my imperfections, looking doughier and doll-like. My hair is glossy. Bouncing the light with every swish. The thing that catches my eye the most, *is* my eyes.

There almost seems to be a glow to them. My dank green eyes now shine like the brightest emeralds. Just like mother.

I wish she was here. She would have loved this ball. She always wore some type of fancy dress. As a kid, I would hide in her skirt as a game. We would play peek-a-boo for hours. She would often wear black. It looked classy on her, an elegance that followed everywhere she went. I thought at some point; the contrast in her eyes had to do with the black she wore, but they never seemed to dull with any other color. She was just… the best thing that ever happened to me, but now…

A knock sounds at my door. I try my best to walk with grace, Axil's insult from this morning fresh in my head. I open the door. Outside stands Axil, more handsome than ever. He is in his normal colored suit, but everything looks more sophisticated, embroidered with gold lining, his crown newly polished.

"M' Lady."

"Your Highness." Curtsying, I hold out the fabric of my dress, the feeling again being very odd.

He offers out his arm. "May tonight be a dream to remember."

Chapter nine

Interlocking his arm with mine, he leads me down to the ballroom. People watch us as we pass. I try not to let their stare make me feel self-conscious, but I can't help but question what other people must be thinking. A lowly advisor, a commoner, being escorted by the prince. Sensing my stiffness, Axil gives my arm a squeeze. The gesture makes my heart flutter. Is it possible that tonight I can be someone for just one moment, be the person I have so longed to be? I guess tonight I will find out.

We step inside together, melodic harps being accompanied with a piano. Axil is right. This does seem to be some type of dream. The smell of jasmine fills the room, just like the soap in the bath. I still can't remember where I have smelled it, but it relaxes my muscles the second I breathe it in.

I look around seeing some familiar faces. I spot Rosalyn in the corner. She stands next to a vase of gold dipped roses. Her pen pointed at them, counting. She writes something down on her notepad, scanning the rest of the ballroom. I sure do hope she lets herself enjoy tonight.

I scan around some more, trying to recognize anyone I might have seen at the village. Lo and behold, standing next to a table of goodies, the old woman stands in simple dress. It is nothing special, but I can't draw my eyes away from it. Something about her humbleness reminds me of a distant memory.

I leave Axil for a minute, searching through the vases. I miraculously find a daisy; just like the one she had the day Axil and I went into town. Pulling it from the vase, I walk over to her.

"You made it." I call out to her.

In the same steady voice, she responds, "I told you I would." Winking at me, she continues; "You're a lucky one."

"What?"

"You can't get that prince to leave you alone."

I look over my shoulder glancing at where Axil stands. At that moment he catches my gaze and smiles. Noticing the old lady, he nods and waves.

"Oh, it's not what it looks like," I ramble on, making a fool out of myself. Turning back to the old lady.

Interrupting me, she holds out her hand grasping mine. "I know young beating hearts when I see them. Don't waste your time on childish games. You'll be my age by the time either of you say anything to each other."

I let my hands loose in her grasp for a moment, listening to her, before I clear my throat, collecting my thoughts.

"This... uh... this is for you." Holding out the daisy to her, I finish my sentence. "For your generosity."

She takes the delicate flower, cradling it gently in her withered hands. "I have lived in my village for a long time. Never have I come across a heart like yours."

I don't know how to react. This is what I asked for. To be myself, not the person Damian has shaped me to be, but it is still part of me. Part of my past, and I have no idea how to run forward.

"I... uh... hope you enjoy the ball this evening. I'm sure everyone will like your sweets."

"You too."

Walking away, I try to find Axil without looking like a lost lamb. Through the sea of people, my heart starts to race. Surrounded by a crowd, I am reminded of how secretly I have been living my life. All the eyes, all the bodies, making me feel as though I am caged, and then I am grasped.

Gasping, I quickly turn around.

"Woah, are you okay?"

It's just Axil. I allow time for my heart to become a natural beat before I respond.

"Yeah... just a little crowded."

He grabs hold of my hand, soothing me with soft strokes.

I look around for Crista. I don't see her yet. I hope everything is okay. She will probably come in later. Making a last minute spell, I presume. I don't see John anywhere either. I hope it stays that way, but I know he will question me, pry me for answers. I—I thought he would be happy if I decided to go against Damian. I don't understand his new found desire to be like him, to be in control. I can't blame him. It's how Damian raised us, but I thought he would follow my lead. I thought—

The music cuts off, all eyes wandering to the grand staircase. I must say that thing looks like my worst nightmare. Trumpets wail, echoing in the huge room. The King and Queen arrive hand in hand.

I remember when Damian used to hold my mother's hand. Over the years, it started to fade. I have vague memories of when life was not as it is today. When I had a mother and father. When we would pack a basket, sit in the meadow, and have a picnic. When I would watch old films cuddled between them. Where did it go?

The expanse goes silent, the King raising his voice.

"We welcome all here today with open arms. To celebrate this kingdom. Celebrate our union, our hope, and our dreams." The King stands tall, a broad smile on his face. "This kingdom will always stand strong. Not because of us, but because of you. A kingdom is not a building, or fancy silverware, or jewelry."

He looks at his wife, his eyes softening towards her as he speaks, "It is a community, our family. So let tonight be about family. Something we shall all honor." Raising his hand towards the Queen, he bows to her.

Cheer breaks through the silence. Life filling the room. The Queen speaks this time.

"I hope you all enjoy the ball. I had some help from Rosalyn and Zaria. Without you two, this ball would not have happened."

Axil squeezes my hand again, looking down at me smiling. I look back at him wishing I could relieve this moment over and over again.

"May all of you have a great time, and safe travels back home."

People bow in response to the Queen. I follow their lead. The music starts back up again, louder this time signifying the start of the ball.

Axil turns to face me, all jokes from this morning fading away into a light and sweet smile. "May I have this dance?"

I take his hand. "You may."

He sweeps me far into the ballroom, swaying to the music. I don't know how to dance, he guides me with the music. Following Axil's lead, I relax into the melody.

I have longed for freedom for my whole life, and only now I can say that this is the feeling I have imagined. Being lost, yet found. Being broken, yet repaired. Axil holds onto me. Feeling him here is like an anchor to my lost ship. Even if I am nothing more than a friend to him, even if he just invited me to be polite, I feel free. To be me, and only me.

"I must say, you look absolutely stunning."

I blush trying to hide my face. "Thank you. You don't look… too bad."

"I'll take that as a compliment." He smiles in return, his own cheeks now turning blushed. "You seem different tonight."

I feel different tonight, and I don't have to keep lying.

"I haven't had a celebration in a while. A night to wind down and have fun was long gone in my life."

"That's terrible," he says.

I look down wondering if I should ask. I could ruin everything. This is what I need. A night to be myself, to feel peace, but it itches at my mind. Before I can even really think, I say it. "Why? Why did you invite me?"

He looks puzzled. "Did I not tell you when I asked you this morning? I wished to invite you, so I did."

"Yes, but why?" I hang my head. "I don't want anyone's pity. I have told you my story, and it's not the best one. I don't need you to fake your kindness just to make me feel better."

"Zaria. I did not ask you here tonight out of pity. Nothing I have done has been out of pity. I invited you because I enjoy your company, because it has been a while since I have made any friends my age. You have only been here a short time, but you have helped so many people, my mother and I included. You are so special. Don't let anyone sway you otherwise."

I lean my head onto his chest. We stay like that, swaying to the music, the world around us fading. Someone cares, someone hears me and listens. My throat starts to close up. I don't want to cry tonight, but I can't contain my relief. Relief that there is something else out in the world. There is love. There is hope.

The music ends. We separate from each other. Looking into his eyes is like sailing on open waters. Not a cloud in the sky or rocks blocking the path. Just deep water with no end. But every water has its dangers.

I see Axil's relaxed face turn from a dream into a nightmare. My skin chills as I already know what is about to happen. Turning around, I am met with John. Dressed in the suit he came here in, he splays a fake smile. One that would fool a thousand people.

"Do you mind if I steal Zaria for a dance?"

Disappointment runs through my veins along with something else… fear. I never thought that I would ever be afraid of John, but my heart starts to run, not in excitement, but panic.

I wait for Axil's response, hoping, praying that he will kindly shoo John away, but I know he won't. Because that's who he is. He would never let his own emotions stop him from taking me away from who he thinks is still my friend. Looking up at him, I now see *him* put on a fake smile. "Sure. I need to speak with my parents." Looking to me, his eyes soften. "I will be back." With one last squeeze of my hands, he walks off.

As the next song starts to play, John wraps his arms around me. At one point I would have felt safe in his embrace, but there is no warmth. A stone wall separates us, cold and lonely. It makes me unsettled.

"So what do you have?"

I feel a moment of pause, because as I listen to the voice in my head though it is the same, it is my voice. Not the pleads of my mother but of myself. Do what is right, even if it hurts.

"Nothing." I look him right in the eye. "And it's going to stay that way."

"What!"

"You heard me right. The mission is off. You can go home, do whatever you want. We are not robbing the palace."

He looks all around, shock written plain on his face. "You can't be serious. What are you going to do? Huh? Are you going to live life on the streets? End up dead like your mother?"

I take a deep breath, swallowing my anger back down. "What I do does not concern you. I am calling off this mission."

His tone goes completely low, dangerous. "You can't do that."

"Why not?"

A smirk plays on his face, a small laugh coming from his throat. "You are forgetting one thing. Damian didn't put you in charge of this mission. He put me in charge. You have no control over me."

"Now you are just being dumb. Since when do you care about what Damian says?"

"Things have changed. I warned you. I warned you that I would take over if you fail, and it seems you have."

"So what? What are you going to do? Kill me? Good luck. Guards line every entrance and exit."

"Ah, so you got your little prince protector. Really, I thought more highly of you." He circles around me in tune to the piece being played, but there is nothing enchanting about it. He is trying to intimidate me, to take control. "So clueless. Are you forgetting that I am a guard? I can ask permission to any room I need. As for your life, I want you to see this kingdom fall. The kingdom you so desperately are trying to protect."

"What happened to you?"

An evil smile appears on his face. The face I found comfort in. The face I looked at and saw my equal. Now I see the devil staring back at me.

"All in good time, you will figure it out." Continuing his monologue, his eyes drift off behind me. "Feeling stupid, you will beg to be a part of my plan." Leaning in close to my ear, he whispers, "And then it will be too late."

"Am I interrupting anything?"

Axil's voice sounds from behind me. John looks up at him, finally letting go of me.

"She's all yours." John walks off slowly, like a fox waiting for cover. Axil and I follow his path standing frozen. John looks over his shoulder one last time, and with a wink disappears.

I see the anger that suppresses within Axil's eyes but sweeping me back up again, he tries to smile. My mind runs a mile a minute, trying to connect the dots. "Are you alright?" Axil asks. "You seem a bit pale."

I need an excuse. Time to think things through. "I am going to go to the bathroom. I will be back."

I walk off, a bit more of a jog. Tripping over every step, my breath quickens as I fight my way through the sea of people. My eyes set on the door, I don't even see Crista. Grabbing my arm, she stops me.

"Is everything ok?" Crista looking as beautiful as ever holds my arms. She, herself, dresses in a white and blue dress, a true complement to mine. If I wasn't in such distress I would have commented on her floating tiara instead of hat. She's royalty. I find that slipping my mind more often then not.

I can't hold back. "No, nothing is okay. I don't—

I stop short, my eyes fixed on one thing in particular. My mind stops, all external problems fading.

"Your necklace." A golden pendant holding a blue gemstone hangs from her neck. Almost everyone else, I would brush off, but this necklace is nothing ordinary.

"Yeah, this is the last thing I have of my mother. Everything else was taken except for this, she gave it to me."

I pull my mother's necklace out from the inside of my dress. They are a matching set, mind the color.

"That's not possible." Her eyes widen, calculating.

"What? What's not possible?"

"That would have to mean—"You need to come with me."

Once again, I am being dragged off. I look back, glancing one more time towards Axil. Before we exit the door, I see that brunette bitch from before approach him. I wish I could go back and speak my mind to her again, but Crista's grip is tight.

This night is not what I had thought. Not at all. I just want the craziness to end, but that will take a lifetime.

***

She pulls me through the halls. They look like a ghost town compared to the ballroom being so lively.

"Please, Crista. What is going on?" I ask in a pleading voice.

"Just wait. I will explain everything in my chambers."

The run there seems excruciatingly long, each click of my heels sending a shock of pain, but it is the only thing that is keeping me locked in reality. The world blurs together as my mind runs through the possibilities of what could have happened with John. Damian. I bet he has something to do with it. He always has something to do with it.

When we arrive, we make quick work of shutting the doors and windows. Everything, so that we are completely isolated from the outside world. It is not me who speaks, but Crista. She grabs the photograph that was set on her nightstand. The one I saw when I first met her.

"That can't be. It doesn't make sense."

"What! What is going on?!"

She takes a deep breath before speaking. "This necklace is the necklace my mother gave me."

"And…" I egg her on, my patience running thin.

"She explained that there was a magic only chosen sorcerers could possess. My mother was one of them, I am as well."

A long pause fills the air. "Zaria. Only sorcerers own these necklaces. It is a gift, for being accepted by the gods. A protection." She rummages into her nightstand drawer. "Here. Here's mine." She holds up the same golden chain, with hers having a purple gemstone.

She hands me the frame that holds the photograph. I look at it, memories flashing before me. The picture is of a woman, presumably Crista's mother. Another woman stands beside her. A black dress billowing to the floor, green eyes shining at the camera. My mother. My mother looks back at me.

"That's... it's—

"Your mother," she finishes for me.

I can only nod my head, my mind totally blank. A void. What is true? How does any of this make any sense?

Crista goes on, "That woman in the picture was my mother's best friend. They were chosen at the same time."

"What— what is chosen? What does that mean?"

"Chosen is when the gods bless you with every type of magic. Most sorcerers can only possess one, maybe two powers at most. If you are chosen, the gods leave you access to all types of magic." She trails on, "You know what this means?"

I don't answer. Everything I seem to know has all been a lie. John, my mother, it's all been hidden. Hidden from me.

"Zaria, you are Maria's daughter. You are a sorcerer. A descendant of the chosen ones."

"No! No, this can't be true! Why did I never know? Why did she never tell me?"

I break down on the floor, spiraling. My father the mafia boss. A ruthless, coldhearted leader. John, my best friend, turned villain. My mother, the wife of a mafia boss, and a chosen sorcerer.

***

"What do I do now?"

Crista shakes her head. She looks more worried than shocked. We sit in silence both thinking the same thing, yet none of us dare speak. I want to believe the necklace my mother wore was just a fake. A phony copy of the real thing. I don't want to live a life knowing my mother lied about something so important. Something so life changing.

"Can you… test it? To see if there is magic, I mean."

"It's not that easy. To test if it is hers means tapping into the necklace. Their souls are locked inside when they die. I would be looking at all of her emotions, all of her memories." She pauses, trying to look out the window, but quickly remembering it is closed. "It seems too private."

"I don't care! I need to know." I grab her shoulders, forcing her to look at me. "I need to know who my mother was."

I look deep into her midnight eyes. Guilt washes through me. I can't just ask her to look into someone's life. Something that should not be seen. If I made her do this, how much different would I be from Damian?

"I'm sorry. I can't make you do this."

"No!" She stands up facing away from me. "I have to know too."

I reach for the lock on the chain, gently unhooking it. Taking it off, I realize the weight it had been putting on my shoulders this whole time. Something heavy. Not just in weight, but in meaning. The second I feel the weight of the necklace leave, the longing of wanting it back around my neck becomes strong.

My hands shake, dangling it in her direction. With both hands she takes it from me. How will she know if it's true? How will she see my mother? Part of me wishes it could be me. I wish to see her. Feel her presence. Hear her voice other than in my head. I watch her like I always do. This time she grabs a dropper. The contents clear like water, but the aroma insists that it is some type of oil. She takes a dried sage roll, lighting it. I watch the smoke billow in the room. She sways the sage in a circular motion around the necklace's middle. There is a flash of light that comes from the ruby. A brief second, a snippet of time.

My mother. My mother is in there, trapped forever. I wait in silence, frantically picking at my nails. I dig so deep, I make myself bleed. I stop, staring at my blood. Am I magic? Is it part of me? Never before did I ever think I would ask myself such a ridiculous question.

Chosen. My mother was chosen. I still don't fully grasp the idea of what all that means. My mother knew Crista's mother. Maybe even knew Crista. A sting of jealousy courses through me. I only had my mom till I was twelve.

I remember now, there would be times where she would take a day trip. Probably once every week. Was she visiting Crista? She was supposed to be my mother, and she spent her time with other girls. I didn't nearly have enough time with her. I just want her back. Back!

Crista comes back to reality, her eyes flying open. She takes a deep breath of air.

I run to her, holding her up, wobbly on her feet she still blinks, coming back to earth. "What? What did you see?"

"I — I saw her."

Numbness flows through me. I had still wished that maybe Damian had killed a sorcerer on one of his jobs and stolen their necklace. Twisted stuff, but that's just the kind of thing he would do. I wouldn't put it past him to gift my mother a necklace stolen from a murdered corpse. He had told me it was a gift for her. That he got it for her. What a liar. They were all such liars.

"I saw her — All the things — I saw you."

She spoke in broken sentences. All I want to do is smack her across the face. Get some answers, and move on. I take a deep breath, slowing my thoughts. Walking over to her sink, I fill a glass for each of us to drink. I hand it to her.

Grabbing it, she takes big gulps. What did that spell do to her?

"I do have one question."

She looks at me, exhaustion on her face.

"Why did you say, you needed to know as well?"

She takes a long pause. The water bringing a little life back to her skin.

She talks in almost a whisper, "Why do you think our mothers were murdered at the same time?"

I looked at her shocked, "Your mother was murdered too!"

"I didn't want to scare you when I told you she died. I like to believe that she died peacefully, but I know that is not the case."

My eyes snap back to hers. I, too, had not told her that my mother was murdered. "Did you see it, her murderers?"

She sits still for a while before slowly nodding her head.

The adrenalin comes back. The want to know who did it. I have stolen from many people, many companies, all things that could be replaced. Whether it be jewels or cash. All the things I stole had limited value, a value that could be replenished with even more if they so desired. They stole from me. Stole something that could not be replaced. Something that had a priceless value. Something that would leave me in shambles for the rest of my life. For a long time I wanted to know, to get back at them. Do to them what they did to me.

Every time I listened to the thought or planned something out, all I could see were my mother's eyes. A peaceful spring day. I would then look down at my hands, blood dripping down. The hands of my father. I had to choose. Two conflicting sides pulling me in a game of tug of war. It's just a matter of who will win.

***

We sit together collapsed on the floor in our puffy ball gowns. Tears flood her room, sobs echoing in the hallway. I have never felt as lonely as I feel now. Even after her death, I knew she was gone. That she had moved on into the sky, looking down upon us. Now I don't know where she is. Crista said their souls were sealed into the necklace. Is that part of being chosen? It's the only logical explanation I can come up with, then again, logic is pretty much out the window at the moment.

"I miss her every day," Crista wails softer than ever. "I wish she was here."

I try to dry my tears. We can't both wallow in our grief. Someone has to keep it together. Another wise phrase from Damian. I try to concentrate on anything else. Counting the wood tiles seemed like a good distraction. My eyes follow the lines, the grain of the wood flowing like the waves of the sea, and like the crashing waves, I am never able to catch a break.

I get up from the floor, cranking open one of the windows. The starlight shines through her dark room, and instead of finding peace in them, I can only see a chaotic mess. A bold representation of how I feel right now. Broken, alone, and burning.

I can hear Crista's soft snooze. I'm glad she was able to doze off. The guilt of having her look into the necklace sits odd in my stomach, ripping at my insides anytime I move. I didn't force her, she chose to do it, but it doesn't make me feel any better. The horror on her face when she came to from the spell will forever be burned into my memory.

It's not just the guilt from the necklace, but something else doesn't sit right. If our mothers supposedly had access to every magical ability, how could they die? Why couldn't she just save herself? I try to imagine life with my mother back, here in the palace with me. What would it be like? Would it be like old times with her stories and cooking? Would we live here? With Crista and Axil? I try to call out to her now more than ever. Call out to her hoping to hear something from her, but she remains silent. The thought only bubbles up another round of tears. Suppressing it, I go back to counting the tiles.

I stir through the whole night until both Crista and I are startled by banging on the door. My heart speeds, sweat forming all over me. Please, don't have it be John. I wish to curl up and die, but if I did, would I ever see my mother?

Crista and I huddle together under her bed, it being high enough off the ground for a perfect hiding place. Neither of us know what is going on, but we both are in agreement that it can't be good. A loud crack rings through the palace walls, light shining into the dark bedroom. The door has fallen to the floor, unhinged. Quick footsteps run into the room. A glint of light shows off the polished shoe. Axil?

I peek my head out from underneath the bed, Crista still holding on tight. I am met once again with those blue eyes. A wave of relief rolls through me.

"Zaria?!" He kneels down grabbing hold of my hand. Sighing, I scurry out from under the bed, dragging Crista out as well. "What happened!?" he asks, flustered. "The two of you look a mess."

Crista is the one to answer, not in words, but with the photograph.

"What are you trying to tell me?"

Finally able to talk, she speaks up. Her voice firm. "Look closely… very closely."

He looks at me before studying the photograph. "It is a photo of your mother and Maria."

So he knows my mother's name. Interesting.

"Does anything else look familiar?" Crista continues.

His eyes wander all over the photo, looking for any clue as to what to look for. He catches my eye again, looking back and forth in quick motions. "No way."

"There is a way, and it's true," Crista says, snatching back the photo.

"You are Maria's daughter?"

I nod my head in agreement. I stand still not knowing how to function.

"How did you find out?"

I cradle the amulet that hangs down my neck. Crista does the same. I can tell he doesn't quite understand, but he tries hard to put the pieces together.

"Isn't that the necklace your mother gave you?"

"Yes, and it's magical. You know my mother was chosen. Maria was too. Zaria is her daughter, with her necklace."

It still takes him a while to comprehend all that is being said.

"Listen, I know this is a lot to take in, but Zaria and I need to go." Crista grabs my arm, ushering me out.

"We do?" I question, looking back and forth between Crista and Axil.

"I'm coming with you."

Crista takes a long look at Axil, sharing some sort of message I can't identify. Axil reciprocates Crista's glare.

He uses his "prince" voice now. The one I always heard in council meetings. "I am coming with you."

Crista's grip tightens around me, taking her aggravation out on my poor arm.

"Where are we going?" I ask, trying to break the intense glaring.

"Fine!" she shouts, breaking eye contact with Axil. "You guys follow me."

We follow her. All of us in our best clothes. A runaway ball. Three lost souls on the run for justice.

***

The three of us run outside to the pumpkin patch. Crista stops, examining all of the pumpkins.

"Please don't tell me we're booking it out of here Cinderella-style," I say sarcastically, trying to lighten the mood.

Axil speaks up, "She's not looking for a carriage." I look back at Crista, hunched over the rows of orange ground ornaments. "She's looking for a key."

An explosion roars through the air. One after the other. A giant orange firework. Crista balls both her hands in tight fists, her hands glowing with deep purple magic radiating pure rage.

Slimy guts fly through the air in every direction. Covering my face, I turn my back towards the explosion. It doesn't do much to save my dress. I face back towards where Crista still explodes pumpkins, and Axil flicking stringy pumpkin guts off of my arms. Axil and I catch glances, both of us looking absolutely disgusted. A laugh bubbles out of both of our mouths, each of us pointing at one another.

"You look ridiculous," he points at me, clutching his stomach.

"Me! It's all over you. I should start calling you Prince Pumpkin."

He steps closer pulling strips of exploded pumpkin off of my dress.

"It's ruined. I'm going to have to bake cupcakes for the Queen for a year to pay off the cost of this dress."

"My mother is not like that. Besides, if she were, she would have me to deal with."

He winks at me, quickly going back to picking pumpkin guts off of our clothes.

"I got it!" Crista emerges from the patch just as gutty as we were, if not more. Each one of her steps squishing the leftover pumpkin on the ground.

"Did you have to blow them all up?" Axil looks at me. "They are Lucy's. She works very hard on them."

He used my words. Acting like an angel, he completely skims over the fact that he was doing the same thing just earlier today.

I pick up a slop of guts that had dripped down. Throwing it at him, I watch as it hits the center of his suit. Sliding slowly down, his eyes un-squint.

Crista puts the key in front of us. A shiny thing it is for living inside a pumpkin. It lies in her hand, taking up most of her palm. Gold, like everything else in the palace, it has intricate swirls at the top. Jewels line each swirl, the moonlight dazzling off the cut and polished edges.

"Why did you hide a key in a pumpkin?" Axil asks.

A smirk falls on her face. "It's absurd. No one would have found it."

Looking around, Axil responds, "Clearly, neither can you."

Shoving his arm, Crista walks off, leaving us to follow her.

We walk through the night. Neither Axil nor I ask where we are going. It doesn't seem like the time to ask questions. The unknown eats away at my stomach. I trust her, I do. But growing up in Flesherg has taught me to always know the plan even if you are not a part of it. Knowledge is gold. A good brain can get you out of a jam.

We walk for a solid twenty minutes in silence. The only noise coming from the rhythmic crickets. The hoot of the owl startles me, making me shiver. The moon hangs overhead, a full moon. We are lucky in that it illuminates the path we trek, wherever that path may lead. We had entered the woods a while ago. I question if Crista knows where she is going. To me, it looks like we are wandering God knows where, but she keeps a steady pace. I have to trust she knows what she is doing.

All the while, Axil breaks into a whistle. The action calms down the tense air we breathe. His melody is slow, relaxing. The notes try to break into my memory, the tune a little familiar. Mostly I think about the ball that we are supposed to be at. The music and food that we are missing. The sways back and forth as the melodies would carry us into the night. It was all so perfect.

"I'm sorry I abandoned you at the ball," I whisper as to not hinder Crista's concentration.

His soft tune comes to a close to answer me. "I am just glad I found you. I tried to look for Crista thinking you must be with her, and I couldn't find her either."

Crickets fill the air, as if this conversation wasn't awkward to begin with. He looks over his shoulder.

"So it's true? Maria was your mother."

"Yes." In five years I have never once heard her name be spoken. It's like she was hidden in a box, collecting dust all these years. Most of all, I feel guilty. I had never forgotten her, but I had agreed to not mention her. I would say to myself that the loss was damaging my training, but I think it was just an excuse I made up, not to talk about her. The more I would shove her away, the easier it was to deal with her absence.

The busier I got with training, the more it intensified. When I started my first few jobs, I swore I heard her voice. Her disappointment, her tears, her warning. I did not want to do jobs after that. I couldn't bear to hear her voice when I knew she was dead. It would give me too much hope. After one of my jobs, I had a breaking point. I could not go on being so emotional. I snuck into Damian's room and stole her necklace. *The* necklace. I thought if I carried a piece of her, the voices would stop, and that's exactly what happened. I now wonder if it was all in my head, was it all just a delusion?

Now all I want is to hear her voice. Make me feel a little less lonely. A little less lost.

"I remember when she would visit the palace. Crista and I were just little children. She would read us stories, and bake cookies. She was a wonderful person."

I knew she was. I knew she was one of the kindest people on the planet. A heart of gold that prospered to everyone in need, but she had left me. She left me to Damian even when she was alive. While I was being beaten again and again until sundown, that was what she was doing? Mothering other children? Reading stories she was supposed to be reading to me? Baking cookies we should have been sharing at home?

"It must have been nice for you. At least you had a mother that stayed with you when you were a child." My voice comes out colder than I thought.

"You know that's not what I meant —

I hurry up to Crista's pace, walking with her rather than with Axil. Wiping tears from my eyes, I try to compose myself. It's too much. Too much to handle, but also not enough. The explanation is not enough. Some of me doesn't even want to believe that it was true. One night of supposed truths won't make up for five years of what I *thought* to be true.

We trudge through the forest for another twenty minutes. The only track of time is the moon moving overhead. Another twenty minutes, and it will be over the mountain. I will have no guide, no clue. Only guesses, and I am tired of guesses.

***

Crista stops walking when we make it to a hedge in the woods. She bends over, crouching on her knees to knock on a tree. She waits. Still feeling irritated, I almost scoff. This whole thing seems stupid to me until my thoughts are interrupted by a tiny voice. A high-pitched voice coming from the tree.

"What are you doing here so late? You're going to wake up my pups."

A fox opens the door that had been on the tree. The trunk has been hollowed out, fluff lining the inside. Four little baby foxes curl together in one fur ball. The sight softens my heart a bit.

"I brought you the key. I need to borrow your motorcycles," says Crista.

Motorcycles?

"Let me see it," he says. Snatching the key out of her hand, he examines it. Flipping it over, his eyes roll around every inch. "It's a deal. I need them back by the next full moon."

"You got it." She holds out her finger. Grabbing it, the fox shakes her hand in agreement. A deal.

She walks away without a word, the fox gently closing the door.

"What is that key to?"

Crista once again walks off. I get no answer. I look to Axil, but he isn't helping much, refusing to look at me at the moment.

I raise my voice again, "What is that key to?!"

Axil speaks up in a monotone voice, "The treasury to the palace."

The treasury? That has been what I had been looking for, or not. No. I'm not looking for it, but John sure is. I guess unless he happens to kidnap a talking fox, and have him cough up the key, he won't get it either.

"Why would you do that, Crista?"

She doesn't look at me, her eyes still set in front of her. "The fox's most prized possession is his motorcycles. A fair trade would be to give over our prized possessions as well."

"Why did we need to borrow a fox's motorcycle? Why can't we just use the royal carriage?"

"We are going to be gone for a couple of days. Taking one of the carriages could cost the people in the kingdom. A loss of resources is the last thing we need right now."

We circle around the forest even more. It's amazing Crista isn't getting us lost. We come to a halt when the trees don't hang above us anymore. A thick layer of vines covers a stone wall next to us. Crista opens the vines, parting them down the middle. Behind the magic curtain sits two mean motorcycles miniaturized to fox height. The thought of the fox we met earlier riding on one of these makes me have to hold back a giggle. Axil goes over to assist Crista, lifting them out of the semi-cave. The moonlight reflects off of the shiny metal, the handlebars reflecting beams of light.

Setting them down, Crista backs away from them, her hands glowing again with deep purple magic. Right in front of us the metal starts to stretch taking a new form. I've never seen her in such control. Her gaze focused on the motorcycles she grows them until they look exactly like the ones I would see in the side alleys of Flesherg. After she's done, Axil gives her an amusing nod and clap.

"We walk these the rest of the way out of the brush, pick up on the main road, and ride to our destination."

I have never heard Crista so demanding. Why is this so secretive? Earlier tonight I was dancing with Axil in a ballroom, flowers everywhere, living my dream, but now I am as lost as I was when I first came to the palace.

"Where are we going?" I ask for the final time, my patience running thin.

"We are going to Flesherg."

Tonight was supposed to be a dream, not a nightmare.

***

"What?! Why?"

Interrupting me, she keeps on her powerful mask, "Damian has something we need, and we are going to get it."

"What is going on here? Who is Damian?" voices Axil.

My blood heats up, locking eyes with Crista. The only way she could know who Damian is, is by my mother's memories. If she saw her memories, then why would she take me there? She should know how bad he is.

"We are going, and that's final," she says, voice tightening.

I pick up a nearby stick, throwing it into the air. I strain my arm, but I don't care. Why? Just why? I crash my fists into my eyes. I try to squeeze out all the anger, but it's no use.

"Take her to cool off. I got these," Crista tells Axil. She walks away, the motorcycles floating up into the air. Levitation.

I hear the footsteps behind me, ever so faint. He waits for me to turn around, my face bright red and hot.

"Who is Damian?" he questions me, looking off into the distance.

I try to lower my voice, hoping to sound as calm as possible, "My father."

Our previous conversations run back into his mind, mine as well.

"Your father? The one that—

"Yes, and I have no interest in seeing him."

He reaches out to me. I try to ignore him for a second, but his open arms are pretty convincing. I step towards him, bundling into his warmth. Wrapping his arms around me, I try to remember the cozy feeling from the ball, try to hear the music, and try to smell the flowers.

"I made a promise to you," Axil insists. I raise my face to meet his eyes. "I told you I would protect you. Neither Crista nor I would ever intentionally put you in danger. You know that, right?"

I don't know how to answer, my mind drawing a blank. I wish I could believe his promise, but it's a big promise to maintain, and no one but me knows what exactly Damian is like; How dangerous he can truly be, because there was a time… a time that I was just like him. Right after her death I went psycho. I still fall asleep thankful I survived that gruesome year.

"Don't get mad, but why do you call your father by his first name?" he asks hesitantly.

I remember that day. The day I had stopped calling him my dad. The same day of tragedy. He was supposed to be home. Home with us. Instead, he had one night off, so he had decided to go drinking with his friends. He was getting drunk and gambling, while someone came into the house and murdered my mother, his wife.

When he came home, he was drunker than ever. He heard my screams and told me to shut up. He was tired of hearing me whine. It wasn't until then that he saw what had happened. He shoved me in my room, locking me in there. I wasn't let out for three days. During that time, I could hear people coming in, people I didn't know the identity of. It sounded like a male and female.

They sounded nice. Hearing the female speak reminded me so much of my mother. I wanted to break down my door and cry all over again. Letting me out was never an option though. John wasn't even allowed to visit me. I remember the one night while I was crying, Damian yelled though the door. He told me that my mother was dead because I couldn't protect her. I always wondered if that was why training was so hard. I think he was genuinely mad that a twelve-year-old couldn't protect her mother from murderers. That was the day I had lost all respect for my father. The day I decided that no man who blamed their daughter for her mother's murder could be called my father. Ever since then, it has always been a card game. A question of who is the dealer, and who has the upper hand.

I explain all this to Axil. He listens, still holding me. I let it go. Let it all go. I didn't have the heart to tell him about the whole mafia gang business, but I told him everything he needed to know. There are no words said. Personally, I like it better like that. More than having to try to understand someone's meaning behind their words. We stand there in the open field, holding onto each other like we both fear for our lives, and who knows, that might be exactly what we are doing.

We walk hand in hand to the open road. My breathing has calmed down a little bit, but I still feel shaken to the bone.

When we make it to the road, Crista is crouched over by one of the motorcycles. Using the trim of her dress, I see her polishing the body of them.

"Oh come on, they are shiny enough," Axil says sarcastically.

"Oh dear cousin, nothing can ever be too shiny. You're a prince. You should know these kinds of things."

I turn to look at Axil, "Won't the King and Queen be looking for you?"

"When I went to go looking for you, I told them there might be trouble. They will probably be worried, but I have left for longer lengths of time."

Crista and Axil share another one of their looks, a full conversation happening between them.

Once she is done she gestures towards the bikes. "We should get on the road. I'll ride this one," she points to the one she has been polishing, probably the whole time we were gone. "You guys take that one."

Riding into the night sky reminds me of Flesherg. I was never safe there, but that was always part of the fun. Breaking the rules, feeling no restrictions. One could call it freedom until it bubbles back to the surface. The consequences. I'm not talking about legal consequences but Damian's. Because, when he asks for something and does not receive, he lights up like a bonfire, and we are three little match sticks.

Chapter ten

We ride for hours, at least I think it's been hours. For a moment I could have sworn I blacked out holding onto Axil, riding on the back of the motorcycle. When I woke up, it's like all of Lumbridge was some faded dream. There were no flowers, no bright sun, no warmth lingering in the gentle breeze. It's cold. Well, not cold but being awoken by the chill air gusting in my face was definitely a shock. The sky is dark, the whole world looking as if I'm seeing it through sun glasses. No, we are just in reality again. A reality that I wish I could curse.

I think about the thoughts running through people's heads as we ride by. Crista and I still in our billowing dresses, and Axil in a baby blue suit.

I see Crista pull into one of the gas stations. We are going to need a lot of gas for this trip. To get to Lumbridge, John and I took a plane. It will take us hours to get there. My hair is a mess from all of the wind. All eyes draw to us when we pull in. We all must look like little lost ducklings.

Crista scrunches her nose, the smell of gas probably potent in the air, unlike the faint smell of roses that was always in Lumbridge. "Axil, you go inside. See if you can find any type of clothing."

I speak up, my voice a little hoarse from the gusting wind, "It's a gas station. You're not going to find anything in there except packaged food and slushies."

Upon my words of advice, Crista changes her request, "Go inside and get any food you can, also try to see if there are any bags, so we can bring it along on our trip."

Axil trots off to the store. I look at Crista, who looks absolutely exhausted. I offer to pump gas into the motorcycles, realizing I am probably their best bet for city life.

"Why don't you just use magic on everything? I mean, you say you are also a chosen one. Why can't you just teleport us there, or make our own food, or fill up on gas without lifting a finger?"

A slight sigh leaves her lips. "If only it was that simple. We have to have a bit of normalcy living in the world. Yes, technically I can use magic for everything, but it comes at a cost. The gods give you your gift, they can take it away as well. If the magic used seems fit to them, they will allow it. If not, you're not powerless, just a little more human."

More human. Her words almost make me laugh. She looks a little different, the spunk of her floating tiara gone, or maybe she's just hiding it with her magic. Processing all of the information makes my head spin. I have no idea how I'm going to keep up with all of this new-found magic.

"You said that I am magic as well. How come I have never been able to do it?"

She looks away, like I had hit a nerve. "I hate to bring this up, but the reason is because your magic has been immobilized. Social stress can trigger this response. Technically, your body got so weak physically and mentally that all your power went into fighting the next day. At the time, you were not strong enough to do both."

I realize I had not hit her nerve, but my own. Out of all words, weak, stings the most. Frail, delicate, fragile, tired. None hit as hard as weak. It's what I have trained my whole life not to be. My mother was delicate and fragile, but she was not weak. She was one of the bravest people I know. Strong, courageous, kind. Never weak.

"I have to confess something." I eye her up and down, waiting for her to spill whatever beans she has. "I never struggled with my magic."

I snort, looking back to how many gallons I have pumped. "Yeah, I gathered that."

"No, I'm being for real. Remember the first time we met when I ran into you in the hallway?"

"I think it would be hard for me to forget."

Rolling her eyes, she shuts me up. "I felt some sort of pull. Something I couldn't explain. I asked you to come by again, to see if I could figure out what it was. It had been a while since I had been around anyone that had magic that I didn't know of, with my mother being gone and everything. It was only then that I realized I could feel your magic, ripping and tearing at you, trying to get out."

I take my eyes away from the machine, fully listening to her story, but she doesn't dare meet my eyes.

"So, I fabricated a lie. Something that would keep you coming back to spend time together. I... I wanted to see if you knew anything about it and were just hiding it, or if you genuinely didn't know anything about the magic inside you."

I don't respond. Slowing my breathing, I try to just play all the times we had spent together in my head. Another lie. Another truth I was kept from.

"I just want to apologize... for everything. I know what I did was pretty invasive, and I can tell you don't really like feeling vulnerable, but I... I—

"Wanted to know the truth." She nods her head, her lips drooping into a frown. "It's okay. I asked you to do it. I feel sorry for even suggesting the idea."

A silence falls over us. Once the motorcycles are all filled up, Axil conveniently walks out of the store. A bag is in his right hand, filled with goodies I hope. My stomach growls at the thought.

"I got a box of cookies and some bottled water. It's all I could find."

Crista takes the bag from him, "That's okay, thank you."

I smile at him, trying to get a clue as to how he is feeling. A weak smile comes from his lips, and I guess I have my answer.

"How did you pay for it anyway?" I ask, a little curious. Knowing him, he probably traded one of the chunky gold rings on his finger for some fifteen dollar food.

"I was supposed to pay?"

"Hey! You! Get back here!" shouts a woman storming out of the store.

Without thinking, Crista jumps on her motorcycle almost causing a car wreck on the road. I quickly follow after, dragging Axil along with me.

It's weird. My whole life I did illegal things, especially stealing. So, why do I feel so shitty about leaving the worker running in the parking lot? I think about her life, or what I can imagine it is like. She looked fairly young. Probably getting paid way less than she should. Now she is going to have to explain to her boss that someone in a silly suit robbed the store of some cookies and water.

Axil holds on tight to me as I catch up to Crista. I need to get in front of her. We need to make another stop. I rev up past her, cutting in as close as possible to get her attention. I need everyone to trust me. If there is one thing I know about stealing, it is that you need a disguise. It's not going to be hard to find the royal brigade along the road, with all of us looking like this. You won't find clothing at the gas station, but you will find it at the mall.

I would have to say about two hours had passed. I finally started to see signs along the road that suggested that there are stores around somewhere.

Crossing my fingers, I take the next exit hoping that Crista will follow. Then again, she doesn't really have a choice.

Luckily, I find a strip of stores. It's not going to be the best of clothes, but Mr. Prince is going to have to deal, especially after making a huge scene at the gas station. I park in another parking lot, waiting until Crista comes rolling in with us.

"Why are we stopped again?" asks Axil.

I turn around dumbfounded, "We are here because of you." I advance towards him, my finger poking at him. "You can't just steal food out of a store."

Saying it out loud, I hear it. Not the voice of my mother, not even my own voice, but just a fact. *You can't just steal food out of a store.* Hypocrite, it says. Hypocrite, hypocrite, you're a hypocrite. I can see the guilt on his face, but nothing still makes it right.

"It's not going to be long until your face starts showing up on the news, cops looking for you, and you are pretty easy to spot right now, us included."

"What is going on?" Crista finally joins the conversation.

"We need a disguise. Not even a disguise, just something that is not our formal wear. Now, come on."

I walk towards the store feeling like my old self again. The one that barks orders, and the one that can take charge.

From behind me, I can hear Axil's sarcastic tone, "Aren't you forgetting one thing? You don't have any money, either."

I guess he really is stupid. Who does he think payed for the gas? But, he might also think that gas is free, just like the nice old lady back at the village.

A sly smirk displays on my face, "Let's just say, I'm taking more from Damian than just what we came for."

The whole point is, if Damian even notices. All the money he has in his account, it would take a big dent for him to even notice something was gone. Even if he does notice, how can he be mad? He is the one who taught me memorization in the first place. I couldn't help myself. When I had seen his credit card number, the pin was a picture in my memory ever since. Some would say that what I am doing is rude or arrogant, but I say I'm freshening up on my training.

"Yeah, Zaria for the win," Crista semi-sings.

"Stealing money from her dad is not a good thing."

We all look at Axil in disbelief.

"Yeah, says the person that just walked out of a gas station without paying. You also didn't see what I saw when I looked into Maria's family life, so back off, cousin."

That last part draws his eyes towards me. I know it must be hard for him to consider growing up with such a rough childhood. He was always sheltered.

"We don't have a choice," I say sincerely. "If there was another way out, I would definitely suggest it, but as of right now, I don't see any other alternative." The last thing I need is for the King and Queen to question me where we have been and why their son was in jail. That would be a headline no one would forget. *PRINCE LEAVES PALACE WALLS AND IS NOW BEING HELD PRISONER.*

We try to walk into the mall as discretely as possible although it is hard to not stand out with the way we are dressed. As soon as we make it inside, the smell of soft pretzels fill the air. My favorite part of the mall.

In unison, Axil and Crista both ask, "What is that?"

I look back at them. Their eyes wander all over for where the smell could be coming from.

"Those are the soft pretzels." I point over to the stand.

Like little children, they both take off after the amazing buttery smell. Screeching to a stop, they halt behind the people who have formed a line. They both look over the people's heads to see the "magic" that is happening. When I walk up behind them, the questions roll in.

"Can we get one?"

"Please."

"I will never steal again, please."

"We just got cookies, guys." That doesn't stop them. They both shrug their shoulders in unison as if they were identical twins instead of cousins. My eyes roll into the back of my head. "Alright, alright. Don't choke on your own saliva."

So, we wait. In line, the looks keep coming. Some from older fellows, but most from teenage girls. They take their phones out, flashing their cameras at us. I make sure to step in front of Axil as much as I can to protect his image. These pictures will no doubt end up on social media. It's a good thing Axil and Crista don't know what that is, but more than half the world does.

I am surprised that no one recognizes him as the Prince of Lumbridge. If I recall correctly though, neither did I. I had never even heard of the palace. I can only bet, it has something to do with Crista's magic, keeping the kingdom a secret and all. The thought of that brings somewhat of an ease to my mind.

"Hey Crista. How come no one recognizes you guys. It seems like no one even knows of Lumbridge."

Axil cuts in before Crista herself can explain. "I guess you could call it another world. Our fantasy, compared to this reality, but it is more like a barrier. People can know of the palace from outside sources. It is in plenty of books. Our founding, our history, but unless you know that, Crista keeps the whole kingdom on the down low."

"Why is it on the down low?"

"Invaders. We try our best to keep out any unwanted guests. Assassins, thieves, you name it. It's for the protection of the people in the kingdom." My heart stops, my blood turning cold. I try my best to keep eye contact. To nod my head, acting like everything is fine, but for a moment I look away, knowing exactly what he could do to me if I got caught.

"I guess that's how you knew about the palace, right?" From your mother?"

Stumbling for my words, I try to speak, "Y—eah." Peeking my head around, I act as though I am looking for stores. Anything so that I don't have to look into his perfect eyes, full well knowing that I just dipped my toes into some hot water.

When it comes to our turn, I am relieved and speak for them. The same pretzel pop-up is in Flesherg. I remember doing eating contests with John back at home. We would order every type of pretzel they offered. Whoever threw up first was the loser. Most of the time, I was the one who lost. My pretzels making a lovely reappearance. But I knew the ins and outs of the menu and exactly what they would like.

Before I start talking, I can already see the shock on her face. The question of, "What the hell is going on?" But, she refuses to say that out loud.

"May I get one cheese stuffed pretzel and one cinnamon sugar one?"

Crista whispers in my ear, "Get one of the bubbly yellow drinks."

I look at her annoyed. She only looks back with an innocent face, pouting her lips.

Grudgingly I tell the food worker, "And one lemonade."

"What size would you like?"

"Sm—," Crista cuts me off before I can finish.

"The largest one you have."

I look over at both Crista and Axil. Smiles are on both of their faces. All it takes is a little bit of food to get them back to normal. I'm going to have to remember that.

"Okay, you can scoot over to the other counter top. Your food will be ready shortly."

I guide them over to the pickup line. I hear their toes anxiously tapping away at the tiled floor. It's only now that I realize I am still in my heels. As my adrenaline runs out, I can feel the pain from them more prominently.

"How was prom losers?"

A group of teens pass us by laughing and pointing. As if I expected something, I look over at Crista. Her dark cheeks become the color of burgundy. Her attitude changing within seconds, she balls her fist and starts stomping over to them. Quickly I try to pull her back, but she manages to slip by. My muscles tighten as I brace for whatever scene is about to go down.

The teen boy, obviously the leader, wears a proud devilish smirk as Crista stomps over to him. "What are you going to do, little girl? Cry your mascara down your cheeks?"

Without hesitation Crista raises her arm, backhanding the dude right in the face. His group of friends back away, but I can't tell from whom.

"Hey!"

A mall cop comes up, approaching Crista. I run over to her as fast as I can, Axil following close behind.

"I am so sorry, sir. That was out of line. We'll be on our way now."

He gives me a nasty look before checking on the boy who got his ass handed to him.

"Your order is ready!" A shout from the pretzel stand, and I sprint back to receive our food.

"Thank you!" I shout, smoothly grabbing our order and running away.

Making it to a clearing, I slow my pace.

"How can you navigate the city so well?" Crista asks from behind me.

"The same way you navigate the forest," I tell her, reigning in my frusturation.

I take a sidelong glance all around us to see if there are any suspicious eyes wandering. Looking like we are in the clear, I put the food and drink down on a nearby bench. The warmth from the food immediately leaving my palm.

"You guys stay here. I'm going to get us some new clothes." I go to walk off but turn looking back. "You guys think you can handle that?"

Axil nods his head, "Yes m' lady."

My look of annoyance is back. This time raising his hands, he responds more appropriately.

As I enter the store, I lay my plan in front of me. New mission. Get the royalty back to the palace in one piece.

***

I frill through the racks searching for anything that matches their style. Sure, I might be wasting my time, but there is no point showing up at Damian's house without making a statement. I pick Crista's outfit first. I know she likes black and purple, so that's exactly what I get her. Purple leggings, a black blouse, and a gold skater skirt to go over top. For Axil, I get light washed jeans that replicate the color of his suit, a white shirt, and a yellow flannel. I want them to be as comfortable as possible in a place that is not comfortable at all.

I now shop for my look. I go for my regular. Nothing too special, just a nice way of saying *I'm back.* Black leather pants, a red shirt, and a leather jacket. I shop for all the gold accessories I can buy. On top of that, I get us all a pair of combat boots. This look is going to be strange to them, but I feel a bit of relief that I am back in my own skin.

I pay at the register perfectly fine, and as I type in the pin, I wonder how much exactly is in his bank account. One million? Maybe two? I don't feel any remorse at all. I can steal a few hundred dollars from him. He stole the most important thing away from me. My hope.

When I exit the store, I walk out with my head held high. Feeling the weight of the boots under my feet keeps me grounded. I had changed in the dressing room after I paid. I come out to tell the crew to do the same. I go over to the bench where they sit. I hear giggles coming from them, so I take that as a good sign. Somehow they got another straw and are now slurping the lemonade together, doing what looks to be a staring contest. When Axil sees me coming, the snap Crista throws at Axil proves my hypothesis correct.

"Wow. You look…"

Crista finishes for him, "Like a street rat."

Axil shoots her a shocked look, slapping the back of her arm.

"Mmm. Well I'll let you change. Then you can all be street rats with me."

I don't know what reaction I should expect. I wouldn't be surprised if I got a look of disgust from them. I definitely don't expect them to be jumping for joy like I am. I examine their faces as they open their boxes. I don't get much of a reaction, but more of what I could call an understanding. From what I know, they have never had to wear anything like street fashion ever before. They pick at every piece of fabric, looking at the color, feeling the material.

"You can go into the store to change, I'll wait out here."

"You better not eat my leftovers!" Crista shouts.

I examine the remains that had been left on the bench. Little stubs of pretzels and two sips of lemonade are left.

"And if I did…" I daunt, her expression priceless. The whites of her eyes bulge out of her sockets, her face turning a bright red. "I won't… I won't." Pointing her finger at her eyes, and then at me, she slowly backs into the store until she needs to round the corner. Axil scoffs, shaking his head in disappointment.

***

I must wait for twenty minutes. What could be taking them so long? I can get dressed in less than two minutes. I try to tell myself to relax, that they are new, and this world is very strange to them. How was everyone so patient with me when I first arrived at the palace? Interrupting my thoughts, they both walk out of the store. They look truly magnificent and, to my surprise, they looks as average as any other group of teens in the mall.

"How do you like them?"

Neither of them talk. They look at each other, then back at me. I see their eyes wander down to their new clothing. Were they dressing for so long, or were they just standing in shock? Something tells me the last one might have some truth.

"Do I look like a street rat?" ask Axil shyly. He picks at the seams of his shirt, moving his arms back and forth.

"Yes."

"Then I guess we're good. Where to next?"

Crista snaps back into reality after her fits of rage and excitement, "We should be arriving at his mansion tomorrow evening."

A groan comes out of all of our throats. We are all exhausted, deprived of sleep.

I propose, "How about we ride for the rest of the afternoon. I know of a campsite nearby. We can make a pit stop there and recover our time in the morning."

Everyone shrugs their shoulders, "I guess we have a plan then."

***

Settling in at the campsite was tougher than I expected. It's a lot easier for royals to act normal when around, well royalty, with their expensive habits and fancy palace. Try bringing that to the wilderness, and the attitude starts coming out.

"It's hot out here," whines Crista.

Axil is next, "The bugs keep getting into my eyes."

"It isn't like this in the palace woods."

This all started when we stopped at the camp store on the way here. All we needed was to pick up a tent, pillows, and some blankets. Then, Crista had to come out just like she did with the pretzel, and demand we get marshmallows. Axil continued to complain as I explained to him that we would be sleeping on the ground.

Their idea of camping had been renting a hotel, but I can't do that.

If there was ever a doubt in Damian's mind as to what was happening with his money, I wouldn't want him to be able to track us right to an easy location. At least at a campsite, he would have to be desperate enough to have to find us in the middle of the campground.

My eyes go wide, my lips forming a sharp line. I can feel my blood starting to boil, each comment taking it up a degree. Before bubbles pop out of my pot, I say through my teeth, "How about you guys go into the tent. I'll get the firewood and start a flame. I'll call you out when dinner is ready."

Crista with her unnecessary sass flips her hair and crawls into the tent. Axil, looking a bit ashamed, holds his arms limp at his side and looks me in the eyes.

He's just uncomfortable, I try to tell myself. This is all new. You were new once, too. Yeah well, I had to put on a mask. Act like everything was okay. It seems as though they aren't even trying. Hanging his head, he steps into the tent after Crista. This is going to be one hell of a night.

I trudge through the forest marking trees, with the knife I had purchased, so I don't get lost. The knife selection held both their attention enough for me to get us some food, and the rest of the ingredients for s'mores to go with Crista's marshmallows.

I feel the weight of every piece of wood I add to my arms. Just another thing to burn, to end up in ashes. A snap comes from over my shoulder. All the wood in my arms drop, holding up the largest log defensively. Everything in the woods makes a sound, but this sounded big. My throat dries as I prepare to swing.

"Hey."

I come slamming down on whatever has approached me, quickly wishing I didn't. Axil hunches over, his arm cradling his left side.

"I'm so sorry." I rush over to him to help bear his weight.

"That's okay. I probably deserved that."

"What are you doing out here? You are supposed to be in the tent." I talk through gritted teeth.

"It's not right for you to do everything. I know I'm not much help, but at least give me a chance to try."

A twinge of guilt comes crashing into my heart. I really shouldn't be so hard on them. I'm just angry. Angry at the world, angry at where we are going, angry I have to take them with me into my own nightmare. I drop my eyes down, slowing my breath.

"We will also try to stop complaining. It's just... I have only been outside the kingdom once, and it was nothing like this."

"What for?"

He looks away, "Ah... you know... the usual prince stuff."

If it was usual, he wouldn't have only gone out once.

I bend down back to the ground, picking up all of the wood that had been dropped.

"Here, let me get that for you."

He bends down with me, his arms awkwardly trying to replicate the way I hold the wood. "So, what are you going to do? About your father, I mean… Damian?"

I stumble in thought. I try to convey so much confidence that I even fooled myself for a little bit. I can't simply walk into his mansion, mission failed. He will surely want to get rid of me. The only advantage that I have over him, is two royals on the run with me.

"I… I don't know."

"Whatever happens we are both here with you."

I take a long look at him. I miss the trust. What I used to have with John. I could always count on him, until I couldn't. What is he doing right now? Scouring up and down the walls for a potential key that only a fox in the woods has. The thought almost bubbles a giggle. That fact that he is so sure of himself, to most likely fail as well. That's the karma he deserves.

"Thank you… for everything," says Axil.

"I could say the same to you."

"No, no. I mean it." Reaching his free hand out, he stops me, pulling me back towards him. "The only time I left the kingdom— the magical barrier created because of my sister. She—

"I know… the Queen told me." I say softly. "I'm so sorry."

"We spent so long looking for her. There was… so much blood… and she just laid there…"

The memory of my own horror plays in my mind. No wonder he is so sensitive out here. I can't believe I didn't put the pieces together sooner.

When I had been finally released from my bedroom, it took me a while to even look into the living room, none the less go inside of it. Stepping over the threshold felt like I would be swept back in a loop, only to keep reliving that horrid night. I couldn't bring myself to it. The only thing that got me to cross that line was the first time John ever got drunk. Not just drunk, but wasted. Like my mother, I wasn't sure if he was just going to collapse on the floor and die right there from too much consumption. I took him to my room, laying him down on my bed. I tried to concoct some ancient traditional medicine I used to see my mom make for Damian often. It wasn't exact, but it seemed to do the trick, it kept him alive.

The next day when a doctor came to the mansion, it was discovered he was not drunk, not a drop of alcohol was in him, but he had been poisoned. Since that day, I had never let a nightmare of mine stop me from what I set my mind to.

"I okay to still be shaken. And if someone should be apologizing, it's me. I'm sorry. I'm just—

"Nervous." He finishes for me. "I get it… I really do."

Smiling, we head back to the campsite. In that moment, again comes that feeling I do not recognize. Like I could scream. Both from being happy and scared at the same time. The feeling of wanting to crash into him, embracing in a hug, but also wanting to run far away. All I can do is focus on my steps. Putting one foot in front of the other. Because if I do take off, I don't know where I would even go.

With each step we take back, the more something smells as though it is burning. I look up into the sky. Black smoke billows. My feet lead me back to the camp faster, my arms and legs getting cut on every little bramble as I roar through the brush.

Stepping out into the clearing, I see a huge flame licking at the sky. Next to it, Crista sits popping marshmallows in her mouth.

"Crista! What did you do?" The flame is probably twice my size, roaring and devouring anything in its way.

"You said you needed fire. Here's fire." She pops another marshmallow in her mouth, satisfied with herself.

"You can't burn a fire that big!"

"Why not?"

Agitated all over again, I walk over ripping the bag away from her.

"Hey!" she shouts.

"See those trees?" I point above us to where the fire is growing. "Those trees will catch fire, and when they do, we might as well shove ourselves in an oven."

Shock plasters on her eyes. Fumbling with her hands, she holds them out, trying to dwindle the flame, but it is no use. Either from nerves, or the heat of the fire, sweat start to form on her face.

Throwing the wood down, I run. Ripping a water bottle out of the grocery bag I splash it onto the fire. Letting out one final deafening hiss, the flame disappears, wet wood smoldering in a pile of flaking ash.

"WHAT IS GOING ON?!" One of the next door neighbors yells from his tent. My breathing intensifies again, every nerve in my body alive.

"I... I just wanted to help."

Axil comes up from behind me, placing his hand on my shoulder.

"We all do. It's going to take some time."

I listen to his words as best as I can, my angry breaths getting in the way. I can't look at them. If I do, I fear I might reveal just how violent I can be.

"I... don't... I don't want to see him," I say quietly. That's the whole point of going this way. I still don't know what's happening afterwards, and don't even know if I want to find out.

Closing my eyes, my tears squeeze out of my squinted lids. They hit the ground like an earthquake. I must be losing it. I knew I had to go back at some point although while I was at the palace, I was strongly considering not going back.

What if I end up dead? I don't fear for my own life but theirs. If I'm gone, what will Damian do to them, especially if he finds out that these street rats usually wear crowns *or floating top hats*? They won't make it out either.

Both their arms wrap around me as I cry. I feel as though I am trapped in a snow globe with no way out, and someone keeps shaking it. A violent storm engulfing me, until my demise. We stand completely still. I didn't do anything to deserve their kindness. Growing up with Damian was all about a power struggle. A constant battle of which one of us had more control.

Control…

I know what to do.

Chapter eleven

Huddling around the *small* magical fire, I feel a little more at ease. As the sun goes down, they tell stories of their childhood in the palace.

"There was this one time at breakfast that mother told such a funny joke, Axil spit out all the milk he was drinking. His suit was so ruined, not even the royal staff could get the stains out."

"That was one time! Plus, do you remember when you fell down the stairs so excited to get a new stupid top hat?"

"They are not stupid, they complete my look."

Branching out her arms, she puffs out her curly hair. Laughing, I listen to their back and forth argument.   Staring at the fire, I try to remember what it was like to have a happy family. That was years ago, maybe when I was six. What was most sad, was watching the life dwindle out of everybody. My family who used to laugh and sing was now a ghost town filled with murdering zombies.

"So, what about you? Any funny childhood stories?" He waits, his cheeks still held high from the smile that graces his face.

I try to think, I would have to search deep in my memory. When training was sped up, my brain was used for more skill. Things like funny memories weren't really remembered, so I tell them about the pretzel competitions with John. It could never equate to some of their stories, but it's one of the only ones I got.

"So, I'm guessing you guys have been lifelong friends?" Axil asks curiously.

"Kind of, we are more like siblings. He was an orphan when my mother took him in. Being around the same age, we would often call each other twins."

He nods smiling until he sees that I am not.
Like he's reading my thought, "And then…"

Staring back at the fire I continue, "Then, I guess you could say we went our separate ways."

"That's pretty recent, isn't it? Since you've been at the palace."

"Yeah."

A long pause fills the air, the crackling of the fire serving as the entertainment.

"How about I get the marshmallows back out and make some s'mores."

Puppy eyes again look back at me like they did at the mall. "What are s'mores?"

I laugh, keeping my mouth shut about what they are, "I guess it will be a surprise."

***

Never before had I seen the royal crusade messier. Melted marshmallow glues to their hands, chocolate lining the corners of their mouths. Watching them explore the outside world is almost poetic. Seeing the crown prince and the royal sorceress have a blast sitting at a fire eating marshmallows is humbling.

I am glad they can experience the outside world. A world where there is no roof over their head, a world where you have to fight every day. On paper it sounds really bad, but it's those experiences that make us feel truly free. The days that we work so much that we can't keep our eyes open any longer. The times where adrenaline takes over our bodies until we collapse with exhaustion. I feel blessed to be able to share this with them.

"I have never seen so many stars in the sky," Axil voices. His eyes in awe of the sky's masterpiece.

"It's truly amazing," says Crista.

I stand up to beat the logs that are crumbling in the fire. "This should be safe for us to go to bed."

"You just let it burn overnight. What happens if it grows like earlier?"

I look to Crista, "It won't. There are only embers left. It will stay warm overnight, then I will be able to cook on it tomorrow."

"More s'mores?" she asks, a cheeky grin on her face. Standing up, she stretches her limbs, extending her arms over her head. "Well, I've got to get my beauty rest. I will see you all in the morning."

Giggling, I wave her off, making sure she climbs in safely.

"How does her attitude change so quickly?" I say under my breath.

"I've been asking myself the same question for years."

From the tent comes a yell, "I can still hear you guys!"

We laugh until the soft zipper of the tent closes. Taking that as his que, he slides closer next to me, wrapping his arm around me. For the first time, I allow myself to relax, to not worry about anything, and just enjoy a moment of happiness. Laying my head on his chest, I listen to his heartbeat. The same way I did as a little girl with my mom, only this time it feels more special, more safe.

Dropping his voice to a whisper, he leans his mouth close to my ear. "Are you scared?"

"I'm never scared." Taking his face away, I can feel his glare shooting in my back. "I'm just... skimming through every possibility that could happen tomorrow."

"That's being scared."
Gritting my teeth once more, I respond, "No it's not."

"It's okay. I'm scared all the time." Leaning back, he holds his hands behind him, propping himself up.

"Why?"

"When is a King ever not scared? Scared for his kingdom, his people, and his family. But the thing about fear, is that you can either let it consume you, or you can harness it. A King is never at rest because of his fear, but instead of drowning in it, a King uses it as a guide."

"So… I should let my fear tell me what to do?"

"You let it tell you what is important. Let it guide you, so you can guide it."

Lifting my head from his chest, I look him in the eyes. They shine from the soft glow of the campfire, making them seem auburn. "How? How do you do that?"

"You surrender. Cast all your fear into the sky. Only then, will you know what to do."

There is another pause. I try to decipher his words, still not fully understanding what he means.

"Do you ever look at the moon and wonder what it is like up there? Is it like here, or is it completely different? Will all my dreams come true if I can one day reach it? Would everything go back to the way it was?"

We both know what we mean by turning the clock back, and the thing is, I have thought that. That same exact thing about the stars in the night sky. That maybe one, out of a million, will hear me, and answer.

***

Curling up in the tent is a back sore compared to the bed I was once sleeping on. I can't even imagine how uncomfortable Axil and Crista must be right now. We each take a corner of the tent, listening to the small crackle of the fire outside.

I swear I drift off to sleep hearing the same lullaby Axil was humming earlier. I wish I could remember where I heard it before.

At some time, the lullaby mixes with the sound of mourning doves, the morning sun already making an appearance. My back payed the price, but I feel very awake. I sit up slowly as to not wake anyone, but when I search around the tent, I am the only person in here.

I scramble out of the tent, franticly unzipping the flaps. Hissing fills the air. Oh please don't tell me —

"Good morning Zaria." I am stunned to see Crista and Axil sitting by the fire. Eggs sit on a cast-iron skillet hissing against the heat.

"Where did you get that?"

"Our neighbors lent it to us," explains Axil, a smile on his face.

"They also called us clueless," corrects Crista.

The smile on Axil's face disappears. I walk over to the group, each step feeling a vertebra crack. "Not bad."

The eggs sizzle perfectly on the skillet. Whether they knew what temperature the fire should be at, or if it was dumb luck, I'll take it.

"Thank you."

"Don't be impressed yet. Axil isn't one to cook."

He hangs his head in disappointment.

"You made me hot chocolate. That was really good," I say.

"Yeah what did he do? Heat it up?"

"And, what exactly are you doing?" A subtle laugh comes out of Axil at my remark.

"I am meditating for the day. You know, super important sorcerer stuff."

"Oh, I bet. Now, I wouldn't want to interrupt your meditation with breakfast, so Axil and I will take care of that for you."

She startles from the ground, "On second thought, I just finished."

Balling up his flannel, Axil wraps it around the burning handle of the skillet. Crista already at the table, sits for her apparently unimpressive eggs, a smile on her face.

"Thank you for getting everything ready this morning." I say.

"Well, we thought that it wasn't going to be a great day for you. Might as well make the morning special."

I look at both of them, smiling.

"It was my idea," Crista states, fanning herself with her hand.

"Like hell it was." Never before had I heard Axil swear. I choke on my bottled water.

"Was it not me who suggested we do something special?"

"Yeah, but who decided on breakfast? Who went over to the neighbors? Who cooked the eggs?"

"I appreciate it." Interrupting their brawl, I dig into my egg.

She turns toward me interrupting her own act, "On a serious note, what is the plan for today?"

I choose my words carefully.

"Damian has… power. Power that revolves in mind tricks and numbers. Our numbers are pretty small, but we are going to have to deal. What I need is for you guys to just follow my lead. Whatever he says, let me answer. Any move he makes, let me counter. Trust me, I cannot mess this up."

They both move in their chair a little uncomfortable, Axil more than Crista.

"What do we need anyway? You never told me."

Back to her normal self, Crista explains. "Every chosen one gets a certificate after their ceremony. We are going to need it for the next step."

"Which is…?"

"We will cover that when we get there. For now you need to focus on today and getting that slip."

I finish my egg silently thinking of every scenario that could play out today, my mind stuck on the worst possibilities. Axil pats me on the back before standing to clean up, reminding me of our conversation last night. His hand warm and steady. As long as they get out, everything will be okay. I can deal with Damian. He is my father, and that's exactly how I will approach him tonight. As his daughter.

Packing up what little we had was simple. Once we were back on the road, the whole thing seems surreal. What are we doing?

A little while after, I start to recognize the roads we are on. All the streets I have left my name on. I wonder if Crista knows where she is going, but just in case I tell Axil to pull in front of Crista and pull over.

On the side of the road, Axil and I trade places, me sitting in the front this time. "I will guide us the rest of the way."

"Should we park close to where he is, or at his house?" Crista asks.

I can tell the closer we get, the more anxious she is becoming. I wish I knew exactly what she saw when she looked into the necklace. Into my mother's memory. Did she see stuff that even I do not know, and if so, what was it?

"I will ride right up to the front door. After all, it's my house too."

I say that in full truth. More truth than they will ever know. I was the sole person who afforded that mansion. If it weren't for my work every night, Damian would be living a very different lifestyle.

Back on the road, my heart starts to beat. Not from the focus on the bike, but the fear of my father. If all goes well, we should be out of there in ten minutes. Fear, fear, fear. Why am I so scared, and how do I not become scared?

Axil said to let it show me what is important, but I can't tell my right from my left anymore. I feel so lost, and that too makes me scared. But I am out of time. This is it. The moment of truth. Time to make some noise.

I roll up in his driveway revving the motor as loudly as possible. I know at this time, Damian is probably drunk like a fish. I try to think if that will be an advantage or not, it depends on the day. I get off the bike, ready to bust through the door. Before I can, Axil grabs my hand. He laces his finger with mine, staring deep into my eyes. The sun is going down, but I can still clearly see his aqua blue eyes. He gives me a tight nod. I can read his thoughts in that moment. The words he has told me before, the promise he had made me, and standing here, with my whole heart, I finally believe it.

I wait until both of them are behind me, expressionless masks covering their faces. I can feel the anxiety radiating off of them, but I have to cross my fingers that this will work.

Punching in the code to unlock the door, I burst through.

"Daaaad! Daaaaaddddd!" I scream. My voice filling the empty halls. There is no way he didn't hear me. I know he is here as well. His black limo is in the parking garage. Just another little thing I paid for. Once my echo fades, I hear it.

His steps are strong, intimidating, how he always approaches me, but this time it is different. This time he is angry. My heart beats fast, my forehead sweating, but a sly smirk falls on my face. He is coming right for me, and I am waiting, ready to fire.

"Zaria? What are you doing here?"

He towers over me, close to my face. He has always known how to make people feel uncomfortable. I curse myself when I sense jitters coming from behind me. Still in his suit, he reeks of alcohol. By his attitude, it sounds like I caught him on a bad day.

"Who are these people?"

He moves back from me to examine Axil and Crista. Surprisingly when I meet their eyes, they are locked onto Damian's. A stone face on each of them. I sigh in relief.

"I have come to pack my things. The mission is done, and I am starting my own gang."

There it is. The moment I have been dreading. I have said out loud that I am starting my own gang, which suggests that I was part of one before. I want so badly to look at Axil and Crista, to know their reactions, but I don't think I could bear to see their betrayed faces.

"You're a liar. I have not heard back from John."

I speak over him, "John has gotten into a little trouble. I have taken care of it, and I have taken care of you. Now it is my turn to take care of myself."

"Where is it?"

I know exactly what he is talking about. Not even a care to what has happened to John. All he cares about is his end of the deal. And I'm not going to lie. I have the gold of the kingdom right here in this room with me, but I would never tell him that.

"It's closer than you think."

"What is that supposed to mean?"

"It means I have done what you asked, whether you like the outcome or not. Now step aside, father."

"Father?" he laughs in my face. A laugh that I know is not supposed to be funny, but a warning.

"Unless I get what I want, you didn't hold up your end of the deal. You know the consequences."
I see him reach for his side. Knowing what he is reaching for, I give the signal for Crista to run. She knows where my mom had been keeping her certificate from the memories she saw in the necklace. She takes off into a sprint. Opposite of that, Axil freezes behind me.

I am met with my fate. Double barrel pistol aimed right at my heart. No one moves except for Crista in the hallway. It is a struggle to keep my face plain, unimpressed. My throat starts to close, fire running though my veins. They scream for me to get out, run. I cannot. I knew this was going to happen, and I knew what to do when it happened.

"Do you think if you killed me, mother would use her magic from the heavens and save me?"

"What!?"

"Don't you think she would save her own daughter, unlike you, who would take my life? I wonder. Do you think she would curse you after bringing me back?"

"I... I don't know what you are talking about."

I laugh, copying his as much as I am able to, "Oh, it was all thanks to you. You are the one that taught me to steal information. Are you not?"

He lowers his gun, finally meeting my gaze. It is now time for me to revel. "It's nice to see I have your attention."

"Your mother was not fit for a world like this."

"You're right. She wasn't." I take a few steps closer to him. "You didn't deserve her."

Axil warns me from behind. I can almost hear his plead to get out of here. At his sound, Damian raises his gun again.

"All she did was love you. I always wondered why she did. My father was never comforting. My father never loved his wife back. My father was never there for me while I bled out on the blacktop."

Slowly, I keep advancing towards him, like an animal stalking its prey. I walk until the cold steel barrels hit my chest.

"You think you have power, building an illegal empire, murdering on the streets. It was all out of jealousy wasn't it?"

"You have no idea what you are talking about."

I continue, "You knew you would never have as much power as her. Once she was gone, you finally got what you wanted, right? You were the most powerful person in the family. In all of Flesherg!"

"There was just one little problem added to the jar though. You feared I would turn out like her. Not dead, you obviously didn't care about that. No, what you cared about was being the most powerful, and I was just an obstacle in the way."

I have never seen his face like this before. Vulnerable? Ashamed? Whatever it might be, it's too late.

"Sending me on jobs was not to make me a successful leader like yourself. It was to hopefully not see me again. To get rid of me, so you didn't have to do it yourself."

"Now, you are faced with a choice. I am here, in the arms of your power. Only one of us can pull the trigger, and it's not me. So… what's it going to be?"

I see him look from me, back to Axil, back to me again. For a while he does nothing. All I can think is that he is wondering how I figured all of this out.

Evoke fear in your opponent.

Footsteps fill the silence. Out of the corner of my eye, I see Crista running towards us with the paper in her hands. I am relieved that she could find it after the mess that he has made of this house. Damian looks at her, then at the paper. His mind moving fast, he takes action.

"Goodbye, daughter."

A sharp pain throbs in my chest. Falling backwards, I feel like I am flying. In slow motion, I hear three more gunshots fire. One after the other, they ring through the hall. My vision and hearing starts to blur, my breathing slowing. Get out, I think to tell them. Run, run far away, and keep running. Run all the way back to Lumbridge. Then you will be safe. Before I close my eyes, I see a beautiful blue color. Like the ocean, it is calming. I close my eyes, hoping to lie in the sand, the warm sun on my back, but all I see is darkness. A black void, with the only thing inside being a lullaby.

***

I feel very calm, like I am floating in saltwater. A world with no worries, no expectations, just this happy feeling. Just relaxation. I open my eyes to see where I am. Looking around, all I see is water. There is no land, no food, just me, floating in the vast ocean.

A rumble roars behind me, creating waves. I raise my body to swim instead of float. Behind me is a boat. I hear a voice. I can't tell if it is inside my head, or real.

"Grab hold of the boat."

Over and over, the voice repeats itself. I have no choice but to give into the pull. It draws me in like a magnet. Moving feels like the whole world is on my back. Each stroke making my lungs burn.

"Keep going. You are almost there."

I swim and swim, trying my best to keep my head above the water. The boat is not even that far away, yet it takes hours for me to get to it.

I remember what Axil had told me about fear. To let it tell me what is important. And in that moment I swim. Swim to hopefully find a way to save them because I am not afraid of what will happen to me, but I am afraid to lose them.

So I listen. Listen to my fear. Listen to it tell me to get on the boat. Listen to it draw me in because there is only one way out, and it is this compiled piece of wood.

All the endurance trainings really help right now. Fish distract me, sliding up against my legs. Taking my final stretch, I put every ounce of energy left to get on the boat. My finger grazes the lip, gripping weakly. Lifting my weight into the boat, brings tears to my eyes. Every muscle hurts, screaming in pain. I let out a wail, as I collapse into the boat. Closing my eyes again, the boat takes off by itself full speed. I don't know where it is heading, but I hope it's to a better place.

***

A loud ringing makes my eyes squint. I hear slurs of words. They sound worried? Panicked? I lie on my back, stiff as a board. I try to lift my head, but it feels like a hundred pounds. Blinking, I keep trying to focus on what is in front of me.

Again I see an aqua blue color hovering above me, but this time there is no music, only a panicked voice. My body starts shaking, the movement almost resetting my vision. Looking around I am met with Axil's face. He hovers over me asking bunches of questions.

"Are you okay?"

"Are you hurt?"

I try to process all of the words. They still sound like a drunken slur. I hear a higher voice. A mumble is all it sounds like.

"Keep an eye on her, I'm not sure if this will work."

Before I know it, I fall asleep again.

***

A dull pain throbs in my chest. This time, my vision is clear, and my hearing is a bit better. A slight ring still left behind. I lift my torso, wincing.

"You're awake."

Axil rushes over to me, his eyes wide.

"How much pain are you in?" His face is squinted like it was when I fell off the horse. His throat bobs up and down, swallowing all the words he doesn't know how to say.

"Less than before," I whisper.

"Zaria, what were you thinking? You could have died!"

"I know." I hang my head, breaking his contact.

"Why… How…"

"Axil, leave her alone. She needs to rest."

He looks back over to me, tears rolling down his face. Leaning over, he wraps his arms around me, careful of my muscle ache.

"Crista healed you. She couldn't do a full recovery, but she did as much as she could."

"Thank you." I try my best to look over Axil, to meet Crista's eyes, but she doesn't look. She sits reading a book on a sofa. A sofa I do not recognize.

"Axil!" she shouts for the final time, her tone something I have never heard before.

Letting go of me, he lingers on my hand. Turning around, he gives one final squeeze. I drift back into a deep sleep knowing that when I wake back up, I am going to have a lot of explaining to do.

Chapter twelve

I sit in a chair, Axil and Crista across from me. They have decided that I am healed enough now to talk, my wounds finally scarred because of Crista's magic. I can tell by their faces and crossed arms that they have thought long and hard about their assumptions.

Crista starts, "Firstly, what did you mean by, I got the job done?"

I knew this was the biggest thing, along with the gang comment. *Do what is right, even if it hurts.* I take a deep breath, preparing to tell them everything... and I do. I tell them about the museum and what Damian said afterward. I leave out anything involving John. He may be angry with me, but I did this mission to keep him safe, and I will finish this mission with him being safe. I tell them about the history of Damian's gang, when I started to do jobs, and what was expected of me.

They listen, not interrupting me once. Their faces have gone blank, a numbness rolling though my body.

"You mean to tell me, you got a job at the palace to rob us!" Axil stammers, his fist hitting the chair he sits on.

"I didn't want to, but I didn't have a choice. I would die either way by refusing or fleeing. Once I got to the palace, I realized you weren't like I thought you would be. I thought it was going to be easy, like any other job. Just another company to rob for Damian but I... I couldn't do it."

"What about John? What is he up to?" asks Crista, her arms dropped at her side.

"John has nothing to do with it. We lived together at the mansion, but the truth is, he was the only one to have a day job at the prison. I just used his job as a cover." I hate it here. Half-truths still filled with lies, but I can't do it. I can't tell them the truth. It wouldn't be fair. Damian had put me in charge. He made that clear several years ago, and I will always try to protect the family who protected me.

He threatened my life, just like Damian had done. Just like Damian had executed. But I can't shake the feeling that something is off with him. Like he is acting in a way that is not fully himself. I wish I could tie him up, question him myself, but I would never do that because for him, I would do anything, even if it means putting up with his attitude.

I glance over at Axil, his arms tightly crossed over his chest. "All I want to know is why. Why rob us?"

"I didn't. Why Damian sent us, I have no idea. Because he's Damian? Because he wanted his name stamped on the palace walls? I... I don't know."

"Was anything real?"

"What do you mean?" His voice registers in my ear. Low and dangerous.

Waving his arms he continues, "This… everything… us. Was anything real?"

I hear the hurt in his voice, as if he were the one that was shot in the chest. "Of course it was," I say raising my voice. "I tried. Tried to be good for my father, but I have never enjoyed what he turned me into. It was either work or starve. I had no resources, no way to take care of myself, so I agreed. I'm… I'm sorry."

I see Crista holding back tears, shifting in her chair. I think she understands the situation, then again the memories probably helped.

"It's okay —

"No it's not!" Axil shouts, standing up. "We have welcomed a criminal into our home, treating her with nothing but kindness, and still she plans to steal from us." He turns his attention away from his cousin to face me, and looking me in the eye, he says, "You know I feel sorry for you. Your whole family is messed up. No wonder you turned out the way you did."

Crista stands as well, "She didn't do anything. She's telling the truth. Like she said, she had no choice."

I lower my head. I can't watch them fight. Just a week ago, we were gathered by a campfire, shoving our faces with s'mores. Now, I wish that bullet just would have left me floating in the sea.

Axil looks right at me. No warmth, no comfort, just iciness like his mother's eyes when we first met. "You are just like him. A manipulator. A liar. You will never be anything, but a criminal."

His words pierce through my heart, sharper than the bullet. Slamming the door, I hear the motorcycle start up, roaring away from the house. We sit in silence, the only sound being the ever so steady tick of the clock. Second by second, I replay everything in my head. How it could have gone differently, how he might still be here if I just would have told him what he wanted to hear like I had the whole time at the palace, but that would have gotten me nowhere. It would only dig my hole of lies deeper than I already am. But even if telling the truth only filled the hole a little bit, it doesn't matter because I am still six feet under.

A gentle hand warps me back to reality. "I believe you," Crista states quietly. "I can only imagine how tough your life was."

"Thank you, but I cannot stay."

Crista had brought me to her aunt's house to recover, before the next step of the trip. Her house was in the city, so when I had my emergency, this was the closest outlet.

"Why?"

I stand up, stomping my foot, "Crista, what is the point? What is so important to keep going? I can't keep dragging you into danger after me."
I stomp away to the corner of the room. Her voice fills the house.

"I'm bringing our mothers back."

I stop in my tracks, wondering if I heard her correctly, "What?"

"We are going to the Magic Court with the request to resurrect our mothers."

"You... you can do that?"

"If they pass it, there is a chance. So yes, there is still something to fight for Zaria. Now I need to know, are you coming or not?"

***

That night, we have simple peanut butter and jelly sandwiches. Still hopeful for Axil to come back, I make him a sandwich. I wait at the table for hours, watching the window. The moon comes into view, just a dark shadow. My mind wanders to last week. Huddled next to each other, Axil spoke of his dreams. The dreams he wishes to find on the moon, but the moon left when he did. Only a vague outline of it hangs in the sky, dull and dreary. It must be a new moon. We must have the motorcycles back by the next full moon.

"Should I put this in the refrigerator?" Crista's aunt asks.

"I guess."

She sits down, the opposite side of me. "Listen. I just wanted to tell you, I knew your mother. I can see her in you."

I scoff at that. I don't know who to believe. Honestly, I don't even think I know myself. I am either my mother to some people, but to the most important person, I am my father. I can't blame him. He has stuck up for me the whole time through everything. Of course I seem fake to him. I want to believe that what we had was real, but what if I was just lying to myself? I had gotten so used to lying, I question if I can even discern a lie from a fact in my head.

"I want you to know that she mentioned you. She was so scared. She never explained why, but hearing your conversation today made me realize why. If you ever need anything, you can always call me. I owe your mother a lot."

I ponder on what that could mean. My mother did a lot for people, more than I think I ever could. She was always kind, the sweetest soul on the planet. Some could argue she was like a walking angel. She was definitely *my* guardian angel during those restless nights. When she died, I felt so scared, so unprotected, so vulnerable. I didn't know how to go on without her, so I changed who I was. I could not be myself, and be a thief. I needed a new me, a new look. A look that scared those who came after me, a look that screamed I was a badass.

That persona took over. It not only frightened me, but it has now frightened Axil. Even right now, I myself am scared of who I am. I will never live up to everyone's expectations, but maybe with my mother, maybe with her, I can find who I am.

She rises from the table, rubbing my back. Slipping the plate into the refrigerator, she walks back down the hallway. That night, I wait on the couch wishing on every star in the sky that he will come back. I wish for him to forgive me. I wish to curl in his embrace, feeling safe and warm. I wish for him back. No matter how many stars I wish on, nothing can change the way I had betrayed him.

***

"We've got to get a move on. Very busy day today."

Crista shakes me awake from the couch. The first thing I do is look out the window. Disappointing myself from the start, there still remains only one motorcycle in the driveway.

"How long a drive for today?"

"An hour."

"An hour?" I question, a little shocked.

"Don't get too excited. The rest of the trip is by foot."

I walk into the kitchen, smelling sweet cinnamon. Three bags sit on the table.

"I hope you don't mind, but I am coming too. I would like to see my sister back as well," says Crista's aunt.

"Of course, I don't mind."

Crista comes up from behind me, a new smile on her face. "See, I knew you weren't all bad."

Shoving Crista's shoulder, I sit down. A plate is set before me. Hot French toast sits on the plate, the steam rising up like tiny little ghosts. The warmth of breakfast tries it's best to heat the ice in my heart.

"How long a walk?" I ask, munching on my bread.

"About two days if we're fast. Another day added if not."

I am excited to see my mother, I truly am. But everything will be so different. I have learned to live with her gone. If I get her back, what will I do? That is, if it even happens. I don't want to get my hopes up for the Court to just deny our request.

"Do you… do you think they will say yes?"

Crista stops mid-chew. The reality hits that we could be doing this for nothing.

"If the offer is right, most likely."

"What is the offer?"

She pauses again, "Leave it to me, just make sure your body is healed enough to make it up the mountain."

The mountain? Dread rolls over my body. I had not gone to the gym in about a month. I didn't have the need to. Now, I seem unfit to climb up a mountain. Not even mentioning the wound I am still recovering from. It's a little sad that I wasn't even surprised. In fact, I expected him to do it. I knew Damian never really liked me. He tried to make his training seem like love, but it was just to wear me out.

Make me weak enough to not argue back the next day. That's why he got so mad when I would cry to mother. He feared she would stop him in his tracks. If she did, how would life be different? I definitely wouldn't be a criminal. She could have maybe lived. She could have introduced me to Crista and Axil sooner. I could be practicing magic with her right now. How much better that would have been. I question, though, if this was fate. If I remember what Crista told me, maybe she couldn't use her magic to stop Damian. Is this the way life was supposed to be, and if so, why?

Crista's aunt, whose name is Rebecca, locks the door to her house.

"You guys take the motorcycle. I'll meet you over there."

I almost ask how she will, until I remember I am surrounded by witches.

"Is that your power? Teleporting?"

She looks at me a little funny, then laughs. "No sweetie. I am taking my car." Unlocking her car, it beeps back at me mockingly.

Blushing, I hide my face. She walks over, taking our bags and hoisting them into her trunk. We wave our goodbyes before we hit the road. The cold wind hits my face again. A twinge of sadness stings me knowing I am not holding onto Axil this time. The pain worsens as the realization hits that I probably never will again.

The wind slows from my face. I have absolutely no idea where we are. My eyes burned from all my tears last night, so I closed them on the way. Getting off the bike, my movements are slow, my mind racing. Will I truly be happy when I get my mother back? What am I thinking? Of course I will. I just fear how things will be different. If I am a disappointment to Axil, I will no doubt be a disappointment to her.

"Crista?"

She turns towards me, awaiting my question, "What do we do? If this really happens?"

Looking up the mountain, she speaks, "We start to live life with them, instead of for them."

I always thought that if my mother was alive, I wouldn't have had to fight. Now that I lost her, I don't think I could live in a world where I don't fight for her.

"Is everybody ready?" shouts Rebecca.

She carries out our bags from her trunk. Handing them to us, I genuinely feel the weight of what we are about to do. How will I walk down this mountain without her? I won't. I will make sure of it.

The hike starts off smoothly. The towering mountain still in view. First we have to get there, then we have to climb it. I try to focus on the crunching of the leaves under my feet, the silence almost suffocating. So many questions race through my head. Questions I want to know the answers to, but don't want to ask.

The sun shines bright in the middle of the sky, beating down on our backs. The cold biting wind makes up for the heat of the sun. I guess it's the best time of year to climb a mountain. I can't imagine scaling that mountain in 90 degree heat.

"We should stop for some lunch," Rebecca says, reaching into her bag.

"Stop? No! We can't stop!" They both look at me like they have seen a ghost. "What happens if we don't get there on time? What if, because we didn't get there earlier, they refuse to grant our request?"

Crickets sing in the background. "I don't think that's how it works."

Crista grabs hold of my shoulder, "We will get them back, but to get them back we need to be able to get up there in the first place. We all need food, and you need all the rest you can get."

I shove her off, "I don't need rest. What I need to know is that I'm not a failure!"

I turn around embarrassed. "Is it because of Axil?" Crista asks.

"It's because of everything! She didn't want me to become a criminal. She didn't want me to join Damian's gang. All I've done, ever since she was gone, was disobey her."

Neither of them know what to say. I can only think it's easy for them. They seem like the people that are perfect angels along with my mother. People that could never do wrong. Crista's mother will be overjoyed to see her daughter and sister.

"What if she doesn't want me? After all I've done. How could she?"

Rebecca comes from behind me, turning me to face her.

"Zaria… you have had a bad history, I will not deny that. But look at all you are trying to do to fix it. You are scaling a mountain, for her. You got shot by your own father, for her."

Crista speaks this time, "She will see what all is in your heart, broken as it is. She will see you, for you. The daughter that saved her, and the daughter that fought for her when no one else could. Now come. You need to eat."

I gulp down my sandwich as fast as possible. Everyone else takes their time in protest. I decide to sit by the little stream. Picking up stones, I throw them in, watching the splash that happens after. All I can hope is that at the end of this, I don't sink like a rock.

Dinner comes earlier than expected. Instead of having dinner and leaving, it is decided that this is where camp will be, and this time Crista does not complain. She apparently got all her dramatics out while her cousin was here. I have tried to be stubborn all day, but I forgot how exhausting going against everyone is. When we set up the tent, I keep my mouth shut.

"Zaria. Since you are so avid about getting up the mountain, you seem like the perfect candidate."

I look to Crista, who is whacking steaks into the ground.

"You mean, the only candidate."

"But isn't it perfect." Rebecca says, smiling.

I roll my eyes. Handing me a map and a compass, she explains, "We are not far away from the mountain. If you want to make tomorrow's trip a little smoother, then go mark the trees in the correct path to the mountain."

I sigh in exhaustion, but I have a bit of relief knowing that tomorrow will be quick.

I take off into the forest following the needle of the compass. Earlier today, we got a little turned around, the exact reason why we are not at the mountain today. The last thing I need is to get lost again tomorrow and have it cost another day. For the big trees, I pick up a leaf and some mud. Slapping the leaf on the trunk, I use it as a guide. I left my knife that I used at the other campsite back with our stuff, so I work with what I got.

If I were not trying to resurrect my mother, this hike would be very peaceful. I wish Axil was here with me, his hand in mine, telling me everything was going to be ok. That even if I couldn't get my mother back, he would always stand by my side. He made a promise. He promised he would always be there for me, but it seems like every person that does that, ends up leaving. The one person that never said it was Damian, and it seems as though he is not leaving anytime soon.

Thinking of him, he is probably in contact with John right now. Questioning him as to what happened. Demanding that he finish the mission, so he can get his cut. Reveling about how he got rid of me. Let him. Let him and John think that I will never come back. It will be one hell of a surprise once I do. For that, I can't wait to see their faces. Especially when I have my mother right beside me. My mother that is supposed to be dead, just like me. They'll have no idea what is coming their way.

Every few feet, I keep marking the trees, my hands especially dirty now. Looks like I'm going to have to visit the stream again before I eat my dinner. After what seems to be the one hundredth tree, they all of a sudden stop. I am met with a huge granite rock. Almost running into it, I reach my arms out in front. My hands on the rock look so tan from the sun. I check back on the map to see if I made a wrong turn somewhere, but all signs lead to right here. Suddenly, the sun disappears, a darkness clouding around me. Looking up to see where it went, I stumble backwards.

The mountain lay right in front of me. A huge gray cone. A thousand mile walkway circling up the giant rock. Tomorrow we climb. It's up to us if we make it to the top.

The bark under my hand is rough. I touch all the trees I had previously marked to find my way back. The sun is going down, and it's a little hard to see. I squint my eyes, using the last bit of light in the sky.

"Oh hey, you're back."

Crista runs toward me, meeting me in the middle.

"Yeah, just let me rinse my hands, then I'll be ready."

She walks over to the stream with me, side by side.

"I saw it. The mountain." Keeping my head down, I try not to be awkward.

"A sight to see, isn't it?"

Dipping my hands I ask, "Have you ever made the climb before?"

Shifting her weight from one side to the other, she stands uncomfortable. I was about to tell her that she doesn't need to answer, when she starts talking.

"Once. I traveled once before."

"What did you ask?" I'm careful of my words.

She doesn't respond for a moment, still rocking on her feet. "The same thing."

"You asked them for your mother?"

Nodding her head, she continues, "They said it was not her time. One day, I would see her again after a great sacrifice."

Sacrifice. She had mentioned an offer before. I wish I knew what she was planning. Not knowing, is driving me insane. I hope it's nothing too serious, and if it is serious, I hope she will let me help like she has helped me.

"You think they will have a change of heart?"

"It's what I'm hoping."

Standing up, I look at my reflection in the water. My eyes have been sunken in again, looking like there is no life in them.

"What if… what if I did this for nothing? What if I ruined…"

"I know you are worried about Axil." She looks at me through the water. "I know you two both liked each other. Give him some time. Like he said, all of this is foreign to him. He wasn't prepared for the girl he liked to end up being a gang master, who got shot right in front of his eyes."
We still stand there, the wind blowing back my dark hair. "He was very scared you know."

"Axil?"

"He carried you out of there, as fast as he could. Other gun shots went off. When Damian saw that he was carrying you out of the house, he shot him."

"What?"

"I was able to quickly heal him. The wound was only on his leg and it wasn't that deep."
Relief rolls through me. "No wonder he was so scared. He got shot one of the first times he was outside the kingdom."

"Zaria, that's not why he was scared."
I look at her beside me, adverting my eyes from the flowing water. The calmness of the ripples already fading.

"He wasn't scared for himself. He was scared for you. We… we both thought that you wouldn't make it." She now looks into the water, her eyelids low. "Obviously he blamed himself. He had told me that you told him about your father. He blames himself for even letting you go in."

"You know I would not let anyone else face Damian for me."

"I know. And for that sake, give him time. If he can't see all the ways you had tried to protect him these past couple of days, he's an idiot."

"He thinks I lied though." I kick the small stones that rest on the shallow cliff, "He thinks I'm still planning on robbing you. That everything I said was a ruse."

"A smirk appears on Crista's face. "If you wanted to, you could have just taken the key from the fox before we even left. I believe you when you say you didn't want to do it. You had plenty of opportunities in the palace. Instead, you spent your time being our friend and assisting the Queen in her ball planning. That is not what a criminal does."

What is left of my heart, shatters. She wipes the tears that fall down my cheek.

"It is what a girl does."

I am just a girl. To some, that is not enough, to not have a title or a reputation. To me, it is perfect. I can just be a girl. A girl who is trying so desperately to find her mother, with her friends.

"Dinner is ready!" Rebecca calls.

Crista smiles at me, squeezing my hand before leading me back to our camp. Control. I don't need it. It's nice to rely on other people. To not always have to carry the weight of the world on my back. Even if all Crista did was take one pound away. The feeling is angelic.

Chapter thirteen

Rebecca prepared a hot meal of potato stew for us. Once the sun went down, a chill graced the air. This meal will keep our insides warm while we sleep. The fire is contained this time, so I guess Crista learned her lesson, although I wouldn't mind a big fire tonight. My mind won't shut up. I stare into the flame, watching it dance, taking a new turn every second.

The flames never die until something forces them to. Just like my mother. I thought I was doing well. Waking up every morning, starting all over again. I thought I was in the right, to never give up, no matter what. But now I have learned the difference between the two. Never giving up, and doing the right thing are two separate tasks. Just because I never gave up does not mean I was right. Not even wishing on stars can change that.

"You never told me about my mother, Rebecca. What was she like?" I ask, breaking the rambling in my head.

She raises her face from out of her hands, "Well, she was one of the nicest people I knew. She would visit me every so often, sharing a cup of tea, talking about the latest gossip. One day I sent her a letter. I told her that I had gotten myself in a little bit of trouble with one of the local gangs."

I gasp. Quickly she raise her hands, "Not your father's gang, but one of the nearby ones. I had been out one night, and, let's just say, I messed with the wrong group of people. I bet that I could beat them in a game of pool. I knew I would win, it was easy money.

"My magic is a form of mathematical understanding. Pool was the perfect way to show off my skills without revealing I was a witch. Like I had predicted, I won the game. They never even got a shot in. The whole night was just me, making circles around the pool table. I thought I was a genius. They had bet a great deal of money. Looking back, I should have known I was in danger from the start. The gang got angry, saying that I was cheating. I guess in a way, I was, but not in the way they were thinking. For "lying to the gang," I had to pay them what they said they would pay me. I wrote a letter to Maria, asking her to make me some money. Before the letter was sent, they raided my house. Through the raid, they found my letter. On paper, it sounded really bad. Illegal actually. They took all of my belongings. From what I know, they went for your mother, as well."

Through the whole story, I can't breathe. I listen, my eyes wide, without blinking. I knew it was the Huva gang. It lines up perfectly from her story.

"I can't keep going on this trip, not telling you. If you want to blame anyone for her death, it should be me. That's what I meant by, I owe your mother a lot. I owe both her, and your life. I'm so sorry."

Now *she* stares into the fire, expressionless. I'm tired. Tired of felling angry. Tired of blaming people. If I'm honest, what she did was exactly what I would do if I crossed paths with the Huva gang. If I blame anyone, it is not her.

"Apology not accepted. You told me yourself. You have a dark past, but you are trying to fix it. In fixing it, you are also helping me. You cannot take back what you did, but you are doing everything you can to set it right."

I am trying, I really am. I just wish it wasn't so damn hard.

As our eyes start to close, Crista starts to lazily hum that same tune, the lullaby that has sent me to peace so many times.

I can't help but ask, "Where is that melody from? It's been in my head this whole trip."

"It's the lullaby from the palace. When the Queen was younger, she loved to play the piano. All of the kids in the palace were born at around the same time. For Christmas one year, she gifted all of us a song she had written. It was this lullaby. I asked her about it years later, she said that she sat in front of the piano for hours, trying to come up with an original lullaby." Taking a deep breath, she continues, "Axil and I still hum it. I hum as a reminder to keep myself calm, that's the whole point of a lullaby, and it's one of the most beautiful songs I know."

I can't help but agree with her, "It truly is."

I wake up back in my room. My old room in Flesherg. Panicked, I run for the door. It is locked. I pull on the handle with all my strength, my knuckles turning white. The door will not budge. I hear muffled voices. A man and a woman. I listen closely, hoping for some type of clue. I can tell Damian has changed his voice. He sounds a lot more emotional than usual, his voice a bit higher and stringier. The muffled voices starts to clear out a little. Not enough to tell what they are saying, but enough to recognize the voices. The woman sounds very much like my mother, a little bit more formal though. Same with the male. It sounds very sweet, but with a commanding tone. I don't tell myself to sit down, but I do. I am trapped in in my body of when I was twelve, right after my mother's death reliving the moment I have feared for so long.

Sitting on the floor, I start crying. My wails echo through the halls. It seems as though my screams have summoned someone. Footsteps sound from the hall, coming closer and closer. Backing away, I am prepared for Damian to come in here and shut me up. The closer I listen, the lighter the footsteps sound. There is a certain grace to the stride. I hear a voice outside of my door. I quickly huddle under the cover of my bed, covering my head. It is silent for a moment; holding my breath, I try not to make a sound. The tears still roll down my cheeks, making them hot.

A soft voice sings on the other side of the door. I am surprised but still don't dare to make a move. The song reminds me of the ocean. One note swaying beautifully into the next. A wave of tunes swirling together. My tears start to dry, only a couple rolling down my face. I don't remember when, but I drift off into a sleep. I then hear a voice. Not enough to wake me, just enough for it to become part of my dream.

"Sleep well little princess." Even in my dreams I can still hear the song. A song of peace and freedom.

A song from the Queen.

***

Placing all of my belongings into my bag, I rub the sleep from my eyes. Perhaps this is the last night I sleep without my mother. Everything will be renewed. It will be as though the time turned back.

"We should be there around two. The Council will have just had their lunch, so it's probably the best time to chat."

Rebecca paces around the camp, collecting all of our things, moving any stick she does not like. I search for Crista. She is very quiet. Packing her things, her hands move with a grace to them. A slow steady pace that lingers on everything she picks up.

"Are you okay, Crista?"

"Me? Yeah. Just tired."

"We have a long hike. Are you sure?"

She flips her hand in the air, "Don't worry, I'll be fine."

I linger beside her for a while.

"Zaria! Can you help me with this tent?"

I nod my head, walking over to where Rebecca is struggling. Together we pull at the rods, folding them intricately into a neat stack.

"Why are we taking the stuff with us? Why don't we just leave it here for the way back?"

She looks at me funny, "You don't know how many people make this trip, do you?"

I shake my head. "I haven't seen anyone else around us, so I thought this mile high mountain was a dare and a half for most people."

"Sometimes, not the greatest people come here." Folding up the fabric of the tent, I listen to her. "What is that supposed to mean?"

"There are some people that will come with… not so great requests. Requests for gain. Not just family, I'm talking, going against the gods' wishes. They ask to change personal power, instead of selflessness."

All I can do is nod my head, "Would they destroy our camp?"

She scoffs, "More like, not leave anything behind."

Her comment is like salt in my wound. These people don't sound that much different from Damian. Not that much different from me.

It's easy to see the damage. The vice of stealing. People never seem to think about why. If they do, they probably think that we are drug addicts or alcoholics. Most of them would be right, but I hate that I have to group myself with those people.

We make sure the campsite is spotless before taking off. The sun is only starting to come up. An early start to a gruesome mountain. I lead through the trail I had marked before. Some of the mud I had placed on the trees, dried and crumbled to the ground. It is still pretty simple to see where I left off, though.

"About how long did it take you until the clearing?" Crista asks.

"About half an hour, I suppose."

Every tree that we pass, I put my hand on, seeing if I recognize the bark pattern. With my leaf trail and Rebecca's map, we make it there in no time.

The peak of the mountain cuts a sliver of golden sun. It looks stunning, yet daunting. I could say the same about a great white shark. I would love to see one, but I would not want to swim up to it. The sight of the mountain is beautiful to look at, but that's about where the beauty ends.

"It looks just the same as last time," Crista speaks, her voice a little shaky.

I can only imagine how stressed she is today. She is reliving one of the most disappointing days of her life, besides her mother's death. She had climbed this mountain with so much hope, only to be sent back down with nothing in return.

"Might as well start." Rebecca starts to walk in front.

"Where even is the entrance?" About fifteen feet up, I see the path start, but I cannot seem to find how to get to it from the ground.

She looks back at me, "Phase one. Climb up the mountain."

Stuttering, "Climb up… you… you mean."

"Yep, straight up. What a wonderful way to start this journey."

I groan, looking up at the top. Curse whoever is in there for making the hike so difficult. I fall into step behind Rebecca, Crista holding up the rear. She drops her bag on the ground, pulling out the rope she had packed. Tying it around her waist, she throws her hands against the rock looking for any holds. I watch her climb surprisingly smoothly. She makes it to the path in a matter of minutes.

"You want to go?" asks Crista, still behind me.

"Um… you know what, you can go." I scoot her in front of me, ushering her up to where Rebecca started her climb.

It's weird. Only two months ago, I was scaling street buildings. I had the wall ladder, but I had no fear. Maybe I was addicted. Not to drugs, but to the action. The rush of running, to not get caught. Now that I am with other people who are a lot more stable than I am, I feel so useless. My training has depleted my magical abilities, but in this moment I can't feel any of my physical abilities, either.

In the time that I was lost in thought, Crista as well made it to the top with Rebecca.

"Now, I'm going to throw down the rope. You are going to tie it to one of the bags, so we can hoist them up."

A job without climbing, I can do that. Rebecca throws down the rope, the tail barely able to reach. I lift up one of the bags, tying it around one of the handles. The weight isn't that much, but holding it in the air, my fingers start to fumble around the string, praying to the sky I will tie a knot. When I get something that seems decent, I shout back to Rebecca to pull the string. I watch it go up, the pack dangling above me. I keep my eye on it until it rests on the rock with them.

"Great, now do that two more times."

And I did. Each bag made its way to the top of the climb, now it is just my turn.
Crista yells this time, "Come on Zaria, you've got this."

Placing my hands in the first hold that everyone has been using, I take a deep breath. Closing my eyes I look down. I hear that same voice. The one I heard when I was floating out to sea.

"Just fight a little more. You will rest soon."

I lift my body off of the ground, clinging to the tiny bits of rock that stick out.

Again, *"That's it, just a little bit more."*

Focusing on the voice, I move my legs up the wall, using my arms as support. I close my eyes, only feeling the way the rock is placed. I make sure I am going up, but the more I look up, the more my doubt starts to kick in.

With every step, the voice keeps encouraging me in my head, getting louder and louder. I get so focused on the voice, I almost fall when I feel two sets of hands grasping my arms. My eyes fly open yelling in terror. Stupidly, I remember it is just Rebecca and Crista.

Pulling me up the rest of the way, my feet walk against the wall. I collapse on the path. The voice disappears, leaving me lying on the ground.

"I didn't think you would be that scared. You got shot for goodness sake."

Crista helps me up. Breathless, I come to a standing position like everyone else.

"That's it for climbing, right?" I ask, still catching my breath.

"For now," Rebecca hands me my bag.
For now? My heart leaps into my throat. With a pat on the back, she passes me walking uphill. I look up, taking note that it is all uphill. For once in my life, I wish I was going downhill.

I would say it takes about fifteen minutes to get around one loop of the mountain. The more we go up, the shorter it will get. No wonder it will take us all morning to get up there.

My calves ache with every step, almost as bad as they did when I was flung off the horse. I wish the voice was here. To cheer me on or help in some way, but it is now my turn to fight. But just because I feel alone, it does not mean I am by myself.

Crista and Rebecca check up on me periodically. I wonder how they are so calm. It's the opposite of what I thought today was going to be like from this morning. Their pace is steady, their breath still in their lungs. I was a thief. I was on the run every day of my life. How are they so… at peace?

"This looks like a good place to stop."

Rebecca starts to shuffle through her bag, pulling out what little food she has. I dare to take a peek over the edge and regret it right away. Guessing, I would say the drop is about one hundred feet down. A fall like that, and you're not coming back.

I tiptoe back over to the inside edge, holding my hands out by my side. While my hands are open, Rebecca slips the sandwich she made for me into my hands. My eyes still wide, I grip around the sandwich and take a bite. We had not had time for breakfast this morning, so the little dinner I had yesterday grumbles in my stomach.

Eating makes me feel a little less dead, but my throat feels very dry. I look in my bag for water. One bottle. Cursing myself, I take a tiny sip, then place it back in the bag. I am going to need that on the way back.

Not ten minutes later do we all stand up and continue our journey up the mountain. Feeling more refreshed, the walk isn't as gruesome as it first felt. Our pace is a little quicker. Whether from the rest, or the anticipation, it doesn't matter.

I am ready to go home. I don't know where in the world that is, but I know home is with my mom. When she died, the mansion was not a home anymore. It was just a house. A house that I was keeping up. A house where I was assured a bed, and a house that provided a roof over my head. There was no comfort. There was no warmth. All of the love in that house had been stripped. Turning what used to be a home into just four walls.

I try not to look down again, but as the path gets narrower, there is no option. The lip of the path only sticks out about two feet. We are almost to the top. The last few laps have to be done with our backs against the rock, sidestepping onward.

"Oh, hell no," I say, my eyes wandering down to the tiny trees. From where I'm at, I could be in a cloud. Birds pass us soaring for their dinner at eye level.

My knees start to wobble, my arms shaking against the rock wall.

"Is everyone okay?" Rebecca asks.

"Yeah," says Crista, her own voice a little shaky. "It doesn't matter that I did this before. It still makes my heart skip a beat."

"How about you Zaria?"

"Please shut up."

"Got it."

Our pace slows by a ton. All we can take are short steps. Slowly creeping our way up. I thought the climb was going to be the worst. The fifteen foot climb now seems like a joke in comparison.

At some point I had closed my eyes just like I had done climbing. I squeeze my eyes shut, every muscle in my face spazzing. Focusing on my breathing, I match my steps to my breath. Inhale, slide my front foot. Exhale, slide my back foot. The noise around me cancels, my mind locked into a rhythm.

I hit a wall. Flinging my eyes open, my balance falters, a quick sweat perspirates my face. Rebecca catches me, pushing me back against the wall. It wasn't the wall I hit, but her. I check behind me to see if Crista is still there. She gives me a thumbs up, a forced smile on her face.

Looking back in front of me, I catch a glimpse of how high we are on the mountain. My breath catches, halting in my throat. Closing my eyes again, I pray for peace. I wait for Rebecca to move, but she doesn't. It may be a mistake, but I open my eyes again.

I had been so focused on Rebecca I had not noticed the cabin that sits upon the ledge. It overlooks the view of how high we have climbed. I don't know if living here would be a constant panic or peace, and I don't plan on finding out.

The cabin is a dark maple color, looking very mysterious. There is no greenery or decorations that line the house. It's just a house. On a mountain. Rebecca holds out her hand, pointing towards the house. "We have arrived."

Chapter fourteen

Crista takes the lead. Extending her hand, she moves to knock on the door. I don't know why, but I was expecting something a little bit more extravagant. When Crista talked about a Council, I thought they would be living in luxury, just like the royals, not a simple wooden cabin.

We both stand behind her. She draws in a long breath, before curling her knuckles. Knocking three times, we wait for a response, but nothing comes. We wait even longer, looking at each other, not knowing what to do. The wind howls, but there is not much to it. In fact, the air is very thin up here.

Lifting her hand again, she goes to knock, but before her hand can hit the door, a voice sounds from the other side.

"You may enter."

It sounds youthful. A high-pitched tone trying to sound wise. Slowly, Crista moves for the knob. Turning it ever so slightly, she opens the door. The smell of rosemary is overpowering. The aroma is delicate yet eye-watering. I swallow my saliva over and over to get the strained feeling from out of my throat.

Crista steps inside, tiptoeing over the threshold. I follow behind her cautiously, Rebecca on my tail. My eyes scan in all directions. The walls are obviously the wooden logs, but it is the pictures on them that catches my attention. Tiny, little photographs hang off the crease of the logs, portrait after portrait. One in particular catches my eye. Nothing about it is special, in fact all the pictures look the same. Except this one has a woman and a little boy instead of a little girl. All the other photos have the little girls' hair in pigtails, with a stern look on their youthful faces, but this one, this *boy* is different. He sits upon the woman's lap holding her hand. The joy in his face almost brings a faint smile to mine, and then there is something… jumping up and down, my brain tries to make the connection as to what I'm seeing, but nothing comes to mind. Rebecca pulls me with her after I had fallen behind, and all I am left with is an empty feeling of mystery.

Pushing those feelings aside, I open my eyes to the common room. A golden chandelier hangs in the center of the room, the warm light reflecting, making the wood glow. Ahead of us I see two chairs that look like thrones. One is definitively bigger than the other one, lined as the centerpiece.

A girl drapes herself in the big chair that I can only guess is not hers. She only looks to be about ten. When she sees us, she plops herself from her relaxed position, folding her legs into one another. "May I help you?" she asks, that same youthful wisdom in her tone.

Crista bows before the throne. I never thought she would bow to anyone other than the King, her uncle.

"Please accept us, on behalf of the moon and stars. We come with a request, and would greatly appreciate to be heard."

She sounds so proper as she speaks, the opposite of what I had known her to be on this trip. Her speech sounds genuine, so I listen on. My eyes still wander. I don't know where to look. Should I also be bowing, or should I be looking at the little girl? Trying not to be awkward, I stay where I stand, slightly dropping my head.

"And, what might this request be?"

"Emma, what are you doing?"

A woman comes from the other side of the room. She wears a red dress that runs like a river to the floor. Her hair is tied up in a bun, resting on the back of her head.

"We talked about this. No talking to the guests while I am not here."

"But mom…"

"No buts."

Frowning, the little girl hobbles back over to the smaller throne. She slumps in her chair, over exaggerating her movements. I look over to the lady again. She stands, looking us up and down. Her lips in a thin line, she takes a sip from the glass she holds in her hand. Again, I get that feeling of power, much like Damian. Power oozing out of every atom they are made of. Just from her appearance, I can tell she knows what she is doing, and I can't tell if that is a good or bad thing.

A slight accent hangs in her voice, making her sound posh. "This request I heard about... would you like to go on?"

Crista bows again, hesitating for a moment before bending over. "I would like to request the return of two chosen sorceresses."

The lady's eyebrows raise, stopping mid-sip. "You know that is a big request. And big requests require big payments."

Crista's voice lowers, "I recall you telling me before, five years ago. I have come prepared this time."

My heart pounds, listening to their banter. When Crista is done speaking, the lady looks at Crista. Not just looks, but stares. It seems as though she is reading Crista. What is in her heart, her soul, and if her words match her true feelings. The thought of it makes me shiver. I can only hope she doesn't do the same to me, because if she did, I have no idea what she would find.

"Hmm. Who might these sorceresses be?" she asks, a slight smirk on her face.

"Maria Farwell, and Mika Norwood."

A sly smile appears on the lady's face. Setting her glass down, she folds her hands, intertwining her fingers.

"Oh, I remember them. Charming girls they were, always sticking together. Now it seems they have died together. How romantic."

Crista's voice hardens, "They did not die. They were murdered. You know as well as anyone, that dying at the hands of another person is not a fair death."

She shakes her head, taking a few steps closer to us. "No. It is not fair, but when is life ever fair? You can try and try every day, and for what? For life to kick you to the curb, throwing you into a hurricane. Doesn't that sound familiar?"

She now is standing right in front of us. She does not look at Crista though, she looks at me.

"Zaria, what would having your mother back *really* do for you?"

My hands ball into fists as she speaks. The fact that she uses my name without asking what it is makes it known that she is violating me. Digging inside me for anything she can find that doesn't settle right with the world, and there is nothing I can do about it.

"I mean really. It seems as though you have… set yourself up." She pouts her lips, bluffing any sort of empathy.

I glare back at her, my eyes in straight lines. "What is that supposed to mean?"

Releasing a dramatic sigh, she takes a step back. "I guess you will find out soon enough. Crista, come." Crista leaves the formation that we have aligned, following the lady. They both rise up onto the steps, Crista stopping before the top. Kneeling down, she lowers her head.

"You mentioned you have a request." Looking around, she looks very proud of herself. "And, you know that there is going to be a price to pay."

Almost inaudible, Crista whispers, "Please don't do this. You already know what it is. Just please, get it over with."

She doesn't look at Crista as she talks, instead she keeps her eyes locked on mine. "Why don't you tell your good friend Zaria what her mother costs?"

Crista lowers her head, refusing to look at me. "Go on, tell her." The lady nudges Crista's shoulder. She wobbles on her knees after the shake.

"I… I am giving up my magic for our mothers."

"You can't do this Crista!" I yell, looking at her defeated body. "Your magic is worth more. Don't do this to yourself."

A cold sweat runs through me, my eyes widening. Crista loves her magic. It defines her, makes her feel herself. Without magic, what will Crista do? It is the way we met. The reason I am alive right now. She can't just give it up.

The lady holds up a finger, silencing me. She waits until it is completely quiet before continuing.

"If it makes you feel any better Zaria," she spits out my name, sounding it out. "That is not all that is the price." She looks towards Crista, waiting for her to finish. Crista doesn't move, her eyes glued to the floor.

"Hmpf. If Crista won't tell you, I guess I will." Stalking towards me, she tiptoes around my boundaries. "After your visit, once Crista's magic is gone, you will have to take care of all of her responsibilities. And no, I don't mean her laundry and dishes. I mean all the magic that goes through the palace."

I try to think of all Crista does. I had never really asked her what all she contributes to. Secondly, I have no idea how to do magic. Like Crista had told me, my magic has been depleted. I have never done any magic in my life. I can't just take over for her.

"You seem confused." She pouts her lips, looking glum. "It seems that you have taken a lot of things for granted. Let's go back, ah yes. The first day you got there, the towels were warm after your bath. Or, oh... how about the fact that there are still flowers in the garden. Flowers that never seem to die."

She is now circling me, like a shark deep in the ocean. "I can grant your request, easy peasy. But is it worth the cost? Come now, you have never done magic in your life. A disappointment you would be to the kingdom. Under your magic, the kingdom will surely die, and there is no way Crista will be able to save you."

"Stop!" Crista stands from the stair she had been kneeling on. Looking the lady dead in the eye, she speaks slowly. "You will do as I ask. Do not look down on me as if I had not thought this through. It is my decision."

"No, Crista!" Rebecca holds me back as I try to advance towards the thrones. "We can go back. Don't strip yourself of who you are, to have something that is already gone."

"One day you will understand why I am doing, what I am doing."

She nods towards the lady. Walking over, the woman pulls out a piece of paper. Crista picks up the pen. She doesn't hesitate, instead she grips the pen firm in her hand. My heart drops as the ink flows onto the paper.

"Sweet child. What a sacrifice you have made. You will get what you are searching for tomorrow, along with your ceremony."

Tomorrow? She dare disrespect Crista. A royal with magical abilities, who has the power to end her in one second. I open my mouth to object, but Crista rushes in. Her eyes tell a thousand stories. I can read her sorrow, her pain, her need for me to not fight. For once in my life, to not fight. All my muscles tense as Rebecca leads me along.

I look back at the woman one more time, a smug face still splayed on her lips. We walk to the other side of the cabin, taking a turn to our right. I wonder what happened last time when they were here. How long did she make them wait in here? What kind of mental torture did she put Crista through? She was just a little girl.

***

I hug my knees to my chest, staring blankly at the wall. The place we were shoved in has to be the most basic four wall room, with a bed in the corner. There must be a leak somewhere. The rain from outside drips into a pail that sits in the corner. The steady rhythm is unsettling, each drip making me more tense.

I can't bear to look at Crista. And from what I can tell, she doesn't look at me either. No one says anything. I wish someone would scream. At least it would give me a reason to start talking. To fight for what is right. I have learned the difference of right and wrong the hard way. I have learned the difference between want and need. I want my mother back, but I don't need her to survive. That has become quite apparent. It's not right for Crista to have to give up something that is a part of her. Something that she was chosen for, just to see our mothers again. Just to feel the pain of them die again.

The sound. The sound of someone finally talking, breaks the silence.

"I don't know how to feel," Rebecca voices, pulling her head up. "Why didn't you tell me?"

"Because I knew you would say no." Crista's voice turns flat, and just like me, her secret had been exploited, and she is now waiting to see the consequence.

Rebecca throws her hands up, standing now. I have to raise my head from its sorrow to see her.

"Of course I would say no! Are you crazy? You were born with magic, you don't know the effects it will have on you, to not possess it."

Crista now stands, holding her hands in fists, "Are you saying that you don't want Mika back? You seemed pretty excited until now."

"Can you please… just think about this?"

"Why weren't you there?!" Crista cries. A silence fills the room, even the drips have stopped hitting the bucket. "Why did you never check to see if I was okay? You lost your sister, but I lost my mother. I lost the person that loved me more than anything, in one second… and you were never there."

Rebecca just looks at her, her face unreadable. Crista turns her back, unable to take anymore. I can feel the tears that drip down her cheek like it's the rain outside.

"I have thought about this. I have no one else. And when I lost everything, you never came to see if I was okay, never stood up to be my role model. The mother figure I needed. I want this, so *I* am paying the price. Zaria wants this, so *she* is paying her price."

I look down again, this room being too small for this argument. Axil. Axil would have known how to help her. He is so kind. So stable. So caring. He would know exactly what to do, and I have no idea. Maybe I am heartless, maybe I am a criminal just like my father, but I am still here. Here trying.

***

The night passes just like a distant friend. Its unusual how the night was tense but peaceful. I can't shake the guilt feeling of Crista's sacrifice. I'm part of the reason she is giving up her magic. In turn, I have no idea how I will ever be able to live up to Crista. The woman was right. Although she was very rude and smug, everything she said was the truth. I will never be able to live up to people's expectations. I will always be a failure in someone's eyes.

We wait again in silence, one thing I have gotten into a love-hate relationship with. In the silence, I don't have to speak, don't have to resist, I can try to catch a moment of peace, but peace almost never comes in this kind of silence.

The outside world may be at peace, but my thoughts swarm me like a colony of bees.

"The ceremony will be starting shortly," the woman comes into the room we have been staying in. She wears another red dress. This one more sparkly than the one she wore yesterday. She must think this is a celebration. I don't understand. This woman is magic too. She knows how much sorcerers treasure their magic, and yet she treats this like a game. Like, she can't wait to suck the life out of Crista.

Crista stands to take the ceremony gown out of the woman's hands. It is a white, floor-length gown, not a blemish to be seen. This has got to be the worst day of her life, and it's all my fault.

"Can I talk to you?" I ask Crista. "Outside please." At my request, I catch the lady give a sly smirk with the same taut vision as yesterday. The eyes of a hawk.

She takes another glance at Rebecca, still a little salty about the argument they had. "I guess," she says glumly, leading the way out of the cabin.
She walks with her head held high, and her shoulders back, looking confidant as can be. When we are outside, she turns around to face me.

"If you have taken me out here to tell me to rethink..."

"No!" I say throwing my hands in front of my face. "I... just wanted to say that I am sorry. For everything. Your loss. My loss. This whole situation. I am sorry to drag you into this mess."

Her expression is tight, "I have told you once before. I will tell you again. I chose this."

"But why?"

She takes a deep breath, like she is holding back a demon. When she lets go, her face softens just a tad, and I know I am now talking to *Crista.*

"Everyone is acting like I am doing something reckless. Who knows, maybe I am, but look at you. You do reckless things all the time. Everyone sees you as a hero. And don't even tell me about how not having magic will hurt me. You are a sorcerer and don't have magic either."

I take in all she is saying, listening to how I am once again the cause of someone's pain. Clouds start to roll in above us. Dark and summoning.

"I want to be able to do something heroic as well. I thought you would be happy. You would be getting your mother *and* magic back. I would finally be getting my mother back."

I reach out for her as best as I can, keeping my voice in a calming tone. "I understand your motive, I really do. I as well would do anything if it meant getting my mother back, but I want this decision to be for yourself. Not for Rebecca. Not for me. But, for you."

Finally she looks me in the eyes, all the exhaustion from the past few days coming back in a tsunami.

I speak over her silent cries. "I have gone my whole life thinking I was doing heroic acts, but none of it was for me. If you do this, all I ask is for you to be happy."

She doesn't answer, but she nods her head. I can only hope what I said has talked some sense into her. When we arrive back in the room, Rebecca still sits in the corner facing the wall. I wish they would just talk. I would hate for them to go down the mountain, in what should be a reunion, and instead be spiteful towards each other.

Crista picks up the fabric of the dress, rubbing it in-between her hands. Her fingers glide like she is memorizing the pattern of the fabric, reading its history.

"This was my coronation gown when I was chosen."

I can see tears start to roll down her rosy cheeks, still cold from the outside air.

"Crista," Rebecca speaks shyly. "I wanted to thank you for what you are doing. What you are doing for all of us. I appreciate your sacrifice. What you are doing is something I can never even imagine giving up.

"You were right. I wasn't there, and for me to tell you what to do now, when I was never there for you then, isn't right. I should have done something. I was so focused on my own loss, I couldn't bear to watch a child go through it. Instead of trying to help, I just disappeared."

Crista speaks now, her voice still softer. "I know. What I said last night was very harsh. I needed someone to yell at." She takes a break. "I want you guys to know that I'm doing this for everyone."

She gestures to each one of us. "For you, for Zaria, for me. I also want to do it for the kingdom. I know it will take time to adjust to not having my magic, but I hope you can all still understand why I am doing this."

I walk over, placing my hand on her shoulder. She still holds the dress, reminiscing on the past. "We do."

I kneel down, bowing my head before her. Rebecca comes next to me, mirroring my action. I do not know how things will go today. I do not know how things will go tomorrow, but I do know that Crista is the friend that has made the ultimate sacrifice.

***

Bells chime through the small room. Crista stands, her eyes wide facing forward. She wears her white gown, looking as though she has seen a ghost. I can only imagine all the things running through her head. For a moment I wonder if she is even going to go through with this.

The little girl from yesterday is here. She is wearing a sparkly red dress just like her mother. All the childlike nature is gone, from the previous day. The woman probably gave her a pep talk about being mature and holding up her reputation. It is just the five of us in the small room from yesterday. Nothing has changed, and yet everything has changed. It is official.

We will be leaving the mountain today with both our mothers.

"Please rise."

We stand from the seats we have been given on the side. Rebecca turns to face the monstrous woman, so I grudgingly follow her lead. When I face her, she once again locks eye contact with me. The stare has more nerve than some of the looks Damian has ever given me. She just seems cold. Like, there is something that is blocking any emotion from her. Yet, something about her looks familiar. Feels familiar.

"We gather here today in an exchange of magic for life. There is a great sacrifice in taking away one's powers, but a giant unity that comes in the form of life. Crista, would you please step forward."

Robotically, Crista takes the step that she had knelt on yesterday making her offer. The woman's face turns into a pleased gaze watching Crista kneel before her. The thought disgusts me, sending my stomach into a turning mess.

"I would also like for Zaria to step forward."

I had not expected to be part of this ceremony. Limbs shaking, I force my legs to move, my body screaming for me to stay put. Every step I take is closely monitored by her and her daughter. I remember not to trip on the carpet that lines the center of the floor, running up the stairs. I slowly bring my weight to my knees, never breaking eye contact with that monster. I bow my head in unison with Crista.

At least she won't be up here by herself. If I can make the experience even a little less lonely for her, I will endure the pain.

"Now usually I would ask for my payment first, but where is the fun in that? Why don't we bring your mothers back first, so they can watch all you are doing for them?"

My heart drops into my stomach. Why? What kind of witch would intentionally make the mother of their child watch them suffer?

No one speaks. Not one dare say a word. Even all of us together couldn't win a battle against her, and I have already tested the waters. The last thing we need is to get sucked into a rip current.

"Nothing to say?"

She now looks at Crista. Taking a few steps forward, she stops in front of her, sticking out her spiny finger, and lifting Crista's chin.

"Do you not want your mother to watch? Scared you will be a disappointment?" Tilting her head back she cackles, truly revealing the wickedness covered by her beauty. "Don't worry, she will find out sooner or later. Might as well make it a little easier. For her, I mean."

She traces her finger down to her neck, ripping off Crista's necklace. The chain snaps in two, leaving it broken. She then steps over to me. With a stern look, I grasp my fingers around the necklace. If anyone is taking it off, it is going to be me. And she will not dare break it.

I reach for the clasp in the back, working my finger to get it open. She holds out her hand, impatiently tapping her heel to the floor. My fingers become sweaty. She clears her throat, obviously annoyed as I am finally able to unclasp the hinge. I gently cradle it between my two hands.

I look at it one last time. Not having the necklace on leaves a bare feeling. The feeling of vulnerability and sorrow. Even in this dank cabin, the ruby pendant still shoots a thousand lights, making a sea of stars. She roughly snatches it out of my hand, her skin leaving behind a cold chill in my palm.

The little girl walks out of the room. All eyes follow her, except for the lady. She keeps her eyes locked on mine. I wish I could figure out that frostbitten stare. I have seen it before, the last time being as chilly as the first. Struggling sounds come from the back, where the girl had disappeared to. Tiny little breaths quickly escaping. The woman rolls her eyes, placing the necklaces down on the nearest altar.

She disappears where the little girl has gone as well. Mumbling comes from the side of the room, with a lot of background noise. I break my position to look at Crista. It seems as though she has done the same. As we look at each other, we try not to laugh. Just then, the woman shrieks in pain. She yells at the little girl, grumbling. A puff of air escapes my throat that cannot be contained.

She comes back into the main room, pulling out the cauldron. Her eyes are sharp, knowing that everyone heard her from out here. The little girl scurries back to her chair sitting ashamed, her face as bright as her dress.

The woman closes her eyes, taking a deep breath. Smoothing her skirt, her attitude comes back as if nothing had happened. "Now, where were we? Oh yes."

She retrieves the pendants that lie on the table. As she snaps her fingers, jars just like Crista's appear on the table, along with both of our mother's slips. Why she couldn't do that with the cauldron is beyond me. It was probably just for special effect. Some of the ingredients I have seen before, like spiders and rose petals. Others are a complete mystery. Yet another thing that I have no clue about. I do recognize one of the mysterious looking jars though. I have only seen it once, but I will never forget it. The star dust. It glows just like my mother used to. Always the center of the room.

Everyone watches in silence as the woman assembles her spell. She needs no book to tell her what to do. To be able to do all this magic, she must be a chosen one. There is no other explanation.

Only then does the voice of the woman break the silence. Even as she casts the spell, her voice sounds more like a curse than a blessing, the thought making my stomach twist into knots.

"Upon this day, life will be given. To one who has passed, a new chance arisen. From sunrise and sunset, every day of their lives. May they be mothers, sisters, and wives."

My heart speeds with every word that is said. This is the moment. The moment of no return. She turns her hand around the cauldron, spinning in a circular motion. A wind breaks out, a tornado of stardust. At that moment she takes both of the necklaces, snapping them in two. For a moment my heart aches. It was the only thing I had of my mother when she left besides the gloves. I can't manage to draw my eyes away from the sight. Two ghostlike figures hover over the giant cauldron. For a moment the voice I had been hearing rings in my ears.

"Well done."

Two words. Simple and short, but mean the world. For once, I have done something right. Done something that was good. I can see her, see her face forming. The aura around her shining all colors of the rainbow. She shares it with Crista's mother, both of them shining now.

When they transform into humans, it is hard to tell. They too wear the same gown Crista is wearing. The fabric swishes in the air, still hovering above the cauldron. A white shining light blinds the whole cabin. I close my eyes, bracing my arm in front of them, then. Everything goes silent.

Chapter fifteen

"Well done."

It is like a dream. All I can see is white light. Did I faint? Am I dreaming? Her voice. It's really there. As real as the moon and stars. My muscles relax. I must be dreaming. I have never felt so floaty in my life. Feeling as though all the weight of the past five years has been lifted. Warmth. I feel warm. Warm arms wrapped tightly around my shaking body.

"Thank you."

I hug them back. Everything is gone. Every lie, every cheat, every crime, every nightmare, gone.

"Zaria, look at me."

I open my eyes. They flutter open, getting blurry on the spot as tears fill them. I see it. The green. Those emerald eyes. Voices surround me. Too much for a dream. I squeeze the shoulder of the arms that wrap around me. Flesh. Living, breathing…..

"Mom!"

The world stops. Nothing else matters. She's here. Finally here. After all this time, she can hold me in her arms. She can guide me through this messed up life. I can have someone to love again.

"You did it. I knew you would."

I wipe my eyes to look at her. She looks the same. The same sparkle in her eye, same soft skin, same angelic smile, same melodic voice. This is her.

"What… what do you mean?"

"I mean, I knew my daughter would go to the lengths of the earth to do what is right because that's who you are."

She smiles at me. Smiles like I have done no wrong. Like, I am truly her daughter, but I'm not.

"I'm so sorry."

I funnel my head into her arms again. Her sleeve now soaked in my tears. She is here. She is perfect, but I am not.

"I did so many things for dad. I wanted to do what was right, but I couldn't. I couldn't…"

She wraps me tighter, trying to release some of the pain that escapes me. "I know honey. I know."

We sit on the steps embracing one another. I force myself to open my eyes and look to the side. Beside me is Crista in her mother's arms as well, Rebecca, Crista, and her in a big reunion. I see the smile on Crista's face. The smile that makes a hundred roses bloom.

The moment is perfect. A perfect moment I never thought would ever happen. Only in my dreams would this happen. Some nights, I would open my window. I would stick my face into the cool breeze, filling my lungs. Wishing on every star in sight, I would squeeze my eyes and pray. At the time, I didn't know who to pray to. Just someone, anyone who would listen, anyone who would hear my cries and one day deliver. I never once thought the day would come.

In that moment, the clouds open, washing away the rain that had once poured down this morning. Beautiful clouds shine in through the windows. Soft colors filling the sky.

"Hmmm. I don't mean to interrupt this little moment, but I still need my payment."
My mother turns to look at the old woman. She looks at my mother the same way she looks at me. A hint of familiarity, with a smidge of hatred.
My mother turns to whisper in my ear, "What did you pay Eden?"

I try to connect the name with the face, still nothing comes. Before I can turn to answer her, Crista rises. Her mother holds her hand as she walks up to Eden. She must know. Know what her daughter has done for her. I'm glad that someone can be up there to hold her hand and walk her through the storm.

I walk up alone as I once did earlier today. The second I leave, the longing for her arms makes me want to run back. I could leave. I could disappear, just as Damian has once taught me to do. I could get us all out. But I can't. Not this time. Not with her.
"Maria, Mika. Do you want to know what you cost? What your brave little girls would do just to see your pathetic faces again?"

I look at both of them. This is the first time I really see Crista's mother. Crista looks exactly like her, deep golden skin with delicate curls. I can see her worry. Crista's worry, in her eyes, but she knows, she has to. It is my mother that is scared.

She summons a cane to her hand. Again for dramatic effect. Swinging it around, she walks with a swag in her step. Her stride is like she has won a game.

"Dear Crista has decided to give up her magic."
I hear my mother gasp behind me. As if sensing another blow coming, she races up beside me, placing her hand on my back.

"And… she has decided to transfer her magic to Zaria, who will take over the palace in all of its magical needs. How amorous. A loss for one," she points to Crista with her cane, she then points it at me, "Still a loss for the other," she says with a sigh.
My mother's grip on my shoulder startles me. She had come up to stand by my side. The grip on her shoulder suggests only one thing. Anger.
A voice rings out. One I do not recognize. Sweet, yet dominant. It is Mika. "Is there really no other way to—

"Agghh!"
A cry roars through the tiny room. Sharp and gruesome. I didn't know what I expected, but I didn't know the ceremony would be painful. I try to wriggle out of my mother's grasp, but she holds firm. My limbs shake, heart racing, as I watch Crista strain in torment. She looks as though she has been shot, the bullet pulsing in and out to elongate the process. Her eyes squint into two sharp lines. She holds herself so tight, the thought of just killing Eden rolls through me. After what seems like an eternity, she finally collapses on the floor.

Rebecca and Mika are at her side at once. I don't know which is better. At least when she was being zapped by Eden, she was standing up. It's over now, but she lay lifeless on the floor.

Hatred is written on my face as I look over to Eden. In her hand, she possesses a purple glowing orb. Crista's magic. It spins like its own little planet. A whole world shoved into that little ball. With a wicked grin, she scoffs, shooting it into my chest.
I feel the whoosh of air before I feel the magic. The force almost knocks the breath out of my lungs. I stumble on my feet, my mother now bearing my weight. I hate this. Hate everything about it. The second we get our mothers back, she makes them watch us in agony. The pain isn't as bad for me, as it was for Crista, judging by her face.

As the magic seeps through my system, I can feel it as it moves, coursing through my veins like a roller coaster. It doesn't hurt, everything just feels alive. My fingertips tingle, my breath quickens. I feel as though I am shaking with energy.

"You'll be alright. It's just the shock." My mother cradles me in her arms, propping my body against hers.

"Crista…" I manage to break out.

Mika looks over at my mother, nodding. "She's going to be okay."

We lie there. All of us broken. A moment of joy, just to get nullified. Why did it have to be this way? Why did they need to see?

"Feel free to leave whenever you want. Preferably sooner, rather than later." Eden walks away, leaving us lying in the room. We need to get out, all of us. It's just a matter of when we can get up.

***

Hobbling down the mountain, we stick together like kittens following mama cat. Both of our parents are anxious to get away from the cabin. I wonder the lore behind it. How did it get there? Who used to live there, if anyone? We all link arms, not letting go of each other. No one says a word; however, it seems as though I am feeling feelings that aren't mine. There is an ambiance around each person. A vibration that I can feel. They all feel in sync, yet each vibration has its own path. Its own rhythm.

Once the trail evens out, we walk two by two. Rebecca generously lets Crista walk hand in hand with Mika. I can feel her. I have never seen her like this, so happy, so alive. The feeling is enough to power me through life, no matter how broken. Here with my mother beside me, I have found home. Our pace never slows until we get down to the part we had to climb up. We come to a sudden stop.

"I had forgotten about this part," mumbles Mika, under her breath.

My mother looks to her, "You take Crista. I'll take Rebecca."

They nod in agreement, my mother rushing over to grab Rebecca.

"Mom? Mom, what is going on?"

She turns around, lifting my hands in between us, "I need you to be brave honey. One last time. I need you to trust me."

That face. The face I had once seen after my hard training sessions. The face of trying to comfort, when she is nervous herself. The calming effect never truly seeming to work. I watch as Mika and her grab Crista and Rebecca. They hover over the top of the mountain, peering over the edge. Heart racing, I watch as my mother walks off the cliff.

"No!" I scream, following them to the edge. My heart stops as I look over. A pile of bodies on the ground is not what I see, but both mothers in the sky. Flying free, airborne flipping through the clouds. What looks to be a dance, the sway and swoop in every direction. Today is not just about us. It is about them. Friendship overcoming the grave. It's about family. We are family. Every single one of us.

After their aerial dance, they come back down to the bottom of the mountain. Looking down now, I can see that the drop is a lot higher than fifteen feet. I don't even want to guess how high I am right now. All I want is to find a way down.

My mother looks back up at me, her eyes shining.

"Zaria, you are going to have to fly down."

"WHAT!"

Crista speaks this time, "You once told me before, about the pen. I needed to feel it. Block everything out except for the feeling of flying."

"But, I have never flown before. How am I supposed to know what it feels like?"

She looks at me, hands held up, "You have to trust me. My magic will not fail you."

I take a step back, my mind drawing a blank. Never before did I think that I would be jumping off a cliff in hopes of flying. The only time I had thought of that, I thought it to be the last thing I did. My legs shake just thinking about it. I close my eyes, trying not to think.

Forcing myself to run off the cliff, I feel the empty space around me. I try to picture clouds, big puffy ones that they were dancing around. I feel the wind on my face. It comes in big gushes, filling my lungs with almost too much oxygen. Fly, flying, birds, I am a bird. Maybe if I keep telling myself that I am flying, I won't hit the ground. It has been a few seconds, I take the risk to open my eyes.

I see orange. Little crumply leaves piled on the ground. I am flying. I did it. Crista's magic has saved me —

My body plunges downward. My head is spinning, my limbs having no control. I tumble down, hitting branches from trees. I shut my eyes, not wanting to see what happens next. I'm dying. I'm going to die. I got to see my mother for one full evening, just to fall out from the sky, cracking my skull into a tree.

I stop midair, a zapping noise startling me. I carefully open my eyes. A green tornado surrounds me. It sparkles, keeping me in place.

I look at it amazed until I can feel my feet on the ground. I had been set into the pile of leaves I had seen from above earlier. The tornado disappears, leaving all four friends surrounding me.
We all look at each other, waiting for one person to be brave enough to speak.
"That was—" my mom starts.
"Just a little rusty," finishes Rebecca.
"You did it. I didn't think you would actually jump."
Crista comes over to me, helping me up. Picking the leaves off of my clothes, it sets in what I had just done. I had done magic. My first magic ever, and it was flying. I can't help but smile. I look over at my mother for approval, her face very satisfied. In a daze, we make it back to the camp that we had stayed at before. Life is the same, but with a purpose now. I just have to figure out what that purpose is.

Chapter sixteen

Around the fire, we curl together. There is not much talking, just a lot of feelings. I can still sense the nerves from my mom that aura that I felt earlier shifting from an angst to a deep focus.

"Mom. Who was that woman? Eden?" I ask, my voice shaking even though I dare it not to.
Everyone's eyes look over to her, leaving the fire as light, instead of their main focus.

She takes a deep breath. "Well, she is a special ruler. She is the Queen of the kingdom that Lumbridge is at war with. We have no choice but to go to her. She was the chosen of the chosen. I guess you could say a hierarchy. She has direct contact with the gods, so when there is a request to be made, unfortunately, she is who you go to."

That's why Crista was so uncomfortable bowing to her.

"How did you know her?"
She looks deep in the fire. Too deep. Maybe now wasn't the right time to get into this story, but I have to know.

"Being the Queen of Malaka, her kingdom had once fallen into a depression. Back then, she was not the villain you see her as today, she was kind, an angel actually, but this hopelessness turned her heart to ice. She had prayed and prayed for the gods to save her from the depression, but there was nothing to be done. Her people were starving, supplies were low, and the streets were filled with people begging for her aid and blessing. She didn't know what to do. She had then decided to reach out to the next best thing, the chosen ones. She begged us all to help her, but when we tried, the gods didn't allow it. Instead of trying to deepen her faith, she took her rage out on us. If we were not able to help her, then we were of no use to her. She thought that what we had done was a betrayal to her kingdom."

Her eyes never leave the licking flames as they glow brighter into the night. As if the fire too could feel her pain.

"We tried to explain. Tried to reason. It was not our fault. What the gods say, goes. It was at that time she had started to send out troops. Troops to find every chosen one she had asked, and slaughter them for the great betrayal of her throne and kingdom. Under her command is why Mika and I were murdered."

The crackle of the fire fills the silence. Malaka troops? I had thought the Huva gang had killed her. Even Rebecca had thought the same.

"So… it wasn't the incident? You know… the one with the gang?" Rebecca asks, myself wondering the same thing.

"I'm so sorry. All this time, you thought it was you, that it was your fault. The only one to blame is Eden. She has always been self-centered, worrying for herself, rather than her people. I just never thought that she would have gone so far as to take innocent lives."

"If she was the one who sent troops to murder you, why did she decide to bring you back?" I ask.

She looks at me again with that same concerned expression. "I… I don't know. Maybe she had a change of heart."

That's my mom. Always looking for the soft spot in people. I wish I could do the same. All I can usually see in people, are their flaws. The things that they had done wrong, always putting myself in competition with them. It would make me feel a little bit better to know there was someone worse than me. Lucky for me, I didn't have to look very far.

Crista raises her voice, still a little hoarse from the ceremony. "Miss Maria, there is something you should know… about your husband."

I shake my head trying to stop her. This is not the time to bring this up. Ignoring it, she continues.

"Your husband had sent Zaria on a mission to the palace to steal the treasury of the kingdom. Anyway, when we had found out that Zaria was your daughter, we had gone over to the mansion to get your slip for your ceremony. When he had seen Zaria back with nothing… he shot her."

Both mothers gasp, listening to Crista's story.

"You… he… did what?" my mother stumbles on her words.

I quickly try to reassure her, "Crista was able to heal me. I am fine."

She places her hand on her head, "What all did he make you do?"

"Uhh… almost all of his jobs."

The rest of the night was spent filling in our mothers on the last five years. Some good, others bad. For me, it was mostly bad. I told her about how I had met Crista, and how everyone in the palace was so kind, so that was at least two good things. I leave out the part about Axil and I. I can't bear to go into another emotional wreck. We weren't even together, so why do I feel as though he shattered my heart, leaving me to suffer?

"I'm so sorry. I should have done something sooner. Should've stopped him, stopped you… I…"

"Mom. There was nothing you could have done. But now we get to start over. Start a new life. All Damian knows is that you are dead, and supposedly I am as well.

We can choose our lives. I know I need to stay at the palace with Crista. She can show me how to take over the magic system there, just please, please, don't go back."

As if it was a promise, her eyes sparkle. "I will keep you safe. That, you can be sure of."
The same promise. A different person. The same promise that has already been broken. I can see Crista flinch as she says it.

Drifting off, we still curl around the fire, no one daring to move. I think we all have the same thought. If we move, if we leave for a split second, we might all wake up from this dream. Crista and Rebecca both snooze on Mika's shoulders, peace finally taking over their faces. I'm glad that Crista is okay. Even with everything that happened, she still lay with a smile on her face as her mind drift into another world.

***

Riding the motorcycle back was a little lonely. I take it back with Crista. It left some time for our mothers to catch up. Also a little time for Rebecca to be with her sister. She had been a little hesitant. After Crista had snapped at her, I think she was scared to be too domineering about Mika.

Eating at rest stops, we talk about everything and anything that runs through our minds. But even through the hustle and bustle Crista pulls me aside at one of the gas stations.

"I just wanted to tell you, I will always be at your side. You know that, right?"

"I do. Thank you. I know it's going to take me a while to adjust to this whole new world."

"Okay Jasmine," she mocks, punching my arm.

We laugh, taking a deep breath. We had done it. The first mission I had completed that had a happy ending.

"Wait. If you are not running the magic at the kingdom, then who is?" She doesn't need her magic powers to see the quick sweat that broke through my skin.

"Relax. My mother is handling the transition for you. She did it before I did, so she knows what to do."

Sighing, I try to focus. I want to get back to the palace, I do… but I will have to see him. See the eyes that ripped my heart out. The stare that crumpled me to the ground, and stomped on me.

"I just… worry…"

"About Axil, I know."

"What do I do?" I start. Stopping me, she butts in.

"You be happy. You have accomplished what you had set to do. You have done what is right. You will be devoting your life to helping the kingdom stand. If that's not good enough…"

"I know. I know. I guess I'm just worried."

She forces me to look at her, "It will be okay. I have your back, and so does everyone else here. Whatever happens, we will always stick together."

"We've got to go!" she shouts to the rest of the group patting me on the shoulder.

Racing the clock, we're back on the road. We must get back tonight to return the bike to the fox. The fox. I almost forgot about John looking for the key. I wonder what he is doing. Things are definitely going to be different when we return.

The sun starts to set, saying goodbye to the world. The moon shines through the pinkish color of the sky. We are almost back at the palace. Now it's just a matter of finding that fox.

When we stop the bike, Crista treks into the forest knowing these trees like the back of her hand. All of us follow her lead. It makes me wonder just how many times she has come to trade with this fox. How many times has she roamed in these woods just to find some peace? The thoughts are short lived as we approach the familiar hollow tree, Crista's knock singing through the night air.

The same little fox opens the door holding his paw to his mouth in a shushing motion.

"I have your motorcycle back in the cave." she says, her voice no louder than a whisper

He sneaks back into his tree, handing over the key. It is still as shiny as when it was given to him.

"From what I can tell..." he starts, "There seemed to be an early return from the prince a few days ago." His fluffy eyebrows stich together, worried.
Crista puts on a fake smile, nodding. "Oh yes. Everything is fine." Giving him a curtsy, she says, "Thank you for your service."

He raises his tiny paw to his head, saluting to her. "Anytime. You take care."

Waving off at him, he closes his door. Making our journey back to the castle, my heart starts to beat, my skin shivering. What if they know? What if he told them about me? Then what? I won't be able to hold up my end of the bargain. I can only imagine the King and Queen summoning me into their office, just to have me imprisoned. I can't argue though. It is what I was planning on doing. It's what I deserve. That was before, though. I hadn't done anything wrong. Never once did I look for anything in the palace. I had never intentionally went out of my way to finish my task. Even when John confronted me, I had still chosen not to do anything. My relationship with Axil and Crista meant more. They came first.

And if I don't end up in jail, what then? What will I say to him when I see him again? It's inevitable. Will I still be his advisor, or will I be stuck in a room to practice my new magic? I just wish I could explain everything, but I already have. It wouldn't do anything other than make him more upset. It seems as though some things won't be different when I return. I can count on that because I sure don't expect a warm welcome back from Axil.

We all walk to the front gate, side by side, my mother holding my hand as we approach.

A low voice comes from the darkness. "Miss Crista, Zaria, is that you?" a guard asks us, placing his hand on the gate.

I keep my mouth shut, keeping my profile on the down low as much as possible. "Indeed it is, and look who we brought."

He examines our group, trying to figure out who all is here. Falling back, he holds up his hat that slips from his head.

"Is… is that Mika and Maria?"

"Surprise," my mother retorts.

"How… but you…"

Crista answers, "We would love to explain everything, but we must get inside. The King and Queen are waiting."

Her words make my throat close. Fumbling, he opens the gate, rushing us inside. Stepping into the common area is like entering a dream that you don't know is good or bad. I can only wait to see what happens. The only downside is, if things go wrong, I can't wake up.

Crista takes charge again, leading us through the palace. "The King and Queen are probably just settling in for bed. I will make a call for them. You guys wait in the throne room."

She leaves us, skipping through the halls. Her words run through my head, *"No matter what."*

"Zaria?"

I turn around to see who the voice is coming from. Mika stands behind me, cautiously.

"I just wanted to thank you for being friends with Crista. As far as I know, no one really gave her a chance. I'm glad she found you."

It's weird to be getting a whole bunch of thanks. And for what? What I did doesn't erase all the things that I have done. I'm not a person who should be getting thanks.

I don't want to be rude, so I force a smile on my face, nodding my head.

"You know, I understand you." I go to look up at her, but she looks at the tiles, fidgeting with the rings on her fingers. "In my younger days, I used my magic for... not so great things. I could cover my tracks, no doubt. I was unstoppable."

I question, "But if your magic is gifted from the gods, why would they allow you to do such things?"

She takes a deep breath, "Just because the gods gift us our magic, it doesn't mean they are going to monitor our every move. They will not tell you what is right or wrong. Some things are bigger, like the great depression of Malaka. With stuff like that, they guide us through. But it is still our choice."

"If they held our hand through the rest of our lives, it would basically make us non-human. We would be robots who never do wrong. They still give us the choice, to learn and grow. Do some bad things, and learn from the experiences. I think what happened was supposed to be a lesson to me."

She pinches the bridge of her nose composing herself.

"Once Crista was born, I decided that she couldn't have a mother that was wandering around the streets. She needed a role model, someone to look up to." She now had a look of despair. Not just discomfort, but like an aching pain was taking over her body. "I tried my best, but I ended up falling back into my old habits. Crista took over the palace long before your mother and I were murdered. She had to pay the price of my actions. While all the other kids were playing, she was learning how to work the system of the palace."

She takes a deep breath, her voice becoming more stable as the memories of the past wash away.

"I guess what I am trying to say is, thank you for finally being someone she can relate to." Her eyes widen after that. Covering her mouth, she looks down at me. "I mean, I didn't mean I'm glad that you… you know."

I let go a laughing sigh, "I know what you mean. And, I could thank her for the same thing."

I look over to where my mother is. She stands with Rebecca, talking about what seems to be the old days. No matter what, I will always stand with these people.

***

The doors to the throne room burst open, the King and Queen puny in comparison. They both wear their nighttime dressing. I hope she didn't catch them during sleep. That could change the whole outcome of this conversation. Waking up John was a nightmare and a half.

"Bless the Sky. Look who it is."

The Queen comes running into the throne room, heading straight for my and Crista's mother. She grabs both of them by the arm, pulling them into her embrace.

"I thought I would never see you again," she says, squeezing them. There is a strain in her voice. Years of tears that were held back, now making a reappearance.

"Likewise," Mika sequels.

She starts the line of questions, now gripping onto her dress. "How are you back? What happened?"

My mother interrupts her, "It is all thanks to Crista and Zaria."

I point to Crista. "It was mostly her."

She looks at me for a second, eyeing me up and down. "Are you — are you Maria's daughter?"

Nodding my head I answer, "I am."

"I thought I recognized you the second I saw those green eyes." She does a sly wink. "You take after your mother pretty well."

Relief runs through my body, my muscles relaxing. She doesn't know.

Crista explains to both of them the details of the trip. She doesn't mention anything about the true reason I was sent here, which I thank her for. The King and Queen listen, gasping at the right moments, adding in questions to the parts that Crista missed. They really are making a production of the whole thing. My mind starts to wander into a daze. I watch the moon through the window. Slowly it moves, lulling to watch. And the night sky, which had once been a happy place, a whole other world at the edge of my fingertips, has turned into a mystery. The stars separate from the moon, trailing a line around it like a boundary.

"Zaria… Zaria…" my mother shakes me back into reality.

"What?" I come back a little groggy.

The King speaks this time, "Is it correct that you will be taking over Crista's duties?"

Bowing, I answer, "Yes, Your Highness. I hope you will understand that it will take me some time. But after that, I plan to be stable on my own feet." My voice is pleading, something I haven't done in a while.

"Arrangements of your new job will be made in the morning."

"New job?" I question, my heart skipping a beat.

"Well, I can imagine it would be difficult for you to balance both jobs."

"No!"

This didn't even run through my head. Sure, I bet Axil is upset with me, but I can't imagine just leaving him. I have left enough people, I have to at least try to make amends. He has made me happier than ever staying here. If I have fought this long, I can fight a bit longer.

"Please, Your Highness. I have loved my job, and would like to keep my position. I will work double time, I will never be late, please. Please let me keep my job."

The Queen gives him a look. It seems as though she is pleading as well. How strange. He looks back at her, sighing.

"We can try to work something out. No promises."

My breath returns to my lungs. "Thank you, Your Highness." Bowing again, I try to remain calm.
I can do this. I have to try, and even if I fail, at least I have tried to do the right thing.

***

My mom and I trek back to my room. It has been a long day, and we both need sleep. With each step up the stairway, my mind runs through all the possibilities that could happen tomorrow. What if he has a change of heart? I mean, we can still be friends, right? He has to understand.

I open my door, welcoming my mother inside. She looks around, seeming to examine all that I have created. The walls are bare, the bed neatly made thanks to Lucy. Since I have been here, I have done nothing with the room.

"Zaria, what job were you talking about?" she talks in a soft voice.

Closing the door, I kick my shoes off. "When Damian sent me here, my job was to be the prince's assistant. The job was to make him fall in love with me and find the information to steal the treasury out that way. As you can see, my situation is more troublesome."

"How do you mean?" She leans against the bed, ready for me to spill.

I sit down next to her, contemplating whether I should tell her. For goodness sake, she was only alive for two days. I don't need to be laying my problems on her the second she comes back.

Laying a hand on my shoulder, she gives me a light squeeze. She wants to know, and I can't disobey her wishes.

"When we first started our journey, Axil was with us. We were very close. Closer than John and I have ever been. Everything was great until I needed to talk to Damian. My only plan was to tell him that I had decided to start my own gang, and that I had completed his mission.

I thought I could fool him, but it was stupid of me to underestimate him. When I got shot, it had really scared Axil. He thinks that the only reason we had anything was because I was doing it for Damian."

"Honey, I'm so sorry." She brings my face closer to her, embracing me.

"He… he said I was no different. That I was just like *him*."

It all comes out now. All the sobs that have been suppressed inside come exploding out of me. It is hard to breathe, hard to think. I have tried so many times, but it is never enough. I can never do the right thing, it's always bad for someone else.

She cradles me like she used to, the memories flooding back. She has always been my rock, and when she was gone, it had turned into John. Then he had abandoned me, and then Axil showed me love and kindness, and now he is gone as well. Everyone leaves. No one can stay forever. I just wish he was one of the ones that had decided to stay.

***

I rise early before the sun has come up, the inky sky a beckoning call. This time it is not for danger, but for peace. I move as silently as possible exiting the room, as to not wake up my mother. Her soft snooze fills the dead room with a bit of life. Just hearing her breath sends a calmness to my beating heart.

Stepping outside, the cool air calms my nerves. I was heating up inside, so much I could burn. My feet move in a rhythm I do not recognize. They are slow, inconsistent. Things were bad before, but at least I had things figured out. I knew what the next day was going to be like. I could feel the mood of the people around me and act accordingly. Training, nap, eat, steal, sleep, and do it all over again. That was life. It wasn't the best life, but it was mine. Now, I don't even recognize myself. I can't rely on my brain. I can't even rely on actions. I have turned into a train wreck.

Can I even blame him, I mean, look at me. I'm absolutely broken. A lost, weak girl who can't find her way home. I... don't even know if I have a home.

"Hey."

Even now, I must be losing my mind. How did I become so fixated so fast? I have no control. I gave up control a long time ago, now all I want is to earn it back, even just a little bit.

"Hey."

This time it seems real. A little too real. I turn around prepared to be disappointed, but there he stands. In the dark, the moonlight shines upon his light hair, illuminating every strand, making him seem like he's glowing. He stands a bit awkward, his hands in his pockets. His shoulders are hunched as if he is in pain.

"Axil, I—

"Don't." He stands a bit straighter, preparing for whatever he is about to say. "I just wanted to tell you, John has been put in the royal dungeon."

His words pierce my heart, if there even is one anymore. This is all my fault. How did he know? How did he see past my lies?

"I'm guessing you want me down there as well," I say in a low voice. I don't want any suspicious ears overhearing our conversation.

"I… um…"

"It's okay," I say, interrupting him. "I deserve it."

He takes his hands out of his pockets, "Look, I made a promise to you. Consider it paid."

I don't know whether to feel relieved or hurt.

"I just want to say that I am sorry. For everything. I know it must seems like it was all —

Interrupting me this time, he spits out, "I don't want to hear any more apologies." He stumbles on his words, trying to form the best way to say them. "Listen, I'm not going to say anything, so just please… let it go."

I don't know where it comes from. I have been beat down more times than I can count, I won't let it happen again.

"No."

"No?"

"You heard me."

He takes a step forward, lowering his head. "I am your Prince. You do as I say."

Glaring down at me, he stares as he did the night before he left. I can't help but feel ashamed. Why did I ever think I could be anything more than some worthless criminal?

"You will forget that I ever went on that stupid trip with you."

"Do you even know what happened? Crista resurrected our mothers together. We both finally have our family back."

"Congratulations. I hope your mother is proud of the little criminal she has raised."

He turns to walk away. Stomping my foot, I stammer, "That's all you'll ever see, isn't it? What about everything else?" I feel fire. It's not just heat rising in me, but fire. Part of my magic coming out that I can't control.

His face is angry now, angrier than I have ever seen. "How do I know any of it was real?"

Without thinking, I run towards him, slamming my lips into his, trying to tell him all I can through the action. Yes, it was real. Nothing we had was fake. I'm so sorry for everything. It doesn't last long though. Shoving me away, his stare burns through me. His hands turn to fists, his body starting to shake.

"Axil..."

Before I can talk, he turns away. He walks, setting flames to the ground with each step, my flames. Tears well in my eyes. What have I done?

A lonely owl hoots its lonesome call. That is all I'll ever be. A creature that dwells in the night, begging for someone, anyone. Together we will burn in silence.

Chapter seventeen

The moon illuminates my path back to the palace. My days have just gone from bad to worse. I shove my head under my pillow, silencing any ounce of pain that may escape. I am supposed to meet the King sometime this morning, I might as well get ready. Get ready for the tsunami I am about to be swallowed by.

Once the sun has come up a little bit more, I drag my feet to the dresser. I flit through all the clothes Axil has given me, every piece of fabric being a memory. A memory I don't wish to relive.

Looking deeper into my closet, I find a dress that Lucy has hidden back against the wall. It is a white dress with floral lace, making the ensemble seem very dainty. The sleeves rest on my forearm, straps securing it to my shoulders. I brush through the mess of my hair, letting it flow down my back. My eyes wander from the flats, to the heels. Rolling my eyes, I slip on the flats, grumbling.

Maybe the King will be at breakfast by now. I hear he always rises early. I pray to the stars I can catch him while he's not busy.

Making my way to the dining hall, I try my best to keep my steps in an orderly manner. My heart quickens as I near the double doors, my breath hitching as I try to calm myself down.

Closing my eyes, I take a step into the dining hall, bracing myself. When I step in, voices stop. I open my eyes to see not just the King of Lumbridge, but his son as well. As soon as he sees me, he looks away. I can see his mood, a deep red color boiling around him. Watching it go from the light pink of his love, to a blood red. "Ah, Miss Zaria. Would you like to discuss future plans?"

Biting back the tears, I take one last look at Axil. "Excuse me." I bow in their direction. "It seems I should come back another time."

"Nonsense." Lifting a finger in the air, he calls out to one of the servants. "Jessica, get her some breakfast."

I can see the hatred radiating off of Axil. I can't blame him. He sees me as a monster.

The King sits at the head of the table, Axil to his left. I scurry over, sitting on the opposite side. No reason for me to agitate him even more. Sitting down, I fidget in my seat, remembering to cross my legs, and sit up straight. The action makes him glance in my direction. He looks me up and down, his face softening, just for a brief moment. The tightness in his face flinches, his jaw relaxing, but I pay no mind to it. He wants me to forget, then fine. I will forget the niceties that he has done for me, just like he has forgotten all the niceties I have done for him.

"So, you had questioned if, with your new job, you could still be Axil's advisor."

Hearing the King say it out loud after what happened last night makes my face heat all over again in embarrassment. His eyes widen with pure rage. It seems as though only I can tell. His face is fuming, but his father only looks and smiles. It must just be the magic. It can do that right? Amplify feeling?

"Yes, Your Highness," I answer hanging my head. This is not how I wanted any of this to go.

"Well, I only feel inclined to include my son in this conversation. If he feels comfortable with you balancing both jobs, then I have no problem."
He speaks up, locking eyes with his father, "I would like to send in for a new advisor."
My heart drops into the pit of my stomach. It has been doing that so much lately, it concerns me what the side effect could be.

He continues, "If she is getting a new job, I would like to know that I have someone who can stay focused and on task." He bites the last part at me, but again his father doesn't pick up on any of it.
The King just listens, considering everything his son is saying. When Axil finishes, he stands.

"Congratulations on your new job, Miss Zaria."
Miss Zaria. Not just my name. With that, he walks out of the dining hall. I watch as he leaves, not even caring if the King is watching me.

"Your breakfast." Jessica arrives behind me, placing my food down in a delicate manner.

I sit numb in my chair, rage bubbling up. I thought I had escaped people talking to me like that. The way someone talks when they have the upper hand in a card game. They sound innocent, but if you lean in close enough, you can hear the sting, the bite, the punch. I am tired of being thrown around like a ragdoll.

Pushing my plate away, I stand. I don't say anything to the King. Anything I would say, would end up being a lie anyway. I march out of the room. This time, my steps are in check. Steady, and powerful. I glower through the halls, my arms swinging to the beat. For a while, I don't know where I am walking, just that I need to get out.

My legs end up leading me to Crista's room, the heavy wooden door always a masterpiece. I knock on her door, hoping for an answer. I wait a second, then two, then ten. I knock again, but there is still nothing. I raise my arm to slam on the door for good measure.

"Good morning Miss Zaria."

The Queen startles me from behind. I turn around, my hand still in the air. Looking at it, I quickly tuck it behind my back.

"Is Crista not inside?" she asks.

I shake my head. "I don't think so."

"Well I'm glad I found you anyway."

Great. Put on a smile. Act presentable.

"In honor of the return of your mothers, the chosen ones, I want to host another ball. Since you did so well planning the last one, I was wondering if you would help me plan this one as well."

Another ball? Why? Why now? Of course it has to be now.

"With all due respect, Your Highness, as you know, I have training I need to attend to. Crista and her mother are supposed to be teaching me how to work the system."

Her eyes light up. "Marvelous! You can practice your magic with the ball. That should make planning a lot faster."

She smiles wide, excitement in her face. I try to match her energy, but it falls short… way short.

"Yeah… that is such a good idea."

Clapping her hands together, she jumps on her toes. "I'm so happy you are on board. I have so much I want to ask you."

Great, just great.

***

I follow the Queen as I once had before. Since when did I go from feared thief to royal ball planner? I have disconnected from my father, and still I seem to be leading the same life. Always hiding, always lying, I am forever going to have to keep an eye on my back. To say people want me dead is an understatement. For the things I have done, people will want me to suffer, just like John had said. I can only imagine he's sulking at this exact moment in his cell, his plan falling apart. I need to find a way to visit him without looking suspicious.

"So how does it feel? You were able to resurrect your mother from the dead. That's not something most people can boast about."
She looks at me and smiles. I can tell she is trying to be nice, and I try my hardest to be kind as well.

"Resurrecting my mother is one thing I will certainly not boast about. People would find me crazy. As for having her back, I… don't know."
We now walk side by side, strolling through the empty halls. A maid crosses into the hall, but with one look from the Queen, she changes her direction.
"How do you mean?"

"Having her back is the best thing that has ever happened to me. The part of my heart that was buried with her is now alive. I guess, for her it is like time just keeps going on. I feel as though I am struggling from the change. The past five years…"

Looking down at me, she speaks, "I understand, dear. You have to rearrange everything in your head, like meeting a best friend after five years. Your lives have totally changed, and when you try to come together, catching up can feel like a hurricane."

"Yes."

I follow her back into the planning room. It's funny how it has only been a couple of weeks since I was last in here planning a ball. The room looks totally different than it once looked. It is still lit by candlelight, but all the papers are gone. My guess is, that will be today's project. Coming up with ideas. "Will Rosalyn be joining us today?"

Closing the door, she answers, "She will be coming later today. Family event, I think."

I press my palms against one of the wooden desks, the smooth edges running against my fingers. "So what will the plan be for today?"

She sits upon the throne-like chair in the room. It's a little silly to see her sit so properly in what looks to be an uncomfortable chair. Adjusting her weight, she lifts her head, "That is what I was going to ask you, dear. We need to figure out a theme. I would have liked if Crista could have been down here as well, but she and her mother are probably catching up somewhere. I couldn't bear to separate the moment."

"She really loves her mother. Oh…"

"What is it, dear?"

Sheepishly I recall, "I didn't even congratulate you on getting your sister back."

Folding her hands, she replies, "I didn't know you knew. Who was the one to tell you, Axil or Crista?"
I cringe at that name, still keeping a smile on my face, "Crista. She had told me that she was cousins with Axil."

Taking a deep breath, she replies, "It was always hard for me, knowing that I didn't have magic."

"I thought it was something that ran in the family."

Steadying her voice, she continues, "It is. Mika was adopted into the family. Our mother had tried to make me feel better. No magic in the house, no bragging about abilities. She had tried to make everything as fair as possible, and Rebecca just had to be a special case, a golden goose. I was the only one left with no magic. I guess now you could say that things have evened out." She points to her tiara, smiling.

"That must have been hard for you."
She clears her throat, "What about you? You said you must train for this magic, were you born without it as well?"

I rub my arm, looking at the tile on the floor. "Crista had told me that she could sense the magic inside me, but it had almost been... put to sleep."

"Oh dear," she says gasping. "How does something like that happen?"

"I never knew I had magic. She said when it was time for me to be learning how to do magic, my mind had been focusing on other things. I had gotten so tired that the magic went to sleep. Now I have to work at waking it back up and also dealing with Crista's magic on top of that. I just hope I won't be a disappointment."

She takes a sip from her teacup. I hadn't noticed it until now. "We will be patient as long as you need, darling."

Nodding, I respond, "I appreciate it."

A moment of silence fills the room. I had not thought it would be so easy to talk to the Queen of Lumbridge. There is something so calming about her demeanor, calmness that I long for from someone else.

"It seems I have gotten off track. I wanted to ask you, what is it your mother would like at the ball? Any specific theme or color?"

"Jasmine."

It had only clicked in my brain last night. Of course that is why my mother had smelled exactly like the soap from this palace. It's because she was here, helping Mika. All those sleepless nights, the scent of jasmine had lulled me to a hypnosis. Never quite asleep, but a peaceful world where I was safe.

"Jasmine and emerald green. That, I think she would like."

She stares into me, like she can see straight through me. She cocks her head, taking one last sip. "I couldn't agree more. Why don't you start making a list of things, then when Crista and Rosalyn come, they can look at what we have started."

I grab one of the pens that rest on the desk, knowing that it is not Crista's pen. The sight of my handwriting is still atrocious, and I have no idea how to cast my own spell.

"Thank you for including me. Anything to make my mother feel welcome back, I want to make as special as possible."

"And, you were so good at it last time. Truly, your talent for design is remarkable."

Writing down the things we have talked about, I start thinking about the last ball. "I had left before I was able to truly thank you for the gown you had made for me. It was lovely."

"I'm glad you liked it. I wasn't sure how the girl that wears shirts and pants, was going to react to a puffy ball gown."

I look down at the dress I wear today. I can see when I tilt my head, that she has taken note that I am not in my usual attire.

"You look very beautiful in that dress, dear." Hanging my head, I answer, "Thank you."

"Wanting to dress up for your mother?" She asks, her voice rising, as if to poke fun.

"No, I… just wanted to feel more cheery today."

Her face falls into a frown, "Why are you upset? I'm sorry to drag you here. If you need time with your mother, I totally—

"No, no. It's not that. It's just... I haven't been feeling well the past couple of days. I had thought... maybe dressing up would help... lift my spirits."
She doesn't say anything. Nodding her head, she takes another sip of tea. The aroma of chamomile dances through the room.

"I sure hope you feel better."

This time, I don't say anything. I nod, continuing to scribble down our list.

***

About an hour passes, the Queen and I talking about the ball, and also just life in general. I answer questions carefully as to not raise suspicion about my past. She asks questions about my childhood. Luckily for me, Damian has drilled a fake story into my head. The one I always tell people on the rare occasion that they ask. I feel bad lying, but I also don't want to be locked up the second my mother has just been risen from the dead.

"Hello?"

A knock comes at the door, a familiar voice filling the room. Crista pops her head into the study, quickly smiling as she closes the door.

"You asked for me?"

"Yes. Have a seat."

Once she sits down, she faces me. "My mother said she is ready to start teaching you whenever you're ready."

I glance over at the Queen for her request for me to stay or go. Turning towards me, she nods in my direction.

"Don't have me holding you up."

Nervously, I stand pushing in the wooden chair I had sat in for the past couple hours.

Bowing, I tell her, "Thank you for the conversation. I enjoyed your company."

"A thanks comes from me as well. Good luck, Miss Zaria."

Rising, I close the door behind me quietly, a new conversation already blossoming between the two of them. I never knew the Queen was such a chatter box, but not in a bad way. A chatter box in a way that makes time stop, or in our case, speed up. It's relaxing.

Just then I realize, I did not ask her where Mika is. I double back down the hall to ask.

Before I turn the corner, I hear voices. One sounds very angry, the other, a serene melody. Both voices sounding familiar. I can't help but stop and eavesdrop.

"So what?"

"So what? Are you kidding me!? Why does everyone think this as some foolish game?"

"Maybe you're blind?"

I take a risk, peeking around the corner. On the other side of the hallway, Axil and Lucy stand. She stands tall, even a little taller than Axil. She stands, her arms crossed. I recover back behind the wall, pushing myself into it as much as possible.

"Once she comes back a new person, she is not going to want anything to do with you."

"No one can change like that."

"Oh yeah? What about me?"

A silence fills the hall. I hold my breath, shadowing myself into the wall.

"Pull your act together, or you're going to end up crumbling."

"Stop acting like the boss of me, sister. She is bad news, and the fact you can't see that, is exactly the reason you got broken in the first place."

I gasp, quickly covering my mouth. The conversation continues, so I take that as a sign, I was not caught.

"Yes, I was broken. So listen to me when I say, so is she. She did what she did to survive, and I will still treat her with as much kindness, regardless of her past."

Another silence fills the air. I shouldn't be here.
"From what you're telling me, it seems to me she didn't have a choice. Doesn't that sound familiar?"

"She had a choice. She told me she had a choice, and still she chose to do this."

"Did she? Because as far as I can see, the treasury is in balance, and thanks to her idea at the meeting, Malaka has no idea about our extra forces. Give her some credit. Stop acting out of fear."

He had promised. He told me he wouldn't tell anyone.

"I am not acting out of fear." He snarls at Lucy.

"Fine, then go talk to her."

"I am not going to do that."

Again, another sting that jabs me straight in the heart.

"Then, I guess you are not as brave a prince as father says you are."

After that, I hear the steps of Lucy get fainter and fainter. Now I really need to get out of here, and fast. Slipping off my shoes, I run barefoot down the hallway. My mind focuses on getting to Crista's room, thoughts blurring my mind.

Number one, Axil broke his promise. Number two, Lucy is in alliance with me. Number three, Lucy is the dead princess.

Chapter eighteen

Luckily, Mika is in Crista's room. She stands observing all the ingredients that line the shelves. When I burst through the door, her shoulders flinch. "It looks as though you have had a fright."

Still catching my breath she walks over to me placing her hand on my shoulder. "Are you okay, Zaria?"

For a while, it takes me a moment to come back to reality. My head spins like a tornado, unable to process all the information that just keeps being uncovered.

"Maybe now isn't the best time..." she starts.

"No!"

I need a distraction. If I am sent back to my room, the only thing that I will be able to do is stare blankly at the wall. I have made up enough scenarios the past couple of days, I don't need another one.

"Now is a perfect time." Trying to force a smile to my face, I look at Mika.

"Are you sure?" She looks at me puzzled, cupping her hands together.

"Positive. What is the first lesson?"

With wary eyes she takes one last look at me before looking into her spell book. Her frail fingers frill through the pages, looking for the right one. It seems as though Crista's love for jewelry came from her mother. Dainty golden rings wrap around her fingers giving her a fantastical look. Starting from the back, she shifts to the front. Once the page is found, she opens the book to me. It is a leather-bound book, the rustic aroma immediately giving it away. The pages have been yellowed over the years, each page brittle and thin. The script inside is almost impossible to read, I have to squint my eyes to even make out the letters.

"Was this all handwritten?"

A smirk appears on her face. "Indeed. Passed down from generation to generation."

I take another look, getting lost in the faded inky letters. It is truly amazing. Magic seems so tight-knit, like a family. Someone had taken the time to write down every spell they knew, just to pass it down to their children to learn as well.

"Where do we start?"

"We start at the beginning," she says tapping the page to my left.

Too busy flipping through the middle pages, her sentence catches me off guard. "The beginning is so boring though." I start rolling my head back. When my eyes come back up, I am greeted with two stern eyes. Tilting her head, she continues to glare.

I change my attitude, knowing it's time for me to shut up. "On the other hand, starting at the beginning sounds like fun," I quickly flip back to the page she had chosen. "Lesson number one."

Finishing her glare, she finally releases me from her death trap. "Lesson number one," she repeats after me. "Vocalization techniques."

Pointing to the page again, her finger hovers over a drawing of a little girl saying a spell. "Vocalizing your spell makes it a whole lot easier to concentrate. All beginners start out by using their speech."

"What's the difference between just doing the spell in your head?"

"Zaria, your mind can become a dark place, and by the looks of things when you came into the door, your mind is in no place to be reciting spells."

She nods her head at the page, filling a glass of water, setting it on the table. "Well, let's see what you can do."

"You mean..."

"Mmhhm."

"Right now?"

"Isn't that why we are here?"

Inhaling, I fill my lungs, looking at the page. The script has become a little clearer. The first sentence I read in my head. *Liquid pool that fill this glass. Turn the contents into brass.*

"Do I just say it?"

"Just say it."

I hold the book a little closer to my face. "Liquid pool that fill this glass. Turn the contents into brass."

We both stare at the glass of water. As the seconds pass, I grip the cover of the book tight. Mika just stands there, looking at the cup.

"Nothing happened."

She still looks deep into the glass, still waiting for something. Not taking her eyes off of it, she tells me, "Try again."

Sounding stupid, I recite the spell again. All that follows is silence. Not the start of a wind, or a trickle of water. No sparkles are in sight, not even an explosion. I would rather have this water blow up, glass breaking everywhere, than have it stare back at me like a failure.

"How do we even know I am chosen?" I ask impatiently. "I mean, even with Crista's magic inside of me. How can I wield the magic if I am not chosen?"

"You are definitely chosen, Zaria. It's something that all witches can see. It's your scent, your aura. It shines around you like a fireball. I can see the magic in you. It's almost screaming to get out, we just have to find a way to do it."

"And how come I was able to fly? That didn't take as much effort."

"As cool as it seemed, you did more falling then flying. We will figure out a way, don't worry."

"Uggh!" I throw my hands up, flopping onto Crista's bed. "I don't have time to figure it out. I need to do this."

She lowers her voice, following me. "And, why is that?"

I turn my face away from hers. It seems everyone is right. I don't know who I am, and if I don't know who I am, I am nothing. Just like everyone keeps saying.

"Zaria. What did you see before you came in here?"

How? How is she so good? How can everyone see straight through me?

"Stop analyzing me."

She lets out a breath. "For once, I am not. I can tell you are not yourself. You looked as if you had seen a ghost while you came rushing in here." The lightness in her voice changes a pitch higher. "Don't get me wrong, if you did see a ghost, I wouldn't be surprised. But, something tells me, that's not quite it."

Sitting down next to me, I hug my legs to my chest.

"I didn't see anything."

"Okay, so what did you hear?"

I look at her, eyes blaring. "Okay, I might be analyzing you now, but come on. Tell me. These kinds of things affect your magic, and as your teacher, it is my job to get to the bottom of it." And there's that sass that Crista had inherited.

Picking at my nails, I start talking. "Axil knows why John and I came here. It hasn't been the same. He told me he wouldn't tell anyone, and now, he is breaking his promise behind my back. I heard him. I heard him talking about me."

"And… what happened?"

"Well, he was talking to Lucy." I don't mention anything about her being his sister. It seems too private. "She seemed to think he was overreacting."

"So, at least there is one person who agrees with you."

I slam my fist on the bed. "I shouldn't be here, Mrs. Norwood."

"Why not?"

"It's not fair," I say closing the book gently, a little bit of my anger out. "John is in the dungeon. He's down there because of me. I guess that makes me no better than Axil."

"Zaria, he is down there because of his choices. Axil saw that you didn't do anything. John, on the other hand, was in the process of making plans. For him to be down there, they would have had to find something. His actions are not your fault."

"It doesn't matter. It's what everyone wants anyway. Everyone I have ever cared for seems to have some sort of sin against me. Why don't I just make them happy?"

Her eyes drop to the mattress. The tension in the room is pulled as tight as possible. "Do what you think is right. I won't judge you no matter your path. Whatever you decide, we will always support you."

Do what you think is right, she said and my thoughts have now been able to finish that quote, *even if it hurts.*

Who was I kidding? I am no hero. All my life I have been told to do crime. It runs through my blood, making my heart pump. I am no sorcerer. I am a thief. A criminal. And that's all I'll ever be.

Mika told me to take a rest in my room. She said I wouldn't be getting much work done anyway. I can't shake the feeling that I am not where I am supposed to be. I don't know where home is. I thought having my mother back would be everything I dreamed, and more. But, it seems as though everything has gotten worse. There is only one person to talk to, and I am not looking forward to it.

***

"Ah, Miss Zaria. Have you come to turn in your paperwork?"
Bowing my head, I feel the weight of what I am about to do. "Uh... no Your Highness. I have something else to turn in."

He looks up from his desk. I relish in that kind face. The face that he has always shown me. The kind smile I wish my own father would have given me. I take it in for one last moment, knowing that my life is about to change.

"What else do you have to turn in?"

Here we go, "Myself."

The papers he was holding drop to his desk. Just as I have suspected, the kind smile vanishes, never to be seen again. Instead, what I see now is the powerful King I should have always feared, and it becomes a toss-up of who is scarier. My father, John, Axil, or the King.

"You wouldn't have anything to do with the crime that John was put in for?"

Hanging my head, I accept my defeat. "Yes, Your Highness. I have come to turn myself in for intent to steal on palace grounds. I welcome my punishment with a stable knowledge of what is to come."

***

Never before have I heard so much yelling. My ears ring loudly, I only recall the King calling for his guards. Tight fists wrapping around me, around my arms, my legs. There is no way to escape now, no way to disappear. Restrained, I look up. The anger in his eyes left as quickly as it came. Now what is expressed on his face shows something of disappointment and sorrow. Seeing his hurt face stings more than someone being angry. When someone is angry, I can feel angry back at them. But when someone is disappointed, I can't help but feel guilty and small.

The guards that aren't strangling me, are wrapped around the King like a force field, their bodies acting as his shield. I shift my gaze all around me. Five guards surround me, which means ten hands at most. I stop myself mid-thought. No. I am not escaping.

Axil needed to learn how to fight. That's easy. Get mad at something, then take it out on your opponent. Resisting the urge to fight though, is a whole other ball game. Giving up all control, leaving everything in the hands of your enemy, is something I was never trained for.

I don't have to stand still for much longer. I am lead down a flight of stairs, one after the other. I wouldn't be surprised if all these stairs lead to the burning fires of Hell. Might as well prepare, it seems to be the only path my life will bring.

My feet give out on me, looking down to see at least three more flights of stairs. I am not allowed to fall, one of the guards pushing me back up yells in my face.

"Stay in line, you little rat."

Restrain, restrain. It's for the best. Once I regain my balance, the grip on me becomes tighter. The further down we walk, the darker it gets. The only light I can see are little bulbs above cells. I guess this is the bottom. The hall is made of pure stone, iron bars as welcome gates for the criminals. At least now I know where home will be for a while. Doesn't look like I'm leaving anytime soon.

"Looky here. You and your partner in crime are next door neighbors." They laugh in unison, mocking our situation.

John looks up as we pass. If they wouldn't have mentioned it was John, I wouldn't have guessed it was him. He doesn't look like the brother I had named him to be. Instead, he looks like his face could be on a wanted poster. His sneer when he sees me, shakes my bones.

The guards shove me in my cell. Oddly enough, I'm glad there is a wall that separates us. *You are nothing more than a manipulator.* Axil's words run through my head as they lock the door to my cell.

Then, I am alone. Alone in the most filled hall I've ever seen. When do people come down here? And do they ever come back up? From the smell, I can guess that even though we are in a royal dungeon, we get treated the same as every other criminal. Little water privileges. No bathroom privacy. Nothing to do but complain about the heat, and stink.

This is everything my father had warned me not to do. Everything I have done is going against what I have been taught. Never walk into the hands of the enemy. Never fess up to any crime, even if the odds are against you. Don't get caught, because if you get caught, you will be wishing you were dead. Never, never, never. I hate it. I hate rules. I hate this dungeon. I hate the fact that I will never see my mother. I hate John. I hate Axil. I hate Damian. I hate myself, because no one is to blame, but me.

Hugging my knees close to my chest, I regret not changing out of this dress before I came down here, the dainty white fabric being stained a mucky brown.

I have grown up in a house full of men, but that does not make the smell any less rancid. I tuck my head further into my legs, inhaling the residue of soap on my skin, instead of the death gas.

***

"If only daddy could see you now."

John has been taunting me ever since my stay. I know he is just trying to scare me. Make me feel small. Although, there is not anything better to do, so I decide to play his game.

"Damian would scream if he saw me in here."

"All his training, and for what? Look where it got you?"

Lifting my head, I continue, "I could say the same about you. And if he were to look for me, he would look underground."

"If he found you here, you would be dead."

A smirk forms on my face, "Considering the bullet he put in my chest, I think he already considers me dead."

A silence fills the halls. I can feel all the curious ears that are listening in. Let them. I've got a story to tell.

I wish I could see his face. To have the stone wall between us crumble for just a second.

"You're a liar."

"Am I?"

"Damian wouldn't shoot anyone unless he knew he would walk away with their stagnant heart."
Now I am in the story, ready to let him in on a little secret. "Oh, he sure did leave me dead. If it weren't for some magic, I would have been invited to the underground party."

I can feel him rolling his eyes through the wall. He's not buying any of it. Also part of the plan.
"Well thanks for ratting me out. If it weren't for you, we would be rich."

"We?" I correct. "From the last time we talked, it seems I would have died either way, and I didn't rat you out, you did that yourself. What was it that gave you away?" I take a moment to let him simmer in rage. "Was it your snooping, your pathetic little lies, oooh or was it the fact you couldn't keep your damn mouth shut?"

He struggles against his chains on the other side of the wall. "I should have killed you then. It's your fault we are both down here."

"And here we will stay. What a lovely time, old friend."

He scoffs. "You are no friend of mine."

Nodding my head, I press a little harder, "I sensed that at the ball. Although, I can't seem to tell where we fell apart."

No response comes. I have played my cards right. As long as I am going to be stuck down here, I will make it a living hell for John. It's payback time.

There is no way to tell time down here. There are no clocks, and the sun doesn't shine underground. The only way I can feel it is nighttime, is by my exhaustion. But with the way I have been carrying on, tiredness doesn't even mean the moon is in the sky, it just means my body is giving up, and I can't give up. Not yet.

My eyelids feel heavier than they ever had before. I decide to close my eyes just for a second. As I do, all my muscles seize. I would like to think myself strong and tough, but I have been holding myself so tense. Even behind bars, I don't feel safe.

I can wear a pretty strong mask during the day, but at the end, it starts to disappear. All the comments start to file into my head. Comments that I couldn't even process during the day.

My mind shuts off. Why did I do this? Even if it was the right thing to do, it solves nothing. John still wants me dead. Axil is still probably furious. I have abandoned my mother, leaving her alone in a world I brought her back to. I have betrayed Crista's friendship, and I have betrayed my promise. I guess I could still try to learn magic down here, but what would be the point? No one wants a criminal to be running the magic system of the palace.

I had seen the King's face. I had let him down. I let him down doing the right thing. The more I think about it, the more the right thing, seems to suck.

***

Gunshots ring though my ears. It's happening. It's happening again. I cover my face, bracing for impact.

"Wake up, you lazy slugs!"

My eyes fly open. The shots have come closer to me. It's only then, I realize that the noise isn't gunshots.

The guards are walking the halls, shaking everyone's cell doors. "Up! Up! Up!"

"Oh come on! Ten years, and you still won't let me sleep!?"A man started shouting at one of the guards. He was an old guy, rough looking. His crime must have been bad. Ten years is a long time to be locked up.

"You want to sleep in? Maybe you should have thought about that before you kidnapped the princess."

They stare at each other for a while. A stare I have never seen before. His eyes look at the man, wishing him dead. The guy does not budge, though. This must be a regular argument that happens over the years.

The princess? Is this the man that kidnapped Lucy?

A guard comes to my cell. Backing away into the corner, I keep eye contact on the man. He holds his hands up, an innocent expression on his face. He looks younger. Must not be as tough as the older guys, and for once, I am thankful.

He slips a copper cup into my cell through the bars. The cup is bent on all sides, surrounding the brim. I can tell it has been through lots of prison doors. The thought makes my stomach twist. What all happens down here?

He sets it down on the floor of my cell, reaching inside his cloak. Pulling out a canteen, he pours it into the cup, filling it half way.

"Drink."

That is all he says. I don't move from my corner. From what Damian has told me, prison guards try to poison the prisoners to make their job a little easier. He looks around, his hands twitching impatiently. The guards continue to make a racket through the halls. It is all for show. Everyone was awake from when the first door got shook. It's their way of torturing us without consequence.

"Hurry. You need to drink."

Kneeling on the floor again, he nudges it closer. I don't know how I ended up near the cup. My mind kept retaliating, but my legs pushed me over to the door. My hands shake as I pick up the cup, gulping down the water, I notice how dry my throat was. Sleeping on the dirt floor made my lungs and throat a raspy mess.

The water quenches my thirst, pouring down my esophagus like a waterfall. When I am done, I slowly put the cup back on the floor.

"Hey! No stealing. You should know water is only served in the afternoon."

The same guy that offered me the drink is now yelling at me, snatching the copper cup out of my hands. His face does not change though. He still looks innocent as he yells.

"Is that girl givin' ya trouble, mate?" Another guard comes standing beside him.

"Nothing I can't handle, boss."

Looking back at me, he winks. Then, he is gone.

The day passes just like yesterday did. There is some chatter, but there is mostly silence. Comically, there is another bucket under a leak in the roof. Time is spent just hearing the water drip into the bucket.

I wish to drift off to sleep, but I don't know what will greet me if I do. Will another guard come slamming into my door, like the other guy? It surprises me how many criminals the King has right under his palace. If we all decided to plan a heist, his kingdom could be in our hands faster than the snowfall outside.

I hope Crista is enjoying the snow. I overheard the guards talking about it when they came down here, complaining about how cold it was going to be. I can picture her sledding, or ice skating on the pond. She deserves to be a normal girl. To enjoy the seasons with her family instead of being cooped up all day perfecting her magic.

John doesn't say another word. I would be lucky if he was dead, although I wouldn't have anyone to pick on if he was. I'm sure I could find someone. All I can see out my bars is a solid wall. I venture my way to the edge of my cell, holding onto the bars. Spending all my hours in the corner is suffocating.

Once I am at the threshold, I look around. From where I am, I can only see one cell across from me. It is an older man. Not as old looking as the other guy that started the argument, but he looks like he has been down here a while as well.

He catches my glance, getting up from an upside down bucket he had been using for a chair. That's the kind of thing the guards see as a reward. If you behave, you get a bucket. Do with it as you wish. He advances towards his bars, locking eyes with me.

If I were to ever see a pirate, this is exactly what I imagine they would look like. "What are you lookin' at, kid?"

His teeth have yellowed over time, some falling out. His beard is a mess, making him look like some sort of caveman.

"I'm just meeting my next door neighbors," I say, my mask back on again.

"Nice to meet ya. Now do me a favor, and leave me the alone."

I place my hands on the bars. "No can do, sir. This place seems a little boring. I'm looking to spruce it up."

"You have completely lost your mind."

Nodding my head, I answer, "Oh, I have. That happened a long time ago."

His voice a little raspy, he points at me, "Well, you can say goodbye to your games. They don't put up with people like you here."

"I guess I'll see for myself," I say winking. I walk back toward the corner of my cell, curling up again. How long can I keep this up?

I drift off. Not to sleep, but a depressed coma. My time is spent mostly staring at nothing. My mind draws a blank but also can't seem to shut up. Thoughts swirl around my head in a tornado, making me queasy.

Lunchtime rolls around. The only way I can tell is because water is being poured, just like it was for me this morning. When the guards make it to my cell, they fill the canteen. Instead of giving it to me in a cup, the water is thrown on me. Water drips down my clothes, the air a lot chillier than it was before.

Laughing at me, a guard points in my direction. "*That* was for this morning."

I remember the guy that gave me the water. It seemed like just a minute ago, but also an eternity. All I can do is stand. Other guards gather around, pointing and laughing. Even now, I have done nothing wrong, and yet I am paying the price.

One of the guards leans into my door. "Next time, I would watch your behavior. Nothing gets by us." Gaggling on, they finish doing their rounds. It doesn't take them much more time, being at the far side of the hall.

I sit back down, balling up my skirt. Sure, it has been collecting sweat and rolling in the dirt, but it is my only source of water. I put the skirt into my mouth, sucking out all the moisture I can. Even with the half cup I got this morning, I am very dehydrated. It is a million degrees down here regardless of the season outside.

Damian used to tell me that heat made people go insane. They would usually crank up the heat before a hearing or as a lesson from the guards. Made them stationary, exhausted. Too hot to do anything. If anything, the guard might have done me a favor cooling me down. The effects of the water only last a little while though.

I drift back into my slump. Do people spend years like this? Maybe John was right. Maybe I am weak. But if I am weak, that makes him weaker than me. That's the reason Damian put me in charge. It wasn't just about his name. It was about getting the job done, and getting the job done was something I could do, I guess until now.

"Zaria!"

I must be delirious. The lack of hydration finally getting to my head.

"Zaria!"

I have longed to hear his voice, but I knew he wouldn't come. Not for me. Not after everything.

"Zaria!"

The footsteps have grown louder, quicker. The voice keeps calling my name. The angelic voice I have obsessed over. I look up, to see it all stop. The yelling, the footsteps, all of it. Because there he stands in front of my cell. The Royal Prince of Lumbridge looking upon his criminal.

Chapter nineteen

"What are you doing down here?"

I stand from the slouching position I have adopted, my muscles retaliating against any movement. "What do you think?"

"How... I didn't..."

I correct him. "You did. But I am not in here because of your mouth. I am in here because of mine. I turned myself in."

He looks at me with distress, his ocean blue eyes turning into storms. "Why?" Now his voice is pleading. A plead to know what I have done and why.

"Why? Do you not remember your own words?" I shoot back. "I am just a manipulator. A liar. I will be nothing but a criminal."

He puts his hands against my bars. "You can't be serious."

"I am very serious. And if you are going to be King one day, I would suggest keeping better memory of what comes out of your mouth."

His lips are in a thin line listening to me. Letting out a sigh he starts.

"I wanted to talk to you." He tries to stay calm, but his nerves take over. "Then I am told that you are down here in the dungeon. What were you thinking?"

I step towards the door, now right in front of him. "It is too late to talk. As for what I was thinking, I decided to make things right. A criminal I am, so a criminal's price I shall pay."

He doesn't say anything. All he does is just stare into my eyes. His grip loosens on the bars, his shoulders falling from their harsh square. "I'm sorry…" he trails off.

Feeding his words back at him, I spit. "I don't need your apology. You got what you wanted right? Why should you be sorry?"

He throws his hands up, "*This* is not what I wanted."

I look at him blankly. "And what exactly did you want?"

Again, he does not answer. His breath hitches as he inhales, water coming to his eyes. He examines me, my wet hair and clothes from the splash just a few moments before he came down. He looks under my eyes. Dark circles must be there. Hollow and empty like they were when I first got here.

Seeing him in front of me, separated by bars, makes the reality of the situation quite clear. I will always be a prisoner. A criminal who deserves pain. And he will always be a prince. Despite his flaws, he will carry a crown on his head, with smiling faces adoring him.

He stammers off as he had last time. But this time is a bit different. I can hear soft murmurs as he walks down the hall.

Sniffles echoing off the stone. I try to convince myself that the air pressure has just made him develop a sniffle, but as I look to the ground there are drops of liquid that paint the dry dirt that covers the ground. Once again, the right thing feels like a stab in the chest.

***

I hope my mother is happy. She will be with her best friend and Crista. I pray that they can take care of her. When Axil came down, he said that he was told I was down here. Did he need to ask, or does everyone know? It's not like life can get that much more embarrassing.

***

What I've learned, is that it gets pretty boring, really fast. That's the whole point of prison. For one to reflect on the crimes they have done. Do they really expect us to do that, though? I for sure am not thinking of all the crimes I have committed, but instead thinking about all the things that I didn't do. I don't know how long I will be down here. Years? Decades? If I even get out at all, it might be too late.

It is an eternity until dinner is served, if I could even call it dinner. All our rations are crusts of bread. The chunk I get is about the size of my palm. Again, this is on purpose. A way for them to torture us, with no consequence. After all, their job is to keep us alive to serve our time. Other than that, they can do whatever they want.

I nibble on my crust slowly, trying to savor every moment. If I can drag out this crust over several hours, I might not be as weak.

***

There is a certain head space behind bars that I never prepared for. The feeling of every emotion, every thought entering your head, but feeling helpless. I can't do anything about the things I am concerned about, so I might as well just stop, but it doesn't matter how many times I tell myself to stop… my mind just keeps babbling.

It also doesn't help that despite our previous conversation, John has not said a word. I don't know whether to feel relief or be afraid, but what should I be afraid of? Like the guards said, nothing gets past them.

"I have a letter for a Zaria."

The same guard that gave me water that one morning calls out down the hall. Walking over to the door, I hold out my arm. "That's me."

My body is slow, it feels like a ton to hold myself up. I would try to exercise. Remember some of my training from Damian, but I can't seem to find the energy. Also, if I did, I would burn off all the calories of the bread and have nothing in my stomach.

When he walks down the length of the hall, he hands me the letter. It is in a crisp white envelope, sealed with a wax stamp. The guard waits for a while, staring at the letter. He doesn't move, he just waits.

"You can go now," I stammer, my voice irritated.

"I am supposed to return a response." Leaning against the wall, he stretches his arms. "Take your time."

Every movement that comes out of this guy, makes my body twitch. I feel as though I am already going insane. Is insanity in just a couple of days possible? If it is, John would be right. I would be a weak little thing that couldn't handle the pressure of prison.

Breaking my glare from the guard, I rip open the envelope. Inside I find a neat handwriting that I do not recognize. The letters swirl around each other, mocking the way I write. It is formally addressed to me, reading Miss Zaria. It can't be my mother or friends.

Outside my cell, the guard has started to tap his toes on the dirt floor. The action brings dust to my lungs. The particles burning my throat like a roaring fire. Holding back a coughing fit, I focus on the letter.

Dear Miss Zaria,
It has come to my attention that you have turned yourself in for a crime that was not committed. I have heard about your past, this so-called mission if that's what you would like to call it. If you're up for it, I have a mission for you as well. Learning the magic system of this palace is quite a tall order for someone who doesn't know how, but if you can prove that you can master your powers, then I might be able to strike up a deal.
Master your abilities. Show that you can provide for yourself. Speed and agility is what I am looking for. If that is accomplished, you are free to go.
So, what do you say? Will you accept my mission?
From, the secret server

I read over the letter. Over and over. It doesn't make sense. Master my powers, to get out of jail free? Why? There has to be something more to this. Something they are not telling me.

"Is this all?"

"Yup. If there was more, it would be included in the letter."

I fold the paper back up, pointing it at him. "Who sent this?"

He puts his hands behind his back, rocking back and forth on his feet. "That is confidential information Miss."

"So, I am supposed to answer to someone I don't even know?"

He rolls his eyes up, "Uh… yeah."

I slip the letter back into the envelope. Handing it through the bars.

"Tell them I am in here for a reason. For doing sketchy missions in the first place. I put myself in here. Now, leave me the alone."

Slowly, he takes the letter back. I have a feeling he knows exactly what was in the letter. Giving me a second to reconsider, he stands in front of my cell a bit longer. I stride back to the corner of my cell, but he still stands.

"Do you need an invitation to leave?" This time my voice being more angry than irritated.

Just like everyone else, he walks away. It's funny how people do that. They are there until they aren't. And somehow, I have no idea how to escape the escapees.

Nighttime falls upon the prison. The only nice thing they do is dim the lighting of the bulbs. Our bodies follow the rhythm of the sun. Without sun, there is no rhythm, and with no rhythm, there are exhausted prisoners incapable of doing anything.

Before I drift off to sleep, I do my nightly routine of staring at the wall separating John and I. I can't even tell if he is on the other side. I decide to give it a try.

"Hey John."

No answer. "John?"

"What do you want Zaria?" he answers flatly. The only thing I heard him say in days.

"How are you holding up?"

He scoffs, "Better than you, that's for sure."

The second the words leave his mouth, I wish I never said anything in the first place.

"You seem to be quite popular," says John.

"Ah, they'll get over it." Our voices have now gone to a whisper.

"It was nice for your little boyfriend to visit you. How romantic."

I am quick to answer, "He is not my boyfriend." "Mmhhm."

I roll my eyes. My vision starts to go blurry. Fighting to stay awake, I shake my head.

As I shake my head, little dots appear in the air. I close my eyes even more, squinting them shut. The harder I squeeze, the more my eyes want to open. Through squinted eyes, I peek them open.

The tiny dots are not just dots, but sparkles. My eyes relax as I examine the fall of sparkles. They come down in little flurries, all colors raining down. They start to spin together. Faster and faster into a ball. I brace myself again, waiting for what might happen.

The ball bursts open, another letter floating in the air. Fingers shaking, I take the envelope.

It reads,

*You do not know who I am, but know I am trying to help.
I have now shown you I have magical abilities as well.
Take this as a peace offering. This mission is not just
about you getting out of jail, but being prepared. I cannot
tell you for what, but I need your help. You can trust me.
Can I trust you?*

I hold the letter in my hands. As I do, a pen appears midair where the letter came from. Be prepared for what? I have fallen into the trap of misdirection before. I do not feel like tiptoeing again, but I also don't want to be stuck down here in this hole.

I examine the handwriting again. It has to be someone I know, though. I just have to figure out who.

***

I barely get any sleep throughout the night. Mostly from my thoughts keeping me up. John snoring next door doesn't help, though. That guy could drown a city with his snoring.

My mind races. Do I accept? I wish I knew how urgent the matter was. What do I need to be prepared for? I could just stay down here. Keep out of trouble. I will get out eventually… I hope. The letter is from someone in the palace. Someone that needs my help. Correction. Someone who needs my magic. But that still raises the question. Why?

The only person I ever helped was Crista, and this is definitely not her handwriting. One of the days during her training, we were taking a break; she had decided to prank the royal chef. On a piece of paper, she wrote a note asking for two chocolate cakes. Once the cakes were delivered, she pretended as if she didn't write the letter. Asking the chef to return with the letter, he walked away.

Crista had made the letter disappear. She liked training like that. Making it as fun as possible. Raising her spirits always seemed to help with her magic.

Maybe I should give that a go. There is plenty of space to practice magic. Mind spells anyway. And, I might know a few candidates for some pranks.

I was already awake by the time the guards came in for their *gentle* morning call. The same routine as every day. Banging on every door, angry prisoners yelling at the guards. They might as well give up. The guards actually find the arguments quite amusing.

Ready, I stand at my cell. I hide the letter and pen behind my back as I cross my arms.

Just on schedule, the same guy comes to my cell. His face is shocked to see me up and ready.

"Restful sleep?"

"Oh, I wish." I take a step toward him, bringing the letter and pen between us. "Tell the secret server I accept." I make sure to keep my voice at a low monotone. The last thing I need is John to bribe me to get him out as well.

"Pleasure doing business with you." He copies my volume. He extends his arm for the letter. Pulling back the letter, he grasps the air.

"I have a condition."

Rolling his eyes, he takes a step back. "Continue."

"For me to complete this mission, I am going to need to be in good health. And, as you could tell from my stay, I am pretty dehydrated. I am also starving. Give me a good supply of food and water, and you have yourself a deal."

Crossing his arms in front of me, he shrugs his shoulders. "Well Miss, I am not the one to make that call."

"Don't worry." I form my lips into a pout. "I wrote it all down." I shove the letter and pen into his hands. "I expect my answer by this afternoon." Taking the letter, he moves on. Once he gets out of the prison, I know he is going to read what I wrote before he delivers it, so I gave him a little surprise.

Hello secret server, and Guard guy,
I have accepted your mission on the account that I will be provided for while I train. I'm guessing you can relate to how much mindset is a part of magic. If I cannot have a good meal in me, I will not be able to work. Let me know my deadline, and what magic I need to master. You don't trust me, and I don't trust you. Let this be a sign that I do want to make things right. I hope you will at some point make an appearance to check up on my progress. As for the guard guy, I will see you later today.
Have a better day than me,
Zaria

If I am agreeing to this, it is going to be on my terms. I am tired of not being in control. When I stopped having it, everything fell apart. Including my mother's life. I hope she is okay. No doubt, she is disappointed in me. I hope she knows she is part of the reason I decided to do what was right. I want to be a better person for her. As long as I can make her happy, I'm happy.

My answer arrived that afternoon. The same guard came to my chambers, concealing a platter of fresh water and bread with berries making it as discreet as possible.

"For a prisoner, you sure do act like a princess," he whispers.

"When there is work to be done, I make sure it's done right."

I look down at the platter, my mouth watering looking at the delectable food. It's not much, but it is better than having to drink water from my soaking clothes.

"By the way, do you mind bringing me some clothes from my bedroom?"

Opening my door, he fumbles with the keys, the platter wobbling in his hands.

"There still has to be rules, Zaria. You can't just ask for anything you want."

Accepting the platter I respond, "Oh thank you. I would also like my moisturizer. My legs are getting very dry from this dirt."

He holds the food tightly in his grasp, looking at me blankly. Pouting my lips, I look back, my grip also tightening. We stand there both holding the platter, looking as if we are about to duel, which is more possible than I had expected.

Sighing, he rolls his eyes. "New clothes, nothing more."

In his response, I force my lips into a smile. I pull the tray towards me, careful not to spill the water that is filled to the brim. I slurp some of the water, not wanting to lose a drop of it. It tastes like water has never tasted before. I might have died and gone to Heaven. That is exactly what this tastes like.

The guard briskly leaves my cell, swinging the door shut behind him. He pulls out his keys again. Locking the door, he tugs on it, checking that it is indeed locked. Even if he had left it open, I probably wouldn't risk going back on palace grounds. Not without a way to escape.

He starts walking away. Stopping him I ask, "What is your name?" in a not so quiet voice.

Retracing his steps he smirks, the left side of his face turning up. "From your letter it seems that my name is Guard guy. You can stick with that."

With a flick of his finger, he starts towards the other end of the hall. Now that he leaves, I admire the food on the table. Never had I wanted bread before, but now looking at the puffy inside, a smile comes to my face.

A jingling noise sounds from outside. There is a scrape, then nothing. I don't dare look to see what had just happened. I will eat my food, then get to work. All I know, is that the prison just got very quiet.

Chapter twenty

Butter still coats my mouth as I try to work, leaving me wanting more. Tonight I should be getting more food, and it's the only reason I'm putting in much of an effort.

I try to concentrate, focusing as much as I can. But, there is not much to focus on. My eyes keep adverting to all the specks of dirt that cover the stone walls. It is so dirty, but I guess nothing in here is very clean. The dress I still wear has become somewhat of a rag more than a garment. I can't even see the floral design on it anymore.

Each speck is like a sin. A sin I have committed and have had to live with. I close my eyes. I wish I could have a fresh start. No gang. No jobs. No training. No palace. Just life. The life of a girl who braids her friend's hair. The life of having a picnic in the meadow, making flower crowns with my mother. The life of a girl who went to school and sat doing homework. It all seems like a distant dream. A star, hiding in the clouds that cannot be wished upon. Everything. Every little thing, has now come back to bite me. I feel no love. No comfort. There is only the thoughts in my head.

They swirl around, taking over me. Any sentence I had said. Any action I had done. It all replays in my mind.

I squint my eyes ever harder, a slight cry escaping me. Then, there is nothing.

I awake to shouting echoes down the halls. Two prisoners are fighting back and forth about who is stronger. A stupid thing to argue about. If you wanted to prove it, break us out of here. Then I will believe that they are strong.

My eyes sting as I open them, my head still turning. Feeling like a ton, I slowly lift my head. The sight is the same, but as I squint I can see the definition in the stones. No dust sits upon it. No spider webs collecting in the corners. All that remains is a slight shimmer that hangs in the air. I reach out to touch one of them, the light sparkling before it disappears. I had done it.

***

Dinner had rolled around. The same old routine going about. Guard guy had brought me clothes, but not the clothes I wanted. He had brought down the first outfit I had worn when Axil gave me clothes. The only thing he had changed was the fact that the pants were black. It would be a little silly to sit on the dirt with white pants. From the dress that hangs over me, we both know that is a bad idea.

I had been fed again. He tried to come down the hall as discreetly as possible, trying to not draw attention to the fact that I was actually eating meals. None of the other guards would be okay with that. He comes either a few minutes early or a few minutes later, but he always comes, and no one dare say a word about it.

He had brought me what seemed to be the scraps of meat left from dinner in the dining hall. The smell of alcohol lingering on the dish. Next to the meat was some green beans, and another hunk of bread. I had savored the food as much as I could, my hunger disappearing as I slowly eat it.

I had been in a zone, until the plate was empty, reality hitting again. I had promised myself a routine. Eat, then practice until I get something right.

***

It has been a week of the same routine. I must say, I surprised myself a bit. I kept my cell clean, focusing on the little specks being washed away with the waters from a stream. I had learned that I was a very visual witch. For my spells to work, I had to envision what I wanted to happen, and they would.

I had pranked the guy that was down here for kidnapping Lucy. He was also the one that was arguing when I woke up, so I say he deserved it.

I had put a curse on him, for his limbs to be paralyzed when the prison guards came. A reasonable curse for a kidnapper. Let him know what it feels like to be helpless. The guard had come to give him water, but obviously, he couldn't accept. Eventually the guard had gotten mad and thrown the water on him as he once did to me.

Guard guy had given me a wry smile as he realized that it was me. He kept his end of the deal, delivering me food, and clothes when needed.

I had not heard from John at all. He has stayed pretty quiet, even though we are right next to each other.

Through this week, I had learned to levitate objects, make my hands invisible, and every now and then, I got permission to teleport to my room and back. For that to happen, I had to give up one of my meals. It was their way of making sure I came back. Their reasoning was flawed though. I could always teleport to a restaurant and get all the niceties I wanted while gone. But, I had stayed. I had to constantly remind myself that this was for the better. I just had to trust that the secret server wasn't playing with my head.

I would get a letter from her every now and then. They would check in on my progress, congratulating me, when I had learned something new. I was quite a fast learner. Always have been. They had made sure to send a grand meal at the end of the week when I had mastered six new skills.

Levitation

Invisibility

Teleportation

Telekinesis

Materialization

And... well, flight was still a problem. Mika had been right. The day we had left the cabin, I had done more falling than flying, and every day, I am feeling the pain from it. I had made it about two inches off the ground, before I would start to panic, falling back onto the floor.

I have started a collection of bruises that cover my body. It was another practice to make them disappear, so I counted it as part of my training.

I have stayed pretty healthy, but my mind constantly wondered what I was doing it for. Why am I blindly following some magical letter that was sent from the *secret server*? I don't even know who they are, or what they have planned. I could be starting from square one. But just like the mountain, I have to take the jump.

***

"Good morning Zaria."

"Always nice to see you Guard guy."

Opening my door has become quite a habit for him. He has stopped being so cautious while coming in, and going out.

"Am I ever going to know your real name?"

Setting my morning tray on the floor, he responds, "Maybe when you get out. For now, I would focus on your training."

He doesn't even bother to be quiet anymore. Everyone in the prison knows that something is going on, but none have said a word.

I look down at the tray. It is filled with the usual bread and berries. This time it has a cinnamon dusting on top. It is a little suspicious how much food I get. Also considering the quality. This is fresh out of the kitchen, the memory of when Axil and I went in there, flooding into my mind.

"Hey." He stops to turn around and listen. "This whole mission… is it for a good cause?"

"What makes you think it is for a bad cause?" he counters.

I do not hesitate. "I have been shown no evidence of this secret server. The whole reason I am in here is because of past missions. I want to make sure that I am actually doing this for a good reason, and not for some selfish personal gain."

He takes a moment collecting his thought. "I know the secret server very well. She has not said anything about the mission to me, besides serving you. I can say without a doubt, there is no ill intent behind her request."

With a slight nod, I watch as he leaves. Pulling out his keys, I notice a cool silver gleam instead of the regular copper shine.

"Are those new keys?" I ask pointing down at the new set.

Following my gaze he concurs, "Yeah. I apparently misplaced my old ones. They were getting rusty anyway. It was a good excuse to get new ones. I'm surprised you didn't notice sooner. I've had them for a couple of days."

I had not been looking. I had been so set on waiting for my food, I never paid much mind to the smaller details.

He leaves me in the quiet cell. Almost a little too quiet. I nibble on the berries, the juices exploding in my mouth.

He did reveal one thing. It is a female. Secret server is a woman in the palace. Now it's just the question of who in this castle would give me a second chance.

It would have to be someone who knows me and my past. Someone who knows I have magic. Then it hits me. My mother. Gathered around the fire, she had promised that she would keep me safe. Why did it not click sooner? Of course the guard would know her too. Apparently everyone in the castle knew who my mother was. My heart goes numb. If this is the case, I really need to know what is going on. I had also made a promise. I might not have told her, but I promised that I would keep her safe too.

Every hour today, I had spent training. Focusing in on the little bits that would fall apart. I practiced flying again. I had turned my two inches into two feet by the time dinner rolled around, but each time, I still fell.

When I hear the footsteps, I am at the door right away. Guard guy comes. My dish having a lid on top, so no one can see in. He whistles, his steps having a bounce in them. The second he makes it to my door, I grab his shirt through the gate.

"Figure it out! I need to know. What is going on? What will happen?"

His face squishes up against the bars, wincing in pain. My food had been dropped to the floor, spilling out onto the dirt.

He makes an effort to keep his voice low, mine still echoing down the halls. I don't care. I don't care who hears, or who wants to pick a fight after the guards leave. I need to know. I need to know that my mother is safe.

"I already told you before. I don't know anything."

My voice is very firm now, my grip on his shirt tightening. "Well you better find something. I don't care what it takes. Tell me what I am preparing for."

"Hey!"

The guards that usually lined the exit caught onto my scene. Racing towards me, he rips Guard guy out from my fists.

"You little rat. Bribing guards to get you food. No food for two days."

He scolds me through the bars. I never leave eye contact from Guard guy. Regardless of the consequences, I will get my answer.

"Hey you... would you like some fresh food? You've been pretty quiet all week."

He looks towards John's cell, offering grapes he had picked up from the ground.

"Would love some, sir."

I go back to the corner of my cell. Everything is taken from me. No food. No water. A guard comes in, his arms the size of half the door. His face is very stern, his eyes ready to kill. Grasping my arms, he easily shackles me to my chains again. Getting out of them had been from good behavior, but once I act up, back in the chains I go.

The metal cuts into my arms and legs, biting my skin. I internally cry. I would never let these evil prison guards see me shed a tear.

Kicking me on the floor, my face hits the dirt. Once again, I am alone, in pain, huddled on the floor. Maybe this is my destiny. A fate that I cannot escape. And, there is no escape once my eyes close, and I fall into a deep sleep.

***

"Zaria!"

My head is pounding, thunder rolling in my head. Shouts of my name ring in my ear. I have worried nonstop about what was to happen. My eyes fling open, but I cannot see. I try again, but my eyelids won't budge. I can't move a muscle.

"Zaria! Come on."

Her voice swirls the clouds in my head. A voice I recognize, but do not entirely know.

"I'll be back. I'm going to get help."

I fall into a slumber again, but my mind remains restless. I have to… have to get up. I try to lift my hand. If I can support my weight, maybe I can lift myself up the rest of the way. My breath starts to quicken as I realize I am completely paralyzed.

I have to. I have to. The voices in my head won't stop. The voices of John and Axil. My father chiming in at times. I am weak. Worthless. Not enough. I lie. I manipulate. *Weak. Weak. Weak.*

I don't know how much time has passed, if any passed at all. I can faintly hear voices, voices coming towards me.

"Zaria, darling."

Mom? What is she doing down here?

"I'm going to help you up. We're going to get you out."

Get me out? What is happening?

All of a sudden a shock of electricity courses through my lifeless body. Tingles run down my skin, air rushing into my lungs. Is this what it felt like to come back from the dead? I see the boat again. The one I saw when I got shot. This time I have to row the boat, all the strength in my arms leaving me.

Taking a deep breath, my eyes finally fly open. The world around me is hazy, pictures blurring together. Two figures hover above me. A pain in my back registers when I sit up. The pain clears my sight.

My mother and Lucy kneel over me. I muster up all my strength. "What is happening?"

Lucy turns to my mother, "You better leave now. Go to Zaria's room and lock the door."

I see her look at me, hesitation in her eyes. Lucy continues, "She will be fine. This is her duty. Let her make things right."

Her eyes are still locked on mine. I try to communicate, tell her to be safe, and to not worry. A whisper is all that comes. "Go."

My mother squeezes me tight, my body crying out in pain. She notices my wince and quickly releases me.

"Be safe, my little witch."

She stands, towering over me. Lifting my head to meet her feels like bench pressing two hundred pounds. I watch her as she walks away. Looking at the ground, it seems as though I am mistaken. She is not walking, but floating. No tracks being left in the dirt.

Lucy grabs my attention now. Placing her hands on my shoulders, she helps bear my weight. "I need your help. Those letters you received were from me. There is going to be a disaster tonight."

My heart speeds even faster than before, unable to catch any breath. "How… how long have I been asleep?"

"You've been unconscious since last night after dinner. We need to get out of here. There is not much time."

I grip onto her arms, more or less, my feeling still coming back. "What is happening?"

"John has broken out of his cell. He took all the prisoners with him. They are planning on attacking tonight."

I scurry to get up, still crying in pain. "What is tonight?"

Placing her hand around my torso, she helps me stand. "The ball celebrating your mother's return."
I hang my head. That is why John has been so quiet. I should've known. All this time he had been scheming a plan.

"What is he planning on doing? How do you even know that he is planning to attack?"
She pulls me out of the cell, dragging me down the hallway. "Seeing the future is my magical ability. I had help from your mother to send the letters down here to you. I am not chosen like you, but I know that John is going to be holding someone hostage."

"Who?"

"Axil, my…"

"Brother."
She gasps, looking my way. "How did you know that?"

"I wasn't that far away when you guys were talking in the hallway." A blush goes to her cheeks. "Don't worry. I won't tell anyone."

Nodding, she faces forward, leading me up the stairs. Looking up, I see the eight flights of steps that await. "This was the plan, wasn't it? Use my magic to stop John. How did no guards see him escape?"

Her voice shakes as she explains, "I don't know, and there is no reason to alert them now. If we do, they will take action right away. I can sense the anger in John. He would kill my brother right on the spot. The way to end this is to be as quiet as possible."

"Where is Axil right now?"

Hauling both of us up, she breathes the words, "He is in his chambers getting ready."

"And John? Where are the prisoners?"

"They are taking refuge in the library. Somehow, John figured out there are secret rooms in the shelves."

That must have been what he was doing while I was gone. He wasn't looking for the key to the treasury, but looking for an escape route for his own mission.

For a while, we don't speak. Both of us focus on our breathing up the stairs, our minds both spinning.

"Why don't we just alert Axil now? We could hide him. Make sure, at least, he is safe."

Tears well in her eyes as I look over, "I have tried. Many times, I have told him what I have seen. Every time he blew me off. He thinks I am making this up to make him feel worse about all that has happened."

"Your powers. Doesn't he know about it?"

"My mother had asked me to keep it a secret. I had used it to warn Crista about the Malaka troop. I had hid her with me. Along the way, I was kidnapped by one of the troop leaders. Crista had made herself disappear right in time, so they made the mistake that I was her. They beat me to death, but I wasn't quite dead. That is, thanks to your mother. She had healed me enough to be stable before I was found in the woods outside the kingdom walls. After that, my mother told me to never use my powers again. Instead of princess, I was now turned a maid. A lowly servant that was nothing more than a depressed slave. It was the best disguise against them. Axil never knew of my powers, and it was never spoken of again."

My mind draws a blank, staring at the steps we keep trekking up. "I'm so sorry. I can't even imagine what you went through."

"That's the thing, though. You *do* know how I feel. Why do you think I stood up for you? You know exactly what it feels like to be behind some mask. Expected to act a certain way. If there is anyone that understands, it is you."

My feeling comes back a little more. I can now walk on my own, the magical effects from my mother's spell kicking in. My eyes dart in either direction. "How is he…?"

She looks at me, her face bright red. "Axil? He is… not himself."

Silence fills the air. "This is all my fault."

Grabbing my hand, she squeezes. "John's plan is not your fault. This is one giant mess that needs to be fixed, and you are the perfect person to do it."

Looking back I question, "Why? How would I ever be able to be the hero when all I know is how to be the villain?"

"A villain is exactly what we need right now. Someone who can be sly, yet precise. A person who seeks revenge for power, to show the world who they truly are. Not revenge for evil. But revenge, against the evil. We need you, Zaria."

If she needs a villain, then a villain I will be. A villain who will save the Prince of Lumbridge from my rascal of a sidekick.

***

In Lucy's room, we plan. A plan to stop my former best friend from certain doom.

"You know him better than anyone else. Why would he want to do this?"

Guard guy asks the question so flatly. A part of me is pissed that he stands here planning with us when he refused to say a word to me down in my cell.

Taking a deep breath, I sigh. "I couldn't even try to guess. When I had first mentioned to him about not doing the mission, he had already changed. When we got here, he was still his normal self. What changed his mind in a matter of hours, I have no idea?"

"Lucy, what was the last thing you saw with your magic?"

Her voice lowers. Her eyes darting back and forth over the tile. "Gunshots."

No one needed to respond. The thought entered each of our minds.

"I will do whatever I can to protect your brother, Lucy." I pause, "No matter the cost."

He might still think me a criminal. A lying, manipulative girl, but there is one thing he doesn't know about gangs. We protect the ones we care about. Even if the love is not reciprocated, we will stay loyal to the ones that bid us well.

"When is the ball starting?" I ask, trying to change the subject.

"Music will start in about two hours. The ball starting in three," Guard guy responds.

"So… what is the plan?"

Everyone goes quiet. Guard guy scratches the back of his head, looking up at the ceiling. Lucy, rubbing her arm, looking down.

"You told me to be prepared. I have trained as hard as I could, but what exactly am I training for?" Lucy finally speaks up, "I have done the best I can, but the future is still hazy. Zaria…" she looks up at me, her eyes bloodshot. "I have no idea what is going to happen tonight."

She starts pacing around her room, her heels clacking on the marble tiled floor. "I have always had things figured out. Always one step ahead. This time… when he truly needs me… I have no idea."

I sympathize with her. Every day of my life in Flesherg was spent not knowing if I would make it back home. The heart dropping feeling of a life-threating job. But, I had learned to block the feeling. I had learned to step up, and be the leader the gang had needed. The one they went to when trouble sprang up. The one they went to, to organize a plan that was foolproof.

"Here's the plan." I stride over to her side table, a clipboard the same as mine resting there. I flip to an empty page, clicking the pen. "I know John's routine. He will arrive right on time within a crowd, as to not be spotted. He will act just like any other guest, a smile on his face, a drink in his hand. If he is planning to make a strike, we must be prepared for any movement we see. To counter his move, we will do the same. Act as normal guests. Do not alert any guards or extra security. The smoother his plan goes, the better ours will run."

Guard guy starts to talk, sounding out every word, "That is one plan." His sarcasm shows in every syllable.

I throw the pen at him. "Without insight to what exactly John has planned, there is no way for me to make one."

"Isn't that what you used to do? Throw yourself into danger with a plan in your left pocket?"

I glare at him, my cheeks burning. "As a matter a fact, that is exactly what we did. But, our missions were carefully crafted over a set of weeks.

Checking security, mapping out the area. Things like this take time. Last minute, there is not much you can do except wait out the evening."

"So now we are just going to walk into the ball blind? I don't like that idea." He strides towards Lucy, comforting her.

Lucy stands in the corner biting her lip. She looks so frail. Danger had almost cost her life before. She doesn't want the same for her brother.

"You said they were in the library?" Looking up, she nods her head.

Setting down the clipboard, I approach the door.

"Where are you going?" Guard guy asks.

"I'm going to go be a criminal. Make sure that when all of this is over, I have a cell to my name."

Walking towards me, his eyes widen. "You can't just go out there. People might see you."

"It seems you are forgetting all the training I have done. I will teleport there, and back once I am done. Stay here, and lock the doors. We don't want any surprises."

I disappear into the void. The void that connects the world to outer space. There is not much here. It is mostly just dark, like walking through an unlit street at midnight. The map I drew, at the top of my head. The library is just left of the ballroom. I wouldn't even be surprised if there was a secret passage way into the ballroom through the library.

My heart is set. Protect the ones I have learned to love. That should be simple enough. But, I never thought that protecting the ones I love, would come at a price of me betraying what I promised I would never do again.

A spy. Lucy needs a spy. It's not like I don't know how to do it, more I don't want to. If I spy on him, how am I any better than where I started?

I warp into the library, the wind cold against my face. Transitioning from the void is still a little tricky, but I try to make it as discreet as possible.

I gather my thoughts. I am not wearing the appropriate clothes for this, but at least I am not in the dress from before. My hair stays down instead of being in the tight braid. All the things I could rely on are against me, but maybe that is a good thing.

No doubt, John will have his eyes out for me. Just like I did, he will be looking for my usual movements. It's time to shake things up a bit.

I quickly hide behind a shelf before anyone can see me. Turning invisible is easier than it was to teleport. It had actually come as the easiest for me. Part of me wondered if that little bit of magic was with me all along, and I just hadn't realized it. It was always a mystery of how many times I was able to get away from certain doom. So many situations that should have earned me a spot in the ground, but I always somehow escaped.

Tiptoeing across the carpeted floor, I make my move.

"So, what is the plan?" Someone asks. A low burly voice, shaking my bones.

I use the void to teleport inside. Any sign of the door moving, invisible or not, he will take action. Inside, I look around to see all the prisoners dressed in fancy suits. Some recognizable, some not. The only other girl that was in prison also wears a suit. Smart move. The black and white symmetry reminds me of a prison I would see on TV. Black and white stripes lining the people, marking them as criminals.

John steps onto a pile of books he has splayed on the floor for his own personal stage. "Tonight, we take back my kingdom. No matter the cost, round up the "Majesties" and their royal little one. We will be holding them hostage until this palace is back in Malaka's control. Kill anyone who stands in your way."

One man raises his hand in question, "What happens if the guards catch us before we strike?" He stalks towards him, the same way he did in my dream. I never realized how much of a predator he is. Sly, and controlling. I had never imagined him as a real crook, a bad person. His jazzy steps were the one thing that would brighten my day. Any music that had been left in his heart, is now gone.

"What do you think I got these for?" He holds up a skinny sword. From the size, it doesn't look like much, but Damian had taught us about them. With enough force, the sword can cut through anything, making the perfect stab to end someone's life.

Holding the sword up against the guy's neck he whispers, "Do you understand, or do you want me to demonstrate what to do?"

The guy fitfully moves his head back and forth as much as he can without receiving a slice to his neck. Stepping away, the man lets out a breath he had been holding. His face still pale, he holds his eyes open and straight, still in shock.

"As for me, I will be in charge of the prince. Those two old hags shouldn't be too hard to round up, so I will leave them to you. The last thing I need is the heir to the throne, ruining my fun."

"How exactly are you going to do that?"

John's eyes dart to his, just like the other man before. "Do you know what a bullet is, or am I going to have to show you?"

The whole room goes silent. Rolling his eyes, John continues, "As far as the guests, keep them under control. I want them on the floor, in the ballroom. No one goes in or out." He looks around, meeting everyone's gaze. For a split second, it looks like he looks right at me, a sly smirk forming on his face. I try to calm myself down. *You are invisible. He can't see you. You are safe.* After a moment, he looks to everyone else. "Am I understood?"

"Yes, Your Majesty," everyone responds in unison.

With all the information I need, I quickly teleport back to Lucy's room.

A bonk on the head, I fall back in.

"What took you so long?" Guard guy comes, helping me up.

Rubbing my head, I look back to the glass lamp that now lies on the floor in broken pieces. "What took so long, was all the information we need for tonight."

Lucy still stands in the corner of her room. Rushing over to me she asks, "What did you find out?"

I sit on her bed, recovering from my crash. "You were right. He is planning to take over the kingdom. All of the prisoners are armed with swords, and John with a gun. The prisoner's job is to take care of the King and Queen, while he is going to go after Axil. He is planning for him to put up more of a fight than your parents."

Catching my breath, I continue. "From what he said, it looks like you are safe. I don't think he knows that you are alive."

I see her eyes soften, going limp at the same time. I reach into her aura, trying to understand her emotion. I see grief. Grief that is filled with a sense of calm. I wish I could comfort her. Tell her everything is going to be okay, but I learned the hard way, never to say that. When things go wrong, it hurts a lot more to remember someone saying that all would be fine.

"If we are going to pull this off, we need to start getting ready." Her face takes back control.

"Zaria, we are going to need to disguise you. The guards will recognize you the second you walk in. You can borrow one of my dresses. I have plenty from… you know."

"Thank you for the offer, but I have an idea."

***

"Are you sure this is going to work?" Lucy asks standing behind me.

I look at her face through the mirror. I had forgotten how tight I had braided my hair before I went to complete a job.

"It has to. If anything goes wrong, I am going to need my training clothes."

"Won't he recognize you?" Guard guy tries to protest.

I glance over my shoulder, tying off my braid. "That is the point."

"You *want* to be targeted?"

"Think about it. He is not expecting me to be there. According to his plan, I am 90% sure that I am still supposed to be passed out in the dirt. If I can throw him off, it can give you more time to warn everybody."

Lucy hangs her head. Shaking it, she starts, "I just don't know how he could have gotten out."

Butting in, I answer for her. "I do." All eyes go to me, but I only look at Guard guy.

"A certain someone lost his keys, and a few days later the prisoners were able to escape. To me, the pieces fit together perfectly."

A blush fills his face, making him look like a tomato. He lowers his face, Lucy looking at him. A glare in her eyes, she shoots a hushed curse in his direction.

Looking back in the mirror, I check my braid for any loose hairs. "I have my magic that can protect me, but I would feel a bit better if you two were armed as well."

"That would be a perfect plan if the whole prison didn't raid our weapon stash."

Crossing his arms, he tries to push the blame over to me. Lucky for him, I am too focused to have a brawl. Digging in the vanity, I find two gold chains. Waving my hand over them, I transform them into sun-kissed swords.

"All fixed." I keep a straight face, somewhat annoyed looking. Deep down I silently pray that my magic instilled the swords with protection for Lucy and Guard guy. I can materialize swords, but will they hold strong is a different question.

"You guys get dressed. I am going to check how filled the ballroom is."

Guard guy leaves my room, Lucy grabbing onto my arm. "Please be safe."

I give her a tight nod before watching her leave with him. "You can come out now."

"Honey, I don't think this is a good idea." My mother comes out of the bathroom, concern written on her face.

"What other choice do I have, mother? This is my chance to make things right."

Her hands on her hips, she replies, "Risking your life is hardly a way of making things right."

"So, I let the whole royal family get murdered." She goes silent, hearing the rise in my voice. "I need to ask you a question."

Her lips still a tight line, "What is it?"

"John had said that he was taking back his kingdom. All the prisoners had called him "Your Majesty." Do you know what any of that was about?"

Sighing, her voice is back to normal. "I had always known John to go to the extremes when he was upset. I can only think that would be a possible explanation."

Hugging her goodbye, I can only wish the same thing.

***

Walking with Lucy and Guard guy, we enter into the ballroom. I curse my leather pants for making noise through my invisibility. Thankfully Guard guy had corrected his step to mine, making the noise sound like it was coming from him.

Just in case, I hold my breath while walking past the two guards posted at the doors. Lucy gives them a warm smile, bowing slightly. Guard guy, giving a tight nod. My eyes are busy, looking for any indication that someone can see me. I had only had a week of practice, my magic slipping up once in a while.

I am going to have to stay invisible for quite some time. Until I feel the anticipation at its peak in John, I will appear, hopefully throwing him off his plan. The second we enter, I split from them, patting good luck. I sweep around the perimeter, looking for any indication that John is already here. Peace fills most of the air, music bouncing off the walls. The harpist and pianist from the last ball, play their beautiful melody. Their eyelids fluttering in bliss. If I was not here to stop a murder, I would feel calm myself.

I look around, surveying the decoration. Despite my betrayal to the throne, emerald green tablecloths accent the fondue table, vases of jasmine being the centerpiece. The sting of knowing that this ball is for Crista's and my mother hurts. They can't even attend their own ball.

Crista! I never told her. Frantically fighting my way through the gathering crowd, I am careful not to touch anybody. I look through the whole ballroom, but there is no sign of Lucy. Guard guy stands by himself, a half glass of champagne already in his grasp.

Tapping his shoulder, I whisper in his ear. "Where is Lucy?"

He speaks under his breath, barely moving his lips. "She went to aid Rebecca in part of the last-minute ball planning."

I make a note. She better get back soon. "Do you know if Crista and her mother are coming?"

"Lucy had notified them not to arrive."

I release my breath. I need to keep as many people as I can safe.

One of the other prison guards comes up to Guard guy waving and ushering him over. I take that as my cue to leave. I return to walking in circles around the ball, my steps taking rhythm of the music. I look up at the clock. Giant roman numerals hanging on the far side of the ballroom. 9:45 is the time that shows. At least, that's what I think it says. Lack of school has made me a little ditzy to stuff like this. All I know is that the minute hand is getting dangerously close to the tenth hour.

Chatter fills the room, echoing off of every wall. As the ballroom fills with guests, the more my heart speeds. Some of these people might not make it out alive. If anyone dies, will I have failed? Failed at the one thing I had tried to do right? Then what? What will I do with myself? What is left if I have nothing?

There is not much time to think about that. A dark looming cloud fills my stomach, swirling all my guts. Into the ballroom enters John and his gang.

Chapter twenty-one

They start to trickle through the doors, two or three at a time. The guards smile, waving at them like they are some old friends. How? How did he do it?

I watch as all of them file in, looking completely different than how they did behind bars. I count thirteen before he finally arrives. Coming in last, John takes the floor.

My senses were right. The air shifted the second they walked in. Not enough for a normal person to tell, but a dreadful feeling for someone who can magically feel emotion.

I don't let my eyes leave from him. I feel the unsettling around me, circling me. My body screams to look. To make sure that everything is still okay. But my mind is focused. Never leaving my target. Because my target has his eyes out for the person that meant the most to me.

A gaggle of girls swallow me with their puffy gowns. They gossip about the village men, dipping their bread in chocolate fondue.

I huff and puff through the heaps of fabric, my movements as discrete as possible. Once the chatter had filled the ballroom, I had not had to worry about the rubbing of my leather.

Almost falling to the floor, I finally make it through the heap of people. Immediately my head shakes. Frantically, I try to spy for John. I run the outside of the room again, but he is nowhere to be seen. Along my path, I had spotted Lucy again with Rosalyn. Mentally checking that off the list, I keep searching. Black and white. Black and white. Every man looks the same. Every suit the same color, but one thing is for sure. Axil is not here yet. Nowhere do I see a blue suit. The thought calms me a bit.

I run around about two more times, still to no avail. I look back at the clock. One line away. From what I remember, that means I only have a couple of minutes. I try. Try to levitate off the ground. The air swoops around me, holding me a couple of feet high before I collapse to the ground.

Tucked in a ball, I stay until I am sure no one is looking. I can't even fathom if someone has caught me. After a couple of seconds, my heartbeat goes back to normal. Voices sound the same. Calm, joyful. I take a risk and stand up.

I slow my steps. Maybe I was searching too fast. I take my time to examine everything. Every person that is in a suit. Their height. Their weight. The way they hold themselves. The only thing I find are most of the prisoners and guards. Some of them mingling with each other.

There is something not right. Something that does not add up. I look again for Guard guy and Lucy. Thankfully I find them together, exactly where they had planned to be. As close to the thrones as possible, still looking like commoners. I can feel Lucy's blood heating by the second. I worry she might boil over.

Everyone's emotions are so intense. Everyone except John's. I try to tap in. Reaching as far as I can into my magic, but nothing shows me what I need to see.

Sweat starts beading on my forehead, my breath hitching on every inhale. I cannot feel his anger. Only my own. My fury and nerves. I am ashamed to admit it to myself, but I am scared. Fear takes over my mind, making me feel like I am some kid again. It feels as though a dark presence is looming over my shoulder, pushing me to my breaking point. I take a breath, but on the way out there is nothing. I cannot breathe. Heart pounding in my chest, I try to move. Again, nothing follows.

In my right ear, hot air brushes my skin. A whisper that sends nightmares. "I found you."

***

I try to kick, scream, do anything to escape, but there is nothing. John holds his grip around me tight. As far as I can see, there is not even a John. Just a panic cloud wrapped around me. My feet catch along the bottom of the floor. Pushing as hard as I can, I move to dig my heels in.

All that happens in return is his grip tightening. He drags me out of the ballroom in a little corner, behind a table. The hole leads straight into the library. No wonder he held his camp in there. My legs start to burn moving from the glassy ballroom floor to the now carpeted floor of the library.

We enter the same nook he had been in before, while he was sharing his plan. The plan that would take action any second now. I had failed. Failed my mother. Failed the royal family. Crista, Lucy, Axil, the King and Queen. I failed myself. What was it all for?

After closing the bookcase, I am thrown into a chair, rope magically wrapping my limbs to it. I resist as much as I can, fighting against him, whatever dark magic he seems to have acquired, but it is too strong.

I wince as the knots tighten me to the chair, giving no wiggle room. My skin starts to sweat. Hot, then cold. My invisibility is shut down under his control, showing my Flesherg clothes.

"Ah. It is nice to finally see you Zaria. After all your hard work spying on me this evening, it seems as though you were the first one to be caught. A surprise, really. I thought you were going to be the hardest one."

I scream, but nothing comes out. A force blocking my throat. He scoffs. "The more you struggle, the harder I push my magic on you. Now please do me a favor, and let me take back what is mine."

I am able to move, but not much. The rope cuts in to my skin like a raging flame. When I look down, it is not just my imagination. Around my wrists, black ash of my own flesh starts to accumulate. Burn marks searing my skin.

"Take that as a minor lesson of what is to come if you interfere with my plan."
Without lifting a finger, the walls separate for him. He looks back, giving me a wink. "Let the games begin."

***

He leaves the passage open, leaving me to see out into the ballroom. Just after he exits the library, trumpets start to play.

"Please welcome your King and Queen to the ball."

A shout of people start. Whistling and clapping. So much joy for a fateful end. I bend my head to see where Lucy and Guard guy are. There they stand, right at the stairs doing their job, counting on me doing mine. Here I am stuck, unable to do anything. The King and Queen emerge from the curtain, hand in hand like last time. The sight almost brings tears to my eyes. All they had done was love. Love their children, their people, but most importantly, each other. It is their love that kept this palace alive. Their love that spread kindness all throughout the kingdom. And their love, which will now be the reason for their demise.

"Now, please welcome your kingdom's future King, Prince Axil."

Unlike the last ball, he enters with his family. Perfect for John's plan. I curse him under my breath, hanging my head. The cheers break out again for Axil. Looking up, I catch a glimpse of his face. The face that was once filled with so much joy. The face that seemed to glow at all times, leaving a mystic resonance with people. Now, that face is a mask. A mask that looks the same from the outside but is truly breaking on the inside.

It is my fault. I did that to him. He didn't deserve this. No one deserves any of this. But now all these people will pay for the price of my partner's rage.

The King starts speaking, his voice filling the whole ballroom. "The Queen and I are so happy to welcome back our old friends. The friends that have gone away and now come back. Mika and Maria. To the two of you, we celebrate your return. The union to this kingdom again. May you always feel safe and welcome in these walls."

Clapping fills the room. Not the crowd. Just one lonely clap. The clap grows louder, the sight of John stepping towards the thrones at the head of the room.

"May I help you, young sir?"

It must be his magic. Otherwise the King would recognize him right away. John raises his voice, making it loud for all to hear.

"Correct me if I am wrong, but it is the criminal's mother we are celebrating. The mother of the child that has just been thrown into the deepest dungeon for treason."

The King keeps a level head responding, "That is correct."

John prowls closer, slowly climbing up the stairs to face the King. He goes on, "What kind of king are you to welcome the family of a criminal into these walls? If we welcome her back regardless of her status, you might as well open up the whole prison to dine with you."

Guards start to circle in on John. Taking that as a warning, he stops before the King, looking him dead in the eye.

I look around. Axil stands to the side of his father, eyeing up John. He, too, doesn't recognize him. The only people who seem to not be under the effect of John's control are Lucy and Guard guy. I watch them, trying to call out to Lucy's magic with my own, but my magic is so weak. Nothing would communicate. I watch as they frantically start looking around, waiting to spot me at any moment. They start to get antsy. Shifting from one foot to the other, their eyes wandering all around. Lucy stands on her tiptoes, searching for any indication that I am near. I close my eyes, unable to see the faces on them when they find out that once again, I had betrayed them.

The King's voice is sharp this time. A commanding tone only a King could bear. "I would do no such thing. I will not shame a person for the action of their loved ones. As for the prisoners, they are kept locked up. They are of no danger to this Kingdom."

Though I cannot see it, I can feel John's face rise into a wicked smirk. "Are you sure about that?"

Just then, four prisoners jump from the back of the curtain. The guards immediately swarm around their crowns, but to no avail. Gasps fill the room. Screaming and shouting quickly following. Through all the chaos, John somehow uses his magic to force my head up. Making me watch all the horror, tears roll down my face.

I watch as two of the prisoners shred at the guards. Stabbing into their chests, their hearts bleeding out. The other one goes for a different route, decapitating their heads right off of their neck. Blood spatters everywhere, the prisoners tightly grasping onto the King and Queen.

Even through everything, I am relieved that I had spent the time with Axil to teach him how to fight. I watch as he draws his sword from its hilt, his eyes locked onto the approaching prisoner.

Their swords clash, the noise ringing in my ears. I watch in horror seeing him fight for his life. The fight that he shouldn't even be fighting for. I hate to admit it, but if I just would have done the original mission, Axil would be safe right now. Everybody would be. They would be poor, but safe. They would go to bed tonight hungry, but they would live to see the morning sun.

I gasp when I see Axil deliver the final stab upon the prisoner, the little rat falling at his feet. His breath is ragged, his face glistening as he looks down upon what he had just done.

A shrill fills the air. A pitch I had heard before. It is Guard guy. Running towards Axil, he screams.

"Behind you!"

Like it happened in slow motion, I see Axil turn behind him, expertly blocking the next prisoner's attack. The scene is so horrific, even if I wasn't forced to watch, I wouldn't be able to take my eyes off.

I am so focused on Axil that I almost miss another horror.

"Adam!" Another cry. Another cry I recognize. This time from Lucy. I follow her gaze seeing the prisoner that had kidnapped her, throw his sword right towards Guard guy.

By the time her scream cries out, the sword has already pierced his back, Guard guy falling to the ground.

"Everyone on the ground! Hands Up!" another prisoner cries. This is a nightmare. A sick, cruel nightmare.

I scan to see Lucy on her hands and knees crawling over to Guard guy's body.

"Adam!" she cries again. "My love, stay with me."

At that moment my heart sunk. Lucy's love had just been murdered, stabbed in the back, left to die. I had asked him when he would tell me his name. He had replied that he would consider after the mission was done, but I had never envisioned it going this way.

My eyes snap back up to Axil. He was not fighting anymore, but now being restrained by John. Just like me, he had not used any weapons or outside forces. Just his own magic. Dark witchcraft that suffocates all the life out of one's body.

Aside from the hushed cries of the guests, all the action has died down. The prisoners tie the royal family up for good measure, John holding them in the air. I can sense their fear, their anger. I need to stop this, but I have no idea how.

John looks my way, winking again. Proud of all the evil he had unleashed. "Come with me," he says with his snide voice. "You," pointing to one of the nearby prisoners he commands, "Make sure no one leaves this room. I want an audience for when I take back my crown."

"Yes sir."

I angrily watch as he ties up the royal family, just like he had me. We now are stuck in the same room. My speech has come back. I can only think that's because he wants to fight, and a fight I will give him.

"Do you know why you are here?" He speaks to all of us, pacing around. He waves his gun in his hand, spinning it around his finger.

He pouts. "No answer? Well, I guess I will just have to tell you. A long, long decade ago, Lumbridge was not the palace you know today. No. For it was another kingdom. A kingdom that was strong, that was wealthy, but it didn't belong to Lumbridge. It belonged to Malaka. I'm sure you have all heard of the great depression that fell over the kingdom, but it was not the Malaka you see today. During the depression, Lumbridge took control of Malaka, forcing us afterward to bow down to a new throne, or leave. It was this kingdom, right here. Malaka owns this territory, and it is time to get it back."

I speak up, meeting his devilish gaze, "And what does any of this have to do with you?"

Lifting my chin, he levels his face to mine. "Really Zaria, I thought you would have been smarter than this. I am the rightful prince of Malaka. The palace that just so happens to be already occupied. And what prince would I be to leave my people in the hands of some crook?" Spitting at the King, he smiles.

"Stop telling lies. You are just some orphan my father took in, because he felt sorry for you. There is no way you are a prince."

"No need to get jealous now, Zaria. I will admit, at first I did not know either. My mother had abandoned me because I was born while she was told a depression would fall. She wanted a better home for me, far away. It was only when we entered this magical place that my mother was able to get in touch with me. She was able to talk to me through my thoughts, walk me through flashes of the past."

That had to have been his headaches.

"When I found out I was a prince of the sworn enemy of Lumbridge, what better way to take over than to have you steal the treasury of the kingdom. One way or another, it would fall. Leaving me to be the saving grace."

He stalks back over to me, "But you just had to be stubborn didn't you." In a high-pitched voice, he mocks me.

"Stealing is wrong. This kingdom doesn't deserve it." His face goes cold, leaving nothing to hide. "We could have been something, you know. I could have taken over this kingdom with you by my side, but one thing got in the way. A little fly buzzing around."

He turns his attention away from me, to Axil. Cocking his gun, he looks right at him. "I don't understand what I did wrong. Why you were the better option. I saw the way she looked at you. The way she started to morph into one of you. Kind and poised. Uggh!" A smile forms on his face again, laughing to himself. "What a sight it was to see you visit her in prison, after you had brought me down there yourself. And then, she was dumb enough to bring herself down as well. She wept for days after you left. Visions of her clouding my dreams as I slept. I thought, for a moment I had the upper hand. Everything I have ever wanted, but she still chose you."

My memory slipped back to the top of my head. I had once said that I would do anything for him. Anything at all to keep him safe. But, I could never love him. Not in the way he had expected me to.

He strides back over to me, his gun still in hand. "You had taken me by surprise. For one of us to have magic powers, that would have been the talk of the century. But both of us? In a different world, we could have been a new kind of partner."

I speak under my breath, uttering through clenched teeth. "I would never be your partner again."

"I know dear. You have picked your fate. It's just a shame yours doesn't have a happy ending."

His finger hovers over the trigger. The world goes in slow motion again as I see him pull the trigger, aiming at Axil's heart. I pull at the restraints, the flames coming back to sear my skin. Crying out, the fire of his gun rings loud in my ears.

My eyes widen, the breath leaving my lungs. Axil braces himself for the impact, totally helpless. His eyes squint, his mouth tight. Unlike before, there is no way for him to fight now.

Right before the bullet hits his chest, a flash of light blinds the room. It is there a second, and then it is gone. My eyes focus to see not the bloody mess of Axil's dead body. But the bloody mess of my mother's dead body.

Teleporting in here she had stopped the bullet from entering Axil's body. Everyone screams. The King and Queen for their son, but me for seeing my once again dead mother lying lifeless on the ground.

Something in me snaps. The man I had once considered a brother, stands eyes wide looking at my mother.

My skin tightens, I cry out in pain, my bones cracking from rage. I feel on fire, and it is not just because of John's little magic. From the inside, a flame has been ignited, and it is morphing into the fires from Hell.

Never before had I made it five feet above the ground flying, but now I take off. Flying feet into the air, I reach the ceiling, his restraints seeming like a joke now.

I have transformed into a new body, a new being. Black scales cover my body, strong wings flapping in the air. Papers fly, books falling off of the shelves. My new tail whaps against the bookcases, the strength behind it, knocking over anything that stands.

My eyes focus on that scared little face. Not coming from Axil or the King or the Queen, but from John. His mouth is gaping open, his legs backing him into the wall.

I let out a laugh, but the only sound coming out as a frightening roar. This is what I have been waiting for. My proper revenge. At my laugh, it triggers something inside of John. A monster of his own. He, too, takes on a dragon form. Rushing over to me.
Escaping his grasp, I break through the stain glass roof. Shards of glass fall to the ground, none of the shards making me feel pain. I am beyond the point of feeling pain. The only thing that matters is ending this.

He follows after me, racing on the edge of my tail. Before breaking this down, I need to make a detour. I fly back over to the palace, breaking into the windows of the ballroom. All I need to do is trudge through, making as much of a scene as possible. People start to follow my plan. I had made the perfect escape route for them.

In herds, people jump out of the broken windows. The prisoners standing awestruck are now the ones to fall to the floor taking cover.

Once the majority of the people are out of the room, John decides to join me in the ballroom. Last ball he had stolen me for a dance. I wouldn't mind another tango.

He snarls, breaking another window. At the ready, I blast his face with fire, his nostrils flaring at the smoke. I will give him no move to win. It is my turn. My turn to see victory. A victory in honor of this kingdom, and a victory in honor of my mother.
His claws extend outward, scratching at my neck. The pain is enough to feel, but nothing to falter my next attack. Sweeping up, I free dive down on top of him, pushing all of my weight into him. He stumbles over, landing on his back. I pin his wings to the ground, breathing fire right into his face. He thinks searing my wrists is funny, I'll show him real fire. Not letting him breathe, I keep exhaling suffocating flames.

His head moves back and forth, avoiding the flame as much as possible. I don't notice it, until it happens. His tail whips around, constricting the breath out of my lungs. Now rolling me onto my back, he uses his claws again. Ripping at anything he can, blood starts to stream out of my body.

We spar time after time. Attack after attack. Neither of us giving up. The next time I have him pinned, enough is enough. I come free diving like I had once before. Falling to his back, I extend my claws. Bracing for the sound, I use all my strength, ripping off both of his wings.

He roars out in pain. Undecided, I can't tell whether the bones cracking or the cry was more painful to hear. I stare deep into his reptilian eyes, all the pent-up anger showing in my stare.

From the side, I see arrows start raining down. Not on me, but on John. Piercing his body, they sink straight into his scales. Footsteps sound from around. Rope dragging along the floor. Lumbridge guards surround us, hooking the rope around his limbs.

I wait until it is my turn, but no one lifts a finger upon me. One of the commanding officers looks me dead in the eyes. I do not recognize him. Walking through the halls every day, I had started to pick up on the little things that differentiated them, but it is then that I realize, this is what we had planned for. What I had planned for.

An attack against Malaka, with inside soldiers ready to attack back with no mercy. "Whenever you are done Zaria, we will take it from here."

He is giving me the choice. After all I have done. This man gives me the choice to either let John live or die. All my life, I had seen death. So much, that it didn't really phase me. If I were to kill John, I would eventually get over it. He deserves it. Killing my mother right in front of me, doesn't come for free. Even if the bullet wasn't for her, it was still for someone else. Someone whom I love. But, love is the whole point. Killing John would not make anything better. I had sent myself to jail for one thing, and it was to make things right. Who would I be, to break that promise when it matters most? Because I may not love John. I may not like him one bit. But, I have one thing he does not, and it is love. With one last snarl, I slowly dig my claws out of him. I am unaware how much damage I have inflicted upon his human body, but he will live. He should consider that enough.

Looking around I see the royal family lined up behind me, Lucy included. The King stands in the center, giving me a bow. The rest of them follow. Out of one eye, I see the respect upon saving their kingdom, and in the other, I see John being dragged away. Regardless of what is in front of me, the image of my mother sacrificing herself plays in my mind, taking over my thoughts. There is too much going on, the ballroom lights sweeping in, blurring my vision.

I stumble backwards, slipping on the glassy floor. Quickly I turn around, flying out of the window. High in the sky, big tears escape my eyes. Falling to the ground, they come down as hailstones. The cold air freezing them before they hit the snow.

The cold wind howls through the night sky, the atmosphere giving a little relief to my broken heart. There is nothing to do. Nothing I have left. As I allow my pain in, all the scratches, all the wounds, send me in a downward spiral collapsing on a hill. I close my eyes, not wanting to open them again.

***

"Zaria?"

"Zaria, wake up."

Every bone in my body is sore. The gentle shake on my arm feels like a violent stab that shoots through my body. I squint my eyes, the sun now up.

"My goodness."

Arms wrap around me, holding me up. For a moment, I relax. The world settles around me, finally falling into place. When I open my eyes, I see those two confusing oceans I have longed to see again.

Tears cloud both of our eyes, smiles forming on our lips.

"I'm so sorry… I…" he starts mumbling in a ramble as if there is not enough time. As if I would disappear off the earth at any given time.

"I know. I know."

His tears collect on my now ripped jacket. I'm glad that's about the only thing that got damaged.

"With… with John and… and your mother. I can't even…" He falls off, not knowing how to finish what he had started to say.

"You don't have to be sorry."

Holding my head up he responds, "But I do! I had lashed out. I didn't have any reasoning to make you feel so upset. I guess… the only reason I got so angry was because…"

Again, he trails off. His cheeks start to blush, a light pink gracing his face. His eyelashes flutter, looking from side to side. "I meant to tell you at the ball, before everything happened."

Holding my hands, he looks me straight in the eye. "I wanted to tell you, that I care for you. And with everything that happened, I understand if you hate me now. Zaria, you scare the crap out of me sometimes. I never again want to see you in danger. I have seen you come close to death countless times, and I can't stand back and let you do that on your own."

Taking a deep breath, he loosens his grip on my hands. "Can we please just start over? Friends again?"

His eyes are steady, calm. Countering to the sweat that beads at his brow. My magic might still be strained, but I don't need my powers to see the genuine plea for forgiveness. The brokenness that is not only in my heart, but in his. My mother had sacrificed herself to save Axil.

I choose to take that as a sign of peace and hope. Her last message to me, before she met her demise once again.

I guess Eden was right. I had set myself up to fail, and in a way I did. I couldn't protect everyone, and I couldn't stop the free will of my mother. If I could have, the night might have gone differently. Maybe she would be standing here right now, holding me, telling me everything was going to be okay. But she had helped me. Helped to save the person I care for, following in her free will. I can without a doubt answer with purity in my heart.

"Friends."

***

"Wake up Zaria! It's Christmas!"

Crista busts through my door, flopping herself on my bed. I peer out the window, greeted by snow falling gracefully from the puffy clouds. The snow brings back a memory of my mother and I. Christmas day was one of the only days I didn't have training. That day, my mother and I would do everything. Frolic in the snow, catching snowflakes, and making snow angels. We would drink hot chocolate and make cookies. On the coldest day of the year, my heart felt the warmest.

It pains me to not have her back. To celebrate a day of what could have been our first Christmas in five years. Even though she is not here, I can still feel her. Her magic guiding me through the actions that I do, the choices that I make.

"Come on, get dressed. Everyone is waiting by the Christmas tree."

My lips forming a smile, I wave her out of my room. I dress myself in a silk red puffed dress. Axil had once again gifted me clothing to wear, the other ones being too dirty to fix. We have been on pretty good terms. We talk to each other a lot more. The King stated that he would gladly have me back as Axil's advisor. His words exactly, "I feel comfortable with my son in the hands of a knighted dragon."

I guess I have now become somewhat of a soldier. Something I had told the King I would never do. Axil and my days are mostly filled with tasks and meetings as he is preparing to take over the throne. There is much stress being put on his shoulders, so I make sure to plan special activities for us.

I have gotten a whole lot better at riding horses, and I had even had time to pick up a few hobbies while sitting at meeting. One of them being a surprise.

I pick up the box that holds all the presents I had collected for the royal family and headed down the stairs. It seemed a little awkward when Axil invited me to his family's special holiday party. He had played it off by saying that his family wouldn't be here if it wasn't for me. After an explanation like that, I had no choice but to abide.

"Merry Christmas, Zaria." The Queen greets me by the door, taking the box from my arms. After that fateful night, everyone has treated me with more respect. Some I appreciate, and some feels like a chore for other people to do. The royal family has always been sweet about it, though.

For about a month, I have been getting used to living in the palace again. Time in the dungeon, as small as it was, really messed with my head. Some nights are still filled with the nightmares of John, but there always is a hero in my dreams.

"Merry Christmas, to the best of people."

"Merry Christmas, Axil." I turn around to see him fully decked in red and green, a Santa hat flopped on his head. That. That is my hero.

I was a little shocked how quickly the King and Queen learned to trust me again. I guess seeing their kingdom almost fall at the hands of one person, really put things into perspective about how bad things could have been.

Waiting for Crista and her mother, Axil and I talk while munching on some cookies.

"This is one of the best Christmases I have had in a while. After my mother died, the spirit of Christmas died with her."

Hanging his head, he looks at the bite marks in his cookie. "I am sorry to hear that."

Looking at him, I reply, "I want you to know that you shouldn't feel guilty about what my mother did. In fact, I am very grateful for what she did."

Looking up, he meets my eyes. "How? How can you be so understanding of what everyone has done? I don't know how you can stand in this room. A room full of people who have treated you as a criminal, and welcome them with open arms. *Especially* me. That bullet wasn't meant for her, it was…"

"You're right, it wasn't meant for her. But she decided to take it from you. She saw in you what I see. Hope."

Bringing my attention back to my cookie, I feel his eyes still on me.

"Zaria? May I speak with you?" The Queen looks at us both, her lips forming a shy smile. Axil gives us some space to talk, and that's exactly what she does.

"I just want to thank you. Without you…"

"I know. I know. You've told me a thousand times."

She hushes her voice, "I don't mean that I am not thankful for you saving the kingdom, but that is not what I wanted to thank you for." She takes a deep breath. "I want to thank you for being honest. When you first came back, I wasn't sure what you were going to do."

I chew my cookie slower, the soft dough sticking in the crowns of my teeth. "What do you mean?"
She leans in, "I may not have magic that sees into the future like Lucy, but I did happen to know your truth before you told it."
My mouth becomes agape. "How? Why?"
"When Axil returned, I knew something was off. He can't keep anything from me, I always find a way to pry it out of him." She winks at me, smiling.

"Why… why didn't you do anything?"

Taking a deep breath, she responds, "I wanted to hear from you. The day you came back and we discussed the plans for the ball, I saw the real you, not the fake Zaria you were trying to fool us with. I saw how much you cared. That is why I didn't say anything."

"I'm… sorry."

She cups my face. "But, look at you. Look at who you have become. Not only a woman, but a protector." This is what everyone has been trying to do. Congratulate me on saving the kingdom, completely skipping past the point that I was in the dungeon just weeks ago. "I saw what was in your heart." She points to my head, "Not here." Pointing to my chest she continues, "But in here. And that's what truly matters."

A loud crash stumble through the door.

"We're here. Let's start."

The Queen gives me one last look before winking at Axil who only blushes.

After everyone greeted Crista and her mother, the celebration began. We sang songs, danced, ate food, and played games. It was truly one of the best days I have ever had.

"Let's do presents!" Crista is so excited for today. I am glad to see that her spirits are fully back. Lucy huddles out from the corner, a slight smile on her face. Ever since Adam had died, she has been quite quiet.

Gathering around the tree, we all sit in a circle. The King and Queen start first. Everyone gifting them with their best present. No matter what is was, I am sure that they would be thankful. We take turns going around. My best gift is to Crista.

"Da da da da duhhnn... what is it?"

That one hobby I had picked up, I can say I am still trying to perfect. "I sewed you a new hat."

Inside the box, I had packaged a little orange witch hat. Attempting to embroider a leaf onto it, I had tried my best. "To symbolize the first time we truly met."

"The leaf trail! Aww. Thank you."

This is what I had missed. The excitement of watching someone's face light up with pure joy. It's not even the present that mattered, but the thought behind it. The love and care that it was wrapped in, all to celebrate a day of love.

The King and Queen had gifted me a pearl bracelet, which I am very grateful for.

"The complete set will be given out later today." With a wink, the King wraps up the present giving. I am reluctant to take a walk out onto the snow. The quilted blanket being fluffed up by my footsteps. My heart speeds as I pass by the rose bush, which is now poinsettias. The exact spot where Axil had asked me to the ball. Bending down, I run my hand along the velvety petal. Sprinkling a bit of magic onto it, I lift it from the ground.

"Can you not take from Lucy's garden? She works very hard on that."

Axil walks behind me, his sudden presence startling me. "Ah. But this time, it was magic."

"I guess I can let that slide." After his comment, a new poinsettia blooms where the previous flower had been.

"Did you enjoy the morning?" he asks, his voice going a little high.

"I must thank you for inviting me. The morning was quite lovely."

Stepping forward, he continues. "I'm glad to hear that, because I must ask you a question." Reaching for my hand, he looks me in the eye with those two blue diamonds.

"Will you go to the Christmas ball with me?"

"So many balls, I would think the Queen has nothing better to do."

Rolling his eyes, he squeezes my one hand. "I'm being serious."

"Is there going to be some hidden secret about my past uncovered this time?"

Tilting his head, he ponders. "Maybe. Because I didn't ask you the best part yet."

From his other hand, he retrieves a pearl tiara that he had been hiding behind his back. The blush appears in his face again, his lip starting to quiver. "Will you go as my princess?"

Here he stands before me, a tiara in his hand, asking me to be his princess. The girl that was thrown behind bars for suspected treason is now being asked by the prince to be his princess. My heart starts to speed, my limbs shaking a bit.

The direction of the wind shifts. Before I blink, I swear I see a trail of emerald green magic. Closing my eyes, Axil falls in front of me, kissing my lips.

It is not as before. The last time a cry. A plead. But this time, it is about acceptance. A chance to start over as who I really am.

Releasing me, his breath hitches. Looking from one eye to the other, he tries to gauge my reaction. But he already knows, the smile on my face a dead giveaway. He doesn't even have to ask because the answer is "Yes."

***

Dressing in my red ball gown, I am unable to wipe the smile off my face, and I don't even try to. It is time to be happy. To find life in the little things and slowly mend my heart back together.

Axil waits outside of my room like he has done previous times. From the outside, it seems as though nothing has changed, but on the inside, everything has changed.

Hand in hand we walk down to the ballroom. A place where a nightmare had once happened. But a place where I can spend the best days of my life.

Lucy passes us in the hallway, smiling at both of us.

"It seems like you two are on the same page now?" I inquire.

"She told me about her magic as well. Making up was filled again with lots of unnecessary apologies. I am glad to have her back."

When we enter, he points his finger to the window. The one that had been shattered that night. I am amazed when I see it. The same exact tapestry I had seen that night after Lucy had left.

The tapestry of a dragon with emerald green eyes. I had always pictured it to be my mother, not knowing anything like that was ever possible.

"Merry Christmas, Zaria." Lucy stands behind me, but not as her normal self. Tonight she wears her princess gown and tiara. Showing the world the princess she really is.

"You did this?"

"I had a dream about it one night. A dragon flying high in the sky. I had not realized at the moment, but I see no better gift to give you, than one of yourself. The day you saved us all."

She is right. I had saved the palace, but it was not just me. It was the courage of Adam that saved the honor of this palace. The love of my mother that saved the people of this palace. And the bravery of the mighty soldiers to preserve this palace from the roaring beast.

In all that has happened, I take those little bits of them. As I piece myself back together, I sew a little part of them in me, so that one day, when I can officially be Axil's princess, I can have that courage, love, and bravery in me. And as I look out the other windows, the stars shine bright in the sky. A wish for everyone. A glittering green star shoots across the window. My heart at the exact moment filled with energy. Reaching out for it this time, I was not burned. This time, I felt the love of my prince behind me, wrap his arms around my waist.

We sway to the music all night, hand in hand. Tonight is a night of dreams. May it never be forgotten.

Author's Note

The Stars of My Heart is a story that is very close to my heart. Not only are the characters people I already know, but also people I hope to become. The journey of writing this really made one thing clear to me; we must remain having hope. A hope for something bright and beautiful, and a dream to make it happen, and though we must have hope for the future it is also important to make peace with the past. Zaria had to allow her heart to forgive and never once did it make her weak like John had accused her to be, but it made her into the strong young woman her mother raised her to be.

In this book Zaria is finally able to discover who she *is* and how to cope with who she *was*. Change is inevitable and natural in all of our lives. She finds a way to embrace love, friendship, forgiveness, and hope into her heart and at the end, she finally became part of a family like she had always dreamed of.

At the time I wrote this I was fifteen years old, and publishing it I am now sixteen. I would like to think that there would be other teenagers out there that will be able to find themselves in the characters I have written and be able to feel not so alone. I have learned that there are many truths we can find in fiction works, and every story has a lesson and message that can be found. I hope that I was able to portray that in my story.

Acknowledgments:

My parents, Dan and Heather for helping in every step of the way through this book and also through my life as we have faced many challenges.

Thank you to my sister, Sam for offering a beautiful cover, and fun illustrations. Not only is your art beautiful, but you always find a way to make people smile, and that's the most beautiful thing.

Thank you to my friend Luke, who's editing skills saved my story. Your patience and kindness will always be captured within this book.

And a special thank you to God who never gave up on me and showed me that love can be found when least expected.

Place me like a seal over your heart,
Like a seal on your arm;
For love is as strong as death,
Its jealousy unyielding as the grave.
It burns like blazing fire,
Like a mighty flame.

Song of Songs 8:6